GIVE *a novel* ME
STRENGTH

GIVE ME SERIES, #2

KATE MCCARTHY

Give Me Strength

Copyright © Kate McCarthy 2013

ISBN-13: 978-0-9875261-3-7
ISBN-10: 0987526138

Please note that Kate McCarthy is an Australian author and Australian English spelling and slang have been used in this book.

Cover Art courtesy of Okay Creations http://www.okaycreations.net/

Interior Design by Angela McLaurin, Fictional Formats

Table of Contents

To Dan
My lighthouse…

Prologue

A knock came at the door of my apartment as I hopped about the bedroom trying to squeeze into my jeans. I sucked in a breath, did up the button and yelled, "Come in!"

Lucy, my new neighbour, was coming over, and we were going to settle in for a night of Australian Idol and popcorn. Despite her being twenty-four to my eighteen, it was turning into a great friendship. Lucy pretended to like my singing, and I pretended to watch her *Step Up* movies when she played them until I almost lost the will to live.

I loved music. When I had a favourite song, I would put it on repeat and play it a thousand times. When I was young I dreamed of being a singer because music took me to another place. Growing up in the music of the nineties, I was going to be the next Destiny's Child—a Beyoncé in the making—only white and with less hair. Reality was a bitch though because I couldn't sing. I couldn't even play an instrument. Lucky for me I was smart, but even smarts sometimes let you down, and according to my mother, Beth, my life was now fucked. F-u-c-k-e-d. She spelled it out, her smirking lips taking relish in the word.

She was wrong. I didn't care what she thought. She didn't care what I thought either, or cared period. Any idiot could raise a child, and why my mother thought she could do a stellar job of it baffled me.

The sucky reality was that I'd been dealt a shitty hand in life, but the way I saw it I could choose to either fold my cards or raise the stakes and play on. I chose the latter, and because I didn't do anything half measure, I played hard.

Parties, drinking, boys—those three things became my new mantra. It was almost like a three step self-help program. The touch of gentle hands on my body felt good, and I didn't care who it was as long as I felt wanted. The results were somewhat successful because when the hard slap of my stepfather's hand or fist came, it felt more deserved.

My stepfather David was like Charlie Sheen. Initially he appeared like a normal person, but the exterior was hiding something completely whacked. He and my mum were a matched set, except he held jobs like they were hot potatoes. One day he came home throwing around cash that had my mum upgraded from her customary chardonnay special to drinking high dollar vodka in fancy glassware. It was obvious he was caught up in bad deeds, but I kept my mouth shut because they were so busy spending it all they were never home.

Then a year ago I met Ethan at a party. He came up and wiped away a tear from my cheek that I hadn't even noticed was there. My glazed eyes met his, and seeing concern in their depths, I forgot how to breathe. Ethan clearly didn't belong at the party. He looked clean and sober and far too sweet for the bitter circles I ran with.

At seventeen he was a foot taller than my tiny five foot frame, all lanky muscle and shiny, dark hair. He had everything I didn't: good friends, good grades, parents who loved him, and a home.

I was offered a mere glimpse into his world, and it was beautiful. It was like the kind of wonder you would feel if you ventured inside your wardrobe and found yourself in Narnia. My world was more like Middle-earth; angry fists and cruel taunts reigned supreme. There was no love, no beauty, and maybe I had a roof over my head, but it wasn't a home.

Somehow Ethan and I came together, and I had a crazy thought he would be the Patrick Swayze to my Jennifer Grey. He laughed at me when I told him just that, but I didn't care because inside I felt something blooming so large I struggled to contain it. Ethan breathed hope into my already jaded life and it changed me into the type of girl he deserved. It was a relief to drop the bad girl act. The drinking and partying stopped, I dressed more appropriately, and grew my white-blonde hair into long waves.

Just when I thought I might actually deserve a bit of special, life proved me wrong when Ethan died three months ago. My heart broke when his parents told me he went down in a rugby tackle and never got up. I almost folded my hand then and there, but fate decided to give me the chance to do something Beth could never do—be a real mum. I was having Ethan's baby, and there was no way I'd bring something so precious into the fires of hell. In the middle of the night, I packed a suitcase and descended on Ethan's parents' house.

They became my new family, but I struggled under the shower of love. I wanted to stand on my own two feet, prove I was the person Ethan thought me to be. Having just finished high school, they helped me find a contract reception position in the city, loaned me money for a bond in a half-furnished townhouse in Campsie—south of the city—and after two weeks I was finally free.

That was when I met Lucy. She came over offering biscuits she'd baked that very morning, but the results were bitter, hard missiles. She confessed that she'd never baked a biscuit in her life, and I could only agree it was obvious. Lucy was nosy, crazy, and like a lioness. In the space of a week, she knew more about me than any of my so-called friends ever did, including my new dream of working in the music industry. Lucy became my first true friend. Her dream was being a dancer, but unlike me, she could actually dance. We even pushed the coffee table aside so she could show me her moves. She cried with me over Ethan, shopped with wild enthusiasm for baby outfits, and vowed retribution over my upbringing.

"Their time will come," she'd tell me with eyes so steely she belonged in a Quentin Tarantino film.

Having finally finished squeezing my rapidly expanding belly into the too tight jeans, I hit the living room. The smile died on my lips like yesterday's news. It slid from my face, and had it been tangible, it would have splattered on the floor.

A hand was planted on my chest and shoved, making me stumble backwards.

"'Bout time you showed your whore face," David slurred.

My lungs constricted in fear, and it was almost a relief because he smelled like he'd taken a dive in a dumpster. His hair was filthy, his clothes rumpled and rank, but despite his obvious stupor, he looked mean and mean usually equalled pain.

I straightened my spine and growled, "Get out."

"You just invited me in, so fuck you," was his reply.

I looked for my phone and saw it on the kitchen counter behind him. I'd have to get passed him to reach it.

"I'll call the cops," I warned, my threat as useless as it sounded if his smirk was anything to go by.

"Sure you will, Quinn, and when they get here an hour later because you're not worth their time, I sure as shit won't be here."

I took a step backwards. "Why *are* you here?"

David followed, jabbing his finger in my chest, and my skin crawled at the touch. "Beth left me and it's your fault. Your..." jab "...fucking..." jab "...fault."

Beth adored David's dirty money, why she would say goodbye to it surprised me.

I narrowed my eyes despite my stomach rolling in fear and let all the contempt I felt show through. "What's the matter, David? Your well of cash dry up? Has she moved on to someone who can—"

My head exploded into fire when his fist made contact with the side of my face. Staggering backwards at the force, my hands made a desperate grab for the couch to hold my weight. I shuffled back a step but his fist was a blur as he came at me again. I tried to let out a shout for Lucy, but with the lack of air, it came out as a breathless moan of agony.

I made a run for the door, but he planted both hands on my back and slammed me hard into the wall. My forehead hit the plaster with a loud crack, and I fell to my knees. Then he started kicking me, and when

I rolled into a ball, his foot came down on the side of my face, and he crushed it into the floor, laughing. He fucking laughed and I wanted to rip his face off.

I clawed my fingers into the carpet in an effort to get up, as his fists pounded me. When a shout came at the door, he kicked me in my side.

"This isn't over."

The world shifted, I heard yelling, then Lucy was there chanting, "Oh God, oh God, oh God."

"Hurts." I struggled to breathe. Then another pain came. The kind of pain that made everything else fade into the background. I clutched my stomach as agony ripped me apart from the inside. "Lucy," I moaned.

I felt a brush of her hand against my hair. "Paramedics are coming, honey."

I rolled over and swallowed, trying not to choke on the fear. "I'm losing the baby."

Lucy's panic stricken eyes found mine. "No."

Chapter One

Three and a half years later...

My last chance of escape took off in a squeal of tyres. Were the hounds of hell on his heels? Hardly. He was a Sydney cab driver. The fact that Lucy and I arrived at our destination in one piece was proof that seatbelts did, in actual fact, save lives.

My hands trembled as they smoothed the front of my dress. It was bright yellow, short, and backless. It was also brand new. The crafty salesgirl had appealed to the inferiority complex within by telling me it made me look taller. According to her degree in Fashionista 101, it also made my brown eyes big—like Bambi—and as much as I wasn't aiming for a deer in the headlights look, I got sucked in anyway. Not that I actually owned the dress. That honour belonged to my bank when I handed over my credit card. It sounded good in theory, but guilt for the one-off splurge was overwhelming.

I fiddled with my hair, and Lucy smacked at my hand. She'd worked hard to create the tousled waves I was busy destroying with nerves. "Stop it, Quinn. Tonight is your bitch. Act like it."

My spine snapped straight, and I curled my fingers tightly around the borrowed clutch as my eyes fell on the front entrance of the Florence Bar—a venue renowned for featuring hot, new Australian bands. The doors opened and the heavy bass ricocheted outwards, filling the busy city street and pounding into my chest. It increased my anxiety and my breath came in little pants.

"Quinn, this is your first night out in so long. Live a little." She frowned at me when I gifted her with my fake smile. "Now say it. Tonight is my bitch."

I sighed. It was true. I never went out, but losing Ethan and then my baby soon after, made recovery an endless process. Every time I found something special, it was snatched away. I was afraid of that happening again. It became easy to retreat from life and simply watch from the sidelines. Special never found you when you hid yourself away, and that was how I liked it. Lucy wouldn't give up on me though, and now here I was, unsure of myself but putting one foot in front of the other, each step bringing me closer to the bar. Maybe that meant I wasn't ready to give up on myself just yet either. Unfortunately, admitting to that didn't appear to be making tonight any easier.

I frowned back. "Saying it doesn't make it true, Luce."

"Sure it does." She took my arm and herded me towards two bouncers who were busy guarding the bar's inner sanctum as though God himself was inside having a few. "I don't care if you have to lie," she declared. "Lie. Lie your ass off. Just say it."

"Tonight is my bitch," I repeated dutifully.

"Say it like you mean it," she demanded.

"Can we just get this over with?" I snapped, eyeing the long line of impatient people waiting to get in. Flash bulbs dotted my vision as people famous enough to get caught by the paparazzi paraded by. I blinked rapidly to restore my sight and eyeballed bouncer one and two, wondering whether they could scent fear. Then the fear took a new turn as the hairs on the back of my neck stood up, sending goosebumps down my spine. Breathless, I turned and scanned the street, but I couldn't pinpoint anything that would give cause for alarm.

I pushed the eerie feeling aside, but Lucy already noted my panicked expression with an exasperated sigh. "You're not walking the green mile, Quinn. You're simply here to have a good time."

Rubbish. Absolute, utter rubbish. When a rare night off from work heralded its arrival, a good time was had by welcoming it warmly with wine, reality television, and sweatpants.

Her fingers dug in as we reached the bouncer on the left. The man looked like Wolverine, complete with fierce glower, wild hair, and a beard. Despite the scruff, he rocked a suit. It didn't surprise me. It was only fitting a bar like this had bouncers tipping the hot scale of the spectrum. According to Lucy, getting inside this place was the equivalent of winning a golden ticket, but apparently she knew one of these two burley sentries, and it appeared that Wolverine was it.

The doors opened and I peeked around his massive bulk and into the deep recesses of the bar. Inside was an atmosphere that was now so foreign to me it was like watching one of the nature documentaries I loved.

"Here you will find the Australian Man, a generally good looking human specimen, drinking in his habitual environment, socialising, laughing and talking, waiting patiently for his moment when the female breaks rank from the herd and—"

Her eyes on me, Lucy muttered, "Stop it."

"Stop what?"

"I can see your mind ticking over. You're doing that David Attenborough thing again, aren't you?"

"No," I lied and folded my arms.

Lucy bit her lip but the laugh, full and throaty, bubbled out of her. "You're such a dork. We really need to get you out more."

"Good luck with that," I murmured to myself.

Lucy turned to Wolverine and dazzled him with her smile. "Hi, Sean."

The lines of people, shamelessly queue jumped by Lucy, watched us with hissing resentment. I averted my eyes and focused on my feet. They were encased in navy coloured shoes: peeptoe with a heel the height of a small building. They were the shoes that went with everything, even the bright yellow I was wearing. I couldn't do the

slinky black look the way all the women waiting to get in could—
rocking the sex vibe like they were all born to it. Maybe when I was
young and looking for trouble black was the only colour that fit me, but
now colour was the only thing that gave me life.

I peered up at Sean from beneath my lashes and caught his
returning smile and nod at my best friend.

"Luce," he said, then he turned his gaze my way, his eyes travelling
the length of me.

I shifted uncomfortably but thankfully it didn't take long. My
stature was tiny enough that I didn't usually attract attention, and I liked
it that way. His eyes returned to mine, and they were packing heat. The
kind of heat that should've singed my skin off if I got too close. It made
sense. Make the customer feel good, they'll come back. By the looks of
the line to get in, Wolverine spent a lot of time making the customer feel
good. "Who's your friend?"

Lucy pulled me close and introduced me to Sean.

Ever polite, I offered my hand and said, "Nice to meet you."

He took my hand and leaned close. "How come I haven't seen you
here before?"

I looked at Lucy. She nodded at me, her wide eyes urging me to say
something. "Oh, well, I uh…don't go out. Much."

Sean nodded and released my hand. He opened up the big door to
usher us through, and I breathed a sigh of relief. It was short-lived. His
big hand came out and landed on my stomach. The light touch halted me
in my tracks. "Shame."

I met his eyes and he smiled at me, removed his hand, and turned
back to face the street. The interaction had my nerves returning with full
force, and I stumbled through the entrance.

"Booth or bar?" came Lucy's loud question.

Nerves had me beat and already I needed to take five. "Neither," I
shouted back. "Bathroom."

We pushed our way through throngs of people crowding the glossy
black bar and rows upon rows of button leather booths and found the

bathroom. I washed my hands and met my eyes in the mirror as I waited for Lucy to finish. Midnight black mascara highlighted the lashes surrounding my brown eyes. Foundation had done its best to cover the small smattering of freckles across my nose, but I could still see them. Rose blush gave colour to my fair skin, and hot pink lipstick with a slick of strawberry flavoured gloss covered the one feature I couldn't complain about—full lips. My hair was blonde, but not a beautiful golden colour. It was pale, almost white, and the long waves had long since gone.

When I'd returned home after David put me in hospital, I stood in front of the mirror and hacked it all off myself. My eyes watched dispassionately as each lock dropped carelessly to the ground. My outside needed to match the ugly on the inside; therefore, the long, pretty locks needed to go. I'd let it grow a little, but the choppy style was still short enough it barely touched my shoulders.

Lucy reached across me for a paper towel to dry her hands. A long sheet of black hair hung to her waist, piercing blue eyes sat in a striking face with deep olive skin, and boobs that preceded her into the room by at least a minute. I eyed mine. They were a handful, but that was according to my small hands. I sighed and we returned to the bar, rapidly snatching a booth that a group of people were currently vacating.

"Sit," Lucy said. "I'll get the first round."

My eyes followed her movements and that was when I saw him. He caught my eye because he was by the bar talking and laughing as his friends spoke to him, but his eyes weren't smiling. I recognised the look because I'd seen it in the mirror. My heart gave a small tug, and I was sure a bomb could've gone off and I wouldn't have noticed. Realising I was blatantly staring, I closed my mouth and looked down at my hands.

Come on, Quinn. You can do this. There's a social animal inside there somewhere just waiting to cut loose.

I looked up and let my eyes wander the room, knowing where they would land before they'd even stopped. They found him again and took in his tall length, wide shoulders, and tapered waist. Arms bulged with tanned muscle and thick veins. He had a head of blond hair, shorter than mine, but long enough that it just scraped into a ponytail. Loose strands were tucked casually behind his ears, and it gleamed like spun gold under the lights of the bar.

Girls—tall gorgeous ones with long, fluffy hair—hovered at the fringes of his group. Their slinky dresses were black or navy and their lips red and shiny, making me feel out of place in my golden yellow, hot pink lips, and fair, creamy skin. One of them, tanned and dark haired, said something, and he shouted with laughter. Hearing him laugh was beautiful, but seeing someone like her hold his attention brought me back to reality. I dismissed him and let my eyes move on.

Lucy arrived at the table with a tray of eight shots and two wine glasses. Obviously her aim of the evening was not to smooth my nervous edges but lay them out flat.

"Thank God," I muttered and reached for the shot, knowing I had the whole day off to pay for it. I tossed the vodka back and almost choked on the burn.

"See anything interesting while I was at the bar?" Lucy asked as she sat down in the booth opposite me, waiting for me to catch my breath.

I fixed my eyes on her. If she knew I'd been eyeing that hot guy she'd be all over it like tinsel on Christmas.

She downed her own shot and hissed.

"Nope," I replied.

My traitorous eyes wandered sideways, and Lucy followed my line of sight, her eyes widening with glee. "Are you shittin' me, Quinn? That guy is holy fuck me gorgeous." Her eyes narrowed on the hovering fangirls and she pursed her lips. "Could be a player."

I raised my brows at her and pointed my finger. "Exactly."

I picked up another shot and brought it to my lips.

"But that's good," she said, tossing back her long sheet of hair. "That's what you need. You're in a man drought of epic proportions. You need someone like him to clear the cobwebs."

I choked again on my second shot and sputtered. "Lucy! I'm not a...a floozy!"

Lucy snorted with laughter and grabbed her phone. "Who says floozy? I've gotta text that one to Rick." Her fingers started stabbing letters as she texted her husband, chuckling all the while. "Next thing you'll be calling yourself a lady of the night because you had sex once in all of two years."

"I haven't had sex."

"That's why we're here," she muttered as she hit send and tossed her phone back on the table.

"I thought we were here to have a drink and then go home."

She ignored me and picked up another shot, drinking it down as her phone buzzed. She read the message and her smile was smug. "Rick's going to come down for a drink. Then he can keep me company while you make your big move."

I bit my lip to stop the bark of hysterical laughter threatening to burst out at her statement. If any moves were going to be made, it would involve me running for the door.

"I don't belong with a man like that, and I don't belong in a place like this, Lucy."

We both looked his way. He was wearing dark blue jeans and a stretchy T-shirt that emphasised his muscled chest. It was white and had a band's name on the front with a picture, but what the thin, tight material revealed had me straining my eyes. It looked like a tiny little bar pierced his right nipple. Complete and utter lust punched me in the gut, and Lucy's eyes widened when I let out a breathless squeak. Until I'd met Ethan, hot bad boys had always been my thing, and this one appeared to lead the pack.

She flared her nostrils. "Rubbish. Let's not start this bullshit again, Quinn. You're not worthless. You're beautiful, inside and out."

"Not tonight." Nerves curdled my stomach into a tight knot, and I fought past the usual wave of self-loathing. For once, I was trying not to let it beat me down.

She pursed her lips. "Okay. Well let me tell you something. Maybe you aren't a tall sex goddess. So what? You have the market cornered on sweet and adorable. People pay big dollars for a hair colour like yours. Then there's your huge, Bambi eyes, and bitch, you have the cutest smattering of freckles across your nose. You'll always have that youthful look about you no matter how old you are, and compared to all those hos at the bar…" she waved her shot glass around and then looked at it as though she wondered how it got there "…they look fake in comparison, with their hair extensions and orange tans. I swear to God I was watching one of them laughing just before, and her face did not move. I was fucking scared. Scared," she repeated, jabbing her shot glass at me with emphasis before sucking it back.

I chuckled and resisted the urge to kick off my heels, tuck my legs underneath me, and get cosy. "Thanks, Luce, but you don't need to butter me up because it won't work. I'm staying right in this booth."

Two large hands slapped down on the table. I followed them up and into Sean's dark brown eyes. "Having a good night?" He smiled at the both of us, but his question was directed at me. It was probably obvious I was socially inept, so perhaps he felt sorry for me.

Not wanting to encourage any pity, I returned the smile. "If I wasn't, the tray of shots here will make sure I am."

I didn't need to see Lucy's grin at my flirty comeback. I could feel it. I bit down on my lip so I wouldn't laugh at her.

Sean's eyes dropped to my mouth for an uncomfortable moment before he nodded at the door. "Gotta get back out." He slid a small slip of paper across the table towards me with his large hand. "If you wanna change that good night to a great night…" he winked "…then you have my number."

"Oh my God," Lucy hissed at me as he walked away. "Sean is so into you."

The thought had me a little giddy, but it might also have had something to do with the shots. "He's hot, but how many girls does he proposition on the job? I'd just be one in a long line, but…" I grinned as my eyes fell on his retreating back "...I'm sure it's a line most girls would be happy to queue in."

Lucy giggled. Lucy hardly ever giggled. Her laugh was more the rich, throaty kind, so I knew her shots were kicking in. "Well he obviously wants you at the front of it. It's that sexy mouth of yours, Quinn. A man takes one look at it and instantly imagines how it would look wrapped around his—"

"Lucy!" I squealed.

"Okay, so save Sean for another night. Make it a buffet. Start with the hot player at the bar."

I sighed and my eyes sought him out. His friends were still there, but he wasn't. Ever since my eyes had found him, my spine had tingled with awareness. Now it felt like the bottom had dropped out of my stomach.

I turned back to Lucy, knowing my disappointment was obvious. "He's gone."

"Well here..." Lucy grabbed at the bit of paper Sean had left behind and tucked it in my clutch "...there's always Sean, and he's better than a consolation prize. I've seen him without a shirt, and his muscles rival Rick's."

This was true. Rick was the sort of guy you looked at and then expected his shirt to tear apart as he transformed into The Hulk. They were married straight out of school and had been together almost eight years now. I'd met the pair of them when I moved into the townhouse next door four years ago and they'd both been my best friends, my only friends, ever since.

"Speaking of Rick, if he's coming down for a drink, will he still be able to give us a ride home?"

"Honey, you are getting a ride home with someone else." She grinned wickedly, her behaviour getting less refined as the night went on. I could only imagine it was tame in comparison to what went down on an ordinary night at Screamers, the nightclub where she worked. The place was at the Cross in Sydney's red-light district and stripping and cage dancing featured heavily. That was how Lucy got her start, dancing in a cage and working her way up the chain to bar manager.

"Oh, he's back," Lucy said and enthusiasm had her clutching my arm.

My eyes whipped to the bar, and sure enough there he was talking again with his friends. His eyes lifted, flashing with laughter and scanning the room. When he caught me staring, my pulse raced like I was lined up in pole position at the Grand Prix. His gaze wandered over me curiously, and I flushed with embarrassment, lifting a hand to hide my face. The sudden movement sent my wine glass flying across the table and sprayed Lucy. Thankfully she was acquainted with my spatial awareness affliction and used to the drama, so she didn't bat an eyelid. My eyes whipped back to the man at the bar to see if he'd caught the embarrassing display. The amusement in his green eyes and the way he saluted me with his beer told me he had. I cringed as I wiped up the mess with napkins, determined never to show my face at the bar again. Not that that would be a problem.

"Well get over there before he disappears again, Quinn."

"I...what?"

"You heard me." She flung a napkin at me. "I'll give you fifty bucks if you go stand by the bar next to him and order a drink."

"What are you, like a reverse pimp? I just embarrassed the complete shit out of myself. I'm not standing by the bar. I'm leaving."

Her eyes flattened menacingly. "Then what? I get to drag you out again in another two years, making your drought double to four years? Stop running away."

"Thanks for the math lesson, Lucy."

"I won't let up about this so you may as well just—"

"Okay!" I held up a hand. "I'll do it. Just...don't watch me like it's some big deal. I'm going to the bar, buying a drink, and coming back. Nothing more."

She let out a deep, gratifying sigh and slid fifty dollars across the table. "The guy's name at the bar is Vince, okay? I know him so tell him I sent you."

"Keep your money," I hissed. Then I gave my dress a once over and cleared my throat. "Do I look okay?"

Her eyes softened sadly at my question. "You look perfect."

I reached the bar and tried to catch the barman's eye.

"Vince," came a voice from behind me. It wasn't a yell but somehow the deep rumble carried along the bar, and Vince looked up. My chest thumped with nerves, and I grabbed the bar with my fingertips. "Four beers, mate."

Did he just cut in?

Vince nodded and winked in the direction over my shoulder telling me that he had, in actual fact, just cut in. My eyes narrowed and I spun around, having to tilt my head, even in my skyscrapers, to meet his eyes. Up close their colour was a bright, leafy green with a starburst of topaz reflecting the light. He had a straight nose and a strong jaw covered by stubble, but long, golden lashes and gorgeous, full lips changed his features from hard to almost sensual.

Realising I was standing there absorbed in his lips, I dragged my eyes back to his and found him staring at me intently. I cleared my throat, feeling awkward and unsure of what to say.

Then he opened his mouth to speak.

To me.

Oh God, he was going to speak to me. *Please don't. Please don't. I'll have to reply. I can't do this.* My breathing escalated into silent little pants.

"You're not gonna toss your next drink at me, are you?"

My mouth fell open.

Say something, Quinn, I ordered myself firmly.

"My drink?"

His eyes crinkled slightly when he smiled and leaned towards me, enough that I could feel the heat of his body. "Yeah, your drink."

"Oh…" I paused. "I don't have one."

He nodded at the bar, so I turned and saw a glass of wine sitting there right in front of me.

I shook my head. "I didn't order that. It must belong to someone else. Excuse me," I muttered and did my best to get Vince's attention.

I couldn't do this. Being someone that smiled and flirted and made instant friends didn't come easily anymore. Watching everyone else around me do it so naturally just reminded me how little I belonged.

I turned the other way to check on Lucy. Rick had arrived and now they were both sitting in our booth eyeballing me.

What? I shrugged at the both of them.

Lucy's expectant expression evolved into a wide grin when a hand touched the small of my back. Tingles of warmth spread through my body at the unfamiliar touch. Lips brushed against my ear, and I almost moaned. "I ordered it. For you."

Breathless, I asked, "You did?"

"Uh huh," came the soft rumble of reply, and I swallowed. "When I saw you throw your drink at your friend, I thought you could do with another."

I spun back around. The man was completely in my space. Heat radiated from him and sucked every chill from my body. "I didn't throw it."

"Sure you didn't," he said. Then he smiled, slow and lazy, and I wanted to taste it on my lips. "You know, you could just say thank you."

"What?" I muttered.

He leaned in towards me, and I held my breath. Then he stretched his arm out and picked up three beers, called over my shoulder, "Thanks Vince," twisted to hand them to his friends behind him, and returned to me.

"Now," he murmured. "Where were we? Oh that's right. I believe you were thanking me."

"Umm…" He was watching me expectantly. "Thank you," I answered with a flustered smile.

He shook his head and the light spun in his silky hair. "Pity."

My smile dropped at his tone. "What?"

"I was hoping I'd get more than words."

More than words? My eyes dropped to his lips. "What were you hoping for?"

With his beer in one hand, he used the other to reach out and grip my hip lightly as he leaned in and said, "You."

I pulled back and looked at him. The man was a player. That was obvious, but I couldn't bring myself to care. The way he was looking at me made me *want* to be the one he was hoping for.

Is it him you want, Quinn, or just the touch of another man after going without for so long?

Oh God. I didn't know. Was I already reverting back to my old ways, drinking and sleeping with anyone just to feel wanted? Because that wasn't the person I wanted to be anymore. My throat felt thick and my eyes burned as he waited for me to reply. He stood there so patiently, so utterly beautiful, but all he wanted was a warm, willing body. Any woman in this bar would jump at the chance.

"Excuse me," I mumbled. "I have to get back to my friend."

I turned but my heel caught on the stool next to me, and in slow motion I watched my glass of wine pitch all down the front of his shirt.

"Oh God," I cried. *Stupid. You are so stupid!* "I'm so sorry."

I stared in horror at his sopping shirt. The cold liquid made it cling to his skin, revealing muscled ridges that begged to be touched. In that moment the absolute one positive I could gain from this disaster was that if this were a wet T-shirt competition, his rivals would be eating dirt.

He glanced downwards at the mess, brushing away the wet with his hands. "Vince?" he called out over my shoulder. "Towel, mate."

I could hear his friends behind him giving him shit as he peeled it back from his chest with his thumb and forefinger. They must have thought I'd been insulted and done it deliberately.

My first, *and last,* embarrassing foray into the world of socialisation was now complete, and in that moment I prayed really hard for Dr. Who to arrive with the Tardis, but guess what? He didn't show. So I sat my now empty wine glass down, grabbed at the towel Vince proffered, and handed it over.

"I'm really sorry," I mumbled, averting my eyes.

I turned in a sudden rush to leave, but a firm, warm hand grabbed my arm. I paused and met determined green eyes. "Leaving me?"

You should only be so lucky, Mr. whomever you are. "I'm really sorry," I whispered. "I can't do this."

His brow furrowed, confusion clouding his eyes as the towel he held hovered over his chest. "Can't do what?"

"Life," I muttered under my breath. "It wasn't meant for me."

I spun on my heel, nodded to Lucy that I was heading for the front doors, and I left.

Chapter Two

"Running away?"

I turned and pressed my lips together. Oh God. There stood the hot guy from the bar, damp shirt and all. *Why are you standing outside with me? Isn't it enough that I threw my drink all over you and ran away?* Perhaps I was entertainment and he wanted to see what amazing feat I could perform for my next trick.

"Absolutely," I answered honestly.

"Me too."

My eyes widened at the thought of him running away from the fluffy, botoxed beauties inside. "You are?"

He nodded seriously and looked down at his soggy shirt. "I bought someone a drink, and they threw it at me. Seems like a good excuse to ditch my friends in there and head home." He looked back up and chuckled when he caught the flush heating my cheeks. "Share a cab?"

Before I could speak, he lifted his arm, let out a piercing whistle, and a passing cab squealed to a stop. It must have been a slow night because I'd only seen that happen in the movies. Still, I was impressed. Lucy and I hailed a cab together once on a night out a long time ago, and we'd practically had to stand in the middle of the road at the risk of becoming human speed bumps. Even then, I was sure the driver only stopped because he thought Lucy was about to throw herself on the hood.

He opened the car door and looked at me expectantly. I tucked the clutch tightly under my arm and glanced back at the bar before looking back at him, weighing my options.

"What were you hoping for?"

"You."

Was there really an option? Because my mouth was saying okay, my legs were walking towards the car, and I was climbing in and scooting to the other side before I could even think.

He slid in beside me and pulled the door shut. His bulk crowded me, making me hyperaware of how close his leg rested near mine.

"Where do you live?"

"Campsie."

"Campsie, mate," he said to the cab driver.

Remembering my speedy arrival at the bar with Lucy, I hastily buckled my seat belt and sat back in my seat as the driver roared us off into the night.

"Campsie's a bit of a hike for a cab ride," he said.

This was not news. Rick and Lucy were supposed to be my ride. Now I'd need to take out a small loan to cover the cab fare home.

"Do you mind if I get dropped off at Woolloomooloo first? I need to get out of this wet shirt."

"Um…sure," I said with a nod and turned to stare out the window, not wanting him to see my obvious disappointment.

"Woolloomooloo now, mate," he said to the cabbie. The driver waved his hand in acknowledgement and changed direction.

I grabbed my phone from my clutch and messaged Lucy that I was already cabbing it home. It buzzed soon after in response, but I tucked it away without reading the message. Instead, I risked a peek to my left and found the man's eyes appraising me intently, as though trying to figure me out.

"So…" I tried not to fidget under the scrutiny. "What do you do?"

That was witty. *Great start, Quinn.*

"I'm a consultant," he said with a wave of his hand as though it wasn't important. "What about you?"

"What about me?" I grabbed hold of the armrest as the driver spun us around a tight turn. The manoeuvre had him leaning slightly towards me, and I inhaled the spicy scent of his skin underneath the haze of wine I'd drowned him in.

His eyes crinkled in a smile. "What do you do?"

"I'm uh… in between jobs at the moment."

"So what do you do when you're not in between jobs?" I focused on his lips as he spoke and realised that I wasn't hearing a word he was saying. I bit my lip, flushing when his eyes lowered to my mouth.

"Sorry?"

He repeated his question.

"Um…I just finished uni doing business management actually, but that was part time. During the day I worked full time as a receptionist."

Long days of work and late nights of university by correspondence had given me my degree—one thing in life that was working out for me because in two days I had a job interview lined up as assistant manager to Jamieson, one of the hottest up and coming bands in the country.

He directed the cabbie towards his address and then turned to me. "Sounds like you're a busy girl. Who did you work for?"

"Jettison Records," I replied.

His eyebrows flew up in apparent surprise. "Oh yeah? That's—"

The driver squealed around another tight corner. Lost in a pair of green eyes, I wasn't holding on for dear life. My head cracked into the side window with a painful thud.

"Ouch." I winced.

The man cursed under his breath. "Are you okay?"

He held my cheeks gently with his fingers, tilting my head to check for an injury. My heart tripped over at his concern and the tenderness of his touch.

"Godammit, mate," he growled angrily at the cab driver. "You bastards need to learn how to slow the fuck down."

The driver squealed to a stop out the front of a renovated block of warehouse apartments and said, "Time is money, man."

"Come on." The man threw some money at driver, and then he unbuckled my seatbelt and hauled me out of the car as though I weighed a feather. "I'm not sending you home with this speed demon."

He took my hand, lacing our fingers and led me towards the entrance of the building. "I'd drive you home…" he said, punching in some numbers on the security panel and the door unlocked. "…but I'm probably over the limit."

One minute I was pitching my drink at a random hot guy, the next I found myself about to enter his apartment. How on earth did that happen? He pushed the door open, and I tugged my hand free. He could be a serial killer for all I knew. "Well that's okay. I can just get another cab."

He paused and looked at me, concern furrowing his brow. "You think I'm gonna leave you out here wandering the city streets waiting for a cab to pass by?"

I bit my lip and scanned the dark, cold streets. They were quiet and empty and in no way appealing. I turned to face him, about to tell him I'd just ring for one when he exhaled audibly, his eyes burning into mine, and said, "You've gotta stop doing that."

"Doing what?" I asked breathlessly.

He let go of the door, and it closed with an audible click before we'd even stepped inside. "Biting your lip like that."

He took both my hands in his and inched closer until the heat of his body chased away the chill in the air.

"Oh," I muttered.

He spoke, his eyes concentrating on my lips, his voice low. "Your mouth gets all red and swollen until I want to lick it better."

My breath hitched because it looked like he was about to do just that. He let go of my hands and cupped my face gently, his body slowly angling mine towards the red brick wall of the building. I stumbled in my navy shoes, and he cursed, his hands shifting to grip my hips tightly.

"Sorry," he muttered.

"My fault," I breathed as his touch burned right though the pretty satin sheen of my dress and deep into my skin. My chest fluttered up and down as he used his bulk to crowd me into the wall. "I ahh...should probably get going."

"Uh huh."

His chest pressed against me, and I stopped breathing. I licked my lips and he groaned and leaned in, ducking his head until his mouth hovered a mere breath apart from mine.

"Can I kiss you?" he whispered against my lips.

Before I could even finish saying "please," his hold on my hips tightened and his lips crushed down on mine. He wasn't sweet or gentle. His touch was hard and rough, as though he needed his lips on mine to breathe. I moaned when one of his hands moved from my hip to fist in my hair, tilting my head as he pressed me into the wall.

When he pulled back, we were both panting.

"Jesus," he gasped, his green eyes wide and lips swollen as he swallowed.

I had a second to breathe before he slammed his mouth back on mine, pulling back only long enough to breathe against my lips and ask, "Do you want to come in?"

Do I what? I was sure he was asking me something but I was lost. His body was too busy reminding me I was alive and I wanted more.

The early light of dawn brought me awake with a thumping head and a groan. My eyes felt rusted shut, and I squinted them open. Without care at the pain, they flared wide when I took in my surrounds. I was lying naked in an enormous bed with sheets the colour of tropical water. I turned left and caught a white wash bedside table in thick timber, a wallet, coins, and random receipts littering its surface. Oh my God, where the hell was I?

I turned to my right and there he was—the drought breaker. The holy fuck me gorgeous guy. The man I'd dazzled with my lack of wit and wine glass handling skills. He was on his stomach, one arm curled under the pillow with the sheet barely covering his firm backside. I ran my eyes up the tanned, muscular back to the wide, beautiful tattooed wings of an eagle that spanned his shoulders. I'd never seen anything like it: the detail, the raw beauty in the colours, the haunting shadows. I liked looking at him while he was sleeping. The hardness in his features appeared almost peaceful. There was no trace of the saddened expression I'd caught a glimpse of last night. Perhaps it had simply been my imagination running away with me.

Floozy! I shouted silently.

The mute scream reverberated painfully in my head until I remembered last night and how much care he'd taken with giving my body more pleasure than I'd ever known. I felt the shame die away at the memory. The man was…wait a minute. I didn't get his name. I let a guy take me back to his place, and I slept with him, literally, and I didn't know his name!

Floozy! I shouted again.

Oh God, oh God, oh God.

I closed my eyes but all it did was bring back memories of last night, and they were hot. He hadn't just broken the drought; he'd exploded me out of it in a fever so hot I felt almost blistered.

He groaned softly in his sleep and turned his head to face me, one hand shifting from under the pillow to rest near his face. My breathing quickened as I remembered those hands. They were strong and calloused, and he'd used them to shove me up against the wall and push his way inside my body. All the while his soft, full lips travelled hungrily along my neck, biting down on my ear until I thought I'd pass out. He'd ripped his shirt off hurriedly, exposing smooth golden skin covered in muscled ridges and a little silver barbell piercing in his right nipple. When I'd boldly tugged on it with my teeth, he groaned and the sound set me on fire. When I threw back my head and banged it hard on the wall, he simply turned us around and shoved me down on the bed without missing a beat. The man pushed every single button I had. Well, I only had the one, but he'd pushed it enough so that when I went off the edge, I didn't just fall. I took a soaring dive of toe curling, throat baring pleasure.

Unfortunately dawn was now announcing its arrival, returning me to solid ground with a thud called "the awkward morning after." Despite the fact I never went out anymore, I was aware that one night stand etiquette involved flashy "do not linger" neon signage.

I found my yellow dress on the floor. The pretty satin was crumpled, and I winced at its careless abandon in the cold light of day. Next to it sat my matching lace underwear. I held up the panties, noting they had a tear, not from being completely ripped off, but definitely torn in the desperation of swift removal. I closed my eyes for a brief moment to relive the memory of them fisted in his hands as he yanked them down my legs.

I took deep breaths to cool the surge of heat as I finished dressing. I dragged my fingers through my snarls and ran fingertips under my eyes, all the while prepping my mental fortress for the walk of shame.

I heard my phone shrill loudly from somewhere beyond the bedroom. Shoes in hand, I tiptoed out of the room to go search for it. Unfortunately he lived in a loft that appeared huge, and an immediate scan did not bring my phone or my little clutch to light. I heard a noise and my frantic search began in earnest, upending couch cushions, on chairs, looking behind bookshelves, under tables.

"Looking for something?"

I paused and closed my eyes, swallowing hard.

This was not cool.

This shit was so. not. cool.

On hands and knees I turned towards the voice to see a man in the kitchen that was not the man I had left sleeping in bed—full lips, short dirty blond hair—staring at me as he stood there in nothing but running shorts. My gaze lingered on a trail of sweat that ran down the middle of his chest to sink into his shorts, and I flushed from the tips of my mussed hair to the bottoms of the pretty pink toenail polish I'd applied with painstaking care yesterday.

The man cleared his throat, loudly, and my eyes snapped to his amused gaze.

"Oh." I got up off my hands and knees. "I was just um…searching for my bag."

He chuckled and pointed to my little clutch, sitting on the counter of the kitchen bench as though it was quite happy where it was and wasn't prepared to leave. "You mean this one?"

I ran a hand over the wrinkled mess of my dress, fighting the urge to just let the clutch have its way and leave without it. Instead, I moved fast, snatching it off the bench and holding it to my chest.

The man's grin got wider as he took in the dress that was busy proclaiming my lack of moral fibre.

"I'm Casey."

My eyes fell to the hand he was holding out, and I took it in mine briefly. "Um…Quinn. I'm Quinn," I managed before letting go of his hand and taking a step back. I indicated towards the door. "I'll ah…just let myself out."

"Wait," Casey called when I started to flee. "Can I get you breakfast? Did Travis offer you a ride home?"

My eyebrows flew up. "Travis?"

Casey's amusement returned at my confusion, and he nodded towards the bedroom I'd just come from.

I mumbled a rather unintelligent and nonsensical response and grabbed for the handle of the front door just as it was shoved open from the other side. I stumbled from the force, falling down on my backside with a painful and embarrassing thud.

"Oh shit. Sorry. I didn't know you were there," I heard the door shover exclaim.

I pushed the hair out of my face to see another gorgeous guy standing before me. Wasn't the saying all bad things happened in threes? Was it the same case with guys? Do all hot guys happen in threes? If so, why didn't I get the memo? This one looked a lot like Travis with his green eyes, golden skin, and silky hair, though his was dark brown, short, and mussed, as though he ran his fingers through it constantly.

I grasped the hand he was patiently holding out, and he hauled me up off the floor. I stumbled awkwardly to my feet.

"Why you're just a little thing, aren't you?" He observed, his eyes running the length of me.

I straightened my back, flushing wildly enough under the scrutiny to break out in a light sweat. He turned to look at Casey as I tried tugging my hand free but he held on tight.

"Airport *hotdog*. Five minutes."

Casey let out a groan. "Not you with the nickname too."

My mouth fell open as the other man laughed. "Hotdog?"

Casey looked at me and shook his head. "Don't even ask."

Assuming it was some lewd reference to *wieners* and *buns* I could only agree and shut my mouth.

"I'm Mitch," the man said to me.

"Quinn," I replied politely, tugging my hand free.

Mitch looked between Casey and me with a slight smirk. "So…you two know each other, huh?"

Before I could offer a retort, Casey grinned again and shook his head. "No, but she knows Travis, don't you, Quinn?"

Oh my God.

I did, apparently, know Travis rather intimately. Reflecting back on last night left me with the knowledge he was a man I wouldn't soon forget. It had been so long since I'd stopped giving my body away to anyone that made me feel good. I wanted to tell them I wasn't the person who did this kind of thing, not anymore, but apparently I was. Just one night was all it took for me to revert back to my old ways.

Just to round out my embarrassment, the bedroom door opened and Travis emerged. The unfairness that he looked even better this morning than he did last night was not lost on me. The jeans he'd slid on were only half buttoned up, his hair was mussed from sleep, and his eyes were lowered sleepily, not making me want him any less than I did last night—even without the alcohol pulsing through my system.

Without replying to Casey, and before I could be noticed by Travis, I slipped quickly out the door, pulled it shut, and ran.

Chapter Three

After messaging Lucy, I felt pathetically grateful to see her squealing up the quiet street like Batman. Thankfully it was still early, and I didn't have to worry about being seen by the public in what was obviously last night's outfit. The door of her crappy, beat up Toyota Corolla creaked loudly as I flung it open and climbed in the passenger seat. The car was clean, yet it still smelled like a pair of week old gym socks. No matter how many aromatic hanging trees she had hung over the rear view mirror, the smell still remained. After buckling my seatbelt, she squealed off into the street.

"Holy shit, girlfriend!" she shrieked when she took in my dire appearance with a sideways glance. "You look like you've been dragged through the hedge backwards."

I had no idea where to begin with that statement after the encounter I just had. Instead, I wound down the window and let the fresh, cool air blast away the residual heat of embarrassment on my cheeks.

"This is your fault," I told her.

If it wasn't for Lucy, I'd have been sitting at home last night, completely oblivious that such a man like Travis even existed. Now the vision of him biting down on my skin as his hips ground hard into mine was stuck on the repeat button inside my head, and I feared it would never stop. I didn't want it to stop. Already, my body was craving his touch again.

"Hey!" she shouted when I stole the giant sunglasses off her face and jammed them on. My eyes were still gritty and sore—unused to nights out drinking and hot, wild sex. "How is it my fault? I can't believe you went home with the holy fuck me gorgeous guy!"

I couldn't believe I went home with him either. Travis was pure male perfection from the intensity of his green eyes to the way they'd burned with desire. I knew I had a long way to go with rebuilding my self-confidence, and I was working on that, yet I couldn't help but wonder what it was he saw in me that had him touching me with such heat.

Lucy took her eyes off the road to raise her blue eyes at me in disbelief. They were bright and cool, the first thing I saw when I met her after moving in next door. I didn't know what I'd have done without Lucy. The people I thought were friends found out I was pregnant and the shunning began, as though pregnancy was contagious. Idiots.

"Earth to Quinny." Lucy snapped her fingers in my face, the car swerving dangerously with only one hand at the wheel. This was why I never, okay, hardly ever, got in the car with Lucy.

"What?"

"I asked if the man got your number? Is he going to call you?"

I grabbed a packet of gum out of the centre console and shoved it in my mouth, chewing furiously. The fresh taste in my mouth restored me a little.

"No. He didn't get my number," I replied.

"No? Why not? Does he think he's too good for you?" Lucy pulled over to the kerb with a squeal of tyres, and I jerked in my seat, my stomach lurching. "I should go back and kick his ass," she snarled.

"Lucy! No! I snuck out okay? He didn't see me."

"Oh." Lucy lips pressed flat in apparent disappointment she couldn't get in a fist fight on my behalf. "Well, did you get a photo of him?"

"No!" I laughed at her hopeful expression. "I'm not so depraved that I need to take a photo of his ass to look at every time I feel like being a perverted troll."

She didn't indicate before pulling back out into traffic. A driver behind us tooted after getting cut off, and Lucy took a hand off the steering wheel to give him the finger.

"The photo was for me, moron, so *I* can be the perverted troll."

I rolled my eyes. "As if you'd look twice at another man besides Rick."

Lucy and Rick had something special. I liked to think I wasn't bitter or resentful, but I had to admit that sometimes it was hard to watch without feeling sad at what I once had with Ethan. Would we still be together now if he was alive? I would often wonder how different my life might have been if I hadn't lost him. Lately I found myself thinking about it less and less, and that hurt as well, as though I was leaving Ethan behind.

"Come on, Quinn. I've been married since the end of time. You're single so it's my right as your bestest friend in the whole world to live vicariously through you."

"How can you do that? This is the first time I've had sex in forever, remember?"

Lucy snorted. "Well I didn't say you were doing a good job of it, did I?"

I laughed, but inside I pushed down on the ache that pounded a little harder when I thought of Travis.

"Did you get his number?" she asked, obviously determined not to let this go. "Are you going to call him?"

"No! I'm not going to call him. No relationships for me, Luce. You know that. I'm not ready for anything like that. I don't know when or if I ever will be."

She huffed and it sounded almost sad. "Maybe it's time, Quinn. To let go of Ethan. To let go of your past. To move on. To live. Someone who could protect you—"

"I don't need to be protected," I interrupted.

I'd proved I could stand on my own two feet. The good news was that I'd had time to enjoy my independence because David was gone.

The police had photographed my injuries and charged him with assault. Four years in prison was deemed the suitable punishment, yet I was still struggling to sleep properly at night. Four years didn't automatically give me back what I'd lost, and in six months he'd be out. Despite a restraining order already in place, it was just a piece of paper. David knew where I lived. Soon I would need to think about moving, but for now it was hard to let go of having Lucy and Rick next door. Not to mention I needed a job in order to sign a new lease. While my contract position with Jettison Records had been extended continually, it had ended a week ago with an employee returning from maternity leave. Kind enough not to kick me to the kerb, my employers put me forward for the band assistant position I would soon be interviewed for.

"You know," Lucy continued, "Rick and I aren't going to be around forever. We need to see you settled and taken care of."

"Lucy!"

She was making it sound like they were ready to pass through the pearly gates, when in actual fact they were saving hard for a house. I knew they had enough for a deposit because every time I asked Lucy about it, she averted her eyes and glibly changed the subject. They were wasting money on rent because they were worried about leaving me behind.

"I can take care of myself," I pointed out.

"Not this old chestnut," she said with a huff. "I might appear as dumb as a box of rocks, but I *can* track a calendar. I *know* David is out in six months. Have you forgotten what he did? I sure as shit haven't. And last I saw, you haven't magically evolved into Rocky."

"I don't need to take him on. I need to move, that's all." I sighed and tucked my legs up into the seat. "Just get me home before you kill us both in an accident."

Lucy pursed her lips. "I'm a good driver. I could have been a race car driver I'm that good."

"No," I contradicted. "You are just that fast. You could have been a cab driver."

My phone rang from inside my clutch. I emptied its contents into my lap and grabbed for it.

"Hello?"

"Quinn? Mac."

"Mac?" Who the hell was Mac?

I heard an impatient huff, and I wasn't sure if it was directed at me or someone else. "Mackenzie. Mackenzie Valentine."

Lucy frowned at me and I indicated with frantic eyes for her to watch the road.

My interview as Mac's assistant wasn't for a few days. Was she ringing to tell me the position had been filled? The thought had my stomach lurching, although as the scenery passed by at the speed of light, Lucy's driving was likely a contributing factor.

"H-how can I help you?" I stuttered.

"Actually, it's how you can help me."

"Oh?"

"Look. I'm swamped. I need an assistant ASAP. Can I move your interview forward?"

I exhaled silently, relieved the position was still open. "Of course," I replied. "When?"

"Now," she barked.

Oh shit.

I looked at Lucy in panic. She took her eyes off the road to glance at me, raising a brow in question.

"Sure. That's no problem at all," I lied, doing my best to sound bright and efficient instead of painfully hungover. "I'm just out and about at the moment, and I have a dog at the vet to collect this morning." I also had a vet bill to pay that I knew would have my purse cringing in horror. "Would lunchtime suit?"

"No. We need to be on set to start shooting a music video. Is your dog okay? Can you just pick him up and bring him with you?"

"Bring my dog?" I repeated.

"Yeah. Your dog."

"Um…I guess so."

"Good. See you soon," she barked and hung up.

Mackenzie Valentine sounded *fierce*. I shoved all the contents on my lap back into my clutch along with my phone, feeling rushed now and completely unprepared.

"Well?" Lucy took her eyes off the road again to glare at me, offended I was keeping her waiting.

"I'm screwed," I muttered.

"Dammit, Suzi-Q. Not now," I growled.

I kicked at her tyre in frustration, but she didn't reply. Her silence was enough but if cars could smirk, I could swear she was doing it right now, and I wanted to scream. Mac had expected me long before now, and the five second shower I'd managed to take before collecting my dog was now wasted. I felt the sheen of sweat from my flustered panic. I had no time for makeup, and my hair, according to the panicked reflection staring back at me from my car window, was its customary fairy floss. Nothing clean to wear meant I was wearing my white cap-sleeved blouse that had a pen mark and my beige pants where the hem was coming loose. Quite frankly, if she hired me it would be a miracle because *I* wouldn't hire what was staring back at me from that window.

Rufus, my lazy Rhodesian Ridgeback, sat in the passenger seat, his tongue lolling about as he took in his surroundings with fear. I didn't blame him. He'd just survived an over nighter with the vet. Now he was likely wondering what the hell was next. I could feel his pain because I was wondering the same thing. His big brown eyes caught me looking at him, so he climbed gingerly over the handbrake, settled into the driver's seat, and licked the inside window until it was a foggy, slobbered mess. Then his tongue lolled again as though happy with his efforts.

Rufus became mine not long after David's attack. He was rather menacing in appearance, but that was all show because he was a big softie. Still, his presence was a small comfort.

Twenty minutes later an older man by the name of Stan arrived, proceeding to peer under the hood of my ancient and rusty yellow Mazda as though it held all the secrets of the universe. He tinkered under Suzi-Q's hood while I glared at her. I'd had her for over two years now. When I'd driven her out of the second hand car yard, *Devil Gate Drive* by Suzi Quattro blared from the speakers, so the name had stuck. I'd like to say in all the time we've been together it's been a mutually respectful and loving relationship, but my car hated me.

Stan finished quickly, taking off after divulging me of almost a hundred dollars. Suzi-Q, seemingly satisfied with her new battery, purred contentedly.

"Happy now?" I hissed at her, inching carefully back into traffic.

Twenty minutes later, I pulled up in front of a pretty, renovated duplex in the beachside Sydney suburb of Coogee. The driveway housed a big, blue Hilux and an empty space on the other side, but I chose to park on the street, fearing my car would leak oil.

I stepped out of the car and took in the quiet, leafy surroundings. It appeared peaceful and pretty and in no way the headquarters to an up and coming rock band. At the least there should have been long-haired tattooed types hanging off the front porch, cigarettes dangling out of their mouths, and empty beer cans strewn haphazardly across the lawn.

Hoping I had the right place, I wrestled Rufus onto his leash and we puffed our way up the drive. I rang the bell and despite my nerves, I peeked down at Rufus sitting beside me and giggled. He'd suffered an ear infection, and now at least ten layers of bandage wrapped around his head, covering his ears and winding underneath his muzzle. It wasn't his best look.

"Mac! That'll be your interview!" I heard called out from inside.

A whirlwind flung open the door, and I held tight to the leash to stop Rufus barging inside. I opened my mouth to speak but nothing came out. The girl who stood before me radiated sex appeal in waves. Her caramel hair hung in curls to her waist and her skin was a rich, dusky olive. Instantly I recognised her as Evie Jamieson, lead singer of the band my assistant interview was for. Evie was easily recognisable, having been splashed in the papers recently after being involved in a shooting. Her dark chocolate eyes, warm and friendly, took us both in, and she said something I didn't quite catch.

"Excuse me?"

"Nothing." She smiled brightly. "Can I help you?"

"Is Mackenzie Valentine here?"

"Sure. Come in." She stood back, opening the door wide for Rufus and me to wrestle our way through. She yelled up the stairway to her left for Mac before waving me towards the couch with an apologetic shrug.

"Excuse me. I have to go."

She left in a whirlwind and from the front window I saw her leap into the blue Hilux, reverse out the driveway, and take off quickly down the street.

Feeling sweaty and nervous, I sat on the edge of the couch and fought to pull myself together. With no time to fuss on my hair, I'd tucked it under a knitted beret and brushed carefully at the smudge on my pants from Rufus pawing them. Finished, my gaze fell on the room. Soft, comfortable couches in deep navy filled the living room, and a thick, cream rug contrasted nicely with the timber flooring. The room was large and opened towards a dining area filled with a timber table that could seat eight people. Beyond that was the kitchen, done in glossy white cupboards, and caesarstone bench tops.

"Quinn?"

I turned from my perusal of the downstairs area to face the woman striding confidently towards me.

"I'm Mac."

Mac was beautiful, almost angelic in appearance with her long blonde waves, luminous golden skin, and fresh, pale lemon pants.

I focused on her eyes, rich emerald in colour, and frowned. "Have we met before?"

"I don't believe so." She held out her hand, and I shook it carefully. She let go, her eyes falling on Rufus and widening. "That's not a dog. That's a bloody horse!"

I looked at Rufus who stood as high as my hip. His tail thumped as though taking Mac's words as a compliment. "He *is* big, isn't he? I'm used to it I guess."

"Well let's go sit outside then. Evie has a little daschund called Peter so Rufus can keep him company while we talk."

Mac pulled two bottles of water from the fridge before leading me through the downstairs area to an outdoor deck made up of thick timber planks. A shade sail covered the barbecue and outdoor seating from the bright morning sun.

Letting Rufus off his leash, I answered Mac's question about his injury and watched as the two dogs circled each other as we took a seat.

She uncapped the bottle of water, took a sip, and then picked up her pen, tapping it impatiently on the page in front of her. "So. Shall we start?"

Making sure my phone was switched to silent, I nodded.

"So I've been managing Jamieson since they formed back in our uni days in Melbourne. We moved to Sydney last year, and that's when the band started to take off. Now I'm so snowed under with work I haven't even got the time to find my way out of my own underpants. It's stressful so I need someone on board with me to help lighten the load. You come highly recommended from Jettison Records, so I'm hoping you're that someone," she told me.

I hoped I was too.

Without waiting for a response, she ran through the finer details of the job. "Work days would be Tuesday to Friday and Friday and Saturday nights when we have shows. Shows are almost every weekend lately. Can you handle that?"

I nodded.

"Mostly the weekdays you'll be manning the office. When we have to go interstate or overseas, we'll need you with us. The office is just a couple of desks here in the duplex, but it's easier for us because the band lives here. There's a joint basement below where they rehearse, so having the office here makes sense for now. Anyway..." she paused to take a sip of water "...do you know anything about the band?"

"Of course. They've got a real alternative rock vibe that's huge in the indie music market, but they're signed now, right?" I answered.

Mac nodded.

"Your lead guitarist plays like nothing I've ever seen before. Not to mention he's gorgeous," I added without thinking, but I'd seen the band play on YouTube not long ago, and the guitarist had made an impression with his lean, muscular frame and piercing blue eyes.

Mac grinned and her eyes sparkled with mischief as she looked over my shoulder. Then I heard a male voice from behind me say, "Ahh, thanks I suppose."

I winced, swallowing my embarrassment, and the owner of the amused male voice flopped down in the chair to my left. He shot me a lazy grin that had my lips twitching despite the heat in my cheeks.

"This is Henry. He lives on this side of the duplex with Evie and me. Henry, this is Quinn. Our new band assistant," she added.

He leaned forward and held out his hand. I wiped my sweaty palms discreetly before taking it in mine, glancing at Mac open mouthed in shock as I did so.

"I got the job?"

Mac glared at Henry, who still had hold of my hand. He smirked at her before letting it go.

She faced me again. "Of course. I like you. I like your dog. Henry likes you, don't you, Henry?"

"Sure I do," he replied. He ran his hands through short, choppy blond hair before relaxing back in his seat, tilting his head, and closing his eyes to soak up the rays of sun.

"Look, Quinn. Let's cut the bullshit," Mac said, and Henry snorted. "I need you and I don't have time to waste."

"Oh...uh...don't you want to know anything about me?"

"I've read your resume and references, so what else can you tell me?"

"Uh, like personal stuff?"

She shrugged. "Sure."

"Well I don't go out much," I replied honestly, "and I like to read."

"Great, though this job might involve you going out a bit more than 'not much.' Are you okay with that?"

It would be an adjustment, but I wasn't prepared to give up before I'd reached the first hurdle. Last night had been a good practice run that admittedly hadn't gone as planned, but it wasn't like I was being hired to party and socialise on the weekends. I would be *working*.

Straightening in my chair, I smiled at Mac. "I'm more than okay with it." Approval shone in her eyes at my response, and when she smiled back I told her I was looking forward to it.

"Good, because we've got singles to be recorded and released, albums to be made, artwork and photo shoots to organise, publicity appearances at events, and interviews to arrange with TV and radio shows. Also, we start work on their first music video today. Can you start tomorrow?"

"Sure," I agreed, and hearing a playful growl, our heads turned towards the dogs. In my inattention, Rufus had wrenched his bandage off and both dogs were proceeding to chew on it, taking great delight in tearing the thick threads apart.

"Great." Mac clapped happily. "I'll introduce you to the rest of the band tomorrow then." She turned to Henry, the pleased expression disappearing in favour of an irritated frown. "Have you heard from Sandwich?"

"Um...Sandwich?" I echoed.

"Evie," she told me.

My eyebrows flew up. "You call Evie *Sandwich*?"

Henry just shrugged as Mac picked up her phone, her fingers a blur as she typed out a message. "Yeah, for her name: Jamieson. Jam. Jam sandwich. Now it's just Sandwich. Don't worry, you'll get used to it."

Henry tugged his own phone from the front pocket of his jeans and started typing out a message as well, so I asked to use the bathroom.

Mac waved her hand. "Sure," she replied and directed me to the upstairs location.

I wound my way up the staircase, stepped inside, and shut the door behind me.

Chapter Four

"Hey, Travis," I heard Mac call out as I unbuttoned my pants. "What are you doing here? Didn't you have to drop Casey at the airport this morning?"

I paused, my hands frozen on my button because every word Mac uttered sent a tingle of awareness down the length of my spine.

"I was supposed to but I had company. Mitch stopped by early this morning to pick him up and drop him off," came the deep rumble of a voice that was so familiar my heart skipped a beat.

What the hell? I *knew* that voice. It was both rough and soothing, sending me straight back to last night when Travis, with one arm wrapped around my waist keeping me close, had used the other to unlock his front door, all the while murmuring suggestive words in my ear that had me shivering with desire.

I shook my head. I must have heard wrong. Shrugging it off, I undid the zip on my pants, pausing when Mac spoke again.

"Company?" I heard her snort. "You are such a manwhore."

He laughed and I *knew* that laugh. Travis had arched my body over the bed, flicking his tongue down the length of my stomach, dipping playfully into my belly button and letting out a throaty chuckle when I'd squirmed breathlessly.

My knees buckled and I sank down on the closed lid of the toilet seat, my eyes darting about the enclosed confines like they were on crack—or looking for an escape hatch.

"So where is your *company* now?" I heard Henry ask.

Good question, Henry. I covered my face with my hands, fighting a hysterical laugh because his *company* was currently sitting on the toilet in the throes of a panic attack. I couldn't go out there looking like utter rubbish. My only course of action was to wait it out. I hunched over on myself, disbelief making my face hot.

"She left me," he replied.

I heard Mac snort. "Of course she did, you sorry ass. All the good ones do."

After waiting out a few moments of muffled conversation, I heard Mac call out, "Quinn? Come and meet my brother."

Brother?

I gave the toilet roll an incredulous stare.

Travis was Mac's *brother?*

My hands shook as I tore off a few sheets of toilet paper and dabbed at the sheen of sweat breaking out on my brow.

"Won't be a minute," I shouted.

It was now or never. I had no choice but to go back out there. Hiding out in the toilet for the next however long Travis planned on hanging around would not be a good look for me.

I stood, inhaled deeply, and reached for the handle of the door.

"I have to get going anyway, Mac. I'll meet Quinn another day," I heard Travis call from somewhere inside the duplex. The sound of a phone ringing cut through the silence, and I heard him answer.

"Yeah?"

I stood frozen, my hand hovering over the door handle.

"Can't today, Tim. Tell the AFP to set the meeting up for tomorrow morning okay? Did they say what it was about?" The sound was echoing down the hallway, moving its way towards the front door. His voice trailed off as the door opened and closed with an audible click. Shaky with relief at avoiding an awkward encounter, I removed my hand from the door handle and instead moved to the basin. I flicked on the tap and cold water gushed over my hands, soothing away the abuse my nerves had suffered today.

When I wound my way back out onto the outdoor deck, Mac was sitting there by herself, chatting on the phone.

She held up a finger to indicate she would only be a minute, so I watched the dogs for a moment. Rufus appeared thrilled to have a playmate. Both he and Peter had moved on from chewing the bandage to eating what looked like someone's brand new shoe. This Peter character was utterly adorable, but he obviously knew it; he was going to teach my dog bad habits. If Rufus came home thinking shit like that would fly in my house, he would have another thing coming.

"Are you okay?"

I turned. Mac had hung up the phone and was eyeing me curiously.

No, I was definitely not okay. I couldn't believe the day I'd had today. I needed to go home and have a nice hot shower, an icy cool wine, and find my bed. The problem with that was that I knew the dreams I'd be having tonight, and they would be hot.

I smiled at Mac because after everything I had a job. A great one. "Of course."

Mac remained sceptical, arching her brow at me. "Okay. You just looked a little pale there for a moment, but now your cheeks are all flushed."

"I'm fine, really. So tell me..." I began and resumed my seat, the curiosity to hear more about Travis overwhelming me. "You said you had a brother? That must be nice."

Mac froze from collecting her bits of paper on the table and looked at me. "You think? I have three of them. All older." She shuddered theatrically.

Travis times three? My eyebrows flew up.

"First there's Mitch, the eldest at thirty. He's a detective with the Sydney Police. Travis, who was just here earlier, is twenty-eight, and Jared, who's dating Evie, is twenty-six. I'm the youngest at twenty-four."

Forgetting my curiosity for the moment, I imagined how nice it must have been to have three older brothers looking out for you. Tears burned my eyes and I averted them, hiding the sharp burst of pain. "All older, huh?" I murmured wistfully. "Must be nice to have that."

Mac finished fussing with her papers and folded her arms. "You know, it has its moments, but yeah, it's nice, and if I hear you spreading that shit around, I'll call you a liar." She winked at me to soften the words, but I was pretty sure she meant them.

Clearing my throat, I asked, "So what do uh... Travis and Jared do?"

"They own a consulting business together. Evie's older brother Coby is a partner as well, and so is Casey, a guy that Travis went to uni with."

Considering the size and location of the loft I was in last night—all retro red brick interior feature walls, modern leather couches and a high-tech kitchen—I could only conclude the consulting they did was a lucrative business. Places like that came with a mortgage I was sure would pay off the national debt.

"What sort of consulting do they do?" I asked, sitting back in my seat, imagining engineering or investment banking.

"They consult on kidnapping and hostage cases mostly and are slowly building a security division that Jared is taking over. Travis has a degree in psychology and both have associate degrees in policing practice."

"What do you do?"

"I'm a consultant," he said with a wave of his hand as though it wasn't important. "What about you?"

Travis might have been seriously sexy in bed, smart, and some kind of tough guy, but he was obviously someone who wasn't keen on talking about what he did for a living. "It's not dangerous work, is it?"

"It is," she replied and rattled off all their injuries, which included Casey rolling his car, Jared being knifed, and Travis getting shot. I flinched yet she continued on. "Travis and Casey handle most of the custody cases that escalate into unsafe situations." A small furrow marred her perfect brow, and she gazed off in the distance, her eyes unseeing. "I'm starting to think the job is getting to Travis though."

My heart gave a lurch, which was odd because I barely knew him. To say it didn't sound like an easy job to do was an understatement, but I said it anyway.

Her eyes softened. "I know. Every week he sees abused children and that must be really hard."

My hands shook. Seeing it must be hard? Oh God, try living with it: the anxiety and fear, the pain, locking your door at night yet still unable to sleep, the feeling of being utterly alone and never seeing a way out.

Mac continued, "I think he needs—"

Breathless, I stood up and banged the table, knocking Mac's half empty bottle of water and cutting her off. It tipped, spilling everywhere.

"Oh, I'm so sorry." Tears burned from both my clumsy and emotional behaviour. "I'll just get a cloth," I blurted out and ran inside.

"Quinn!" Mac called. "It's just water."

I grabbed a cloth from the kitchen sink and paused to take a deep shaky breath, trying to push the memories away.

"Quinn?"

Flustered, I spun around, wringing the bit of material in my hands.

"Is everything okay?"

"Sorry," I offered. "I'm not usually so..." I was going to say clumsy, but that was a lie. "I guess I'm just a bit nervous about starting the new role."

"Well being nervous is good, right? Means you care about doing a good job." She tilted her head. "Why don't I show you the office? Then we can talk all the boring stuff, like paperwork, and get your employment forms drawn up."

Mac ushered me into the back office and pointed to a huge black and white photo mounted on a board that took up half the wall. "That's Jamieson," she said. I could hear the pride in her voice, and it thrilled me to know this was something I was about to become a part of.

The photo was of the band playing on stage. "Evie..." she pointed "...who you sort of met this morning. She's mostly the lead singer but is amazing on the guitar too when she gets it out. Henry, as you know, is lead guitarist, but he can play bass as well, and sometimes he sings. I met them both when we were living in Melbourne. We all went to university together. That's Frog..." she pointed to the bass player "...and that's Cooper." She pointed to the keyboardist. "They're pretty tight, and be wary... They're letches." She chuckled but it died off when she pointed at the drummer. "That's Jake," she said and her lips pressed flat. Then I thought I heard her mutter, "the asshole," but I couldn't be sure, so I leaned forward to get a closer look. He was shirtless, with a wide chest and powerful shoulders. His hair was a buzz cut and tattoos covered his entire left arm, his right shoulder, and one around his torso. He looked serious and intense, absorbed in the action of pounding the drums.

Mac sat down at the desk and ushered me over. She tapped on the keyboard and called up the schedule. She ran over the next two weeks with me, handed me a pile of employment papers and a contract. "Check it carefully," she warned. "We have a confidentiality clause in there you need to know back to front."

She handed over an iPad and an iPhone. "Here. That phone is for business calls. When you have to go out, you'll need to divert the office phone to the iPhone, okay?" I nodded and she continued. "It's all synced to this computer and my iPhone and iPad as well. You'll now be in charge of keeping the schedule updated. Here..." she handed me another large envelope. "This is original signed paperwork that needs to go to Jettison Records. That needs to be delivered first thing in the morning, so why don't you do that and then come here and get yourself acquainted in the office first. Then you can meet us on set for the music video at lunch time and meet the rest of the band."

I gratefully agreed, grabbing what I needed from the desk before Mac ushered me into the kitchen where Henry was pouring a cold drink.

"Where's our drink, asshead?"

Henry smirked and levered himself up on the kitchen counter. "Get your own."

Mac glared and then looked at me pointedly. "See what I have to deal with? Welcome to my world." She huffed and opened the fridge. "Do you know if Sandwich is doing the shop? There's no food." She half turned to face me. "Another drink, Quinn?"

I declined and she opened a bottle of Diet Coke. The front door slammed and Evie came whizzing into the kitchen. She looked different then she did when she took off hurriedly this morning. A grin was splitting her face a mile wide. It was infectious and I found myself smiling back as she opened the fridge and grabbed her own drink, and Mac introduced us properly.

"So tell us," Mac demanded, hands on her hips.

Evie raised her brows at Mac. "Tell you what?"

"Chook," Henry said warningly to Evie from his seated position on the kitchen bench. "She's gonna blow!"

Henry chuckled as Mac tried to push him off.

"Jared bought a house and we're moving in together."

Silence reigned as both Mac and Henry froze, so I figured this must be pretty big news. I wondered how it would feel, that sweet burst of love, of sharing it with someone else every day and building a life together. Immediately I thought of Travis and my chest burned. I rubbed at it a little. Was it possible for water to give you indigestion?

"Sorry, did you say you and my brother were moving in together?"

"Uh, yeah, I did," Evie replied.

Henry scooted off the bench, folded Evie in his arms, and whispered something in her ear. I could see her eyes soften, and then Mac was squeezing her hard. I felt like I was intruding on a private moment and took a step back.

"I love you, you know I do," Mac told Evie when she pulled back, "but you know what this means."

"I do?"

She started to chuckle slowly until it escalated into a full on wheezing, tear streaming, hyperventilating moment. "Sandwich," she choked out.

"What?" Evie shouted.

"Your days of chips and chocolate are numbered. From now on it's mung beans and grilled chicken all the way."

Henry also started to wheeze with laughter and looking at the three of them, I had absolutely no idea what was going on.

She flexed her jaw. "Thanks for the support."

Henry waved a hand at her as they both gasped for air. Evie muttered a "nice to meet you" at me, grabbed her bag, and said, "I'll be in the damn car waiting when you're all ready to leave."

Chapter Five

At around six that evening I was utterly exhausted from a day I was still trying to wrap my head around. Putting a tray of chicken in the oven, I started to relax, but a phone call from Mac ensured the day had not finished with me yet. I picked it up, answering absentmindedly as I placed a saucepan on the stove top.

"Quinn?"

"Hi, Mac."

She paused. "There's a slight problem. I missed giving you some of the paperwork today that needs to go to Jettison Records in the morning."

"Oh. Well that's okay. I can just leave a little earlier and swing by to get it first thing."

"That won't work because we'll be out early. They want us on set at six in the morning, and I forgot to give you a key. Can you come get it now?"

"Actually, Mac, I sort of can't leave right now. I'm sorry. Can I swing by in maybe an hour or so?"

Justin was eating dinner here tonight, and I was in the middle of making it. We traded business. He walked Rufus for me every other day, and I fed him a home cooked meal. Food for Justin was a high commodity. It made sense because not only did he share an apartment with three other guys, he was also Lucy's younger brother. Justin never ate anything at their place. Neither did I for that matter, but Justin was moving soon. Finished with uni, he was taking a new job interstate, and I was losing my dog walker.

"Okay. Um…hang on," Mac told me.

I heard a muffled sound as though she was putting her hand over the speaker. "Travis," she hissed.

Oh no.

"I need you to drop some papers over to Quinn's on your way to Mum and Dad's place."

Her words left me feeling like my body had just plummeted through an open trapdoor beneath my feet. I spun around from the stove and glanced down at my very unsexy, but very comfortable, pink fairy princess pyjamas, and I knew that just having washed my hair, it would be fluffed out to wild proportions.

"Mac," I heard him say, sounding put out. "Can't you do it?"

"No, I have to get to Mum's early to help with dinner. I don't have time. Come on, asshead. It won't take a second."

"Mac," I shouted down the phone. "Really, it's okay. I can—"

"No, no," she cut me off. "It's all good. Travis said he'd love to help out." I heard a loud thump and a muffled *ouch*. "He's going to deliver them to you, okay? Just hang tight. He'll be there in half an hour."

"Uh…well I think—"

She cut me off again with, "Anyway, I have to go. Thanks so much Quinn. I'll see you tomorrow," and hung up the phone.

My fingers dialled Lucy in a panic. Yes, she only lived next door, but there was no time for such pleasantries as knocking on the door.

"Yo, Quinny," she answered.

"Lucy." I poured out two wines and tucking my phone between my ear and my shoulder, I raced into the bedroom and sat them on the bedside table. "I have a problem and I need you here yesterday."

I flung open the wardrobe door.

"Calm down and tell Lucy what's wrong," Lucy said in her fake, soothing voice. I know it's fake because it takes on a low, drawn-out pitch when she thinks I'm behaving like a five year old, which quite frankly, I knew I was doing right now, but I had good reason.

"It's Travis," I half yelled as I rummaged through my shelves for something I could wear. "He's on his way here. And if you speak in the third person again, I'll slap you," I added as an afterthought.

"Oh Em Gee, Quinn!" she squealed. "You rang him after all. You sneaky hooha! You told me you never got his number."

"I didn't." God. Where to begin with that? "I don't have time for explanations. I need you."

"Fine, but you better tell me everything when I get there. I'll just grab my bag of tricks and be right over." She hung up.

Lucy's bag of tricks was actually a suitcase sized bag of makeup, hair products, and all types of beauty related, mind-boggling, electrical devices. This bag had wheels and a combination lock that Lucy gave to no one, not even me. Not that I ever had much use for it until now.

I rummaged through all my clothes, lamenting that nothing was clean. All my favourite items of clothing, like the dark, skinny jeans that made me look taller, or the soft pink knit that made my skin less pasty, were in the laundry. I held up a pair of denim shorts that I rarely, if ever, wore, but I bought them for the colour. They were hot pink with black piping along the pockets—bought in a mindless splurge simply because they were a bargain. Emerging from the wardrobe, I found Lucy striding in, wheeling her suitcase behind her.

She looked at me and flinched. "You invited him over looking like this?"

"I didn't invite—"

"Just shut up," she snapped, her eyes flashing. "I'm so disappointed in you. There's no time to perform miracles here."

Crouching, she unzipped her suitcase and pulled out her curling wand. She plugged it in and left it to heat on my bedside table. Next she moved to the wine I'd set out and took a large gulp, leaving me feeling like I had somehow become Jack Bauer, starring in my very own series of *24. Between the hours of six pm and seven pm....*

I picked up mine and took a sip, using my other hand to toss the shorts I was holding at her. "Everything's in the laundry. Are these too short?" She looked at them and opened her mouth to speak. "Don't answer that. I know they're too short."

She set her wine down and held them up. "Rubbish. For a little person, you have great legs and a cute butt. Put them on," she ordered. She flung them back at me and took a turn in the wardrobe, coming out with a loose turquoise cotton top that fitted snugly around the waist and fell off one shoulder.

"What about this thing? It looks casual enough to think you were just lounging around at home looking sexy. He'll take one look at the flawless skin on that shoulder of yours and want to lick it all up like a lollipop. Trust me."

I had no choice but to trust her because I was running out of time. I got changed and she quickly curled my wispy strands of hair, finishing by running her fingers through them to make them look casually tousled. She then attacked my face with some rosy pink blusher, mascara, and strawberry flavoured lip gloss and pushed me in front of the mirror.

"Ta da."

I stood in front of the mirror. The lemon yellow strap of my bra was showing from where the shirt hung off my shoulder, and I glared when Lucy suggested taking it off.

"I look like a liquorice allsort," I announced, looking myself up and down critically.

"Rubbish," she snapped. "Well, maybe a little, but who doesn't love lollies? You can thank me later. I'll let myself out."

"Lucy, I don't want to look like a lolly. I don't want Travis here at all."

That was a lie. Sort of. I didn't know what I wanted. The thought of seeing him had my heart racing a mile a minute, reminding me of how I felt when I met Ethan. Only Ethan had been so young, still growing into himself, whereas Travis was older, packed with muscle, and one hundred percent pure man. His body had tattoos and the scars of someone who'd lived hard.

Lucy began shovelling all her tools back in her suitcase and stopped to give me a dubious look. "Are you sure? Why did you invite him then?"

She zipped her suitcase and started making for the door.

"I didn't invite—"

"Gotta go, fairy princess. He'll be here in five minutes. Good luck. I'll be over later to get the lowdown." With a roll of her wheels and a slam of the door, she was gone. I took a deep breath before returning to the kitchen. I opened a packet of pasta and poured it into the boiling pot of water.

The knock came just as I was pouring another glass of fortifying wine. I'd never drunk so much in twenty-four hours in my life. Apparently that was what being Jack Bauer did to you.

I ran my hands through my tousled curls, inspected my shirt for spots, and exhaling slowly, opened the door.

Travis stood there, one hand in his pocket, the other tapping an envelope impatiently against his leg. My lips pressed together before a breathy, little moan could escape. Tonight's fitted T-shirt was another band, but this time I could clearly see it as Jamieson. A pair of mirrored aviators hung casually in the neckline and long, light beige cargo shorts rode low on his hips. His hair was scraped back in a tie, but a blond strand had escaped and fell down the side of his face.

Travis froze, the impatient tapping of the envelope halting against his leg. His rich, green eyes widened on my face, recognition lighting their depths. His lids lowered as they tracked slowly down the length of me. My cheeks heated under the blatant perusal as his eyes worked their way back up to meet mine.

He cleared his throat. "Quinn?"

I repressed a shiver at the memories his voice evoked, aiming for a nonchalant expression by trying to relax the nerves that locked my body tight. It wasn't working. My hand was gripped so tight on the door handle my fingers would need to be pried away.

I nodded, the movement jerky and awkward. "Travis."

His brow furrowed with confusion. "You're Mac's new assistant?"

Sighing softly, I replied, "That would be me."

A beat of time passed, and then another, as though Travis was somehow coming to terms with this freak coincidence. I shifted my legs as I tried to think of something to say that would fill the charged silence.

"I'm Mac's older brother," he told me.

"Great," I stated brightly, plastering a smile on my lips that didn't reach my eyes. I went to take the envelope from his hands when I heard a sizzle and crackle coming from the kitchen.

"Oh shit, the pasta!"

Abandoning the doorway in a rush for the stove, I found the saucepan boiling over, water running down and hitting the gas cooktop with hissing sparks.

"Crap," I muttered, flinching when steamy drops splattered my hand. I yanked it off the stove and grabbed a cloth to start mopping up the mess.

"Burning dinner?" came the teasing voice.

Flustered, I turned, finding Travis filling the tiny space in my kitchen.

I waved a hand at the stove as I threw the cloth in the sink. "I forgot I had pasta boiling on the stove."

He folded his arms, hand still gripping the envelope, and leaned casually against the frame of the archway.

I could forget everything with him standing there eyeing me just like I was the lolly Lucy proclaimed me to be. He was making me want things I knew I couldn't have. I was too damaged for someone like Travis—broken, missing pieces that would never be found, and put back together in a way that never quite fit properly.

The thought left an empty ache in my chest.

"You can leave the envelope on the counter," I told him. "Thanks for dropping it by."

A bang came from the front doorway, announcing the return of Justin and Rufus from their walk. Rufus charged into the tiny townhouse, yanking at the leash Justin held a firm grip on, anxious to get back to his favourite groove in my old, faded yellow couch. Seeing Travis, Rufus changed direction, making a beeline to sniff out the intruder.

Justin yanked him back on the leash. "Sorry, bud," he said to Travis.

"Hey, Quinn," Justin said, leaning in and kissing my cheek. He unclipped the leash and Rufus, seemingly happy with the presence of Travis inside his domain, leaped onto the couch, circled, and settled in.

I introduced Justin to Travis and the two shook hands.

"Beer?" he asked.

Travis shook his head, frowning. "Thanks, but I have to get going."

Justin shrugged and opened the fridge door, grabbing a beer and popping the top. "What's for dinner?"

"Parmesan chicken and pasta," I answered, picking up my own drink so I had something to do with my hands.

"Yum," he replied and jumped on the couch next to Rufus, grabbing the remote and flicking the television on.

Before I could usher Travis towards the door, Lucy's husband Rick was filling the kitchen doorway, and my tiny kitchen just got that much more crowded.

"Rick?" The only reason Rick would be here at this very moment was because Lucy sent him over to see what was going on. My eyes narrowed on his face and through clenched teeth, I asked, "Everything okay?" I turned to Travis. "Would you excuse us for a minute?"

I gripped Rick's bicep in my hand, ushering him out of the kitchen and towards the front door.

"Sorry, Quinn," he whispered and shrugged his big shoulders helplessly. "Lucy told me I had to come over and borrow a cup of sugar."

My eyebrows raised in disbelief. "A whole cup? Is she baking?"

"Um, I hope not," he replied, his response making it obvious that this was the best Lucy could come up with at short notice.

"Tell Lucy that I'll speak to her later," I said, hoping the irritation in my voice conveyed the knowledge that speaking to her wouldn't entail good things.

"Wait," he interrupted, "I better get that cup of sugar. You know, just in case she really meant it."

"Fine," I said, huffing impatiently.

Rick followed behind as I stalked back into the kitchen, past Travis, and into the tiny pantry. I picked up an unopened bag of sugar and walked out with it clutched in my arms.

"This is Travis. Travis, this is my neighbour Rick," I said in the way of introductions. I could have added that Travis just happened to be the older brother of my boss, but that would only encourage scheming on Lucy's behalf to see me settled—as though all you needed was a relationship to be happy.

Travis unfolded his arms to shake Rick's hand politely. Then his gaze flicked to Justin before resting on mine. His eyes were hard and cool, and it wasn't until the distance in them was clear that I realised how hot his eyes had burned before. "Can we talk for a minute, Quinn?"

His phone rang before I could reply and muttering an apology, he took the call, talking quietly, yet I still heard him say he'd been held up and would be there in a minute.

He hung up and Rick narrowed his eyes, obviously hearing the tail end of the conversation as well. Because Lucy had no idea why Travis was here, Rick must have assumed he was here for personal reasons because he asked, "You're not staying for dinner?"

Travis paused in the act of sliding his phone in his back pocket.

I felt his eyes on me, and my stomach hardened against the hurt I shouldn't be feeling. A one night stand was supposed to be about never seeing the other person again. The distance in his eyes should have been expected. Frankly, I should been welcoming it, encouraging it even.

"I have to be somewhere," he told us.

I smiled, not letting it reach my eyes. "Well, we won't keep you any longer. Thanks for dropping off the paperwork."

My dismissal was obvious and Rick frowned at me, not understanding my cool behaviour.

Travis placed the envelope down on the counter. "I guess I'll see you later," he murmured and with a nod at both Rick and Justin, who offered a brief salute from the couch, he left.

My eyes watched his retreating back, remembering the eagle wings that splayed the width of his wide, tanned shoulders. My mind had pondered the meaning of that tattoo all afternoon. The eagle was a creature of purity, beauty, and a powerful force. When I looked at Travis, I couldn't think of anything more fitting. When the door clicked shut behind him, it felt like I'd just lost something that had never been mine.

Justin rubbed his hand through his overly long black hair, leaving it mussed. "Who's Travis?"

"What? You don't know?" Rick smirked at Justin, smug because for once he was in the loop and knew the gossip.

Shaking myself out of the unwanted feelings Travis had evoked, I cut Rick off. "Rick! Do you want the damn sugar or not?"

I jammed the bag of sugar at his big chest and he grabbed it before it dropped to the floor.

"No?" Justin said in response to Rick.

"He's the guy that Quinn hooked up with last night."

I rubbed my forehead, sore from today's anxiety. "Thanks, Rick," I muttered under my breath. Thanks very much for making it known that I took a paddle through the skank pool last night. I checked my watch. Surely we must be hitting the next episode of *24* by now—*The hour between seven pm and eight pm*—because it felt like a lifetime ago that Lucy had dragged me out to that bloody bar.

Chapter Six

I whimpered unhappily when my alarm went off at six the next morning, desperate for another ten minutes before madness descended. My arm reached out and smacked the snooze button before returning to wrap around my pillow.

My front door opened and then slammed shut, madness finding her way into my room in her workout gear. A bright, cheery smile adorned her face that my tired body wanted to stomp all over.

I hadn't slept well but nightmares weren't designed to be pleasant; they spun fear dizzily through a painful slideshow of memories. Last night was different though. The usual shadowy images had been replaced by skin the colour of liquid gold and the slide of rough, hot hands on my skin. Apparently visions of Travis could also ensure a sleepless night for me. Not only that, I was usually able to savour my own space, but I'd woken to a bed that felt too big for my small frame and entirely too empty.

I grabbed my pillow in one hand, my blankets in the other, and prepared to burrow deeply into the thick, warm covers, but Lucy snatched the pillow from my grasp.

"No," I moaned unhappily, making a desperate grab for it.

"Come on, Quinn. It's exercise time!" Her wide eyes, and her words for that matter, were manic.

My slitted eyes raked her over. "I hate you."

"And I love your face." She held the pillow aloft. "Get up."

"I can't. My feet fell off last night, and I can't find them."

"Har har." She tossed the pillow on the floor.

"And I start my job today, and I'm not organised. You don't want me to be late do you?"

My snooze button shrieked wildly and Lucy stalked over to my bedside table and clicked it off. "Rubbish. I'm not blind. I can see your dress hanging on the door."

"Damn."

I forgot I left it there. It was my best office style dress. After the way I'd barely pulled myself together yesterday, today was my chance to make a better impression.

"That's your best dress," Lucy told me as if I didn't know already. "I thought you said you'd get to wear mostly jeans and Jamieson band shirts at the office?"

I swung my legs over the edge of the bed. "I did but I need new jeans and there's a wait on the shirts. And after yesterday, I want to look my best."

"After yesterday?"

Lucy hadn't yet heard the full recount of yesterday, including the Travis connection. I sighed, knowing that would come out this morning—best to get it over with.

After dressing reluctantly, Lucy and I were jogging the pavement in the damp, chilly air. I huffed my way through the lowdown and reaching the peak of the story—being the arrival of Travis at my front door—Lucy had to stop mid-jog from a stitch. It was tempting to abandon her to the sidewalk as she gasped for air, but Lucy could move like an Olympic sprinter, so I hovered, hands on my hips, while she wheezed and flexed.

"Maybe it's fate," she puffed out as she tilted her torso to the side.

"Screw fate," I hissed with more force than I intended.

Lucy blinked and slowly righted herself in the face of my outburst.

I rubbed at my brow. Four years had dulled my anger of the past, giving me the impression I was moving on, yet here it was, reasserting itself like a long lost friend.

My eyes narrowed on Lucy. "Are you telling me you believe everything in my life was meant to be?"

Lucy paled. "Quinny, I didn't—"

"Just—" I halted mid-sentence and stilled, looking sideways as an eerie feeling washed over me. Deep breaths filled my lungs as my eyes did a rapid scan of the suburban street. Nothing seemed odd except the churning in my stomach and tingles of fear tripping down my spine. Cars were parked up and down the avenue, joggers passed by the path we were rudely blocking, aiming dirty looks our way, and a dog across the road was busy peeing on someone's mailbox. I spun around. The sun was rising brightly, forcing my eyes to squint, and the wind swirled around me, yet something in the air didn't feel right.

"Quinn?" Lucy scanned the street, picking up on my fear like a bloodhound. "What is it?"

I shoved the anger away and forced a smile to my lips. "Nothing, Lucy. Sorry. I didn't mean to jump down your throat."

She fisted her hands on her hips and faced me. "Yes. You did. But I don't blame you. Maybe fate realised it fucked you over and is trying to fix things."

Her eyes were wide with hope. I shrugged her statement off, did another scan of the street, and nodded ahead of us. "Let's just get this over with."

Back home and showered, I slipped on my dress—deep navy and sleeveless with a matching thin leather belt—and pinned my tousled hair into a knot at the nape of my neck. Adding some light makeup and hot pink lipstick to finish the look, I sighed at my reflection, hoping it was an improvement on yesterday.

Fighting snarls of rush hour traffic, I delivered the paperwork to Jettison Records before heading over to the office at Coogee.

Letting myself in with the key that had been in the envelope, I called out hello. My feet echoed along the timber flooring as I headed towards the back office, not hearing a response.

Already the business line was ringing, so I answered it, sinking into the chair as someone spoke to me about the proofs for Jamieson's album artwork. Of course I had no idea, so I switched on the computer and promised to return the call. From then on the phone didn't stop, and it wasn't until I heard a tap on the open door that I realised two hours had passed.

Returning from the printer behind me, I was just sitting in my chair and glanced up. For a split second I thought it was Travis and completely missed the seat, falling to the floor with a hard jolt.

"Oh shit." Laughter bubbled out of him, and he quickly subdued it, taking in the wild flush to my cheeks. "Didn't mean to startle you."

He strode over and held out a hand to help me up.

"That's okay. Seems I startle easily," I replied, taking his hand and stumbling awkwardly to my feet.

"I'm Jared," he told me. "You must be Quinn? Evie said you were starting today."

The third brother, I realised. Did the Valentine men have all women falling to their feet or was it just me? My backside was still a little bruised from meeting Mitch yesterday.

Jared perched on the edge of the desk as I made a second, more cautious attempt at sitting down, taking in his subtle differences to Travis. Jared's hair was golden brown and not as long, he was a little leaner, and a cheeky glint hovered in his green eyes.

"How's your first day going?"

"Good."

"You worked at Jettison Records before here?"

"Uh huh."

"Did Mac show you where everything—"

His phone rang, interrupting the rapid fire questions, so I focused on the computer screen while he took the call.

"Travis. How'd the AFP meeting go this morning?"

Just hearing his name was a rush of pleasure that had my mind losing its train of thought.

Jared's eyes widened as he listened. "What?"

I glanced at him when his eyes slid my way with a frown. Silently, he mouthed he'd come back, and with the phone glued to his ear, he strode from the room.

After about twenty minutes, Jared poked his head in the door. "Lunch?"

I hadn't had time to think about food, but my stomach gave an angry growl at the mention.

"Okay. Thanks," I said with a smile, thinking that was really nice of him to offer.

My mistake.

He came back in with a tuna and mung bean salad and a small dark brown roll that was riddled with what looked like bird seed. I didn't want to offend him after the effort, but tuna was something that had my stomach churning. I picked at it carefully, pushing the food around a little as he told me about the house he'd recently bought in Bondi with Evie.

"So you're staying here until the renovations are done?" I asked.

He swallowed a mouthful. "No. We'll be here for just a couple of weeks. I wanna do most of it while we live there."

I put my fork down gratefully when Mac sent through a message with their location, telling me to head over when I was able. With Jared finished, I cleaned up and grabbed my bag. When my stomach gave another angry growl, I soothed it with promises of a drive through burger on the way.

We both left the house at the same time. Jared told me he wanted to check in with Evie before heading to his own office. Striding out the door, his eyes raked over Suzi-Q parked kerbside and offered me a lift.

Fully prepared to say no—there was burger out there with my name on it—the beep of a car unlocking drew my attention to a sexy, vintage black Porsche currently dominating the driveway. So I arrived on set in style, albeit hungry, just in time to see everyone break for lunch.

Mac waltzed over to greet me, taking in my appearance with a crisp nod. "Look at you, Quinn! That hot pink lipstick looks fantastic, you lucky bitch. I try to wear shades like that and it washes me out," she moaned.

"Wow, look at the colour of your hair," Evie muttered, reaching out to finger a rogue wave that had escaped my knot. "It was all tucked under a hat yesterday, but that's your real colour!"

Fidgeting under the scrutiny, I snatched up the phone with relief when it rang. Jared came up behind Evie, sliding his arms around her waist and they chattered for a moment while I spoke into the phone and made notes in the schedule. The call took a little while to deal with, and Jared strode off to talk to Henry as Mac and Evie waited for me to finish.

"Have you had lunch yet?" Mac asked when I hung up. She nodded in the direction of a buffet style table of food currently surrounded by guys. They were all talking and laughing loudly, confident and cavalier, and my inner social douche shrivelled with anxiety.

Mac grabbed my arm, oblivious to my freak out, and started to drag me towards them. "Let's go push all those wankers out of the way and grab something before there's nothing left but shitty salad. I'm bloody starving."

I stopped, halting Mac mid-drag. "Um…actually Jared made me lunch back at the house, so uh…" I trailed off because my stomach was still feeling slighted.

Mac let out a shout of laughter.

"Jesus," Evie muttered. "You didn't actually eat it, did you?"

My cheeks heated. The man was Evie's boyfriend. Offending her on my first day of work was not on my to-do list.

Mac slapped me on the back, and I stumbled forward. "Come on. Let's get our girl a burger. God knows you must be starving. We can put it on my plate so Jared doesn't see." She winked conspiratorially.

The phone rang again and my eyes widened on Mac. "It doesn't ever stop, does it?"

She shook her head gravely.

All eyes fell on me curiously as we neared the table, the phone glued to my ear. Mac elbowed her way into the group, putting together a huge plate of food while I hovered on the fringes. When I was done she strode over with two forks and shoved one at me. "Eat. Then I'll introduce you around."

I ate furtively until I saw Jared fold himself back in that gorgeous Porsche and drive away, no doubt to his own office—where Travis probably was, at his own desk, legs propped up as he reclined casually in his chair, his deep voice reverberating across the room as he spoke into the phone—

"Quinn? …Quinn?"

"Hmmm?" I murmured, blinking.

"You remember Henry from yesterday, don't you?"

Henry slung an arm around my shoulders, the weight heavy and warm, and winked at me. "Of course she does. Who could forget this gorgeous face?" he asked teasingly.

Mac arched a brow. "Quinn was only joking when she said that yesterday, so keep it in your pants, Henry."

He looked down at me, brows drawn in a wounded expression. "You wouldn't joke about something like that, would you Quinn?"

"Well, I uh…"

A hand grabbed mine and I was jerked out from beneath Henry's hold.

"Quit hogging the new girl," the guy now holding on to me said to Henry. His hair was black and silky. Eyes like midnight were raking me over. Tattoos wound the entire length of his right arm, and my eyes were drawn to them as he pulled me towards him and pressed a light kiss on my cheek.

"You smell like strawberries," he murmured softly, making me shiver before pulling back to look me over again. "I'm Cooper," he announced.

Another guy's shoulder bumped Cooper, and he stumbled, letting go of my hand. "I'm Jason," the shoulder bumper told me, taking my hand and his own turn at kissing my cheek, "but you can call me Frog, or whatever you like, really."

I shook his hand, looking between the two of them. Frog had silky dark hair too, but his eyes were light hazel and tattoos wound around both his arms. "Oh… you two are brothers?"

"Not by blood," Cooper told me.

"Stop flirting with Quinn, assheads," Mac ordered them.

I recognised Jake, even with him wearing a shirt, when he stepped into our huddle.

Mac waved a hand. "This is Jake," she said flatly, her narrowed eyes glaring daggers towards him.

His nostrils flared, yet his eyes followed her retreating back when the set director called her over. After a moment eyes the colour of liquid scotch returned to mine. "Nice to meet you, Quinn," he said, and held out a hand.

I took it in my own. "You too."

"You coming back to the duplex for a drink when we wrap?" he asked as he let go of my hand.

Henry folded his arms. "Of course she is. We haven't seen Mac so stress-free in ages. That's cause for a celebration."

Our eyes fell to Mac. She was wearing deep blue skinny jeans, brown boots, and a fitted, red sweater. Hands on her hips, she still looked all class as she glared at the set director in the obvious throes of a disagreement.

"See?" Henry grinned. "She's practically giddy."

Evie snorted.

"Actually, I-I can't," I stammered.

All those eyes fell to me and once again, I felt my face get hot.

"Sure you can," Cooper said.

They were acting like I was their new best friend, and it was simply too much. I didn't understand it. The need to retreat back to my little townhouse with its reality television and comfy sweatpants was overwhelming.

"I uh…have something going on," I lied, averting my eyes to gaze intently at my navy shoes. "Maybe next time."

Mac returned. "Everyone working hard?"

"Hey! We were only asking if Quinn was coming back to the duplex for a drink this afternoon," Frog told her.

"Are you?" Mac asked me.

The backs of my eyes burned, and my voice was a little thick when I explained again that I wasn't able to make it.

Jake slid an arm around my shoulders and leaned in to peer at me. "You okay?"

"What did you do?" Mac growled at him.

His fingers tightened on my shoulder. "Excuse me?"

Henry took hold of my hand, pulling me away from the bubble of rising tension until we were out of ear shot.

I glanced back, finding everyone's eyes on us. They all looked away, Mac saying something that had them scattering.

"Is there something wrong? I know Mac can be a bit overwhelming when you first get to know her, but deep down, somewhere in there, she does have a heart." His brows furrowed. "I think."

"Mac's been great," I told him. "Really," I added when his brows rose. "It's just been a big day, you know? First day and all."

"I'm sure it has," he agreed, his eyes watching me and taking in the sincerity because it really had been a big day. "Alright. We'll take a raincheck on tonight," he warned me. "*But*, if there *is* something wrong, we're all kind of like a big family. One you're now a part of." He waved his hand in the direction of Jamieson. Evie was shoving at Mac, Cooper was high fiving Frog with a laugh, and Jake was talking intently with the sound technician. "If something upsets one of us, it upsets all of us. That's how we roll."

Chapter Seven

"No! No, don't put me on hold—" Mac huffed. "Goddamn effing asstards," she muttered under her breath.

I looked over the length of my desk at Mac. She was sitting opposite me at her own. Her lips were flattened and her knuckles white gripping the phone. It only took two weeks to get used to her feisty, take charge attitude, maybe because she reminded me a little of Lucy. Lucy could be a lioness, but apparently it was only me that brought out that particular quality. When Mac put her foot down the other day, forcing Evie to change a particular pair of shoes for an upcoming interview, Evie had bitched that Mac was like the blonde equivalent of Ellen Ripley from *Alien*. Right now, I could see it clear as day.

"Mac." Her eyes, narrowed with frustration, found mine. "Transfer the call to me and put the phone down."

She exhaled through flared nostrils and nodded slowly, putting the phone down.

An annoyed voice came through the line when I picked it up. "Mac? Look, the best I can do is next week and that—"

"Robin," I said and forced a smile. I was told in a training session a while back that when you're on the phone and you smile, it carries through into your voice. "It's Quinn here, Mac's assistant. We spoke last week?"

"Oh, hi, Quinn."

"Look, I know you're under the pump, and it's completely our fault for not confirming you received approval for the T-shirt artwork sooner." Mac glared at me for taking the blame. The artwork was approved long before I came on the scene, but apparently Robin had missed that. "We have a huge show this weekend, and we really need these shirts ready by then. If you can arrange to have them delivered by Friday, I'll send out a couple of tickets to the show and give Jettison Records some of your business cards."

I heard an indrawn breath and papers being shuffled madly echoed down the line. Robin cleared her throat. "You know, Quinn, I think I might just manage that. Leave it with me and I'll ring you to confirm the delivery details."

I finished up the call and looked at Mac's expectant face. "T-shirts will be here by Friday."

"Yes!" Mac fist pumped the air. She jumped up and grabbed me from my chair. I was twirled in an impromptu waltz that left me both giggly and dizzy. "I love having you here, but that bitch doesn't deserve tickets."

"I agree, but it's a small price to pay."

Mac twirled me around one last time, and I smacked my hip into the side of the desk. "Oh shit, Quinn. You okay?"

I chuckled. One hand peeled up my shirt and the other pulled the top of my pants down, exposing a fair amount of skin in order to inspect the damage. "See? Nothing but a small red mark."

"Working hard I see?"

My heart kicked wildly at the deep voice from the doorway, and my eyes found Travis. He was wearing a pair of grey and black pinstripe dress pants and a collared navy shirt with the sleeves rolled up, exposing his tanned, sinewy forearms. His jaw was tight as his eyes focused on my exposed hip in a way that left me breathless. I snapped my clothes back in place, and his eyes flew up to mine.

"Damn straight we are," Mac answered for the both of us. "Quinn is kicking asstard ass."

"Nothing to it, Mac," I murmured, tearing my eyes from his and resuming my seat at my desk. My hands hovered over the keyboard, and my eyes fixed to the computer screen in an effort to convey that his presence had no effect on me at all.

You might be fooling them, but you're not fooling yourself.

La, la, la, I told the irritating voice in my head.

"What?"

I turned my head at Mac's question. "Huh?"

"Did you just say 'la la la'?"

Shit. "No."

Travis cleared his throat and I turned back to the computer and began tapping at the keyboard as though my life depended on it. What I typed, I couldn't be sure—hieroglyphics maybe.

"What are you up to, Travis?" Mac asked.

The corner of my eye told me he was now leaning casually up against the doorframe as though my presence was but a minor blip on his day. I huffed silently and tapped a bit more.

"I have a meeting with Quinn about the security for the show this weekend."

My fingers froze over the keyboard, and, yes, they even shook a little.

"No," I told the computer screen with feigned authority. "My diary right here says I'm meeting with Jared."

I resumed my busy schedule of ignoring Travis and typing my hieroglyphics.

"Well," came his drawl. "Change of plans. You've got me now."

How did he manage to make that sound like sex? His words licked every inch of my skin, making me want him instantly. How unfair that I was so seemingly happy on my little drought crusade but one night with *him* and now sex was the recurring star of my world. My face flamed as I stared at the keyboard, the letters out of focus.

"Okay then." I drew in a deep breath and swivelled in my seat, facing him full on. "Let's get this over with."

"Tension much?" I heard Mac mumble under her breath. Louder, she said, "I'm going to make us some lunch." She stood up, already striding for the door.

"Wait," I called. She spun around and with all the attention focused on me, I fidgeted with notepad in front of me. "Uh, Jared's not here, right?"

"Nope. Jared and Evie moved into the Bondi house yesterday," Mac said with triumph. Between Jared forcing his healthy eating on everyone, and Evie in the beginnings of a renovation meltdown—if you currently didn't talk cupboard colours or wall paint speak, you may as well have been talking to a wall—it had been a stressful two weeks. Mac pointed at me. "And we're celebrating. I'm ordering pizza. With extra cheese," she added.

She left the back office, her footsteps echoing up the hallway as Travis moved into the room and took her seat. I fought not to stare, but his presence invaded the small space until he was all I could see. He silently returned my gaze until my eyes dropped to the desk. I picked up a pen and shuffled some papers.

"Okay," I began.

Off to a good start, Quinn.

Would you just shut the hell up, I told my sarcastic inner bitch.

I picked up a sheet out of the pile of papers before me. "This is Friday and Saturday night's show at Sixty," I said, and handed the page over with the building layout. He took the sheet, but rather than look at it, his eyes were on my lips as I spoke. "Uh...there's two entrances covered by their own door security, and they have ten more inside the venue—four to be directed by your uh…firm and the rest to man the stage and crowd."

He nodded at me, finally shifting his eyes downwards to scan the page in his hands. "Crowd capacity?"

"Three thousand, both nights, sold out."

Travis sighed heavily and rubbed his brow, looking like he needed to sprawl himself out in bed and sleep for a week. I wanted to join him there, but sleep wasn't on my agenda. And a week wouldn't be enough to do everything that was clouding my mind as I watched his brow furrow in concentration.

His phone rang and he looked at the display before answering.

"Casey?"

He stood, and indicating he'd be back, left the office. It gave me an opportunity to compose myself. I tucked a wave of loose hair behind my ear and rolled my shoulders, expelling air from lungs that had my cheeks puffing out.

When he didn't reappear, I pulled together the final information of the security detail and compiled it neatly in a folder. Deciding to go in search of a drink while I waited, I pushed back my chair and made my way towards the kitchen.

The quiet murmuring of voices became louder. Mac and Travis were talking. Peering around the corner, I saw Travis leaning against the kitchen counter, arms folded, eyes on the floor. Mac was before him, talking, one arm splayed out wide as though making a point. With no intention to intrude on what appeared to be a private conversation, I took a soft step backwards, yet when I heard my name mentioned, I paused.

"Why are you acting like Quinn's just run over your cat?"

"I'm not acting any way, Mac." He sounded exasperated.

"You are. The past few months you haven't been yourself and now this unfriendly bullshit. Quinn is mine, Travis, and I won't have your attitude crapping all over everything that's bright and shiny and have you scaring her away."

"Not sure I'm liking what's coming out of your mouth, Mac."

"I don't give a flying fuck," she retorted. "At the moment I'm more concerned about what's coming out of yours."

"Shit, Mac. I'm not sure if I can do this anymore." His voice sounded hoarse and I bit down on my lip.

"Do what?" came her softer tone.

"The AFP contracted us on a bullshit assignment that's got me twisted in knots, but it's not just that, I…it's this job. We had the worst fucking case today and I…"

His voice trailed away because I fled, disappointed in myself for eavesdropping.

After returning two phone calls, I glanced up when Travis strode back into the room, overwhelmed all over again at the sheer depth of his charisma. For one night he'd made me the centre of his universe, and since then he'd somehow been the centre of mine—hovering in my conscious during the days and stealing his way into my nights.

"Sorry about that."

I shrugged as though I didn't care, but when he sank his incredibly firm, wonderfully male body into the chair opposite me and tossed his phone towards the desk with irritation, I knew I did.

"Is everything okay?"

He frowned, dark clouds gathering in his eyes. "You heard me talking to Mac?"

"No!" I sputtered. "It's just…" I tilted my head "… you seem a bit worn out."

He closed his eyes for a moment, as though re-building his composure, and when they opened, the cold aloofness had me shivering.

"If you're worried about the security this weekend, Quinn, don't be. We'll have it covered."

"No, that's not what I—"

"Barbecue!" came the crooning yell from beyond the doorway, and we both turned as Mac sashayed into the room. "This Sunday, Quinn. Mum and Dad's place so they can meet you and welcome you to the family."

Travis stood abruptly. He reached out for his phone and slid it in his back pocket before picking up the folder I'd pushed across the desk.

His short, sharp movements had me hesitating. "Oh, I don't think—"

"Rubbish to whatever you were going to say. Right, Travis?"

Travis paused and looked at Mac, then he looked at me. "Right. Gotta go."

That was the last I saw of Travis until Saturday night rolled around when he turned up with Jared to form part of Jamieson's security detail.

It was my first weekend watching them play live. Mac and I stood off to the side of the stage watching Evie hold the crowd in the palm of her hand. With her flirty, outgoing nature she made it look easy, always managing to say just the right thing to incite their enthusiasm. The loud, thumping beat vibrated through my body, and every nerve ending tingled with the incredible sound Jamieson was pumping out. Henry hunched over his guitar, absorbed in the music. Frog and Cooper grinned as they played, making it look effortless as they flirted with the crowd, and Jake's muscled arms thumped the drums like the beat was alive inside his body.

"Set break coming up soon, Quinn. Got your list?" Mac shouted at me. "I can't believe they misplaced the one we faxed the other day."

I shrugged. It just meant a quick trip to the bar to organise what drinks we wanted sent backstage. "I'll sort it out," I yelled back.

At least we had our new shirts now. Mac and I wore matching skinny black jeans and skin tight white T-shirts with short black sleeves. The Jamieson name and logo took centre stage on the front and huge black letters on the back read: Jamieson Crew.

In honour of my first night working at a venue, Lucy had wound a braid along my fringe line before pinning the bulk of the tousled curls into a messy knot at the nape of my neck. Smokey, black eyes finished off the look, along with a pass card slung casually around my neck.

"I'll be right back," I yelled.

Mac nodded.

I jumped off the stairs and eyed the thumping crowd. Drawing in a deep breath, I rolled my shoulders in preparation to push my tiny frame, heightened by the new four inch high black stiletto boots, through their jostling depths.

My elbows helped gain momentum through the crowd until I hit a big, muscled body. The arms attached to said body wound around me and lifted me up until my eyes found the dark, black ones of a stranger.

"Hey, pretty little thing. You're with the band right? I saw it on your shirt."

I struggled, shoving against his chest. "Put me down."

One hand reached down and gripped my backside, and I winced as his fingers dug in painfully. "Oh, come on now. Don't be like that." His breath was filled with alcoholic fumes that had me turning my face away, pushing harder to break free. "Why don't we go backstage and have a drink?"

"Let me go," I shouted over the heavy noise of music, grinding my teeth at the helpless feeling.

A wall pressed against my back and a deep voice thundered angrily. "You heard her. Let her go."

"Fuck off," was the strangers reply.

A fist flew from behind my right shoulder, landing on the stranger's jaw with a loud crack. I flinched as his head snapped back and he stumbled, his hands falling away from my body.

I faltered as my feet sought purchase on the ground. Travis snaked his arm around my waist, his hand spreading across the width of my belly, and pulled me backwards until my entire body was plastered against the length of his. My heart kicked wildly at the touch, and instead of freaking out at the violent altercation, I felt warm and safe—relieved enough to rest my hand over the top of his.

His arm tightened at the contact, turning us both sideways before jabbing a finger in the stranger's face. "Hands off the Jamieson crew, asshole," he growled. I shivered at the furious intent in his voice. "Make one more wrong move and your ass is out that door." His jabbing finger changed direction, pointing angrily towards the exit.

Hands were held up in surrender as the man backed away, and the swelling crowd swallowed him until he was lost to our view. Then Travis took hold of my hand, yanking me none too gently towards the backstage dressing room. Pushed into the room, Travis slammed the door behind us. I spun to face him, the two of us alone as the muffled beat thumped heavily enough to vibrate through the walls. His eyes were no longer cold; they were wild and possessive, and my breathing came in little pants from the scuffle. My eyes drank him in, from the dark jeans to the same tight shirt as me. His was the boy version and on the back, in big black letters read: Jamieson Security.

"No more," he ground out.

"No more what?" I asked breathlessly.

"Trips to the bar on your own while you're working," he informed me tightly. He pressed a button on his ear piece and informed Mac in short, terse words to send Jared to the bar when the band was offstage and secure in the dressing room.

My eyebrows flew up. "Are you serious?"

Travis nodded to me as he listened to Mac reply in his ear.

My spine snapped straight. This was my job and not only did I need it, I was liking it. Damned if he was going to take that away from me.

"You're not my boss," I told him and charged for the door.

His body blocked it before I could reach for the handle.

"Quinn." He folded his arms and glared. "The crowd out there is too much."

"I'm not made of glass," I replied, and the topaz in his eyes flashed at me from beneath the dressing room lights. "I have a job to do, same as you. I don't tell you how to do yours."

His brows rose at the very idea of me telling him how to run a security operation. "My job is to keep you safe. As far as I'm concerned, my job is being done, but you're making it difficult for me by putting yourself in situations like that. Make some changes."

"Your job is *not* to keep *me* safe. It's to keep Jamieson safe."

Travis widened his eyes as though I'd lost all sense. "You *are* Jamieson."

My mouth opened but nothing came out because it was quite possible he was right. I snapped it shut, biting my lip to stop a sharp retort bursting through in the face of his logic.

His eyes fell to my lips, and my lungs seized at seeing the heat in them return full force. He took two steps forward. I counted them as I held my breath.

"Quinn," he whispered. His arm reached for me hesitantly when the dressing room door opened with a resounding bang. The moment lost, he took a step back, his arm falling by his side as Mac strode through followed by the rest of the band.

"High five, dude," Frog yelled at Travis. Travis slapped his palm and said something that made Frog shout with laughter.

"Fucking hell, Trav," Cooper shouted and slung an arm over my shoulder. "We saw you punch that massive dude out there."

My eyes were glued to Travis as Cooper spoke, watching carefully as his eyes changed—cool replacing the heat.

"What a douchebag! Our little Quinn needs the security more than we do." Cooper jostled my shoulder and I tore my eyes away and mustered a smile for Cooper. He leaned into my ear and whispered, "You still smell like strawberries." Then he winked at me before Mac pulled him away.

In that moment—watching everyone chatter loudly and laugh around me—I struggled not to feel alone. I'd been that way for so long it had overtaken my life, yet remembering those eerie shivers down my spine, like I was being watched, made it more prominent. Something fierce was bearing down, leaving me more uneasy than I'd felt in years.

Chapter Eight

Sunday lunchtime rolled around entirely too quickly. My appearance was required at the Valentine family barbecue. I would be seeing Travis there. In a social capacity. Nothing work related. Alcohol could possibly be involved. The very idea was making me late because everything in my wardrobe was utter rubbish—nothing that said "outfit to meet and socialise with the parents of the man you slept with once in a drunken moment of folly" jumped out at me. I shouldn't have cared so much. I didn't *want* to want Travis. I just did.

Juggling my handbag, keys, and the container of peanut butter and white chocolate chip biscuits I was up early baking, I locked the door of the townhouse. It was windy outside and strands of hair were ripped from their bobby pins, instantly ruining the hairstyle I'd taken great pains to put together. They whipped into my eyes, and growling irritably, I flicked my head to dislodge them. No doubt my neighbours, not including Lucy because she wasn't home, would think I was having a wild stroke.

Flicking my head a second time, my eye caught a man striding towards me. Panic seized my body and the keys slipped from my hand and fell to the ground.

Oh God, Oh God, Oh God, I chanted silently as I dropped to the ground, grabbing them with trembling hands. I stood up and jammed them back in the door to unlock the townhouse.

"Quinn!" David yelled.

I glanced his way to see he'd picked up his pace to a jog.

Six months. I was supposed to have six more months! Why hadn't someone done their job and notified me of his release?

"Dammit," I muttered when the door stuck. I shoved at it, kicking the bottom corner hard with my foot. It flew open and I whirled around and slammed it shut behind me, the deadbolt sliding into place with a satisfying thunk. Heart in my throat, I scrambled for my phone and punched buttons frantically. When it started dialling I realised that panic had made me stupid because I'd rung Lucy.

"Shit."

I quickly ended the call before she could answer and dialled emergency.

"Come on, come on," I muttered, impatient for someone to answer.

"Quinn!" David yelled and oh God, the sound was right at my door. Loud banging accompanied the noise. "I know you're in there. I saw you. Open the fucking door!"

The phone was answered and the operator told me to state my emergency. I explained in short, stuttered sentences, fumbling my words as she tried to make sense of their jumble.

"Police are on their way, David!" I shouted as I slid down the wall of the living room into a huddle. Rufus scratched at the back door wanting in, but I couldn't bear him getting hurt if David managed to get inside. He whined at me, sensing something was wrong.

"You owe me over three years of my life in that shithole," was his response.

For fifteen minutes the operator stayed on the line while David shouted, banged the door, and rattled windows.

"I'm here to collect," he yelled. "And I'm going to enjoy every minute of it. When I'm done breaking you, you're going to hand over the money you owe me."

Money? What the hell was he talking about?

My body stopped rocking when the realisation that over five minutes of silence had slipped by. Another five minutes and the police were there doing a brief canvas of the area, asking questions, calling up prior assault records, and verifying the restraining order that should still be in place.

I was told that if they managed to pick him up, he would do another ninety days for the violation, as if that was supposed to reassure me.

My phone rang.

"Excuse me," I murmured and answered it.

"Quinn? You're late!" came Mac's admonishment.

My voice shook as I gave my apology.

"Is everything okay?"

I looked around my townhouse. It wasn't safe to stay here. Not now. The younger officer met my eyes. I could see hopelessness in them, as though he saw this shit every day and it was beating him down. Was it hard to offer nothing more than empty words of encouragement and fill out paperwork?

"Actually, nothing's okay right now," I admitted to Mac, too tired to pretend.

"Quinn?" Her voice lost its familiar intensity in favour of apprehension. "What's going on?"

Rufus whined pitifully at the back door. "I don't think I can make it today. I have to pack," I told her.

"Pack? For what? Where are you going?"

"My place isn't safe anymore. I have to find—"

"You're not safe?" she half yelled. "Who—"

Mac was cut off this time, and after brief, muffled words, Travis came on the line.

"Quinn, are you in danger?" His words were harsh and urgent, yet hearing them had calm washing through me, as though his voice alone had the power to leap tall buildings in a single bound.

"No, I'm not. The police are here."

"The police? I'm on my way."

"No, Travis, everything's under control—"

"Stay on the phone," he told me. "Give me the keys to your bike," I heard him order someone. Mitch's muffled voice replied and after a moment, the throaty purr of an engine growled to life. "Hang on," Travis yelled at me over the noise. The sound of a beep and clicking noise came through. "You there?"

"Yes, I'm here."

"Tell the police not to leave until we're there, okay?"

They promised they would stay, and after relaying that to Travis, I offered the officers a drink.

"No thanks, ma'am," said the older of the two.

I picked up the container of biscuits still sitting by the front door and sat it on the kitchen counter. Prying off the lid, I held it towards them. "Biscuit?"

The younger man looked at the older of the two. He shrugged and they both reached forward and took one each.

"Quinn, you still with me?" Travis yelled in my ear over the noise of a horn blasting and someone shouting. "You'll have to speak up, okay?"

"Still here," I replied loudly.

"Holy shit," the younger officer barked out. "These are f—ah, nice biscuits, ma'am."

His eyes were focused on the container, so I offered him another. He reached for one and when his responder crackled to life, he spoke into it around a mouthful of biscuit.

"Keep talking to me, Quinn. Tell me what you like to do when you're not working," Travis ordered.

"Oh…" Even with the fear and panic, my belly still fluttered just speaking to him on the phone. "Not much at all really. I like going to the beach or the movies, or just lazing around. Maybe that sounds boring to most people, but that's my kind of thing."

The sound of an engine gunning roared in my ears, then I heard, "If that makes you boring, then you can bore me stiff any day, sweetheart."

The officers were focused on their paperwork, yet I still spun around to hide my flaming cheeks from their view. Oh my God the visions that his words evoked. Was he trying to distract me? If so, it worked. After a few more minutes of answering his random questions, my cheeks cooling, a loud throaty growl came thundering down the street and Travis said, "I'm here."

I flew to the window and my mouth fell open, the phone still glued to my ear despite the fact that Travis had already hung up. He was peeling himself off a shiny, black motorcycle. Wearing faded jeans, a soft grey shirt, and a worn brown leather jacket, his powerful body strode determinedly to my front door. The blood in my veins boiled as he got closer, and my cheeks heated all over again.

Peeling the phone from my ear, I tossed it on the kitchen counter and made my way to the door. Seeing my movements, the young officer grabbed me from behind and hung on. I squirmed against his firm grip.

"It's Travis at the door," I explained.

He ignored me as the older policeman gave him a short nod and opened the door to the knock.

Travis stalked through, his presence overwhelming the small space. He ignored everything, his eyes searching my face before taking the length of me in carefully until he stood in front of me. Without moving his head, his eyes shifted to the young officer behind me, staring him down until he let go. Satisfied, Travis returned his eyes to mine.

"You okay?"

I managed a nod.

"Good."

He took a step back, gaining distance, and I felt the loss. Hating that the simple movement affected me like it did, I said to the officers, "Thank you so much for your help today. Please let me know if you find him." I looked everywhere but at Travis. "If you'll excuse me, I need to go and pack."

Leaving the room, muffled conversation followed my retreating form. I blocked it out. I didn't want to know what they were telling Travis. He could charm the pants off anyone—I knew that first hand—no doubt they were busy telling him anything he asked.

I dragged a suitcase from my wardrobe and set it on the bed, opening the zipper. Returning again from the wardrobe, I tossed in a pile of clothes. No more banging on the wall that separated Lucy and I, yelling obscenities and laughing at each other. I returned with another pile of clothes. No more Lucy slipping over in her pyjamas to fight over the remote because Rick was watching the footy on their television. I went back for an armload of shoes. No more cooking for Lucy and running it next door so she could pass it off to Rick as her own work. I tossed the shoes in. Oh my God, I would even miss her *Step Up* movies. Maybe. All of sudden it felt like I was losing her just like I'd lost everything I'd ever cared about, which was stupid, but it hurt. It fucking hurt.

My eyes were burning when a tentative knock came at the open doorway. "Quinn?"

I rubbed angrily at an escaped tear, embarrassed and sickened that Travis was seeing firsthand knowledge of what my life was, *is*, like. From the abusive family to the tiny townhouse with its stained linoleum floors, cheap furniture, and aged bathroom that boasted a tacky shower curtain that stuck to your bum whenever you tried to move.

"I don't know why you came, Travis, but everything's fine. You should get back to your family's barbecue."

I shoved at the clothes and shoes to make more room in the suitcase and turned back towards the wardrobe.

Travis walked into the room and sat down on the edge of my bed. "Talk to me."

"No."

I came back with another armload of shoes to him sitting there, elbows on his knees, staring at his linked hands. I paused long enough for his eyes to find mine. He exhaled audibly.

"Quinn," he began, and stopped, swiping a hand across his jaw. "David, your...stepfather...the police say he assaulted you a few years back?"

The shoes tumbled out of my arms and scattered on the floor.

"Dammit," I muttered. Crouching down, I reached for them, and said, "I really can't talk about this, okay? I'm sure the police are out there doing…whatever it is they do, and everything will get sorted out." I scrambled for the last shoe and once again holding the armload, tossed them in the suitcase.

"Stop," he barked out. "Just stop."

My intention was to ignore the order and keep focused on my task, but he grabbed my arm before I could make another move.

"Do you need me to call someone for you? Lucy? Justin?"

I frowned, shrugging off his hand. "Justin? Why would I want Justin…"

He shifted uncomfortably and suddenly his attitude became a little clearer. "Oh my God."

Travis cocked a brow. "What?"

"You think Justin and I are… You think I slept with you while I had a boyfriend!"

His jaw ticked as he looked away.

"Oh my God, you did. You think I'm a slut!" I blurted out angrily. That made me feel about as fantastic as the old teddy bear my dog chewed on. The worst part was that a lifetime ago, I used to be just that. "Why did you even come here? Maybe you still had to earn your White Knight points for today. Mission accomplished. You can leave now."

He exploded from the bed like a rocket, towering over me as he thundered, "What the fuck was I supposed to think? I woke up wanting to wrap myself all around you, but you were gone. Fuck! And then somehow you reappear and some guy is in your townhouse, walking your dog, making himself at home in your kitchen, lying on your couch while you cook dinner as though he's done it a thousand times before!"

His chest was shifting rapidly up and down, eyes glaring as I stood speechless at the outburst.

A knock came at the front door.

"I wanted to wrap myself all around you…"

"Quinn?" someone called out.

"...but you were gone."

The knock came louder. "Travis?"

"Fuck," Travis muttered, his eyes flaring unhappily at the interruption. "Maybe we need to talk."

That sentence was a bucket of cold water. I took a step back. He scratched at his head before dropping his hand wearily back to his side and left the room. I followed him out, standing by silently as he opened the front door and let Mitch inside.

Mitch's eyes scanned over me. Satisfied, he looked around the room, taking in nothing untoward except Rufus growling and scratching at the sliding door to get inside.

His brows flew up. "That's your dog?"

I nodded. "That's Rufus."

"Huh."

Rufus tilted his head as we watched him for a moment.

"You okay?" Mitch asked.

After meeting Mitch on two occasions since he'd knocked me over with the door that morning, I'd come to discover he was a man of few words.

"Fine," I replied, reflecting his efficient speak back at him.

He cocked a brow, disbelieving. "Read David's file. He's a piece of work."

I nodded at that understatement.

Mitch folded his arms, leaning his hip against my kitchen counter. "When did he start hitting you, Quinn?"

Travis straightened from his casual stance against the doorframe. My eyes flicked his way. His face had paled and his body was locked tight. "This has happened before?"

How did Mitch know? I never told *anyone*, except Lucy and Rick, about the abuse I'd lived with. The only thing the police had on file was the assault that had sent me to hospital.

I cringed, rubbing at my brow as they waited for a response.

"Tell me he didn't physically abuse you as a child, Quinn," Travis bit out.

My eyes fell to the floor. "I can't do that," I said quietly.

"How old were you when it started?" he said equally as quietly, yet there was an edge in his voice.

My lips pressed flat.

"How old?" He roared.

I flinched.

"Travis," Mitch warned, pushing away from the kitchen bench and taking a step forward.

I looked at Travis. His hands were fisted by his sides, knuckles clenching and unclenching. "David married Beth…" I couldn't call her my mother because she wasn't one. She was…I didn't know what really. "…when I was seven. He was always a bully and even at that age I could recognise the malicious undercurrent in his attitude. When I was nine he lost his job and couldn't get another. It all went downhill from there really. Then one day he just started disappearing during the day, so I assumed he got another job. It must have been a good one because suddenly he was cashed up and they were both so busy enjoying it, they were never home. I moved out when I was seventeen. That was when the…when…" I waved a hand. "Beth had left him not long after, you see, and he was... well, not happy."

A beat of silence passed.

Mitch's eyes were trained on Travis. "Quinn, sweetheart," he said, without looking away. "Why don't you go finish packing your things?"

Because I liked Mitch's thinking, I gave a jerky nod and started for the bedroom. Travis reached out and snagged my wrist as I walked past him. My breath caught as I looked from the warm hand wrapped around my skin to his eyes. They were pained. "Pack enough for a few days," he said hoarsely.

"Okay," I whispered.

He let go and I left the room. When the front door clicked open and closed, raised voices could be heard from the other side. I sank to the edge of the bed, wringing a shirt in my hands. Where the hell was I supposed to go?

I wasn't sure how long I sat there, but when Travis came back into my room, the shirt in my hands was a lost cause. I tossed it into the suitcase behind me with a sigh.

Travis crouched in front of me so we were at eye level and rested his hands on my thighs.

"Quinn…" He paused and blew out a breath. "What you told us back there? I don't how you managed to explain it all without actually telling us anything. That's quite a talent you've got."

"I…"

Travis quirked a brow when I trailed off. "You?"

"I…"

His lips twitched and my heart lifted a little, so I smiled at him. He returned it, and just like that, the hardness shifted from his face.

"Justin is Lucy's brother," I told him and explained our business trade. "He moved to Brisbane last week after finishing uni."

Travis nodded. "What about your father?"

"I don't have one," I said simply. "There's nothing listed on my birth certificate, and Beth says…" I looked down at my lap "…she says it could be anyone."

I started shaking, just like Rufus did during a thunderstorm, and gripped my hands together. He rubbed gently along my thighs. It was meant as a comfort, but the soothing gesture only increased my need to fall apart.

"Don't. Please," I whispered and nudged his hands away.

Travis pulled back, searching my face, and he nodded. Somehow he understood that I couldn't handle gentle right now, and that only made me want him more.

Chapter Nine

After a brief phone call with Mac, she told me the duplex had a spare room since Evie moved out. It was decided I would stay there—temporarily I'd replied—until I had time to find something more permanent.

Now I was standing on the sidewalk, leash in hand, Rufus sitting to my left as we watched Travis toss my bags in the back of Mitch's car. Then he proceeded to fit the bag I'd packed for Rufus, and his bed, into the backseat. After he was done, Travis swung his leg over that black, metal deathtrap and looked at me expectantly.

"You..." I shook my head. "I'm not..." I nodded towards Suzi-Q. "My car is over there," I pointed out.

"No."

"No?"

Mitch chuckled from the driver's seat of his angry, black Subaru.

"While David's out there, you're not going anywhere on your own."

"I'm not? But...he's not going to attack me in my car."

Travis and Mitch shared a meaningful glance.

"I mean, look at that car." I gestured at the Subaru. "Rufus can't sit in there. He'll leave fur on that clean upholstery. He'll slobber all over those nice, shiny windows." I even mentioned the sagging passenger seat where Rufus had fearfully ripped out a chunk of padding once when we'd been rear-ended.

Mitch grinned at Travis. "That's okay. It's not my car."

"Then whose is it?"

"Mine," Travis replied.

After I buckled Rufus in and shut the front passenger door, the window licking began. I shrugged at Travis. I *did* warn him. His response was to gun the engine impatiently.

My heart pounding, I swung my leg over and climbed on in a manoeuvre that wasn't entirely graceful. My chest was pressed against his back, and my body throbbed from the contact as he instructed me on where to put my feet.

Travis turned his head. "Hold on."

I hesitated and with both feet firmly planted on the ground to hold us steady, he grabbed my hands and pulled them around his waist. Without thinking, my hand ran lightly over his stomach. The muscled ridges were warm and hard. I closed my eyes when he placed his hand over mine for a brief moment.

"Okay?" he asked.

"Yes," I lied, having to shout over the thundering growl.

After taking the scenic roads to Coogee, we eventually rumbled into the driveway. I pulled away reluctantly and peeled myself off the back of the motorcycle. The feeling had reminded me of when I went horse riding at a school friend's birthday party when I was nine. Beth had been thrilled to get me out of her hair for the day, and I'd been thrilled to leave. Riding that horse had been the first time I felt carefree and happy since David moved into our house. They had to get one of the parents to pry me off because I refused to and all the little girls waiting their turn were getting upset. I'd howled and thrown a tantrum when David had to come early to collect me. Then I was taught my very first painful lesson.

Blinking back tears, I wrestled Rufus into the backyard while Mitch and Travis carried in our things. Shutting the sliding door, he whined as he watched me return to the living room where Mitch and Travis stood talking.

"I'll just take these bags up to Evie's old room," Mitch murmured at my approach. Picking up my suitcase and some bedding, he disappeared upstairs.

Alone again, Travis reached for my hand and pulled me a little closer. "Quinn." He rubbed his lips together. "I really want…" he began and paused. It was the first time I'd seen him unsure of himself. "I can't—"

The door flew open loudly, Mac storming through. "I can't believe this fucking shit," she burst out.

Henry was hot on her heels, followed by Evie with Jared—Peter tucked under his armpit like a football—and the rest of the band until the living room was full.

"Are you okay, Quinn?"

My mouth fell open at the same time my purse started ringing. I ignored it. "Why are you all here and not at the barbecue?"

"Shit seems to be going down, and you're involved Quinn. That's why," Evie answered. "We're experts at shit going down."

Jared looked at her and shook his head, as though remembering shit going down and not wanting to.

Mac folded her arms and Henry found his way to my side. "What's going on?"

Eyes were focused on me as everyone waited for an answer. "I'll tell you later," I murmured softly to Henry.

Jake folded his arms, mimicking Mac's stance, and demanded, "No. If there's something going on, you can tell all of us."

"Quinn," Evie said, her eyes radiating sympathy in tsunami like waves. "If you're in trouble, it's now *our* trouble."

"So you may as well tell us," Cooper added.

I sank into the couch behind me. My legs were like jelly, and not the good kind, the green kind that had your insides churning. "My stepfather is a bit angry with me right now."

Henry flopped down on the couch next to me with a heavy sigh. He swiped the remote off the coffee table and sat back without turning the television on.

"Why is he angry with you?" Mac asked.

"Because he just got out of prison and uh...I was the one that put him there."

Mitch returned from upstairs to a full living room.

"Thanks Mitch," I called out.

He nodded.

Henry turned his head to look at me. "Your place isn't safe?"

I shook my head. "But I have a restraining order."

Everyone went silent, processing what I'd just told them.

"Well," Mac said, "we all know a restraining order is just a piece of paper. We need to teach Quinn how to shoot."

Henry pointed at her. "You're not doing it."

"Jesus Christ," Jared barked and sank into the recliner. Peter curled happily into his lap as Jared eyed Evie and Mac in turn. "Remember what happened last time you two went all Thelma and Louise? Not happening."

Evie's eyes flattened irritably. "Are you forgetting the ace shot I pulled off that saved Mac's life?" She waved in Mac's general direction as though introducing evidence of Mac's living, breathing status to support her case. "If anyone's teaching Quinn how to shoot, it's going to be me. I'm a better shot than all of you."

"Who says *ace*?" Cooper smirked. "That sounds dumb."

"You're dumb," Evie retorted.

"Why don't you just move in here permanently?" Mac asked me.

"Really?" The anxiety lifted a little from my shoulders. "Oh, but...I have Rufus."

"Who's Rufus?" Jake asked.

"Quinn's horse," Mac replied.

Cooper's eyes went wide. "You have a horse?"

Travis sighed heavily, putting his hands on his hips. "Rufus is a dog."

"Holy fucking shit!"

Everyone's eyes flew to where Frog stood by the dining table. The container of biscuits I'd brought with me was wide open and he was busy stuffing them in his face. "Who the fuck made these?"

I cleared my throat. "That would be me."

"Quinn's moving in next door with me," he announced, grabbing another as he came and flopped onto the couch next to me. He shoved a handful of silky, dark hair behind his ear as he bit into another one.

Henry slung an arm around my shoulders, using the other to reach across and grab at the biscuit in Frog's hand.

"Hey!" Frog shouted.

He yanked his hand back a little too late. The biscuit tore in half and Henry crowed his victory as a whole bunch of crumbs from the tussle fell in my lap.

Henry shoved it in his mouth and aimed a smirk Frog's way. "Quinn's mine." Then he turned to me and added seriously, "But we have rules in this house."

My brows drew together. "You do?"

"We do?" Mac echoed.

"You gotta walk around in your underwear."

"Henry!" Evie yelled. She yanked a couch cushion out from behind Jared and flung it at Henry's head. It bounced off harmlessly and settled on the floor.

"Not you two," Henry replied, shuddering theatrically. "God! You're like my sisters. Seeing you both in your itty bitties makes me wanna sandblast my eyes."

"Well think of Quinn like your sister," Mac snapped out.

When my eyes fell on Travis, he was frowning at Henry.

My purse buzzed again and thankful for the interruption, I stood, scattering biscuit crumbs to the floor. Peter was quick to remove himself from Jared's lap and scrambled over to hoover the mess.

"Excuse me," I told the room, and picking up my phone, I answered the call. "Lucy." I left the living room for the back deck. Peter charged out behind me, and Rufus fell on him in a giant, quivery mass of furry elation.

"You called and didn't leave a message," was her irritated reply. Lucy hated when people didn't leave a message, but she had an automated answer service because she couldn't work out her messagebank. No one liked leaving messages on an automated service.

"Lucy." I watched Peter yip as Rufus bounded in circles around him. "David's out."

"He's what?" she whipped out.

I sucked a deep breath into my lungs and let it out slowly. "David's out of prison."

There was a pause. "How do you know that?"

There was another pause where I thought about how to explain without Lucy going all Uma Thurman in *Kill Bill*.

"Oh my God. Where are you?" she asked. "Are you okay? Oh God, oh God, oh God," she chanted. "Answer me, dammit."

"I'm okay. I'm at the duplex."

"Thank fuck," she moaned.

I sat down at the outdoor table and gave her a quick overview.

"I'm coming over," she announced.

I was so relieved tears burned my eyes. "Thanks, Luce," I whispered. Knowing she would drive like a bat out of hell to get here, I added, "Drive safe."

She growled something in reply before hanging up.

"Quinn?"

I looked up. Evie was standing there, two glasses of wine in her hands. She plopped one down in front of me and took the opposite seat. She looked effortlessly sexy in her black skinny jeans and three-quarter sleeved silver top. Her hair tumbled down her back in a wild riot of waves. It made me realise my own was a windblown mess. I brushed at it self-consciously.

"I've sent everyone away. Mac and Henry have gone shopping, and the boys are next door. It's just us—sort of. Jared, Travis, and Mitch are still inside. I just..." She paused, her eyes filling a little. "I know we don't know the full story, but I know what it's like to have someone after you. It's like a black, heavy weight on your chest like you can't get a breath. I had a stalker. It wasn't even a fan," she muttered with a short laugh. "Just some asshole that was pissed off at Jared." She picked up her glass while nudging mine towards me. "In the end I was given an opening and went after him myself." She grinned at me before taking a sip of wine and sitting it back down. "Can you imagine Jared's reaction?"

If he was anything like Travis, I was pretty sure I could.

"He freaked out actually and left me. Blamed himself for the whole bloody thing." She looked down at her hands.

"But you two are so madly in love?"

"We are. It wasn't until later, when I got past the anger, that I realised being apart from me was killing him just as much. We worked through it though."

"The papers say that you..." I trailed off, realising I was dredging up memories for her that were best left alone.

"I did. I shot that man and he died, and I'd never been more scared in all my life. But do you know what Jared said?"

I shook my head in reply.

"He said, 'Courage is fighting fear head on, baby. As long as you have that, you'll get through.'" Her chin pushed into her neck as she growled out the words in imitation of Jared and I giggled.

"But do you know what he doesn't know?"

I shook my head again and took a sip of the warm, red wine.

"Having him behind me, and all my friends..." she waved a hand around towards the duplex "...is what gave me that courage. We're your friends now, Quinn. Granted, we might not know you that well yet, but I know enough. We all know enough to see the sweetness in your smile

95

and the shadows in your eyes. If you need courage, Quinn, know that we're standing behind you."

I didn't know how to respond. "Thanks, Evie."

She nodded and downed the rest of her wine, urging me to do the same. Finished, she grabbed my hand. "Come on. There's a brand new bed in my old room. I bought it and took my old one to our house at Bondi. We can put some sheets on it for you."

We passed through the kitchen where Travis, Jared, and Mitch appeared involved in a heated discussion. Silence fell and I could feel their eyes on us while we raided the linen cupboard. Evie filled my arms with sheets and thick quilts, and I stumbled up the stairs behind her, finally disappearing from their view.

Evie insisted on putting the bed together while I put my things away in the wardrobe, chattering all the while about the single Jamieson was due to release later that month. Soon we were done and could hear Mac and Henry returning, bringing Lucy in their wake because I could hear her talking loudly.

"We're back," Mac shouted up the stairs, "and I've got the makings for mojitos! Arriba, arriba!"

"That's Mexican, Mactard," we heard Henry say.

"What's Mexican?"

"Arriba, arriba," he replied.

"So?"

"Mojitos are Cuban," I heard Travis say.

"What the fuck ever," Mac said, clearly irritated.

I shuddered. Mojitos weren't my thing. It was the limes. Lucy made a bad prawn and lime risotto once, and the four of us—Rick, Lucy, Justin and I—had been up sick all night. I'd hunched over the toilet and tossed what I was sure was every cookie I'd ever eaten in my entire life. Limes and I had never collided since.

When Evie left I promised I would be down in a minute, yet when I left, I wound my way to the back deck to check on Rufus. Dusk was coming. The air was getting chilly and a pink glow was warming the horizon. I pulled my cardigan tightly together and folded my arms when the sound of someone lighting a cigarette came from my right. Glancing sideways, Travis was caught in the illuminated glow. He was leaning back in the deck chair, elbows resting casually along the timber arms as he exhaled a long plume of smoke.

"You smoke?"

He shrugged. "Sometimes. When I need to think."

I forced my legs to approach where he sat. "It hasn't been the best day."

Travis met my eyes without moving, and I thought my heart would beat out of my chest. "You could say that."

"Look," I began, and scratched awkwardly at my brow. "About today. I appreciate you helping out. I'm sorry I got you involved in my mess but you shouldn't feel obligated after...after..."

His jaw clenched as he leaned over and stubbed his cigarette out in the nearby ashtray. He stood up, close enough that his chest brushed against mine. I took a step back.

He cocked a brow at me. "After I fucked you?"

My cheeks flamed wildly, even as lust had the breath leaving my body at the thought of him doing it again. "I haven't made that common knowledge."

"Christ," he muttered.

"What?"

He shook his head irritably. "You think I helped you because I fucked you and now I'm gonna tell everyone?"

God. He needed to stop saying that. I took another step back. "That's not what I meant."

"What did you mean then?"

"Effing hell, Quinn, get your butt inside right this— Oh..."

We turned towards the door. Lucy stood there with her mouth open. She cleared her throat. "Sorry, I'm just gonna..." she indicated behind her with a hand wave. She winked at me and disappeared inside.

My eyes returned to Travis. I had no idea what to say. With one last lingering look at his face, I turned and retreated back inside.

Chapter Ten

"Oh my fucking God, Mac. I thought you said you knew how to make mojitos?" Evie yelled.

Returning to the living room, I passed by Jared and Mitch in the office. Mac and Evie were both busy blending up a storm in the kitchen, and Henry and Lucy were on the couch.

She met my eyes with indecision. She didn't know whether to tackle me to the ground in excitement at seeing me with Travis, or smother me out of fear after what happened today.

"Sit down on the couch, Quinn," Mac yelled over the roar of the blender. "It's mojito time!"

The last thing I felt like doing was sitting around drinking and chatting. Today had been a wild roller coaster ride, and whenever I got off those things I always felt like I was going to fall off the end of the earth. Now it seemed the current plan was to add alcohol to that. And limes. Yet I found myself sinking into the couch anyway.

Lucy stood and leaned over me, wrapping me in a hug. "We can talk about it later, okay?" she whispered in my ear.

I nodded, fighting back tears at the familiar comfort of my best friend. She returned to the couch.

"I'm moving into the duplex," I told her.

"Really?" I could hear the relief in her voice. "That's perfect. I'll visit you so much you won't even get a chance to miss me."

"But I will anyway," I told her.

"No more *Step Up* movies, no more cooking for me all the time, no more—"

"Okay!" I laughed. "You're right. I won't miss you at all."

Her eyes fell on Evie coming towards me with a drink. "Now you sound a little too happy."

I rolled my eyes in reply, sinking back into the comfortable couch.

Evie brought the first drink over with a grin and held it in front of me. In their defence it did look pretty. There was lots of ice, slices of lime, and sprigs of mint. I took the glass and felt everyone's eyes on me, waiting for me to take a sip. I brought it cautiously to my lips and breathed in the smell of limes like they were caustic fumes. My stomach lurched feverishly, yet I drew in a mouthful.

It burned like fire. I swallowed rapidly and choked out, "Effing hell. Oh my God."

Evie nodded, her eyes sparkling. "Good, right?"

"Strong," I rasped, feeling my eyes water.

"Damn straight they're strong, Quinn," Mac yelled as she churned out another batch. Seemingly satisfied, Evie returned to Mac in the kitchen like some kind of evil alcoholic mixer apprentice.

Soon we all had drinks and were piled in the living room with pitchers. Evie was curled up on the floor because Mac had spread herself out, leaving no room for anyone else. Everyone studiously avoided the subject of David in favour of band talk. I knew they were doing it deliberately—the drinks, the gathering, the conversation—and rather than feel manipulated, I felt grateful for the effort.

"Enjoying yourselves?"

We all turned as Jared walked in the room. His lips tipped up as Evie winked at him, and I sighed. Travis and Mitch came up behind him.

"We have to go out," Travis said, his eyes on mine.

I took a sip of my drink to distract myself from the belly flutters and shuddered.

"Where?" Mac demanded.

"Out," Mitch said. "We'll be back later. Don't wait up."

GIVE ME STRENGTH

When they left, Henry put some music on while Mac kept busy refilling everyone's glass with her evil potion. As the night wore on, I realised it really *was* evil potion because it was taking me back to Travis kissing me, his tongue in my mouth and all over my skin. All I wanted right then was him and to tell everyone how hot as fuck he was, and with my eyes on Mac, I blurted out, "I slept with your brother."

Everyone froze while the music kicked on loudly in the background.

Lucy giggled.

I closed my eyes, my face flaming wildly at my drunken admission.

Henry moaned. "Those Valentine brothers don't waste time, do they?"

Evie punched him in the arm. "It was years before Jared and I got together," she pointed out.

"Yeah but that's because you had issues."

Everyone returned their eyes to me; Mac's were wide as she asked the all-important question. "Which one?"

"Travis," Lucy supplied.

Mac's mind was ticking over. I could see it. It was just how she looked when in the office scheming over business documents. Then she asked the all-important second question. "When?"

I downed the last of my mojito and pressed my lips together on a giggle. "I'm afraid that's classi..." I hiccupped "...classified."

Mac pointed at Lucy. "You know."

Lucy pressed her lips together.

"Let's just ring Travis and ask," Evie suggested as she tried to put her glass down on the edge of the coffee table with exaggerated care and missed completely. She watched it tumble to the floor, ice and mint splattering the cream rug carelessly.

Mac started to stand, as though she thought Evie's idea was a great one. Despite my mojito loaded status, my reflexes were like lightning, and I leaped up, tackling her, and she went crashing down beneath me.

Due to my lightweight status, she rolled me off with ease and gasped out, "Grab the phone, Sandwich!"

"No!" I howled.

Henry was shaking his head. "And this is the part where living with girls isn't so great."

"Shut up, Henrietta," Mac retorted.

Evie made a grab for the phone and started dialling. Her fingers stumbled in their haste, and she squealed as I made it to my feet and started coming for her. She started running and dialling and giggling and then the phone was to her ear. When she started talking to Travis, I wanted to sink well beneath the floor and into the dirt until I never saw sunlight again.

Instead, I sank into the couch and covered my hands with my face and wailed, "I'm never drinking again."

Lucy snorted and I pointed my finger at her. "This is all your fault."

She waved her hand at me. "Not this again."

Evie's eyes flattened. "Travis isn't telling," she said with drunken disgust. She tossed the phone at me, and I caught it by reflex. "You talk to him."

I held the phone against my chest to muffle the sound and hissed, "No!"

Evie raised her eyebrows. "He's waiting to talk to you, Quinn."

I put the phone to my ear with a shaky hand. "Travis?"

"Quinn." His deep voice washed over me, making me hot enough to blush. I shushed the girls when they started squealing and making kissy noises like we were ten years old. Henry started throwing cushions at their faces while Travis asked, "Are you okay?"

"All good," I sing-songed.

"Are you sure?" He didn't sound convinced.

"Positive," I replied as a rogue cushion slapped me up the side of the head. I aimed a glare in the direction it came from, and Henry laughed. "You just keep doing whatever it is you're doing, and I'll keep doing…whatever it was I was doing, and we'll just, you know, umm…"

"Keep doing it?" Travis sounded amused.

I grinned. "Yeah."

I watched Evie disappear into the walk-in pantry when he said, "I have to go. Be good, okay?"

"Okay," I breathed out, watching Evie now dance her way back out of it with two big bowls of chips. Henry pounced and she shouted, holding them above her head as she danced out of his way.

The night wore on and curled on the couch, I found my eyes drifting shut as chatter continued on around me. Before I knew it Rick was there collecting Lucy, and Jared was carrying a sleeping Evie out the door. My eyes fluttered sleepily as I was lifted and cradled gently against a hard, warm chest. My body rocked softly as stairs were climbed, and then I was lowered into cool sheets. I stretched my legs out, moaning as my head spun. Forcing my eyes open to halt the earth's wild rotation, they focused on Travis quietly leaving the room.

"Travis?" I whispered and leaned up on one elbow.

He paused at the door and turned. "Go to sleep, Quinn."

Even exhausted I knew I was in for a sleepless night, and I wasn't sure I could bear it. "Will you stay?"

He hesitated.

"Just for a little while?"

Travis nodded and walked back into the room. Sitting on the other side of the bed, he bent over and slipped his shoes off. Then came his jacket and when he peeled his shirt off, I had to close my eyes. I felt the bed depress with his weight as he stretched out.

"Quinn?"

I opened my eyes. The covers were pulled to his waist and he was on his side facing me.

"David's back in custody."

"Was that you were out doing tonight? Helping the police find David?"

He nodded.

My eyes burned and I squeezed them shut.

"Come here, sweetheart." Travis cupped the back of my neck and pulled me against his chest.

The gesture broke open the fear that had me bound in knots, and I clutched at his arms. "I just want him to leave me alone," I choked out, the words muffled.

"I know, sweetheart." He pressed a kiss to my forehead, his arms tightening around me, not letting go.

"I'm sorry."

Travis buried his face in my neck, breathing deeply. "Don't ever be sorry," he whispered against my skin. "Not for that."

He rubbed his hands up and down my back soothingly and eventually exhaustion had me drifting off into a deep, even slumber.

The next morning I woke to gritty eyes, a pounding headache, and an empty bed. My head thumped back into the pillow as I groaned, remembering last night's emotional outburst with embarrassment. Without hesitation, Travis had been there for me all day, and as a thank you I'd cried all over him.

I rubbed a hand over my eyes, startled when the door flew open and Travis stormed in the room in his jeans, his bare chest heaving. His eyes flashed anger.

I sat up. "What is it?"

"This," he growled and shoved a file of papers in my face. I barely caught a glimpse of all the photos before he snatched them away. Seeing those once had been enough. My stomach lurched. Those photos had sent David to jail—my bruised eyes in a face so beaten and swollen I could barely be recognised, stitches through the back of my head, a broken arm, broken ribs, and bruising all down my obviously pregnant belly.

"You knew I'd been assaulted."

"Assault?" he shouted. "That's not assault. It's attempted fucking murder! He would have kept beating you and kicking you until there was nothing left. You lost your baby," he whispered. "And three years was all he got."

"How did you get those?" I whispered, staring at my hands.

"We requested the records. The police faxed them through this morning."

"Uh huh." I nodded carefully, rolling my shoulders to relax my body, reminding myself I was an adult who could control her emotions. "And who's *we*?"

Travis thrust his arm out wide, his fingers gripping tight to the folder. "That doesn't matter. You almost died!" He threw it against the wall and photos and papers scattered everywhere.

"It does matter!" I shouted back, all care of control gone in an instant. "It does. Did you see those? Did you have a good look? My baby died. My baby!" I shrieked, now up on my knees on the bed, the sheet clutched in my fingers. "He broke me. He took every piece of me I had left, and he smashed it apart. Nothing fits properly anymore. That's what those photos are, and that's what I don't want anyone seeing."

Mac stormed in, Henry hot on her heels. "What the fuck is going on in here?"

Travis pointed at the door. "Out, Mac."

She folded her arms as Henry came to stand next to her. Both sets of eyes dropped to the photos scattered on the floor. Henry paled and Mac drew a hand to her mouth. Then she looked at me, horror filling her expression.

I turned dull eyes on Travis. "Are you happy now?"

"Out!" Travis yelled.

Mac flinched. She took Henry's hand in hers, and they left the room, the door closing with a soft click.

The silence felt too still as Travis sank to the edge of the bed, running his hands through his hair as he hunched over.

"Travis?"

He shook his head as though he couldn't speak. I swallowed the lump in my throat and climbed off the bed to stand between his legs. He wrapped his hands around the backs of my bare thighs, tugging me closer, running his hands up and down the smooth skin as he fought to

105

find the words. He pressed his head into my belly, and I felt him shudder.

"I'm sorry, Quinn." His voice was muffled against my shirt. "I'm so angry this happened to you."

"I'm angry too." Travis looked up at me from beneath his lashes. "But I don't want to be angry anymore." I looked away, tired enough to not want to be anything. He let go of me, and I backed away, hating that I was letting everything David had done dictate my life. "That's about the only thing I know, apart from the fact that I can't be anything to anyone right now. I don't know if I ever can."

Travis stood, his eyes red and tired, and he nodded as though he understood what it was I was trying to say. "You'll need to go down to the station today. I'll get Mitch to take you." He inhaled deeply as he looked away. "I'll see you, Quinn."

Chapter Eleven

A week later I was in the basement, curled into the couch with the laptop as Jamieson worked through new material.

Wanting to upload some photos to their Facebook page, I lifted the camera in my hands and aimed it at Cooper.

"What a minute, Quinn. I'll take my shirt off."

"You do that, Coop, they'll shut our Facebook page down from the fan backlash," Evie piped up.

I took the photo just as Cooper was giving Evie the finger.

She smirked at him. "Good comeback."

Uploading the photo to the laptop—Cooper was snarling from his perch on the amplifier and Evie, guitar slung over her back, was hunched over laughing at him—I fiddled with the lighting and colour until a vintage look was achieved. I hit upload on Facebook with a grin and waited for the comments to roll in.

Monday had passed by with Mitch taking me to the police centre to formalise the incident report. Now it was a waiting game to hear the outcome. Tuesday was spent off work packing and moving, breaking my lease with the real estate agent, and formally changing my address. The rest of the week was immersed in work, and I wouldn't have had that any other way. I *loved* my job and now that I lived where I worked, I could sleep in more. Lucy's plan was to stop by two early mornings a week for us to exercise together. Early morning jogs in Coogee were different. People jogged along beach pathways. They smiled or gave you the "joggers club" nod. On Monday morning Mac and Evie had come with us. Lucy was thrilled because on Friday a paparazzi snapshot of us appeared in a national women's magazine with the caption: Evie moving on.

"How'd your night go last night with that whatshername chick?" I heard Henry ask Frog.

"Waste of time," Frog announced.

"Well that's it." Evie threw up her hands. "You've been through all the women in Sydney. There are none left."

Cooper pointed at me. "We still have Quinn."

Hearing my name, I glanced up and he gave me a wink.

Henry shook his head. "That ship has sailed."

Cooper and Frog turned wounded eyes on me. "You hooked up with someone and didn't tell us, Quinn?"

I glared at Henry. "No, I'm not 'hooked up' with anyone."

"Quinn!" Mac shouted down the stairs. "Where's that run sheet for next Friday?"

"It's uploaded into your calendar, Mac! Trying to cut down on all the paper," I called back, ignoring the chatter around me to focus on the laptop.

"Too fucking efficient," I heard Mac mumble as her shoes clicked back towards the office.

When Evie was singing a few trial bars and trailed off into silence, I looked up. She was staring at the entrance to the basement with wide eyes. Turning my head, I saw Casey standing there, his blue eyes drinking Evie in.

"Casey," she whispered. "You're back."

He gave her a short nod.

She whipped her guitar off her shoulders and a moment later was folded in his arms.

"Hotdog!" Cooper whooped.

Casey chuckled and the basement chatter got louder.

I looked sideways at Jake when he flopped down on the couch next to me. "Why do they call him hotdog?" I whispered.

He laughed at my pink face. "It's not why you think. It's just a joke term used for flashy surfing. Evie started it."

"Casey surfs?"

Jake nodded. "He and Evie started surfing together before he went overseas."

The computer beeped an incoming email, and I flicked it open, starting to read when Jake nudged my shoulder. "So who's the guy?"

Without taking my eyes from the screen, I said, "So what's going on with you and Mac?"

He patted me on the thigh. "I'm glad we had this conversation."

"Me too," I muttered at his retreating back.

When Casey and Evie stood alone again, I heard him ask, "Is everything good now?"

Evie nodded, saying softly, "Everything's good."

Casey grinned before tipping his chin at the guys. "Catch you all later. Surf tomorrow, Evie?"

She gave him two thumbs up. "You bet."

Then Casey turned those blue eyes on me. "Quinn. Walk me out?"

"Oh." A few sets of eyebrows rose, and I fumbled with the laptop, sitting it on the couch next to me before standing up. "Um...okay."

I followed him up the stairs, frowning when he led me into the back office rather than the front door. When he shut the door behind us, I folded my arms as he walked towards me to lean casually against the edge of the desk.

His eyes searched my face. "How are you doing, Quinn?"

My brows drew together. "Sorry?" Then I remembered Mac telling me that Casey was a partner in Travis and Jared's consulting business.

I stared at my feet. "You know about David too?"

He sighed heavily and rubbed at the back of his neck. "Quinn, I know we don't know each other, but I wanted to be the one to let you know."

My brow furrowed. "Let me know what?"

"David only got sixty days."

109

"I see," I whispered softly, but inside my mind was reeling. After only a week I'd felt safe here, but safe was just a big, fat lie.

"He'll be out in a little under two months."

My hands shook and I turned, blindly searching for the chair and sat down.

"Quinn," Casey said softly. His eyes were on me, and they looked strained. "I wanted to let you know because I understand what you're going through. I've been there too."

"You have?" My eyes ran the length of him. He was almost as tall as Travis and just as wide. Muscles rippled beneath a soft, grey shirt and dark jeans. Casey was good looking enough to suck the air from a room, but that didn't mean anything when it came to abuse. Pain didn't discriminate.

He nodded, sagging into the desk. "I know what it's like to lose what you love and have nothing left." He paused. "So if you need to talk to someone who understands, I'm here, okay?"

Turning in my chair, I faced the view of the backyard from the window. Rufus and Peter were splayed out on the soft grass, taking in the heat of the morning sun. How easy they made life look. "How do you escape it?"

"I don't know, Quinn. I haven't figured that out yet."

My chest tightened as I turned back to look at him. "I'm going to have to move, aren't I? Not just from here, but further away. Interstate, maybe."

"It's an option," he replied.

Helpless rage rushed through me, and when my eyes fell on the stapler sitting harmlessly on the desk, I picked it up and threw it against the wall. It hid with a loud, satisfying clank.

Casey's eyes shifted from the stapler to me. "Feel better?"

I ground my teeth together. "No. Yes." I looked at him. "No."

"Quinn," he said, his eyes softening.

"Don't!" I shouted. The urge to fall apart whenever Travis gave me that look was enough. I didn't need Casey doing it too.

"Don't what?"

"Nothing." My lips pressed together. "Shit. I can't do this anymore. I can't."

"You can." He took hold of my shoulders. "You can. One day at a time."

I shook my head at Casey.

"Breathe, Quinn."

I sucked in a deep lungful of air.

Shouting could be heard outside the door, and then it was slamming open as Travis yelled at Mitch. "...completely fucked up. Two months Mitch, and you can't do shit."

Mitch threw his hands up in frustration, storming off as Travis stood in the doorway wearing his leather and dark jeans, customary sunglasses hanging in the neckline of his shirt. His chest was heaving, anger making his eyes wild.

He held out his hand, palm up and commanded, "Quinn. Come with me."

My hand was in his before I could think. When his fingers closed around mine and held tight, I was pulled from Casey's hold and led up the stairs and into my bedroom. The door slammed shut behind us, and letting go of my hand, he turned to face me.

"I don't want to talk about David anymore today, Travis."

He searched my pale, drawn face. "What *do* you want?"

You. Because you're the one that eases the ache in my chest. It's you that takes my mind off everything that hurts. You that makes me lose all sense just from wanting you. And if I can't have you, I want to be like Rufus and Peter and lie out in the sun as though I didn't have a care in the world.

"I want a day where David doesn't exist."

He nodded, his mind ticking over. "Okay. You told me you liked the beach, so pack your shit."

"My shit?"

"All that crap you girls pack in those giant bags and cart to the beach with you."

"You're taking me to the beach?"

His eyes skimmed me over in a way that left me tingling. "Don't forget your bikini."

"My bikini?"

Travis started walking towards the door. "And pack snacks with your shit. I'm hungry." He opened the door. "Don't be long," he said over his shoulder with a wink.

I blinked.

I was going to the beach. With Travis.

How did that just happen?

I opened the bedroom door and yelled for Mac.

She breezed in a minute later in a pair of navy Lorna Jayne sweats and a white tank top. "You called?"

"I was thinking about going to the beach today."

"Congratulations," she replied. "Isn't it a bit cool now? Winter's coming."

"I'm going with Travis."

"Oh my God." She hurled herself on the bed and a pillow flew off the other side and landed on the floor. "This is just like old times! What are you wearing?"

I picked up the pillow and tossed it back on the bed. "Old times?"

"Yeah, when Evie and Jared got together." She grabbed the pillow and stuck it under her head, wriggling her shoulders to form a groove. When she was comfortable, she sighed deeply. "That took some serious fucking work."

"Well this isn't like that. Travis and I are…"

Mac arched her brow. "Are what?"

My cheeks puffed out as I tried to think while I opened the wardrobe door. My eyes ran over the contents, forgetting what I was supposed to be looking for.

"I have no idea," I said eventually.

"Well I'm sure Travis has enough ideas for the both of you. Now show me what bikinis you've got."

At the reminder, I rummaged through the shelving of clothes inside the wardrobe. "I've only got one," I said absentmindedly.

"What?"

"I've only got one bikini," I repeated.

"What?"

"Mac!"

She laughed. "Okay, okay, but seriously though. That's fucked up. We need to fix that."

"I don't even know where it is," I told Mac when I walked from the wardrobe empty handed. It was probably a good thing. The suit was faded and tired looking. Lucy may well have thrown it out like she'd threatened to do last time we went to the beach.

"Quinn!" Travis called out from downstairs. "Let's go."

"I'll be right down!" I called back.

"Mac is that the phone ringing?" Henry asked, wandering into my room, head down as his fingers flew across the keypad of his phone.

"Rubbish. My phone is right here, so that only means your shitty guitar playing skills have sent you deaf. Now get out. Quinn's getting dressed."

Henry hit a button and jumped on the bed. "Awesome." He snatched the pillow from underneath Mac, and her head snapped back. With a growl, she wrenched it from his arms. "I haven't missed anything yet, have I?"

The pillow smacked Henry in the face. "We're picking out a bikini. Quinn's going to the beach."

"We're not picking one out. I only have one," I reminded her. "And I can't find it."

"Cool." Henry's phone buzzed a reply, and he propped himself up on an elbow to read it. "Can I come?"

"She's going with Travis."

He sighed dramatically. "The plot thickens."

Opening a drawer from my dresser, I snorted and yanked out a pair of denim shorts. "There is no plot. Besides..." I waved my shorts around "...at this rate I'll be swimming at the beach in my underwear."

Mac scooted to the edge of the bed and sat upright. "Alright, Quinn. Show me your boobs."

"Um, what?"

"You heard me."

"Yeah, you heard her," Henry repeated. He tossed his phone into the middle of the bed and widened his eyes at me in expectation.

Mac reached over and punched him in the arm. "Out, Henry. I need to see what I have that will fit Quinn."

"Ouch, Mactard. You really need to get laid." He crawled off the bed, rubbing his arm, and as he reached the door, called out, "Hmm, so does Jake for that matter."

His phone was hurled at him and with an outstretched arm, he caught it effortlessly in his left hand, laughter following him out the door.

"Mac!" Travis shouted up the stairs. "Leave Quinn alone."

Mac grinned.

"What?"

She shrugged and said airily, "Travis just seems impatient to get his hands on you."

Ten minutes later—dressed in a pale blue floral bikini with a centre tie courtesy of Mac, my shorts, and a rose coloured tank top—my bag of "shit" was stowed in the black Subaru, and I was sliding into the passenger seat.

Travis, wearing nothing but a pair of long boardshorts, gunned the engine. The throaty growl of it vibrated through my body as I buckled myself in, careful to keep my eyes averted from all that naked skin. Instead, I fixed them on the clean windows and upholstery, marvelling that his car bore no ill will from Rufus.

"All good?"

I gave him a nod. "All good."

Arriving at the beach, Travis grabbed my bag and started for the sand.

"You're not actually serious about swimming, are you?" I asked, my toes digging into the soft sand as I trudged after him. A cool breeze was gusting in off the ocean, and the horizon revealed a set of monster waves making their way towards the shore.

He looked at me sideways as I caught up to him. "Sure."

I looked around. The beach wasn't overly crowded except for the relative few I could see bobbing about in the waves. Death by chilly monster waves obviously wasn't on most people's list of things to get done today.

Travis tossed his towel haphazardly in the sand and looked out towards the waves. Trying to stave off my impending doom, I pulled my neatly folded towel from the bag Travis dropped in the sand and proceeded to lay it out carefully, ensuring the edges were neat and sand free.

Removing a book and a bottle of water, I went to sit down.

Travis shook his head. "Uh uh."

"Are you serious?" I pressed my lips together.

"As a heart attack," he said solemnly.

Peeled down to my bikini, I hugged my body, rubbing my arms to keep warm, I muttered, "Well come on then. Let's get this over with."

Reaching the water's edge, icy water rushed and bubbled over my toes and my lungs closed up. I stepped back and turned around, but before managing my escape, Travis took hold of my bicep and grinned at me.

"Leaving so soon?"

"Hell yes," I replied emphatically.

"You'll get used to it in a moment," the big bully told me, dragging me forward until alarmingly cold water splashed around my knees.

"Why are we doing this again?"

"Because it's fun."

I arched a brow of disbelief at him, but a wave rocked me, and my efforts were turned to bracing against the onslaught. "Ice torture is your definition of fun?"

Those monster waves were starting to roll in, and as water swirled around my waist, he said, "Nothing makes you feel more alive than swimming in a cold ocean."

I beg to differ, I thought wistfully, watching as he let go of my arm and dived into the waves. *Nothing makes me feel more alive than when you touch me, Travis.*

Eventually he surfaced a few metres ahead, turning to check on me as he pushed hair from his face. Seeing my chance, I hollered to him that I was hopping out.

"You haven't even got your hair wet, Quinn."

"I'm cold."

His eyes lowered to my chest and running a tongue along his bottom lip, they returned to mine with a cheeky glint. "I can tell."

I laughed. "Would you stop?"

Travis grinned and started for me. I began backing away, poking out my tongue as he effortlessly jumped in the face of a big wave. It crashed into me and I was pitched beneath the surface with embarrassing fanfare.

He was laughing when I sputtered to the surface, wrestling wet hair out of my face as my teeth chattered. "This is crazy. We're officially crazy people." My eyes fell on a wave of tsunami like proportions rolling in behind him.

Seeing my panic, Travis glanced behind him. Turning back, he held out his arms. "Come here."

I didn't hesitate. I climbed the length of him and wrapped myself around his front like a barnacle. I burrowed my head in his neck, Travis clutching me tight to him as he turned his back to the wave. As it crashed wildly around us, the sweet bloom of something beautiful began unfurling in my chest and rocked me hard. My throat worked at swallowing it down, but right then I wanted nothing more than to claw my way inside his skin and never leave.

"Oh God," I muttered.

He pressed a soft kiss against my ear as the water rushed around us and the sweet warmth of his breath made me burrow in a little tighter. "You okay?"

Not trusting my voice, I nodded into his neck as he waded through to the shallows and set me on my feet. The sun was high in the sky when we reached our towels. I spread out on my carefully placed towel while Travis picked his up, flicking it around carelessly in the breeze.

"Travis!"

He chuckled as he spread his towel out, lying down with a thud while I brushed at the fine layer of sand now covering my body.

I rolled on my stomach and faced him. He was on his back, his eyes closed as the sun beat down on his chest. Water glinted over his tanned skin, making me want to lean over and lick the salty drops away.

He squinted his eyes open and peeked at me. "What?"

Flustered, I shrugged. "Nothing. I was just uh, wondering where you went to uni."

Sighing, he closed his eyes again. "Charles Sturt. You?"

"That's in Wagga, isn't it? Mine was correspondence because I was already working full time."

"It is. My dad went there and so did Mitch and Jared."

"But not Mac. She went to Melbourne, right?"

"She was going to but I think with Jared and me still there, she didn't want the quote-unquote 'Valentine testosterone' cramping her style."

"You all must be close though."

"Mac and Jared were always close."

"You were closer to Mitch?"

"Well, no, not really. Mitch was close to Dad. He was the one that followed in his footsteps the most. Jared and I kinda peeled off to do our own thing."

"So who were you close to?"

Even with his eyes closed he frowned. "No one I guess, though I met Casey at uni. After the first year, we shared an apartment together."

"And after that you started doing…what you do."

"Mm hmm."

"So why didn't you and Jared follow in your dad's footsteps like Mitch did?"

Opening his eyes, he rolled on his side and propped his head in his hand. "Wanted something a little less rigid I guess—something that felt like we were making more of difference."

"Are you?"

"I like to think so. Otherwise, what's the point?" he said, rummaging in my bag and coming out with a bag of chips. Opening the packet, he offered me one.

I shook my head.

"What about you? Who were you close to—apart from Lucy?"

"No one that mattered, except for…"

Travis stopped chewing and swallowed. "Except for who?"

"Ethan." I paused. "He…" was the one who showed me how good life could be. The one who, by leaving, reminded me that that good life, and people like Travis, weren't for people like me. "…mattered."

A beat of silence passed between us where I thought Travis would push for information I wasn't sure I could share. I sat up. "We should probably get back."

"Soon," he murmured and finished his chips. Travis rolled onto his back again and closed his eyes. A moment later I followed suit, and we lay there together in the quiet, listening to the waves crash on the shore as the mild sun warmed our skin.

My phone ringing brought me out of what could possibly have been a nap. Travis stirred as I reached into my bag and pulled it out.

"Mac?"

"Where are you, asshead?"

My eyebrows flew up and I whispered to Travis, "She called me 'asshead!'"

He nodded, his lips tipping up lazily. "That's a sign of love, Quinn. Embrace it."

"What's the time?" Mac and I had to be at the White Demon at four.

"Three."

"Shit." I sat up and grabbed for my shorts. "Already on our way, Mac."

"Sure you are." She hung up.

Sandy and rushed, we reached the car and I brushed haphazardly at the sand on my feet.

Travis opened the passenger door, and scanning the carpark, thrust his towel at me. "Here." I grabbed the towel before it could drop to the ground. "Cover me."

"What?"

He hooked his fingers in the waistband of his boardshorts and underwear and yanked them off.

My eyes widened and a bubble of breathless laughter escaped me as I scrambled to hold up the towel. I scanned the carpark and turning back, caught a good glimpse of his firm backside when he twisted to flick his wet clothes inside the car.

"You can wrap the towel around me now."

"What?"

"Come on, Quinn. It's cold and that's not a good look for a guy." He winked at me.

With another breathless laugh, I took a step forward and wrapped the towel around his hips, biting down on my lip as I gently tucked it in at the front. I repressed a shiver of longing as my fingers brushed his damp, warm skin. He cupped my cheek in his hand before I could pull away, and the heat of it warmed me.

"Thanks, Quinn."

"What for?"

"For today. Thanks for giving me today."

Chapter Twelve

"Woohooo Sydney!" Evie raised her arm up high as she yelled into the crowd at the White Demon Warehouse.

They yelled back, the sound reverberating around the huge ceilings of the inner city venue as once again, Evie held the crowd in the palm of her hand.

Jamieson was a regular here and the place was heaving with people, the bartenders frenzied as they hopped between one another to fill orders.

On the opposite side of the stage, Jared let out a piercing whistle. To my left Mac was clapping, and to my right Travis stood silently, his arms folded as his eyes skimmed the crowd with measured calculation. He paused for a moment to smile down at me, and my heart pounded.

Our day together at the beach had been weeks ago now, and we were well into the middle of winter, but a day like that, and a man like Travis, wasn't easily forgotten. Quite frankly, he didn't make it easy on me. When he was at the duplex, or working security, he was pretty much all I could see. When he wasn't, I would get random emails and find myself smiling whenever I saw his name in my inbox. My heart would flutter over the simplest things, like…

The list for security is attached.

or

Did you get our latest invoice?

"We've got a member to the Jamieson team we haven't introduced you to yet," Evie shouted into the microphone after finishing their first song of the night. "Wanna meet her?"

My eyes widened and I started backing away slowly.

Evie glanced over at me and grinned. "Uh oh. Looks like she's trying to do a runner."

I spun around, already running, when I heard, "Go get her, Henry," and the crowd started chanting Henry's name.

Arms wound around me and in my ear Travis said, "Uh uh. You may as well just get it over with."

When I turned in his arms, he was grinning at me. I shoved at his chest but he didn't budge. "I'm not going out there," I hissed. "Are you mad?"

He picked me up and walked me back like a rag doll, offering me up towards where Henry stood waiting. Suddenly I knew how Ann Darrow felt when she was offered up as a sacrifice to King Kong.

Henry offered me his back. "Get on."

I shook my head. "No. I'm good right here." And I was actually. All tucked in the arms of Travis.

"She's being difficult, guys," Evie said into the microphone. "Why don't we offer her some encouragement? Who wants to meet Quinn?"

My stomach churned as thousands of people began chanting my name. Travis hoisted me onto Henry's back, and I clung on, turning to glare at him as I was piggybacked into the blindingly bright lights.

"Here she is. Isn't she cute?"

"I shall kill all of you," I hissed in Henry's ear. "Sleep with one eye open, Henry."

He threw his head back in a laugh, and I almost fell off his back. "Smile and say hello into the microphone and we'll let you go."

Trying to smile, I bared my teeth in what was probably a grimace and said hi quickly into the microphone Evie shoved in my face. Then Henry spun me around in circles like I was about to pin the tail on the donkey.

"Get me the hell off this stage, Henry," I whispered furiously.

Set back on my feet, I muttered something about some of us having real work to do and fled for the dressing room.

My phone rang and tugging it from my pocket, I answered it as I shut the door behind me.

"Quinn, it's John about the Melbourne festival appearance. Sorry about the late call, but I didn't figure I'd catch you and was just going to leave a message."

I rummaged through my bag and pulled out my iPad as he spoke. "That's fine, John. Are you telling me you slotted us in?"

"Thankfully we did," he returned, and I could hear the grin in his voice.

"Yes!" I mouthed silently, jumping up and fist pumping the air with enthusiasm. "Great news," I said calmly. "Can't wait to tell the Jamieson crew." Then I boogied my hips from side to side to the muffled thump of the beat coming from the stage.

A deep chuckle from behind sent a hot flush running from my toes to the very tips of my hair. Whirling around, Travis lazily trekked his eyes upwards, locking on mine.

I cleared my throat and replied casually, "Okay then. If you can email the details through, I'll get the paperwork signed and sent back first thing tomorrow."

Tomorrow was Sunday but this was already short notice. In two weeks Jamieson would be featuring at the biggest music festival Melbourne hosted. Organising the details couldn't wait.

John assured me he was emailing the information through at that very moment, and after promising to talk to him tomorrow, I hung up.

"Good news?"

I grinned ruefully. "You had to ask that?"

Hands in his pockets, he shrugged and walked towards me. "Have I given you enough space yet?"

"Space?"

"Yeah." Leaning his hip casually against the table, he reached out and brushed a lock of hair from my face.

"Space for uh, what?"

"Us. I don't know if you're ready for what this is between us, but I can't seem to make myself leave you alone."

I shook my head slightly. "I don't..."

Travis cupped my cheeks in his hands and leaned in. "You're so guarded and wary, Quinn. I can understand why, but maybe space is not what you need."

"What *do* I need?" I breathed, my heart thundering in my chest.

He pressed a sweet kiss on my mouth and against my lips whispered, "Me."

Pulling back, his hands remained, his eyes taking in every inch of my face as though committing it to memory.

I ducked my head from his gaze.

"Don't," he said gruffly. "You're so beautiful."

"Travis," I whispered, both warmth and confusion warring within me. Confusion won. Why did he think I was so special? I had nothing to offer except a sordid, violent past and a broken future. I was timid, unsure of myself, and emotionally unstable. The sleek, flashy women I'd seen at the Florence Bar were a much better fit for him than I was.

I took a step back and his hands fell away.

"I wish I could see what you seem to because I'm nothing like those beautiful girls you were with at that bar. What's here," I waved a hand at my face, "doesn't matter because that's not what I see. I see what's in here..." I thumped a hand against my chest "...and what's in here is ugly, and I live with it every day."

"Is that what you think?" He shook his head at me, swallowing hard. "Quinn," he said hoarsely. "I watched you. From the moment you walked in that bar, I saw you. Amongst all the shallow and the fake, you looked like spring, and then you got close and I was right because you smelled like jasmine. When you turned around to leave I thought I was wrong because why did someone as sweet as spring think that life wasn't meant for her? There was no light in your eyes, and somehow, even though I barely knew you, it left an ache in my chest. How could I let you walk away?"

"You heard me say that?"

"That life wasn't meant for you?"

I nodded and closed my eyes.

He sighed heavily and reaching out, trailed his fingers through the wild curls of my hair. "Life is hard, Quinn, and the hardest part is being yourself in a world of people trying to make you someone you're not. I saw you standing apart from everything that was the same, and that was beautiful, not sad. When I was holding you and inside of you, I watched your eyes come alive, and fuck spring because you were hotter than summer, and I want to see that again." His voice was low and as I opened my eyes and met his, he brushed his thumb across my lips. "I want to see you smile, and I want to touch you again and feel you burn brighter than the sun while I'm doing it."

My heart swelled until I thought it would beat its way out of my chest. I reached up and covered his hand with my own.

"Travis…"

I stood there, maybe breathing—I couldn't be sure—but wanting to tell him that no one had ever said anything so beautiful to me in all my life. That no one had ever looked at me the way he was doing right now—as though nothing else existed but me.

My lips parted as I tried to find the words, and at the invitation, his mouth slammed down on mine. I moaned at the wild force as he thrust his tongue in my mouth, arms winding tightly around me until I was sure I'd never breathe again and didn't care to. Travis lifted me and turned, backing towards the couch until he was sitting down, my legs straddling him. He groaned as my tongue rubbed against his, greedily wanting more and fearing it would never be enough. My hands slid up the hard ridges of his chest, reaching his neck and twining through his hair until he broke the kiss, breathing heavy as he shifted his lips to my neck, his tongue licking a path downwards as my body burned.

"Oh God," I moaned breathlessly, my back arching.

"Want you so much," he muttered, slipping his hands beneath my tight shirt, frantically pushing my bra out of the way until warm naked skin filled his palms.

Someone's phone rang. We both ignored it. Instead, Travis returned his lips to mine, his hips grinding into me along with his tongue.

The phone kept ringing.

"Shit," he muttered, and it stopped as he pulled away.

It was good that he did because there was no way I could. He could have ripped off my pants and filled me right then and there, and I would have been his. That was not good. Anyone could have walked in. In fact, we were both *supposed* to be working.

I informed him of that very fact and he chuckled. "Maybe you are, but we have enough security out there that I'm not really needed. I'm just here for you."

"Me?"

Travis cocked a brow. "You're a full time security job yourself."

My mouth fell open. "I am not."

His eyes dropped to my lips. "Careful doing that. It seems to get you in trouble."

I scrambled off his lap, brushing at my hair and tugging my bra back into place. Nodding at the table where my iPad and pen sat, I said, "I need to do...some stuff."

Travis stood and my cheeks heated at the obvious bulge he was adjusting in his pants.

I tried not to look. "Maybe you shouldn't go out there with uh, that."

He winked. "*That* is not gonna go down if I stay in here. I'll leave you to your stuff, but tomorrow night you're all mine. I'll pick you up at six."

"You mean like a...date?"

Travis gave me a short nod.

I've never been on a date before. Even with Ethan, most of our time together had been spent at his house, at the beach, or at school.

His eyes widened and I cringed. "Did I just say that out loud?"

"Uh huh." He reached the door and opened it, letting the wild beat of music pump through. "Don't worry. I'll be sure to make it good for you," he said with a wink and shut the door behind him.

I shivered and practised deep breathing for several moments. Minutes later, the door flew open and Mac strode through. She eyeballed the walls of the dressing room with exaggerated fashion. "If these four walls could talk, I bet they'd have a lot to say, but unfortunately they can't." She shook her head in mock sadness before narrowing those knowing eyes on me. "So spill."

"How do you even know?"

"Because my brother came back all tight lipped, but his eyes were telling me a different story."

"Oh? What story was that?"

"The same story they told when he was twelve and got the cadet go-kart he'd been hounding our parents about since he was eight."

I averted my eyes because if she saw all that in his, imagine what she saw in mine?

I woke the next morning to shouts from downstairs and dogs barking in the yard, telling me the duplex was already heaving with activity. This wasn't unusual—what was unusual was that I still couldn't get used to it. Living here was loud and noisy, and if you wanted to be heard, you had to throw yourself into the fray and start yelling. I wasn't quite at the yelling stage yet, but I was getting there, particularly when I found my favourite, freshly washed, pink lace pillow covers gracing Henry's bed. He'd simply shrugged at me and said he didn't care if they were pink; they smelled nice. Frog was always hogging the couch and the remote, making me miss my reality television shows. The season finale of The Voice was on just the other night, and I had no idea who won. Cooking dinner was something I'd found myself doing more often than not and cooking, for sometimes up to six or more people at a time, involved planning. One night I gave up and just cooked poached eggs on toast which didn't appear to bother anyone.

Slipping on a pair of sweatpants and a plain fitted tank top, I scraped my hair into a ponytail as I jogged down the stairs. Mac and Henry were on the couch along with Evie, all eating identical bowls of Coco Pops and watching music videos.

"'Bout time you woke up, you lazy asshead," Mac mumbled around a crunchy mouthful.

I rubbed at my eyes. "What's the time?"

"Early," Henry growled. "Thanks to Evie." He elbowed her in the arm and a trickle of milk sloshed over the rim of her bowl and into her lap.

Evie narrowed her eyes. "If you elbow me one more time, you're going to be wearing my breakfast on your face."

Henry made an "oooh I'm scared" face while she brushed the milk droplets from her jeans. I curled up in the armchair, and Rufus let out a whine from the back door. Peter was standing in front of him scratching at the glass as though zombies were on the attack and they needed inside to live.

"I should feed Rufus."

"Done," Mac announced.

"Oh." I smiled at her. "Thanks, Mac."

"Yeah, well. I can be nice."

Evie let out a shout of laughter, and Mac narrowed her eyes. "I'm letting you stay here, aren't I?" she said to Evie.

"Stay?" I echoed.

"Rats," Evie supplied with a shudder.

"Rats?"

Evie nodded. "There's a rat family living in our house at Bondi. They have a camp at ground zero. I saw it when Jared ripped up the floorboards. It's not pretty. They have tents and sleeping bags and some sort of hi-tech equipment that tells them when we're in bed trying to sleep because they start scurrying from base camp into the ceiling as though it's the holy grail of all places to have fun. I've tried to tell Jared that the whole house needs a wrecking ball, not a renovation, but he just looks at me like *I'm* the idiot."

"You are an idiot," Mac retorted. She clanked her spoon into her now empty bowl and stood up.

"Anyway..." Evie ignored Mac "... Jared and I are here for a couple of days while the place is being fumigated for every pest that ever lived."

"You're the biggest pest that ever lived," Mac shouted from the kitchen as she rinsed her bowl and set it on the sink. "Why aren't they fumigating you?"

Evie twisted in her seat and glared at Mac. "What the fuck, Mac? Someone steal your favourite shoes?"

Mac grinned and tossed the tea towel she'd been drying her hands with on the bench. "My shiny red slingbacks are just fine, thank you very much. I'm just in a good mood about Melbourne."

After informing Mac in the dressing room about the festival booking, she'd still managed to wrangle the date details out of me as though I'd already been plied with her malevolent mojitos.

The date.

My God.

Had I actually agreed to it? I shook my head. No. He'd *told* me we were going on a date, not *asked* me. There was no opportunity to say no. Would I have been able to say no anyway? I shook my head again. When Travis was in my space, all sense went flying out the window. Mac had been excited, even after telling me we'd gone about it all ass backwards—sleeping with each other and then going on a date weeks later but I could sleep at night knowing she approved of my 'ballsy tactics.'

Finished with my internal conversation, I pushed out of the chair and stood up, stifling a yawn. "I need to get started on organising the Melbourne trip."

Mac returned to the living room and flopped onto the couch. "Rubbish. It's your day off. I'll do it."

"But I don't have anything else going on," I said over my shoulder while wandering into the kitchen. I opened the fridge and examined the barren, sad looking shelves. "Maybe I could do a food shop then?"

"Sandwich and Henry are doing the shop today," she announced loudly because Henry was holding down the volume button on the remote until the sound breached decibel regulations.

"So what am I supposed to..." My voice trailed off as an almighty knock thundered at the door, and it swung open before anyone could move to answer it. A petite, dark-haired guy no taller than I was came barging in.

Mac smirked at me over her shoulder. "You're going shopping."

"What?"

"You're going shopping," she yelled.

"Just come on in, Tim," Evie said to the little guy with obvious sarcasm.

He huffed and flung himself in the armchair I'd just vacated. "Lord knows I'd be fucking grey with one foot in the grave before you got off your fat backside to answer it. No point in wasting the day."

"This is Tim, Quinn," Evie called out. "He works reception for Jamieson and Valentine Consulting. Oh, and he talks more crap than a politician, so don't believe a word he says."

"Oh, you are just too funny, Evie," Tim replied. His brown eyes, fringed in the prettiest lashes I'd ever seen on a guy, found their way to mine. "Quinn, my new best friend," he said with a glare aimed at Evie. He came over to the kitchen to shake my hand, Mac hot on his heels.

"So what's going on with you and Travis? He's my boss you know, and hot, so it's my right as your new best friend to get all the details."

Mac took hold of my hand as though to yank me away, and Tim grabbed my other hand, narrowing his eyes on Mac. "Back off, Mac. I was here first, only polite enough not to muscle her into the pantry like your usual M.O."

I had to give the little guy credit for having the balls to stare Mac down. I'm not sure who won because the front door slammed, and Jake wandered through into the kitchen, eyeing our odd little clinch with raised brows before opening the fridge. Mac shoved me into the walk-in pantry, Tim right behind us, and wedged the door shut.

The three of us stood there in the dark, panting a little at the scuffle. I heard a muffled sound and a dim light clicked on before flickering off again.

"Shit. The bulb blew."

"So Quinn and Travis have a thing," Mac announced as we stood in the dark. "That's why you're here, Tim. Quinn has a date tonight and needs outfitting, and I need to get Melbourne organised so it's in your hands."

"Mac, it's the movies. I'm sure I have something suitable."

"No you don't," she replied without hesitation.

"Why are we wedged in the pantry?"

"Because Jake's out there and he's pissing me off."

"But he only just walked in the door."

"Exactly," she growled.

"This little pantry summit is directed at the wrong person," Tim decided. "Seems to me that if Quinn and Travis are going on a date, they're well on their way to getting shit together. What's going on with you and Jake?"

I'd been wondering this myself, so I waited with interest to hear her response.

"No comment," Mac snapped.

131

"Ha! We all know *no comment* is euphemism for shit is going on. Right, Quinn?"

I could hear the withering tone in Tim's voice and replied, "We do?"

"Shove your euphemisms where the sun don't shine, Timmy boy."

"Don't call me Timmy boy," he snapped.

The pantry door flew open, light flooding the little space and I blinked rapidly, bringing Lucy into focus. "What's going on in here?"

"Pantry summit," Tim offered, squinting in the sudden light.

Lucy glared. "Who are you?"

"I'm Tim." He raised his brows and looked Lucy up and down. "And who are you? By the attitude I'm going with Mac's long lost sister, but you look nothing alike."

"Watch it, Tim." Mac shoved past him and he stumbled, grabbing hold of the pantry door to gain his balance. "I'll be in the back office."

"I'm Lucy, Quinn's friend. I'm here to take her shopping."

"Me too and me too. I'm going to make a cuppa. Anyone want one?"

Everyone chorused a "yes please," and he mumbled, "figures," as he trotted back into the kitchen.

"It's just the movies, Luce," I told her as we sat down in the living room where Evie was now splayed out on her own. "It's no big deal."

"You never date," she told me, perching on the end of the armchair. "Of course it's a big deal."

Evie's eyes shifted from the television to me. "You don't date?"

"Enough. No more talk about the date or shopping." I pursed my lips and focused on the television.

Tim came over and plopped a mug on the table in front of me. "No idea if you wanted tea or coffee or how you have it, but hey, you didn't have to make it." Taking a step back, he put his hands on his hips, looking at me with wide-eyed hope. "So is Casey coming shopping too?"

"Why would Casey be coming shopping?" I asked.

He shrugged. "Bodyguard duty. Don't you all get escorted everywhere you go by hot badass guys when shit's going down?"

"Shit's not going down," Lucy informed him. "Shit is currently contained."

"Oh," Tim muttered, his shoulders slumping as though disappointed that shit was not, in fact, going down.

"Why are you so keen on Casey going?" Lucy asked.

Tim looked at Evie and me in turn. "She hasn't met Casey, has she?"

We both shook our heads, Evie grinning.

"Honey," Tim said to Lucy, "Everyone says Casey looks just like Jensen Ackles," he began. I bit the insides of my cheeks as Casey walked down the hall from the office and came to stand behind Tim. "But Casey is so fucking all that, he could have a show all his own and screw calling it Supernatural, you could call it Badassnatural because that guy is so fucking cool he was born an ice cube."

Silence reigned until Evie made a choking sound. Tim closed his eyes and I really, honestly, felt for him in that moment.

"He's ah, behind me, isn't he?"

Everyone did their best not to laugh, but I met Casey's eyes and they were crinkling.

Evie tossed a cushion at Casey. "Hear that, hotdog? You're the man."

Casey showed off his lightning Badassnatural reflexes by deflecting the tossed cushion, and it bounced off Tim's head as a final insult.

Despite his face flaming brightly, Tim pursed his lips. "Takes a badass to know one."

Evie raised her brow. "I thought the first rule of being a badass was that you never talked about being a—"

"Don't start throwing rules in my face," Tim interrupted.

"Enough," Casey growled and stooped to pick up the cushion and toss it back on the couch as Evie introduced him to Lucy.

"I'll leave you kids to it," he muttered after nodding his hello and turned towards the front door. "I'm going home to sleep."

"So that's a no to coming shopping with us today?" Tim called out.

Casey threw an incredulous look over his shoulder as the front door swung wide and he stepped out, shutting it behind him without another word.

Chapter Thirteen

"Stop fidgeting," Mac hissed from behind me.

I watched her fiddle a curl into submission as I stood in front of the mirror of the wardrobe door. Mac had a good foot of height on me, so her look of concentration as she tackled my wispy strands was easily visible. She grabbed the hairspray off the bench. "You and Evie could win awards for being fidget sticks."

"No spray!"

She held it like a weapon aimed at my head and raised her brows as though I'd just said "death to shopping," something I'd come to realise was her holy grail in life.

"What?"

"I don't like it."

"But..." Mac trailed off.

"Beth loved hairspray. The smell makes my stomach churn." Not a strand of her hair dared to move when Beth tossed back her unending supply of booze.

"Beth?"

"My mother," I mumbled.

"Tell me about your mum."

"You saw the photos, right?" Mac paused her movements, her nostrils flaring dangerously. "I don't have one. I never did, not really."

She set the hairspray down and looked at me through the mirror. "Your mother didn't deserve you," she said gravely and squeezed her arm around my shoulders. "Don't let the bitch get you down."

The front door opened and closed when she went back to fussing with my hair, and from downstairs we heard Henry say, "Where are you taking her?"

A deep murmur was the reply, and my belly fluttered.

"Travis is here," I muttered, examining my length in the mirror and my new outfit. If nerves hadn't already exhausted me, a shopping trip with both Lucy and Tim was enough to send me running for a nicotine fix and I didn't even smoke. Both of them had whacked ideas of what constituted an appropriate outfit for a trip to the movies. Lucy steered me towards everything that screamed "tramp/whore/here are my boobs in case you weren't sure I had any attached to my chest." Tim was aiming for glamour goddess, which was actually quite sweet, but I was no Evie. Shimmery backless tops and tight leather pants were a little beyond my reality. Between the three of us, we managed to settle on a pair of dark blue skinny jeans with side zippers, a pair of brown knee length boots, and a low back gold metallic top.

"We want her back by midnight," Cooper said.

"What the fuck, dude," came Frog's reply. "She's not Cinder-fucking-rella."

There was more low murmuring that had my ears straining to hear. Mac's eyes met mine in the mirror after she'd finished glaring my strands of hair into submission, as though hopeful that would do the job hairspray couldn't.

"What are they doing down there?"

Mac winked, her hands turning to her own head of hair as she smoothed the soft, gleaming waves. "Playing big brother it sounds like."

I clutched my hands together, moving to sit on the edge of the bed and slide on my boots. "They're being silly."

Mac sat down beside me and slung an arm over my shoulders. "Do you have any brothers, Quinn?"

"No."

"Wrong answer," she replied.

My vision blurred.

"How about I go tell Travis to bugger off and we have a girls night in?"

I huffed out a short laugh. "Did I do that bad a job on my face?"

She nodded. "It's terrible. Next time let me help you instead of locking your bedroom door. That was really unfair and now it's your own fault because you look really shitty."

I chuckled and she looked at me sideways, grinning.

"No."

"No?"

"I've never been on a date before. I need to just get this over with."

Mac jostled my shoulders. "Okay. Well first you need to relax. You look like you're about to ralph all over your new boots."

There had been no polite, gentleman-like behaviour from Travis when it came to choosing the movie. We'd bickered over the offerings and ended up with something that involved wild shootouts, high tech gadgets, and fist fights. At one point I'd leaned over and joked that it was probably just his everyday life and he could write the movie. He'd chuckled and took hold of my hand, pulling it into his lap so our linked fingers rested on his thigh. He whispered in my ear that he should only be so lucky, and throughout the rest of the movie, he proceeded to pick apart the holes in the storyline.

My mind had barely paid attention to any of it because he was holding my hand. Maybe I was just odd, or the dating thing too new, but the gesture felt more intimate than anything I'd ever done with another man in my life.

Now he was taking me to dinner, which from the outside was a restaurant beautifully lit up in colours of gold and red. Reaching the exterior steps, the back of my neck prickled and I froze. The feeling was the same from before, but that didn't make sense because David hadn't been released. I made a mental note to get in touch with Mitch in the morning just to be sure.

Travis paused, waiting for me. "Everything okay?"

Unease rolled through me, busy telling me that nothing was okay. If someone was watching me, they were watching Travis. They were watching anyone I was with. The question was, who the hell was out there?

The urge to run rose swiftly so I forced a smile, focusing on putting one foot in front of the other. "Sure."

His brow furrowed, but he led me inside without another word. The interior screamed *Michelin star Asian cuisine*, and I felt completely out of my depth. The waiter seated us with menus, paying an exorbitant amount of attention on Travis when he asked if we'd like to start with a drink.

"Wine?" Travis asked me.

At my nod, he ordered a bottle and sat back in his chair when the waiter disappeared, running his eyes over me in a way that told me he was remembering everything that lay beneath the carefully chosen outfit.

I let out a shaky breath and smiled at him. That was about when the text messages began. Evie's came first, the words highlighted across the screen as I picked it up.

E: I bet he's taking you to Mr. Chow's. Bring me back a doggy bag if you want to live.

Henry's followed not long after.

H: Text me if you need a rescue.

I heard more flood in after that, but I switched off my phone with an apology, not reading the rest.

His lips curved. "Friends, huh?"

Something warm settled within me. "Mmm hmm."

The waiter left again after pouring wine and taking our orders, and I looked at Travis across the table. Lucy and Tim had versed me through the art of meaningful dinner conversation during our shopping expedition. Great conversation doesn't happen by accident Tim told me. Lucy's suggestion was to ask open-ended questions. I protested that Travis and I had been alone together before, but apparently wild sex, beach swimming, and work situations didn't constitute a formal dinner environment. In the end I think they made me more nervous than I already was.

"It's good to finally have you to myself," Travis told me.

I frowned. That wasn't an open-ended question. What was I supposed to do with that? Tim's advice was to be myself, but it was firmly established I was socially inept, so that advice went straight to the bin.

"You're frowning. It's not good I have you to myself?"

"No. Yes." I picked up my wine. "No."

His eyes crinkled. "You seem nervous." He reached over and grabbed my free hand in his. "Will it help if I told you all the things I want to do to you when dinner is over?"

I took a gulp of wine as Travis started rubbing his thumb in circles on my palm. I coughed and sat my glass down hastily.

"Um, no," I rasped and coughed again. "I don't think so."

Having pity on me, Travis sat back and asked how Lucy and I became friends.

"I met her when I moved in next door," I told him. The waiter brought our dinner as I regaled him with the story of her barging through my door with a plate of biscuits that even Rufus eyed with trepidation. I'd palmed a couple to him, and he proceeded to trot out to the back courtyard and bury them deep into the rocky layers of the earth. "I had to teach her how to cook." I sighed. I saw Rick the other day. He looked like he was losing weight. "Not sure how good a job I did with that though."

Travis swallowed a mouthful of wine. "Who taught you?"

139

I shrugged, finished chewing a delicious bite of snapper, and set my fork down. "I taught myself." Not wishing to delve into the reasons, I changed the subject. "What about you and Casey? You became friends at uni, right?"

He nodded. "I punched him in the face."

"What?"

Travis laughed. "I did. Casey was wild back then. Drunk at footy tryouts. Took me in a high tackle and gave me a concussion. I got in a solid punch before they pulled me off him."

"Oh my God. What happened after that?"

Travis grinned. "We went out for a beer."

I shook my head, but my lips twitched. "I wish *I* knew how to throw a solid punch."

"You never learned self-defence?"

"No, but I should."

"You want to learn, I'll teach you."

"Really?" I said with surprise.

He nodded. "You're too small to ever throw that solid punch, but there are things you can learn that could mean the difference between getting hurt and getting away."

"Thanks, Travis."

He shrugged. "Want you safe, sweetheart."

When our meal was finished and the bill paid, Travis drove us back to his loft, changing gears in between resting his hand on my thigh. My heart thumped in my chest when Travis opened the car door and held out his hand. "I'd ask you how I did for your first date, but the night isn't over yet."

Once inside, the smile on his lips turned dangerous and nerves rolled through me like an ocean. I tossed my bag somewhere and made a beeline for the kitchen.

"You mentioned dessert, right?" I opened the freezer door. "Ice cream?"

A tub of Ben and Jerry's strawberry cheesecake met my eyes, and I felt thoroughly blindsided. The flavour was far too sedate and sweet for someone like Travis. Although, I imagined if there was ever such a flavour as *badass swirl with tough guy toffee crunch,* it would be the one I'd pick for him.

I reached for it when a pair of hands grabbed my hips and yanked me back. My breathing escalated when Travis put his lips on my neck and nibbled his way upwards to my ear.

"Travis," I moaned and turned in his arms. The ice cream was trapped between us. He plucked it from my hands and set it on the kitchen bench. Then his hands returned to my hips, and I was lifted up onto the bench alongside the ice cream. He pushed my thighs apart and wedged himself between them. Fire blazed in his eyes as he took my mouth, his tongue thrusting inside. My legs wound around his hips, pulling him closer, my body rubbing up against the hardening length in his jeans.

Travis took a hand from my body and rummaged through the drawer next to us. He broke the kiss and waved a spoon in front of me.

"Didn't you say you wanted dessert?"

"Oh," I murmured and took the spoon.

He grabbed the ice cream and peeled off the lid, offering it to me, so I dug the spoon in and scooped out a small mouthful.

I started to bring it to his lips, but he snagged my wrist, jolting me, and it splattered on my forearm.

He shook his head. "You're my dessert, sweetheart."

My body throbbed painfully when he dragged my arm towards his mouth, his tongue snaking out to lick the trickle of ice cream from my skin. The spoon aloft in my hand, I brought it to my lips and licked the scoop into my mouth.

Travis, eyes on my mouth, said hoarsely, "Put the spoon down."

It clattered to the bench when he brought his mouth back to mine. His tongue licked along my bottom lip until I opened my mouth and tangled his tongue with mine.

"Your mouth is hot and cold and sweet," he whispered against me and slid his hands into the back of my jeans. "Fuck," he groaned when my legs tightened around him, my body rubbing against him. "There hasn't been anyone since I had you months ago. I don't know what you've done to me, but I don't want anyone else." He kissed me again. "Tell me you want me to fuck you," he breathed against my lips before moving his mouth to my neck, his hands climbing underneath my shirt.

Travis pulled back and lifted my shirt up and off, his heated eyes roaming over my body with intensity.

"Tell me," he ordered, tossing my shirt to the floor.

My breath caught when he tugged off his own shirt and turned back to me, his eyes expectant as his hands roamed up my thighs.

"I want you," I moaned.

"You want me to what?" he rasped, watching his hands as they slid up my torso to cup my breasts, confined in a new ivory and gold lace creation. He undid the clasp at the back and my eyes watched it join my shirt on the floor. I shivered when his hands returned back to my breasts, his thumbs rubbing across the hardened nipples. "Want me to what?" he repeated, leaning down to take one in his mouth.

My head fell back, tingles shooting through my body. "To...to fuck me."

Travis groaned at my words, his tongue laving over my skin as his hands reached for the button on my jeans. He undid my zipper and with some wriggled movements on my part, he pulled away to yank off my boots and peel off my jeans.

Sitting on the kitchen bench in nothing but a pair of lace panties, I somehow found a glimmer of sense to ask Travis where Casey was.

"Out," he muttered, his tongue licking its way up the insides of my legs. His hot breath and his mouth had me aching when he pressed a kiss between my thighs.

"Oh God," I moaned when he slid my panties to the side and licked me. My hands braced behind me on the bench at the feel of his hot tongue tasting me.

"Fuck," he groaned. "I need to get inside you." Travis tore himself away and stood up. "Bedroom," he rasped and grabbed my hand. I was yanked off the bench, my eyes watching the muscles play over his back as he moved. When I was picked up and tossed on the bed, a laugh bubbled out of me. His eyes on mine, Travis peeled off his jeans and underwear and my mouth went dry. He stalked his way up the bed until he hovered over me.

"What's so funny?"

My hands wrapped around his hot, hard length. He shuddered, his eyes closing with pleasure.

"Nothing's funny," I murmured, watching his jaw clench as my hands stroked him.

His eyes flew open, the green bright as they focused hard on my face. "I want to savour you, Quinn, but right now, I need to fuck you."

Travis rolled over and opened his drawer, coming back with a foil condom packet. He handed it over. "I want you to put it on."

My hands reached for it, biting my lip as I tore it open. "You're so bossy but—"

His mouth slammed down on mine before I could finish saying that I liked it, his tongue tasting me over and over until my lungs fought for air. Travis broke the kiss, sucking in rapid breaths as I slid the condom on carefully. His arms wrapping around me, he pushed me on my back. His hands came to rest on my hips but only for a moment because they ripped the panties down my legs. It was just how I remembered him from the first time, and I didn't care at all if they tore. I would buy a thousand pairs just to feel the desperation of his hands needing to touch my skin.

They slid their way back up my legs, one of them finding its way between my legs, rubbing me, sliding inside as he shuddered above me. He breathed deeply, burying his face in my neck, his tongue snaking out to lick me.

Travis rolled his hips and reaching between us, I took the hard heavy length of him in my hands.

"Need you, Travis," I panted.

"Whatever you say, baby." He slid his hand away, and my body ached from the loss. I shifted my legs, wrapping them around his hips to accommodate his body, and so very, very slowly, he inched his way inside me.

I moaned, my eyes burning at the intense pleasure of him filling me.

"Look at me," Travis demanded. "I want you to see what you do to me." I shuddered, but I opened my eyes and brought a hand up to cup his face as he began rocking his hips. "It's never felt like this, Quinn," he gasped, his movements becoming more forceful. "Not even close."

I leaned up and caught his mouth with mine, sliding my hands up his back. My thighs gripped his hips tightly, urging him harder and faster.

He rolled us over until I sat above him, his hands running up over my ribs and breasts, his brow furrowing as he groaned. The green in his eyes deepened as I began to move over him. I leaned over, my hands holding onto his shoulders as my heart thundered in my chest.

Travis slid his hand between my legs, his fingers hard and firm as they moved and when I felt tingles begin in my toes, I wrapped my body around him, burying my face into his neck as pleasure bore down on me so intense it almost hurt.

"Quinn, baby," he ground out as he began slamming hard within me, eventually biting down on the tender skin of my neck as he shuddered.

After a few minutes our rapid breathing eased, but I remained burrowed in his chest, and he remained burrowed within me, both of us apparently unwilling to break the connection.

Chapter Fourteen

My eyes blinked open sleepily and scanned the room, revealing I was alone. My hands skimmed along the cool blue sheets to my left. The blinds on the window were only half closed, telling me it was still dark outside.

Swinging my legs over the edge of the bed, I found my panties and standing up, I slid them on. Picking out a shirt from the dresser, I pulled it on before leaving the room.

The loft was dark and quiet as my fingers brushed through my tousled mess of hair. I noted our clothes no longer littered the kitchen floor and the ice cream had been put away as I padded softly through the kitchen. Catching movement out on the back deck, I wound my way outside, opening the sliding door.

Travis sat on the outdoor table, his feet resting on the seat. He half turned at the sound, his lips curling upwards. "Hey."

He reached out an arm, snaking it around my waist and pulling me into his body. I wound my arms around his neck and curled myself into his lap, shivering in the cool night air.

He was dressed in only a pair of half-buttoned jeans, and my hands roamed over his bare skin, finding it smooth and warm. "Aren't you cold?" I muttered.

"Nah."

My eyes fell on the cigarette packet. "I thought you only ever smoked when you needed to think." I looked at him. "Do you need to think?"

His hands rubbed circles on my back. "Are you gonna give me shit about smoking?"

I pursed my lips because it was on the tip of my tongue to do just that. "Maybe."

Travis chuckled, the deep rumble vibrating against me, and I shivered again, this time from pleasure rather than cold. "Good."

"Good?"

"Yeah, good." He tucked a curl of hair behind my ear and brushed his thumb across my cheek, a gesture that was becoming familiar. "Shows you care. I like that."

I did.

Oh God I cared. So *much*. More than I should. Enough to know he cared too. But Travis didn't know me. Maybe when he knew all there was to know of me, he wouldn't care so much anymore. The ache in my chest broke wide open.

The hands roaming his chest stilled, and I pushed back a little, but his arms around me squeezed, locking me to him. He pressed a swift, gentle kiss on my lips.

Fighting to block out the ache, I buried my head in his neck and breathed him in. "Tell me about your job, Travis?"

Travis exhaled, the sound deep and heavy. "Okay." He let one arm go from around me and twisted, reaching for another cigarette. "Do you mind?"

I shook my head.

"I don't know how much you already know about what we do. Jared and Coby focus on the hostage negotiation and security side of our business. Casey and I handle the kidnapping and child custody." He lit the cigarette and drew deeply, turning his head to exhale a deep plume of smoke behind him. "The two sometimes even go hand in hand. Custody disputes are common and we get called in when they have the potential to turn dangerous or when they already have. It's our job to diffuse the situation. Sometimes that involves using force. We pull kids out of emotionally or physically abusive situations." He drew again on his cigarette, his eyes on the distance. "How can someone be given a gift that needs so much love and care, and treat it like rubbish? I've seen them starving and broken, Quinn, and every day it tears me apart."

I nodded into his shoulder because I knew.

"I think the guys aren't sure I can do this job anymore, and some days I'm not so sure either. This scar," he said, rubbing at his hip, "reminds me that I let someone down. That someone died because I made a mistake. I hesitated and a kid died. I'm scared of it happening again." I could hear heartbreak in his voice, and my chest burned. He exhaled another plume of smoke and chuckled, but it wasn't a happy sound. "How fucked up is that?" he muttered bitterly. "Look at what they're going through, and I'm the one struggling to deal with it. But if I'm not there to help, who will? Who'll be there for them?"

"Travis." I waited until his eyes, so full of hurt, locked on mine. "You can't save everyone."

He twisted to put his cigarette out in the little ashtray, and turning back, tilted my chin up to meet his eyes. "Wish I could've saved you, Quinn," he said gruffly.

My stomach tightened painfully and Travis disappeared as tears blinded me. I wished to God Travis could've saved me, but it was too late for that. The damage had been done, never to be undone. A single slap, or a kick given so angrily and so easily, the pain and fear it evoked, could never be taken back. It lived with you, inside of you, forever reminding you that you were never worthy of love and care.

"Some of us have to learn how to save ourselves," I whispered, blinking the tears away.

"How do you do that?"

"All I know is that you have to find strength somewhere inside of you and hold on to it, but I'm still figuring out where mine is."

Maybe the strength was in simply getting out of bed because there were days when I had struggled to do just that.

"Quinn... If you let me, I'll be strong for you."

Why are you making this so hard?

Travis was meant for something better than me. The thought made anger twist hotly inside me. I wanted to be that something better, the person who could give him happiness. Already I hated the woman that would belong to him. His arms would wind around her all night long, keeping her warm and safe. She would wake to his smile and the love in his eyes. He would be hers.

I stood up and pushed away. The cool air was a shock, blowing hair into my face. I pushed it away, tucking it behind my hair before hugging myself and meeting his eyes. "I don't need you to be strong for me."

He nodded, the movement slow and careful. "Maybe you don't," he murmured. "But I need you. Every day I get up, tired from not sleeping, and I go to work and do what I do. Late at night I come home and go to bed for another sleepless night, and the whole time there's a weight on my chest that's so fucking heavy it leaves me feeling like I can't breathe." Wounded green eyes found their way to mine. "When I've got hold of you, somehow it doesn't feel so heavy anymore."

My eyes filled and I turned away.

Damn you, Travis.

Damn you for having a chink in your armour like a battered knight—so worn down from being a goddamn hero that you're turning to the one person not good enough for you.

I drew a deep breath into my lungs, lifted my chin and met his eyes. "I can't be what you need, Travis." I hugged my arms tighter, trying to contain the hurt rising in my chest. "Inside of me...there's too much damage. Someone gave me hope once, and it was beautiful. I'd never seen anything like it. It changed me from who I used to be." I shook my head, a tear rolling down my cheek. I wiped it away, unable to look at him. "I used to give my body away to anyone who wanted it...and I didn't care because for a fleeting moment I felt wanted. I was only sixteen and already taking drugs and alcohol to get me through each day. I wasn't sure I'd live to see the end of high school," I whispered. "But I thought acting out would somehow justify all the pain David inflicted."

My tear filled eyes finally rested on Travis. "How could I not see I was only hurting myself?"

Travis was frozen, his jaw locked so tight I thought it would break.

I took a step back. "I met Ethan at a party. It was obvious he didn't belong there. He looked so…clean, both inside and out. It drew me in. I wanted to know what being clean felt like. Ethan had this quiet intensity—a confidence in himself and his future. He made me feel like I could have one of those. A future," I added. "But he…he." My voice pitched and Travis rose to stand, but I waved him back. "He died…" I choked out, "… and I wanted to die with him, but I couldn't you see, because I was pregnant. My baby kept me alive and made me realise that I needed to leave. But David found me. He found where I lived and he was so angry. Beth left him. He…I thought it was Lucy at the door," I explained, "so I called out for her to come in, the door was unlocked. The door was unlocked," I enunciated. "David came in and he…" I took a deep breath. "He broke me—inside and out. I tried to fight, but I fell and he wouldn't stop kicking me, and he killed my baby."

A sob escaped me.

"Quinn," Travis pleaded, his hands fisted so tightly his knuckles were white.

"I'm not finished," I told him and lifted my chin, bracing for the worst. "When I woke up in hospital, the doctors told me there was so much damage that I would never have children. I can't have kids," I said simply. "And after they told me, for a whole month I wished he'd killed me too, because I felt dead anyway. There were entire days I couldn't get out of bed. It's taken me years to get where I am now. Days upon days of pretending to be a normal person that sometimes I even convince myself. If I keep doing it, then maybe one day it'll be true. Can you see now, why I can't be what you need?" I looked at him. "I'm not whole."

Travis sat frozen, his face pale, and I died a little inside.

The need to run, to find oblivion, rose within me.

I moved swiftly inside, and finding my bag, I messaged Lucy. She'd be finished work soon, and in ten minutes I could disappear for a while. Finding the bathroom, I shut the door behind me. I flicked the shower on and stood in front of the mirror, seeing a stranger with pale skin and fear in her eyes—someone who didn't know how to fight, only how to run. I might not know who she was, but even I could see she was missing pieces of herself. I tilted my head at the mirror. Maybe Travis might say that was okay, and just maybe it was for him. But it wasn't for me. He didn't deserve okay.

The door swung open and I turned.

Travis leaned up against the door frame, his eyes were pained and wet with tears.

"I don't know who I am, Travis." I turned back to face the person in the mirror. "I don't think I've ever known."

"I know who you are," he said hoarsely.

"Please tell me."

"You're a survivor, and on the inside that makes you more beautiful than you could possibly imagine. Do you think I want perfect? No one is ever that. Perfect is for people who don't know how to be real, and I don't want any of that. I want you."

My eyes closed against the image in the mirror. "I'm not sure I'm able to give you me."

He flicked off the shower and came further into the bathroom, taking hold of my hands. He pulled them behind his back so I was holding on. Then he wrapped his arms around my shoulders. "I'm so sorry, Quinn," he said thickly. "I want to kill him for what he did to you. What he took from you." Travis closed his eyes briefly and swallowed. "People like that are nothing. They feed off the good in others because it makes them feel like something. You can't let him win. You can't let him take that from you anymore."

The phone rang.

Travis ignored it.

It rang again.

"Shit," he muttered. "Be back."

I followed him out, heard him murmuring something before he held the phone towards me. "Here. It's for you."

Eyebrows raised, I took the phone. "Hello?"

"Quinn, did you or did you not go to Mr. Chow's for dinner?" came Evie's voice.

I sighed, thankful for the distraction of her voice, but I'd completely forgotten about her requested doggy bag.

"Maybe," I hedged.

"What do you mean maybe? Everyone's worried about you. Cooper was trying to tell me you were supposed to be back by midnight, and now I hear from Travis you're not feeling well. Damn that Mr. Chow. I think he's trying to kill off the entire female population."

"He is?"

"It makes sense. He has the hots for the entire badass brigade."

Warm hands rested on my shoulders and my eyes closed at the touch.

"Badass brigade?"

"Yeah. I got so sick once that I had to get an anti-nausea injection to go on stage."

I heard Jared's voice in the background. "Baby, that was not food poisoning from Mr. Chow's."

"Oh yeah?" was her reply as one of those warm hands slid around my belly. There was a muffled crackle from the phone and she said, "You would defend him, Jared. You like it when he plays grabass."

My eyes widened. "Grabass?"

"Pay attention, Quinn. You can't just go waltzing in to that restaurant without expecting death glares. You have to—"

Jared's voice sounded closer when I heard him cut her off, calling out, "He's not trying to kill you off, Quinn!"

The other arm came around me until I was pulled into a hard chest. I let out a deep breath. "Quinn? You there?"

Travis snatched the phone from my hand. He pressed the end call button and tossed it on the floor.

I pushed away from the hold, and not looking at Travis, walked into the bedroom, grabbing for my clothes. I started sliding them on as he followed me in.

I spared him a glance. "I should get going."

"No."

I paused and looked at him. "No?"

He shook his head. "No."

"I can't stay here," I told him. Not now. I couldn't stomach him knowing everything about me. Travis had been right when he'd told Evie on the phone that I wasn't feeling well, because I felt sick.

He folded his arms.

"I want to leave."

"Is that what you really want?"

My chin lifted as I finished dressing. "Yes."

Hurt flashed on his face before he shuttered his expression. "Okay, just give me a minute. I'll drive you."

He stalked to the bathroom and shut the door.

"No need to drive me," I called out through the door as I grabbed my bag and slipped on my boots. "Lucy's out the front waiting for me."

I shut the front door behind me.

"Quinn!"

I flew down the stairs and into the street, shivering in the cool, eerily quiet street. Lucy wasn't there so I shrank back into the shadows.

A hand slapped around my mouth and yanked me back further. My knees buckled in panic as I was locked around the waist with another arm.

"Dammit," came a hard male voice behind me. The hand loosened and I drew air into my lungs. My mouth opened, ready to scream but the hand tightened around my mouth again. "I have a gun. Don't make me shoot you."

I whimpered, fighting to breathe.

"Quinn?"

The apartment door opened and Travis flew out of the building in just his jeans. He scanned the empty street. His muscled shoulders, covered by the eagle's wings that made him look strong enough to carry anyone's weight, slumped.

"Move or make a single sound," the voice hissed softly in my ear, "and I'll shoot him."

My heart beat erratically as I nodded.

Go inside, Travis. Please go inside.

Instead, he pulled a phone from his pocket and dialled.

"Mac." He ran his fingers through his hair. "Quinn's on her way home. Can you ring me when she gets there? Please?" After a pause, he said, "No, Lucy...I don't know," he said impatiently. "Just ring okay?"

He ended the call and my stomach sank when he didn't move, but simply dialled another number.

The stranger's breathing was harsh in my ear, and my nails dug into my palms.

"Mitch, David's still locked up, right?" He exhaled loudly as he listened to the other end. "Yes, I know I've already told you, but the second he's out, let me know."

This time when he ended the call, his fingers hovered over the keypad, hesitating, and I knew he was trying to decide whether to ring me or not. I realised with horror that if he rang, he would know exactly where I stood and the man behind me would shoot. My body sagged with fear, the stranger's arms the only thing holding me upright.

Travis shook his head and shoved the phone in his back pocket. A single tear trickled down my cheek as he did a final scan of the street and disappeared back inside.

"Good girl."

My eyes closed with relief.

"Now you're gonna listen to what I'm telling you and you're not to speak. Just nod your head that you understand. Okay?"

I lifted my right leg and slammed the heel down hard on his foot. As he grunted with pain, I fought to break free, but he didn't budge his hold.

"Asrghoe," I grunted against his mouth.

"Did you just call me an asshole? I told you not to speak," he puffed in my ear.

My breath came in bursts and praying my boots made me tall enough to hit my mark, I drew my head forward and then slammed it back as hard as I could.

"Fuck," he growled. His arms loosened from around me, but the bright burst of pain in the back of my head had my knees giving out. My palms came out to brace my fall and the harsh concrete cut into the skin of my hands and knees. Scrambling to my feet, my hair was grabbed in a fist, and I was yanked upwards. I blinked back tears, my heart racing in fear.

"Here's the deal," he growled in my ear. I nodded so he would know I was listening. "David owes us money and that's not good because that means we in turn owe money. There's a chain you see, and David lives at the bottom. You have a good idea of what David's like, so you can imagine the type of man that lives at the top. We're told you're the one that had him put away. Not only that, it seems you know people in high places. That now makes his debt yours." Then he named a sum that left me reeling. "You've got two weeks before I find you again."

Lucy's beat up car squealed to a stop out the front and I could see her looking for me. She got out of the car. "Quinn?"

"See you get the money and keep your mouth shut about it or your friend here, or even your fuck buddy upstairs, are gonna bleed."

He shoved me away and my forehead smacked hard into the brick wall. I bit down on my lip to stop the moan of pain. My hand came away from my forehead bloody, and I turned to face my attacker. My eyes strained down the dark alley alongside the building, but I couldn't see anything, just inky blackness and silence.

I pushed weakly from the wall and peered up into the light blazing from the loft. For a brief moment I remembered the feel of Travis wrapped around me, the sound of his low breathing and curve of his lips when he smiled because soon, too soon, I would have nothing.

Chapter Fifteen

"Let's go," I murmured, sliding into the passenger seat of Lucy's car. I was careful to avert my face. Lucy was like a bloodhound when it came to sniffing out trouble.

"Uh uh." She tapped the steering wheel impatiently. "I want answers."

I faced her full on, all sense of calm rationality disappearing in favour of panic. "Just plant your fucking foot."

She blanched and as though my bloodied forehead was like a green flag, her foot hit the pedal, and we screamed out of the street.

"Quinn, this isn't fair. You attract violence like flies on shit. What happened? Did Travis hurt you? I swear to God, I'm turning this car around right the fuck now."

"See you get the money and keep your mouth shut about it or your friend here, or even your fuck buddy upstairs, are gonna bleed."

My jaw ached with the effort of pulling myself together. "Nothing happened. I tripped on the stairs, okay?"

Lucy glanced at me. "And face planted?"

"Yes," I replied, both annoyed and relieved when a laugh bubbled out of her.

Lucy screeched the car to a stop at a red light, and I jerked forward, pulled up short from the seatbelt and slammed back in my seat. "Okay then. What about Travis?"

My stomach rolled at hearing his name.

"Quinn, tell me about Travis or when we get back I'll sit on you until you do."

I had absolutely no doubt that Lucy would attempt it. I struggled to find where to start. "He held my hand in the movies."

At the green light, she accelerated wildly, taking her eyes off the road to offer me a look of mock horror. "He didn't! The bastard. I'll kill him."

"Lucy," I said weakly. "He knows."

"Knows what?"

I waved my hand, opening the glove box for a tissue. Pulling down the visor, I eyed the mess on my forehead and wondered how I'd manage to hide it. "Everything."

Lucy's mouth fell open.

"Close your mouth before you catch flies."

"Oh, Quinn," she said, weariness deep in her voice. "And then you ran."

I nodded as I wiped the blood away, wincing when it stung. "And then I ran." Slumping back in my seat, I did my best to wipe at the scrapes on my hands. "Actually, I'm thinking that maybe it's time I moved. Made a change or something."

"A change?"

"Yeah, you know, maybe a move to the country or something." My eyes focused out the window and my reflection taunted me.

"The country? You want to move to what—west bumblefuck? David won't find you where you are. You're not leaving." Her voice was firm but I could hear the panic in her voice.

"It's just an option," I hedged.

"Option, schmoption. Who do you think you are—Daniel Boone?"

"Who's Daniel Boone?"

Lucy glanced over her shoulder before cutting across three lanes in quick succession. "Never mind who he is, just…don't do anything or go anywhere without talking to me first. Promise me."

My eyes fell on the best friend I'd ever had—the one person who had seen me at my worst, walked me through it, and came out the other side holding my hand—and I lied. "Promise."

"Quinn, what are you doing?"

Flustered, I minimised my internet search engine window of country maps and called up the diary. "Working."

I smiled up at Mac from my desk to put her off the scent and heard her indrawn breath. "What happened to your face?"

At the reminder, the pain on my forehead throbbed dully. My hand came up to cover it, and I forced a sheepish chuckle. "Oh. That? I uh, scraped it on the um, driveway."

Her lips pressed flat, suppressing a smile. "Did it leap out at you and smack you in the face?" She went a little pale. "Oh shit. I didn't mean—"

I cut her off. "Pretty much."

"Right. Coffee. Then you can tell me about your date last night."

She left and I rubbed at my eyes. I hadn't slept—at all. My mind had raced over every possible scenario but the problem was, there were no scenarios. The simple fact was that if I left, Lucy and Travis, or anyone else for that matter, wouldn't get hurt. I'd move somewhere cold. They wouldn't expect that. Fleeing people in the movies always made the mistake of disappearing to some warm tropical island. Newsflash— that was always the first place the bad guys looked.

"Quinn?"

"Huh?"

I blinked back into focus and found Travis in the doorway. My heart lifted at the sight of him. "Travis?"

"You've been staring at the wall for over a minute." He frowned. "What happened to your face?"

"I fell," I told the desk after averting my eyes.

Travis came and stood in my space. He crouched down and cupped my face, examining the injury. "When?"

"Is that important?" I could feel his breath on my face, and I wanted him so much. Sheer agony speared through me, and I closed my eyes against the force. His touch on my forehead was gentle, and I jerked my head back. "It's just a graze. What are you doing here?"

Travis sighed, and it was weighted with so many unsaid words that I knew he didn't know where to start. "You know why I'm here."

Of course I knew.

"Don't stand so close," I said firmly but he must have heard something else coming out of my mouth because he didn't move.

"Quinn," he breathed, and the depth of emotion in that single word tugged at my heart. "I can't let you do this."

Travis held my eyes, but I couldn't reply because suddenly his lips were on mine. My mouth opened underneath the onslaught, moaning at the taste of him. He lifted me off the chair, and I hung on as he spun me around and pushed me up against the desk.

"Stop," I choked out when his mouth left mine to nibble on my ear.

"Are you sure?"

"Yes." I moaned as his teeth bit into my skin. "No."

God help me, but I couldn't push him away. I wasn't strong enough and he was relentless. His hands were all over me, pushing under clothes and grabbing at bare skin. I slid my own underneath his shirt, tugging on the waistband of his jeans to drag him closer. His mouth returned to mine and my hand came around his neck, holding him there so he wouldn't take it away.

"Oh that shit is not cool. So not cool." Mac's voice registered through the fog, and I pulled back, rubbing my lips together.

Travis took a step back, his hair mussed, and cleared his throat. "We were just ah...sorting the security detail for the Melbourne trip."

I sat up, straightening my shirt, my entire body heating with embarrassment when I saw Jared smirking at both of us from over Mac's shoulder.

"That's Jared's department, yet here you are, all over it like a rash. I'm not fooled. I can bet by the way you had Quinn spread out all over that desk she isn't fooled either."

Jared folded his arms and raised a brow. "Nice one, Trav."

Mac spun around with wide eyes and pointed in his face. "One word, Jared. Bedroom. Not the pantry, not the couch, not the shower. Bedroom."

He held up his hands. "No idea what you're talking about," he muttered and disappeared.

"Hurry up and finish your fumigating because I'm tired of you and your shitty food in my house!" she yelled after him.

"It's Sunday," she growled and slammed the coffee in her hand on the desk as she sat down, "but you're here so let's get this shit done, and then you both can get down to other business." She pursed her lips but I could see the curve in them as though satisfied that whatever happened last night was now over.

I swallowed and looked at Travis. Soon it would be.

He took a seat in the spare chair by the desk, and I faced the computer, discreetly shutting down the maps on the internet tab. I called up the detailed outline of the Melbourne trip and did what I could to focus on the words.

"Mac," I said, reviewing the accommodation. "Why is my name on here?"

"Because you're coming, asshead," she replied as she tapped at the computer opposite me.

"I can't," I blurted out.

My deadline was two weeks. I needed to be gone by then. The Melbourne trip was the perfect opportunity for me to quietly slip away to the countryside without any interference.

Mac stopped tapping and I felt all eyes on me. "Quinn, this is what you were hired to do. Why can't you?"

"Well," I drawled. I scratched at my head. "Rufus," I said and paused. "I can't leave him here alone."

The excuse was utter rubbish. Rufus would quite happily visit with Lucy for a couple of days.

"Rubbish," Mac said, verifying my own thoughts. "Lucy can take him. You're already booked in so I don't want to hear any more about it."

My fingers gripped the edge of the desk with both hands to hide the tremors. Travis frowned, his eyes moving from my hands to my eyes. I turned my back and called up the map of the festival area and clicked *print* while Mac distracted Travis with talk about the accommodation and travel detail.

I passed Travis the sheet and start collating the contact information of all involved. "Mac, I can't locate the contact info for the roadies driving the truck down to Melbourne."

"Hang on," she muttered and with a few taps, the contact zinged into my email. My fingers tapped efficiently, my mind working hard to block everything else out as I pulled the entire contact and run sheet together for Travis.

When the Jamieson line rang, Mac picked it up for me.

"Jamieson. Mac speaking."

The printer whirred in the background, blocking out Mac's words. My chair spun and I collected the printed sheets from the tray.

"Quinn, it's your ahh…mother on the phone for you."

The colour drained from my face as I spun back around. "I'm not here," I hissed.

In a panic I stood, yanking papers off our joined desks. The frantic movement tipped over Mac's coffee mug. My hands made a grab for it, but I missed. "Shit," I muttered, not even registering the mug was empty.

I took a step back to flee.

"Quinn." Breathless, I focused on Travis. "Maybe you should talk to her?"

That was not something I'd been planning to do for the rest of my natural life.

"David owes us money…that now makes his debt yours…"

The words came back to haunt me. Maybe talking to her might give me some answers about what was going on.

"Wait!" I called to Mac when she opened her mouth to speak. My chin lifted as my hand reached out for the phone. "I'll talk to her."

She handed it over wordlessly.

"Beth," I answered.

"Quinn." Her voice sounded tired, nothing like how I remembered. "We need to talk."

"Yes, because we do that so well." I heard her sigh as though already fed up with the conversation before we'd even started. "How did you find me?"

"You were in the paper. Something to do with that rock band you appear to be working with."

My knuckles whitened as my hand held tight to the phone. "I was?"

Ten minutes later and I was in the passenger seat while Travis drove us to my childhood home. Dread coiled within me as Travis peppered me with questions the entire way there.

"How long since you saw or spoke to your mother last?"

"Almost four years," I answered automatically.

"I imagine you had good reason for that."

I stared out the window. "Yes."

I felt him glance at me while he drove. "Tell me?"

"Why?"

Hadn't he heard enough?

"Because it's part of who you are."

"I wish it wasn't, Travis."

I felt him glance at me as he drove. "Me too, Quinn, but I care about you. All of you. I can't pick and choose which pieces of you to care for and which pieces not to. That's not how it works."

"I have a lot of crappy pieces," I informed him.

"Some people do, but the pieces you try to hide aren't pieces you asked for. They were given to you without a choice. Does that mean you deserve less than the next person?"

"Some of those choices I made myself," I pointed out.

"Choices you were too young to make don't count."

"Just like that?"

He nodded. "Just like that."

"Huh."

"What?"

I waved a hand in frustration. "You seem to have an answer for everything."

His eyes remained on the road, but I caught his grin. "That's because I'm a know-it-all."

"Are you saying you're not as perfect as everyone thinks you to be?"

The smile slid quickly from his face and brows drawn, he offered me a pained glance. "No. I'm not. Don't ever think that of me, Quinn."

Something uncomfortable rolled in my belly, and I didn't like it because I'd never had that feeling with Travis before. His tone sounded a little off.

"Um…okay."

Travis accelerated as I directed him where to turn.

"The good memories of Beth aren't good, and the bad ones are worse," I began. "They don't stem from what she did either, but what she didn't do."

Travis gripped the steering wheel as he turned left, taking us closer to where I didn't want to be. "What didn't she do?"

"She didn't tell me about my real dad. She didn't put my hair in piggytails with pretty ribbon for school like all the other girls had. She

163

didn't read me bedtime stories like I wanted her to. She didn't take me to the park or the beach or shopping." My breath started coming a little faster, and I paused to swallow the hurt. "She didn't scare away the monsters in the dark. She…she didn't do anything when David got angry and hit me. When I got home at two in the morning from a party, she didn't even know I'd been gone." Travis met my eyes and I whispered, "She didn't love me and when you're shown every day you're not worth being loved, you tend to believe it."

My eyes followed Travis as he got out of the car. The passenger door was yanked open and then I was in his arms. "Stop believing it, sweetheart." He pulled back, his green eyes bright and unwavering on mine.

"How?"

The corners of his lips tipped up a little in a rueful smile. "Okay, so maybe I don't have all the answers, but I know how to start."

"Yeah?"

He stepped back and to the side, revealing the house in front of me and it felt like a punch to the gut. "Stop running."

I glanced sideways at him. Maybe I would have, but it wasn't just about me anymore.

"Wait here," I ordered, straightening my shoulders.

I strode briskly towards the front door, jerking backwards when my arm was gripped. I spun around and smacked into a hard chest. "Travis!"

"I don't think so."

My hands came up and pushed at his chest. "I'm perfectly safe in there."

"How about I come in with you, make sure it's safe, then I wait out front?"

As I was already being muscled towards the front door, I figured his words were more a statement than a question. He rapped hard on the door and as if Beth had been waiting, it opened immediately.

I cleared my throat, meeting tired eyes the same brown as mine. "Beth." Her eyes shifted nervously to Travis. "This is Travis."

Travis gave a slight nod, and my mind imagined how it would look to someone meeting him for the first time. His blond hair was tied back, arms were folded with biceps bulging, green eyes were hard, and his stance was busy telling the world, and Beth, that he had no patience for bullshit.

Beth took a slight step back, obviously believing everything he was telling her.

I stood a little straighter, taking care to look her in the eye. "You wanted to talk?"

She swung the door wide and indicated with a nod to come in. Travis stepped in front of me, walking in first, eyeing every part of the interior. Despite the place not being clean, it wasn't shabby. The living room and kitchen had undergone drastic renovations and nothing was familiar. My breathing came a little easier at not being slammed in the face with painful memories.

Beth grabbed a glass and started pouring a vodka without apology. "Drink?"

"No thanks," Travis answered and then leaned in close to my ear, so that his lips brushed the skin softly, and whispered, "I'll be right outside the front door. Yell if you need me, okay?"

I nodded.

With that acknowledgement, he tipped his chin at Beth without another word and closed the front door quietly behind him.

"I can't stay long," I prompted her when she shuffled over with her drink.

"Always thought you were too good for us, didn't you?"

I folded my arms, glaring as she sat her glass down on the table and faced me. "You worked hard at making sure I never felt that way, so let's cut through the niceties, shall we?"

"Alright. I know I've never been a great mother…" I rolled my eyes "…but there are people after David. I know he told them about you because they paid me a visit this morning. I wanted to give you some advice."

165

For the first time in my life, Beth was attempting to impart some sort of motherly wisdom? I snorted.

She ignored me and said, "Pay them the money. I don't have it. I see you are in a situation where maybe you could get it. These people won't hesitate to hurt you. They won't hesitate to hurt everyone you know."

"What the fuck do you care about me being hurt?" I hissed angrily. "All of a sudden you decide it's not okay to sit back and watch me get pounded on? Fuck you."

Her hand reached out swiftly and slapped me hard. My neck snapped and I cried out. "I'm still your mother. Don't you talk to me like that."

My eyes narrowed. *"Fuck. You,"* I ground out.

Her hand came up again and I grabbed it, my fingers digging tight into her wrist. A hard wall was suddenly pressed against my back, and Beth's eyes rose up behind my shoulder.

"Touch her again and I'll make your life a living hell." The words were like a whiplash, and I had absolutely no doubt Travis meant every word. Beth obviously didn't either because she tugged her arm away and took a step back.

"Let's go, sweetheart."

He took my hand and I followed him to the door.

"Quinn?" Her voice was pitched high and cracked on my name. I let go of Travis and walked towards her.

She leaned in and spoke so softly I had to strain my ears. "These people will do more than just hurt you. They won't hesitate in making sure you never see daylight again."

I didn't remember what we talked about on the drive home. All I remember was listening to Travis and the way he laughed and teased me, distracting me from what had just gone down. I reflected back on how it felt riding with him on the motorcycle; spluttering through the waves at the beach while he laughed at me; the warmth of his hand holding mine; his eyes heated as he moved inside of me, and my heart hurt.

Chapter Sixteen

The next week passed by like a ticking time bomb. I was vaguely aware of going about my day. People talked to me, but it was like existing underwater. I baked biscuits to occupy my mind, entire battalions of them—enough that I was sure no one would eat another for as long as they lived, yet they kept disappearing. Jared and Evie moved back into the house at Bondi, yet somehow a container found its way to their house because Evie rang with a shaky voice to say she caught Jared eating one. Travis stopped by on and off during the week to check on me, so another container found its way to the Jamieson and Valentine Consulting office because Tim rang, his voice muffled as he yelled at me down the phone around a mouthful about taking me shopping again. Then it sounded like he called me the badass biscuit bitch, but I couldn't be sure. Then Evie had rung back, sounding pissed about something to do with being in the badass club, saying she had to get shot at and almost die and she still hadn't qualified, yet I could do it with some flour and an egg. Then she asked for the recipe and hung up.

Standing in the kitchen scrubbing baking trays, my phone rang. I wiped my hands on the hand towel next to me and picked it up.

"Hey, sweetheart," Travis said when I answered.

I fought against the flush of pleasure. "Travis," I murmured. "I uh…"

"How's your day been?"

"Well, it's Monday, so my day off."

"And you baked again?"

167

I tucked the phone into my shoulder as I poured myself a glass of tap water. "Yes, but I think I'm over it." I turned around and leaned against the kitchen bench as I took a sip. "I think if I bake another biscuit, I'll turn into one."

Henry, Mac, and Cooper turned from various seated positions in the living room to gift me with matching looks of horror. I frowned and waved a hand at them to turn back around.

Mac smirked. "Is that Travis?"

"Yes," I mouthed at her.

"Is he coming over tonight to talk *security* with you?" Cooper asked with an exaggerated wink.

I rolled my eyes at them, noting that little gem had obviously done the rounds. The three of them laughed before turning their attention back to the movie playing out on the screen.

"Anyway, umm how was work?" I asked.

Mac tittered in the background at my attempt to make conversation.

"It was okay," he muttered as I made my way upstairs to my bedroom for some privacy. "Leaving soon. Thought I'd stop over and see you."

"You are?" I scratched at the back of my head, clearing my throat as I sank down to a huddle on the edge of my bed. "Travis, I'm not sure—"

"Thought I could get a start on teaching you those self-defence moves."

"Oh." I paused. "Okay. Thank you. That would be…great."

After promising to see me soon, he hung up.

I wasn't sure how long I sat there banging the phone against my head.

Leaving, Quinn. You're supposed to be leaving. Not getting giddy over Travis coming to see you.

"Quinn!" Henry yelled up the stairs. "Dinner!"

I sighed and tossed my phone across the bed. Henry's turn cooking usually meant frozen pizza.

Half an hour later, nominated by Mac as tonight's "dish bitch," I was rinsing plates in the sink. My mind was wandering when a soft kiss pressed against my neck, and I shrieked with alarm. The plate I was holding fell into the sink with a loud clatter. The scent of Travis surrounded me, and I breathed deeply.

"It's just me," he said in my ear.

Spinning around, I had a second to hear his breath catch before his lips were on mine. I wrapped my sudsy arms around his neck, stretching upwards on my toes. He picked me up, my feet leaving the floor to wrap around his hips. Travis murmured something as his hands gripped my thighs. He turned and pressed my back into the fridge.

I vaguely heard Mac say snidely to Jake, "Get your feet off the coffee table," but Travis held my attention as his tongue rubbed against mine and his fingers dug into my legs.

"Pause the movie, I need the loo," I heard her say again.

"You've seen this movie," came Henry's voice.

"What's your point?"

Travis groaned as I bit down on his bottom lip. The sound was loud as the silence registered.

Cooper's voice from the living room cut through it swiftly. "Apparently that's how you teach self-defence these days. Think I'm gonna quit Jamieson and start working for those guys."

"Huh," said Henry.

The talk faded as I was carried outside, and that only registered because I felt Rufus press his wet nose against my thigh.

Travis smiled. "Hey."

"Hi." I breathed, reeling from the intensity of the kiss.

"Trust your gut, sweetheart."

"Sorry?"

He set me down, his expression hardening into one of authority. "Self-defence, Quinn." He frowned and I felt like the naughty kid up the back of class, caught for not paying attention. "First rule of thumb. If something doesn't feel right, it's usually not."

"Oh," I murmured, remembering the prickly feeling of someone watching me. That had definitely not felt right.

Mac came out carrying notebooks and pens. "Have I missed anything?"

"We're at the trust your gut part," I replied, watching as she set the stationery on the table and motioned for me to take a seat. Travis was standing, hands on his hips, waiting for Mac to settle. When she began to tap impatiently with her pen, I looked to him with confusion. "I don't get to throw you around?"

Mac snorted. "Not even Mitch or Jared can throw Travis around. I've only ever seen him felled once before."

My eyes gave his muscular physique a ruthless once over and remembered the scar on his hip from being shot. I turned to Mac with a frown. "So you're saying self-defence begins with arming yourself?"

"Mac," Travis snapped. "Do you need to be here?"

Her pen carefully scratched out *Self-Defence* and followed underneath with *#1 – trust your gut* before looking at Travis with an expectant, wide-eyed expression. "You'd prefer me to shoot first?"

I picked up my pen and quickly copied Mac's neat, handwritten notes.

"Be aware of your surroundings," Travis began again, and we dutifully copied it down. "Don't walk alone late at night. If you find yourself in that situation, walk fast, don't dawdle or focus on your phone. If you're nervous, or someone is making you feel that way, head for a busy street." Travis began pacing as he spoke, pausing now and then to wait as we copied it all down. "Weapons."

Mac grinned with a nod of her head. "Uh huh."

"Keys are a weapon." He pulled his keys out of his pocket and showed us how to hold them in a fist. Then he made me do it, and when Mac giggled at my efforts, I aimed a mock punch at her and she flinched away from the table.

"My turn," she said.

"Mac. You already know all this."

170

She waved her hand. "Consider it a refresher."

He sighed and we both waited patiently while Mac did the "keys in the fist" drill. She aimed a mock slash at me in retaliation, and I chuckled as my torso twisted sideways.

"Enough!" Travis growled. Mac sat back down with a brief smooth of her hair and picked up her pen. "Anything else you might have on you. Heels, deodorant to spray in their eyes, be resourceful."

I saw Mac write *#4 – Resourceful* and underline it three times before turning back to Travis. "What about pepper spray?"

"Illegal."

"Well how come Evie gets a can and we don't?"

Travis narrowed his eyes. "Evie has pepper spray?"

Mac folded her arms and arched a brow in reply.

He sighed and scratched at the golden stubble on his jaw. "You get caught with that, or using it, you could end up in a world of trouble."

"More than the world of trouble you could end up in getting caught without it?" I said.

"I'll think about it," he conceded.

"Like Jared thought about it?" I heard Mac mutter under her breath.

"Don't yell for help," Travis continued.

I wrote it down then read it back to myself. "What?"

"Yell 'fire' instead. You'll get a better response."

I nodded as Travis continued talking, soaking it up like a dried out sponge. What he was telling me today was going to come in handy soon going by what bad guy number one and Beth had so helpfully informed me. If I couldn't somehow get away before that deadline was up, a world of pain wasn't just coming for me, it was coming for all of us.

Jared appeared on the back deck just as it appeared Travis was winding up the practical proceedings of self-defence.

I waved briefly in greeting, but Mac ignored him, asking Travis, "When do we get to the physical stuff?"

The words tuned out as Travis spoke, saying something that had Mac rolling her eyes and him chuckling. The sun was setting behind him, making his hair lighter, his skin darker, and I realised that he knew everything there was to know about me and he was still here. My chest constricted. How was I supposed to leave him?

"Quinn?"

"Huh?" I looked at Jared.

He looked nervous, cracking his knuckles. "Can I speak to you for a minute?" He eyed Travis and Mac. "In private?"

I stood, glancing at Travis briefly with a frown before I followed Jared inside and into the office. He shut the door behind the both of us and cleared his throat. "Quinn, I need your help."

My mouth fell open. "You do?"

"Yeah I do." He paused to gauge my reaction and softened. "Is that okay?"

I nodded. "Sure."

Jared resumed pacing and ran fingers through his hair. It was getting long. Not quite as long as Travis kept his, but it suited him. Sighing softly, I waited, watching Jared gathering his thoughts together.

"You might find it odd, me asking you this, but well, Mum can be very controlling, and Mac is…well, worse. Mitch and Travis I'm sure have less of an idea about this stuff than I do, but you…" he trailed off and stopped his pacing, his head cocked as he looked at me.

"But me?"

"Well, you're just sweet, Quinn. I never hear you talk crap about anyone, and you don't have a big mouth like everyone else I know."

My cheeks flushed with pleasure. I picked up the stapler off the desk, pretending to check if it needed a refill. "Well I'm all curious now."

His words came out in a rushed exhale. "IwannaaskEvietomarryme."

"Sorry, what?"

Jared sat down and peered up at me from beneath his lashes. "I want to ask Evie to marry me."

"Oh!" I murmured. My hand reached out involuntarily and took hold of his. "I don't know what to say."

"Don't say anything," he said with a grin. "You're the only one that knows. I need help asking her."

I gave his hand a squeeze and let go. "Why on earth would you think I could help you with that?"

"It's her birthday in a month. I wanted to do it then. I was hoping you could help plan the party with me."

A month.

My heart sank.

Why was everyone making leaving so hard?

I drew in a deep breath. Tonight. I had to leave tonight or I didn't think I'd ever be able to.

"Can I let you know tomorrow? I have a lot of work." I waved my hand at the desk, but it looked rather neat and tidy—no evidence at all of someone in the throes of a work crisis.

"Sure," he replied, the brief smile not quick enough to cover his disappointment. "Give me a call."

Jared left and not sure I could go back outside, I climbed the stairs only to find Travis lying on my bed. His hands were behind his head, his eyes focused on the ceiling. Pink lace sheets surrounded him, only emphasising the hard masculinity of his body. Heat punched through me as I leaned up against the door jamb watching him.

"I told Mac how I felt about you," Travis said, his words startling me because I'd had no idea he knew I was in the room.

Don't ask! my inner voice screamed at me. Hearing it aloud would make what was between us that much more real.

Travis tracked me carefully as I shut the door behind me and moved towards the bed. I climbed over his body until I straddled him.

His eyes fluttered closed when I leaned down to kiss him. It was the first time I'd initiated contact with him, but if tonight was all I had, I wanted to kiss and taste every inch of him. His arms came around me, anchoring me, as he opened his mouth beneath the pressure, and I tasted him with my tongue.

Breaking the kiss, I sat back to draw my shirt up and over my head, leaving Travis in no doubt of my intentions. His hands, hard and calloused, held on to my hips.

"Don't you want to know what I told her?"

Yes.

But I ignored his question. Instead, I cupped his cheeks. "I love when your eyes lose their hard edge. The green in them looks so clear and beautiful."

Travis pulled my hands from his face and grasped them tightly. "Between the two of us, you're the one that holds the beauty. Quinn, baby..." His voice fractured and he looked away, his eyes finding the window. "I'm keeping you, you know that, right?" His eyes turned back to me, gleaming possessively.

I smiled through tears.

"Hey," he murmured. "What's this?"

"Nothing," I lied. "You don't care about my...past?"

His fingers tickled their way up my belly, and I giggled.

"That's better," he murmured. "And no, Quinn, what you did, that was before. Me on the other hand..." his eyes fell to my mouth "... I was an innocent virgin until you corrupted me with those lips of yours."

Another laugh bubbled out of me, dying off quickly when Travis trailed his hands up my back and unclipped my bra. I sat up, sliding it down my arms, baring myself to his gaze.

The teasing glint left his eyes, leaving heat in their wake. "Get up and take the rest off," he demanded. "I want to see you."

Shivering at the way he took over, I stood and peeled off my bright yellow shorts. His eyes fell on the hot pink scrap of lace underneath, and my hands went to my hips, ready to slide those off too.

"Wait," he croaked. He sat up and shifted to the edge of the bed. "Come here."

I moved towards the bed, standing between his thighs.

Travis pressed a kiss to my naked belly, swirling his tongue in my belly button, and I sighed softly. He looked up at me from beneath his lashes, and my breath caught at their heat.

He slid a finger under the waistband of my panties and trailed his finger along my skin.

"Turn around."

Travis ran his hands over my hips as I turned around, giving him my back. His hands slid down the bare, smooth skin until he reached the lacy pink edge of my panties.

"*Now* take these off."

I baulked.

"Off, Quinn," he rasped. "Slowly."

With a flush heating my entire body, I stuck my thumbs in the waistband and bent over as I peeled them slowly down my legs.

Travis caught his breath and the rough skin of his hands brushed over my bare skin. Then his mouth was between my thighs, his tongue thrusting inside my body. His hand splayed over my back, holding me down.

"Spread your legs."

"Oh God," I murmured, doing as he told, putting my hands on my knees before they gave out. "Travis," I moaned.

"So sweet," he muttered.

Only moments later, the unrelenting torture of his tongue had wild tingles of heat roaring through me. "Stop," I gasped.

"No," he muttered against my skin. "Want to feel you come against my tongue."

He didn't stop and I did just that. Shuddering, I cried out his name, his arms holding me up when my legs gave out. He pulled me back into his lap, his hard length digging into my spine. "Feel how much I need you?"

"Travis," I moaned.

I heard his pants unzip and the rustle of a foil packet. "Mmm?"

Grasping my hips, he lifted me up and when I sank back, it was with him inside me.

"Quinn," he groaned, sucking in a loud breath.

My head tilted back into his shoulder, and his mouth fell on my neck, biting and sucking. My back bowed from the pleasure.

"Move for me," he muttered in my ear.

Leaning forward, I did as he asked, slowly, until he eventually grabbed my hips and took over. He ground his hips into me and stilled, and when he moaned my name, I felt it deep in his chest, and I'd never heard anything more beautiful on his lips.

Waking to darkness, a hand pressed into the small of my back, rubbing soothingly. My eyes opened to Travis sitting on the edge of the bed.

"I've got called out to work," he whispered. "I'll be a few hours, but I'll come back."

I nodded, leaning into the kiss he pressed on my lips, opening my mouth to the thrust of his tongue with a moan. He pulled back reluctantly.

"Travis…"

"Shh." He tapped a finger to my nose gently and his lips curved up. "Don't get dressed. I like the thought of you naked in bed."

The door clicked shut behind him, and I knew that if I didn't leave now, right this very moment, I never would.

I shifted reluctantly from the bed that was still warm from his body and covered with his scent. I picked up the pillow he'd briefly slept on and placed it at the end of the bed so I wouldn't forget it.

The duplex was silent as I slid on my underwear and walked inside my wardrobe. I yanked my suitcase from the top shelf. Forgetting I'd loaded it with text books from my uni days, it fell down on top of me, and I shrieked with pain. I grabbed at the hanging clothes, but they came off their hangers and landed with me on the floor. I pushed the suitcase off with a huff, and as a final insult, the wheel caught my toe. Hissing, I grabbed at the clothes strangling me and threw them towards the suitcase.

The light switch came on inside my room and I froze. The wardrobe door flew open, and Mac's eyes found me on the floor in my underwear, my suitcase and a pile of shirts at my feet and textbooks splattered open everywhere. Dressed in only a tiny satin slip herself, she took in the entire scene with pursed lips.

I cleared my throat. "I was just uh…"

"Save it," she hissed and started pushing buttons on the phone in her hand. I heard someone answer the phone. "You were absolutely right. You better get your butt over here pronto... Uh huh... You better believe I'm gonna sit on her."

The call ended, Mac tossed the phone over her shoulder, and my eyes followed its descent onto the carefully placed pillow, watching it bounce off and fall to the floor. My eyes flew back to Mac. Her arms were folded, anger almost steaming from her skin. And then the yelling started.

"What the fuck, Quinn? I mean, What. The. Fuck?"

I stood up. "I have no idea what you're talking about." I waved at the books. "I was just trying to tidy up." I nodded at her phone on the floor. "So uh…who was on the phone?"

She arched a brow, ignoring my question. "Tidying up? At three am?"

I forced a chuckle. "Is that the time? It feels so early."

Henry appeared by Mac's side, clad in only a pair of aqua blue boxer-briefs. My eyes went wide at how beautifully his underwear matched his eyes. Then I realised I was wearing hardly anything myself and his eyes were busy.

"Well damn. This is what I'm talking about," he joked with a grin.

"Sister, asshead," Mac snapped out.

His eyes fell on my suitcase and the dregs of clothes hanging out the sides with a frown. Confused, his eyes returned to mine. "Quinn? What's going on?"

"Quinn's doing a runner."

I glared. "I was cleaning."

Henry raised his brows, starting to look a little hurt. "In the middle of the night?"

I scratched at the back of my head, wincing. His eyes fell on my chest, and I hastily folded my arms over my bra. "Yes. In the middle of the night. You should both go because I'm not dressed."

"I've seen it all before," Mac said.

"Well me too now," Henry offered.

"Sister!" Mac snapped at Henry.

"Christ, Mac!" he yelled. "I may hold some kind of manwhore status in your eyes, but I'm not a goddamn letch."

I cleared my throat. "That wasn't Travis on the phone, was it?"

"No, it was Lucy."

My eyes shifted to her phone, and narrowing her gaze, she followed my line of sight. Pursing her lips, she lunged for the phone, and I found myself diving after her.

"Ooomph." Mac fell to the floor with a thud beneath me, and her arm stretched out for the phone.

"No!" I yelled, clawing my way over her to reach for the phone.

"Arrghhh," she squealed when my elbow caught her in the eye.

"Sorry," I mumbled. My hand clutched around the phone, and my shout of relief was short-lived when I was rolled and Mac was breathing heavy in my face.

"What the hell is going on here?" came Jake's growl from the bedroom door.

We both froze and turned. Jake was standing there, bare chest heaving as though he'd run a marathon. I was thinking that maybe our yelling might have woken up the entire duplex when I heard Cooper from beside him say, "Shut up, idiot. Naked chicks wrestling."

Ignoring all of them, Mac got in my face and growled, "Give me one good reason why I shouldn't ring Travis right now."

Panting, my arm outstretched to hold the phone from Mac's grasp, I closed my eyes against the tears, but I felt one roll out the side and down my cheek as I whispered softly so that only she could hear, "Because if he knows, they'll shoot him."

The lovely golden shade of Mac's face paled, and she scrabbled backwards off me in shock.

"I'm sorry," I choked out. My eyes blurred as they took in all of them standing there, feeling utterly horrified I'd brought this hell into their lives. "I'm so sorry."

Mac nodded towards the door. "Everyone out."

No one moved.

She arched a brow. "Did I just speak Klingon? Out. Now."

All three of them left the room with reluctant frowns, and scrambling to my feet, I grabbed a shirt from the floor and shrugged it on. Bracing myself, I lifted my chin and faced Mac.

"Right." She jabbed a finger in my chest. "Time for a chat."

Chapter Seventeen

Standing off the side of the open stage behind the bulky width of Travis, I peeked around his shoulder, carefully eyeing the Melbourne festival crowd. Was he out there somewhere—watching me? Travis said the first rule was to trust your gut, but mine was so busy doing gold medal winning backflips that it was unreliable. My deadline was up in two days, and Mac, Lucy, and now Evie who'd been apprised of recent events, hadn't been able to agree on a solution.

Even though Travis was working, I slipped my hands into the waistband of his pants and held on. He didn't unfold his arms but he tilted his head and leaned back slightly, his body shielding me from the brisk wind. I shivered at the protective gesture.

"Cold?" he asked.

I nodded. "A little," I replied, because I was. Melbourne was chilly and I hadn't packed accordingly. My mind had been focused on more pressing matters.

"Where's your jacket?"

"I left it in the hotel room."

Travis unfolded his arms and peeled his work jacket off. "Put this on."

I slipped it on and he turned patiently and started rolling up the sleeves. The warmth of his scent wrapped around me, and I bit down on my lip as I breathed it in.

"Quinn," he said.

At the warning tone in his voice, I looked up from watching his hands work to see his eyes on my lips. He turned back, the hard edge returning to his eyes as he once again folded his arms and glared at the crowd.

After my escape plan went south, not even managing to even get dressed or make it out of the wardrobe, Mac had taken me hostage. We'd waited for Lucy in tense silence because every time I opened my mouth to speak, Mac glared at me.

"Quinn. Did you think running would stop them looking for you?" Mac had asked.

"Of course not," I replied, "but it would stop them going for any of you."

Lucy growled her anger. "Fuck me sideways. That's dumb. You're being dumb. Dumb as dog shit." Her look had been one of utter disappointment. "After everything, you still couldn't ask for anyone to help you?"

My body bristled in the face of her disappointment. "And risk any of you getting hurt because of me?"

"How would they even know you spoke to us?"

"I have no idea. What if my phone's bugged? Or my bag? These are the kind of people that have people in their pockets—like the police."

"Oh, that is it. I'm ringing Travis," Mac ground out.

"Wait." I grabbed her arm. "There's got to be another way out of this."

Both of them folded their arms and faced me, waiting for me to tell them what it is.

"I just haven't worked out what it is yet," I hedged.

Mac grabbed for her phone.

"You can't," I burst out. "I don't want anyone involved. Not any of you, not Travis. I didn't want this touching anyone. It's my mess. Mine. I'll fix it."

"That's not how we roll, Quinn."

"It's how *I* roll," I told Mac. "I have no idea what David is dealing with, but you know the person he is. These people he owes money to have guns, and all of you, you're high profile people. Evie stands out in the middle of a stage," I whispered furiously, "and Travis and Jared stand right off the edge, in full view of everyone. He threatened to shoot people if I talked or if I didn't get the money."

Lucy sank heavily onto the bed. "We need to get the money. Rick and I have savings."

"Are you kidding? We need to take these bastards down," came Mac's solution.

"No. I need to talk to them. That's all. I'll just explain I don't have the money and that it's got nothing to do with me."

"You think they'll be happy with that?"

"Maybe," I muttered.

Evie yelled, "Last song!" and it brought me back to the present.

I glanced sideways at Mac. I knew what was churning through her mind. It was the same thing as me. The deadline was getting closer and my idea to just explain I didn't have any money was sounding like a really shitty one. She returned my look with a glare and a nod at Travis, her actions informing me that if I didn't tell Travis, and soon, she was going to.

My lips pressed tightly together, and I returned her nod. It was then I realised Travis had caught our silent exchange, and his brows were pinched together in a frown.

He looked between the both of us. "What's going on?"

Travis waited for one of us to speak.

Mac cleared her throat pointedly.

"I was going to let you go," I blurted out. "I wanted you to be safe, but none of you are because I can't get anything right."

Travis looked from me to Mac and back again. "Who's not safe?"

"No one if I don't get them the money."

He grabbed hold of my arm, frustration oozing from his body. I could actually see the vein pulsing angrily in his neck. I focused on it

182

because it was either that or the anger in his eyes. "Get who the money? Can one of you start talking some goddamn sense?"

"You can't tell anyone, Travis," I replied.

Travis let go of my arm and pinched the bridge of his nose with his thumb and forefinger. "Tell anyone what, dammit?"

His voice had kicked up a level, and I was starting to sense some impatience. "About the bad guys."

Travis flared his nostrils dangerously, and Mac shrugged at me when I glanced at her. After drawing in several deep breaths, Travis spoke.

"You..." he pointed at me "...and you..." he pointed at Mac "...back to the hotel room right now." Mac started protesting and he simply raised his voice over hers. "I will make sure the show is wrapped up and everything is packed away and dealt with." Then he spoke into his speaker. "Sean, need you here right now. Mac and Quinn need an escort back to the hotel."

My brows flew up because Sean and Travis were not best friends, and I somehow felt responsible for that. It seems that Sean, aka Wolverine from the Florence Bar, had quit his job and started working for Jamieson and Valentine Consulting. I had no idea, and really, why would I? It had nothing to do with me, at least until Sean met us at the airport for our Melbourne flight to form part of the security detail. I'd been busy throwing up in the airport toilet. Seems I wasn't a good flyer and that was before we'd even boarded the plane. Lucy said it was a good idea for me to take a couple of sleeping pills to relax the nerves, but they just rolled around in my stomach, finding a friend in the nerves that were already there. Then the nerves and pills combined forces and there I was over the toilet bowl, making a drama out of an hour long flight.

When I made my way out of the public restroom, pale and shaky, I found Sean forming part of the Jamieson huddle. When his eyes caught hold of me, they rounded in surprise. Then he picked me up, hugging me as he spun me around, saying he'd been keeping an eye out for me and was disappointed I'd never returned to the bar. I must have paled further from being launched upwards in his big arms because he set me down hastily. When I teetered, Sean reached out in concern and I hung on.

Travis reached my side about the time Sean decided to ask why I never rang him. Travis slid his arm around my waist, tugging me close, at the same time glaring at Sean. My body leaned into Travis, and I simply told Sean it was because I wasn't dating. His eyes glanced pointedly at the arm around me, and Travis glaring daggers at him, and I hastily tacked on that I was dating now. Dating Travis. Against all my better judgement, but I didn't add that part. It didn't seem the right time.

Not to mention my main focus was on my troubles. Now it seemed my troubles were going to become Travis's troubles. I didn't like that at all. It left the blood in my veins feeling ice cold.

Sean arrived and Travis let my arm go. "Take Quinn and Mac back to the hotel." He faced the both of us. "You get there you do *not* leave that room. If I find you have taken one step outside that door before I get back and deal with this, so help me God, both of you will be fucking sorry."

I flinched at the whiplash in his voice and the anger in his beautiful eyes. Taking a step back, I pulled out my phone.

"I just need to message Lucy so she can come with us." There had been no holding Lucy back from coming to Melbourne with us after our little chat.

"Does Lucy know what's going on?"

I nodded.

"Who else?"

"Evie too," Mac added helpfully while my fingers tapped out a message.

He threw his hands up in frustration, and after Sean arrived at the side of the stage, Travis gave us his back and focused on doing his job.

Moments later, the three of us were in the car with Sean driving us towards what now felt like my doom, but he didn't appear in any hurry, so that was nice.

"Did I stuff up?"

Mac didn't hesitate. "Yes."

"No, I mean, did I really stuff up?"

Lucy took hold of my hand. "The reasons behind your actions were noble, Quinn, and maybe if I thought as little of myself as you do of yourself, I would understand, but I just don't." My lips trembled and she added, "but I'm sure this can be fixed. Right, Mac? I didn't know you'd planned on spilling your guts to Travis tonight. I mean, it wasn't the best timing, but there's never a good time to share bad shit, is there?"

Mac shook her head in agreement. "Don't mind Travis, Quinn. He's just shitty at being kept out of the loop. If you haven't yet noticed, my brothers all have a knight in shining armour complex."

"So what happens when they rescue their fair maiden, Mac? The knight complex doesn't just disappear."

Mac snorted. "You've met Evie, haven't you? She's a full time trouble magnet. Jared chose well." She turned her eyes on me. "I'm starting to think Travis has too."

At the front door of our hotel room, Sean ushered Mac and Lucy inside and held me back. "I'm in the room right next door, Quinn. If you need me, just yell, okay?"

I nodded and slipped through the door, shutting it behind me, and blinked at the utter chaos.

"You're not Evie," a drunk guy pointed at me with a frown. Two more of those were busy partying up by the corner bar in the sitting room. Mac and Lucy were yelling and trying to hustle them towards the door.

"Wow, you're quick, aren't you? And what the hell are you doing in our room? And how the hell did you get in here?"

He held up his hands and winked. "Whoa with all the questions. Waiting to meet the band of course," he slurred. "And Evie."

I took off the bulky, black jacket that Travis gave me and flung it towards the couch. Drunk guy number one followed it with his eyes, catching the big white lettering on the back. "Jamieson Security?" He turned back to me, his eyes roaming over my tiny stature with disbelief. "Times must be tough. You gonna throw me out?"

I pointed towards the door. "No. You're going to walk out."

He laughed. "Good one. Come on." He indicated for me to rush him, and it was honestly tempting, but my self-defence lessons from Travis had been exactly that—there was no lesson on how to initiate my own attack. Drunk guy, tired of waiting, rushed me, and it seemed so easy to just take a step to the side and watch him stumble over his own feet. When he turned again, I remembered Travis telling us to be resourceful, so I grabbed the nearest object, which happened to be a chair.

Narrowing his eyes, he took a step towards me, and in a panic, I flung it towards him and yelled, "Fire!"

The chair missed and crashed into the wall behind him—the legs breaking off carelessly and denting the plaster. Everyone paused for a moment to watch the splinters scatter across the floor.

"Fuck yeah!" yelled one of the guys. "Rock stars know how to live the fucking life!"

I caught a bottle of rum getting thrown, and it smashed across the floor. Mac started dialling on her phone, but it was snatched from her hand and sent to join the rum.

Then I was tackled to the floor, hard. Feeling winded and hurt, I grabbed the packet of Pringles that landed on the floor beside me, ready to bean the closest drunken idiot I could see when a gunshot ricocheted in the room. It wasn't loud, but having watched every action movie in existence, I recognised the popping sound. So did everyone else by the looks of it because it wasn't just me that froze—even the drunk and disorderly realised that shit just got real.

"As fun as this is…" all eyes swivelled to the voice "…Quinn and I need to have a chat. So if you'll just excuse us."

A man stood just inside the door, lean but built. Sunglasses covered his eyes and a baseball cap was lowered on his forehead. He faced where

I lay panting on the floor from the scuffle and nodded towards the door. "Let's go."

Recognising the voice as the Money Guy, I carefully placed the Pringles container on the floor and replied, "I still have two days."

He shrugged and shifted the gun to his other hand. "Two days, two weeks. Whatever. Move."

I didn't move.

"Now!" he snarled at me and pointed the gun at Mac. "Or I'll shoot her."

"Oh you so did not just do that," she snarled and took a step forward.

"Mac!" I shrieked.

"Relax, Quinn. I got this."

"You got this? You *got this?* What the fuck, Mac!" I yelled in panic. "Who do you think you are? Jackie Chan?"

I stood up and inched towards the door. "None of you have got this, because I do."

"So help me, Quinn," Lucy ground out, getting up off her hands and knees, her face pale. "If you take one more step towards that door, I'll—"

Mac scrambled and then all of a sudden she had a gun in her hands and was aiming it towards Money Guy by the door. Lucy paused and her eyes went as wide as mine. All of a sudden our hotel room had become the wild west, and I wouldn't have been surprised to see tumbleweeds start rolling by.

"Holy shit," I heard Lucy mutter.

"Never again," were Mac's words of ultimate steel. "You take one step towards Quinn and I won't hesitate to shoot you."

Of that I had no doubt. Her eyes were flat and cool, and she looked completely badass. I was relieved she was on my side, but he didn't appear to be backing down.

"How on earth did you smuggle that thing on the plane?" Lucy muttered.

"I didn't," she said out of the corner of her mouth. "I hid it inside the truck that transported all of our equipment. You drunk fucktards on the floor, I suggest that now is a good time to leave."

Faced with a real threat from both sides of the room, they didn't hesitate, slinking out of the room without a backward glance.

I inched closer to the door. "Mac, just put the gun down, okay?"

"Yeah, Mac." The bad guy smirked. "Put the gun down."

"Who the fuck do you think you are?" she growled.

"That's of no concern to you, princess. I'm here for Quinn."

Lucy and I stood there, our eyes swivelling between the two of them.

"Yeah, well fuck you, because Quinn's not going anywhere."

"Mac," I called out. "Maybe I should—"

"No, no," she said. "You keep out of this."

When I was halfway towards the door, Sean was suddenly there, slamming into Money Guy from behind. He took the blow full force, his body dropping forward. The gun flew forward and it must have been loaded, cocked and ready to go because it let out another pop, ripping a hole in the wall across the room.

Money Guy spun around, catching Sean with an elbow before scrambling for the gun.

"No!" I shrieked and dived for it. He landed on top of me and my jaw cracked on the floor. "Arrghhhh!"

I rolled and started scratching at his face when his weight disappeared off my body and he was thrown across the room. Sean started after him, but he got up on shaky feet.

"Two days, Quinn." He pointed at me. "Or you're fucking dead." He pushed off the wall and disappeared out the door. Sean took off after him as I struggled to my feet, trying to catch my breath.

"Is everyone okay?" I choked out, my legs trembling. I stared at Mac. Mac stared at me, then we both turned to Lucy who rushed over, grabbing my forearms.

"Ouch," I muttered when her nails dug in.

"Are you okay?" she asked.

"I'm fine. Absolutely fine," I assured her as my legs kept trembling beneath me.

We paused a moment to survey the hotel room: bullet holes, smashed chairs, and glassware littered the floor. A picture was hanging crooked and the bar was strewn with empty bottles of alcohol. Lucy looked reasonably neat, but Mac's hair was a little wild, and her gun was hanging by her side. She caught me eyeing it dubiously and shrugged. "It's not loaded."

Lucy gaped at her. "You were playing chicken?"

Mac raised a brow as she smoothed her hair.

"You were asking Travis for pepper spray when you have that?" I added.

"Well. I did warn him about shooting first."

Mac was picking her phone up off the floor, examining the shattered screen, when Sean returned. He ran his eyes over each of us before surveying the scene silently.

"Fuck," he muttered.

"Damn straight *fuck*," Mac replied.

"The boss's sister and girlfriend shot at, a trashed hotel room, and a gunman on the loose on my first real assignment. I think I can pretty much consider myself fired before I've barely started."

Lucy shrugged, trying to remain positive for her friend. "Well, they're not dead, so that's good for you, right?"

"It's not your fault, Sean," I told him, tears clogging my throat and burning my eyes. "It's mine."

We stood around like survivors in the middle of a war zone, watching Mac as she tucked her gun away carefully and picked her way through the mess to the hotel phone. She picked it up, pressed a single button, and when her call was answered, she said, "This is Mackenzie Valentine in room four-two-oh-six. Can you send someone up with a bottle of vodka and some shot glasses please." After a pause, she said, "Thank you," and hung up.

"Maybe you should've have asked for housekeeping while you were there?" Lucy asked.

"First things first, Lucy."

"I'm thinking that I really like you right now, Mac."

She nodded. "Ditto."

Sean, hands on his hips, eyed them both. "Are we finished with the love fest ladies? Because I need to ring Travis."

Mac sighed heavily. "Just let us get a vodka shot in to brace for the next round of hell first, Sean, okay?"

Leaning down, my shaky hands grabbed hold of the Pringles, and I popped open the lid. "Chip, anyone?"

That was how Jules, the room service guy, found us when he came bearing our alcohol—standing around in the mess, munching on chips, trying to process our shock.

"Um…" Jules glanced about the room in disbelief. I thought that was a bit rich. I mean, the entire hotel was chock to the brim with rockers here for the festival. Surely we weren't the only ones with a bit of damage?

Mac casually shifted her body so it covered the bullet hole in the wall. "So, maybe we should get housekeeping in, huh?"

He sat his tray down on the dining table and said faintly, "I'll have someone sent up. I'd arrange another room for you but with the festival, the hotel is fully booked."

Jules left and Lucy started pouring shots and handing them out. Sean declined and got on his phone. The three of us eyed each other silently and then downed one shot each. It stung the inside of my mouth, and I realised I must have bitten down on my cheek when my jaw cracked on the floor. I wiped at my mouth and my hand came away smeared with blood.

"Well, good news and bad news," Sean told us as Lucy started pouring another round.

"Good news first," said Mac.

"I got hold of Travis."

I reached out and held tight to the chair. "That's the good news?"

"I'm afraid so. The bad news is that they've arrived back at the hotel and are already on their way up."

"Oh shit," Lucy muttered.

"Do you think we've got time to do a quick clean up?" I asked and downed the next shot. When my skin grew cold and my body started to sway, I remembered I hadn't eaten all day. Putting down the shot glass, I watched everyone come alive, racing about the room throwing bottles in bins and trying to right fallen chairs.

My teeth started to chatter. "Umm, guys?"

Suddenly they all seemed really far away as my vision narrowed.

"Shit," I heard faintly. "I think she's going into shock."

"No I'm not," I announced, both hands now gripping the chair. "I'm just peachy. I think."

"What the hell is going on in here?" Travis yelled from the doorway.

"Maybe I'm not so good," I mumbled.

"Quinn?" Travis called from far away.

I turned slowly. "Sorry, Travis. I think that—"

"Is that a fucking bullet hole in the goddamn wall?" came Jared's yell.

"What?" replied Travis as Jared went for a closer inspection.

He strode towards me. "You're bleeding." His voice sounded panicked.

I wiped at the corner of my mouth, but he smacked my hand away. Cupping my face, he wiped at the blood. "Did someone hit you?"

"Oh, that. It's nothing."

He ran his eyes over me, and when the world tilted I realised that Travis was holding me and I was being carried into the bedroom.

"Does anywhere else hurt?" His voice was controlled as he laid me out on the bed, but his hands were frantic as they ran over me, examining my body for injuries. "Quinn?"

"I'm fine," I told him, struggling to sit up.

Travis put a hand on my chest.

"It's just…I cracked my jaw on the floor, that's all, when I dived for the gun."

"When you dived for the gun?" He sank to the edge of the bed and rubbed a hand over his forehead. "Jesus fuck."

"Travis?" My teeth started chattering again as I sat up.

He turned sideways and pulled me onto his lap. "Let me just hold you for a minute, then we need to talk."

Chapter Eighteen

"Let me get this straight. I was there. I was right there in the street when that bastard had a hold of you and you didn't yell out?"

I nodded from my huddled ball in bed. We were back in our hotel room down the hall, and after giving Travis all the answers to his questions, I felt sick for making an absolute mess of things.

"He said he would shoot you."

"I don't care," he burst out, his knuckles white from clenching his fists. "I don't fucking care. Let him have tried. I would have ripped him apart just for touching you." Travis gave me his back, his shoulders moving up and down as he struggled for control.

After a few beats of silence, he said softly, "You couldn't have come to me?"

My chest ached. How could I explain so that he understood how impossibly hard it was to rip open every horrible part of you and expose it to someone, and not only that, but to drag them down into your nightmare with you?

"You don't understand," I finally said, the words sounding empty.

Travis turned around, tucking a strand of loose hair behind his ear before tugging his hands into his pockets. "Wow, Quinn. How will I ever understand when you keep everything tucked so tightly inside that you can't even talk to your best friend? I'm tired of asking you to explain it to me rather than coming to me if you need help or just need me to be there. I feel like an idiot for being the last one you talk to all the time. For it having come to this for you to let me in."

"No one thinks you're an idiot."

"I don't care what anyone else thinks right now, just you, Quinn. But I can only fight for you for so long before you have to start fighting for yourself, and for us, and it hurts that you won't even try. I know I said I'd be strong for you, and I always will be whether you want me to or not, but you have to be strong too because I need you just as much." He paused and drew in a deep breath. "Is that such a bad thing—for us to have each other?"

My mouth was open to speak, but nothing came out.

Travis stepped back and rubbed a weary hand over his closed eyes. For the first time he was giving up. I could feel it. The ties that had somehow bound us together right from the beginning were being sliced in two. But he couldn't give up. I needed him to not give up on me.

"Wait!" I called out to his retreating back.

He stopped.

"Don't go. I'm sorry. I don't know how..." I cleared my throat. "I'm scared."

Travis turned around, his eyes, direct and green, held mine. "What are you scared of?"

I licked my lips.

He stood, waiting.

"You."

"You're scared of *me*?" Travis shook his head, looking at the floor before shifting his eyes back to me. "What have I done to make you scared of me?"

He sounded hurt and tears filled my eyes.

"Already you're getting dragged into my shitty world, Travis, and I don't want any of it touching you. You're better than that. Better than me. And maybe not today, maybe not tomorrow, but one day, you'll realise that."

And you'll leave...

And I won't ever survive it because I love you.

Oh my God. I wouldn't. I wouldn't survive losing him.

How could I be so stupid to let myself fall in love with you?

He'd made it too easy.

As he strode towards me, my eyes ran over his wide shoulders, the thick veins running the length of his biceps, the hard edge in his eyes from the strain, and I knew I would do anything he asked because it was too late now. Too late to let him go and if I didn't survive loving him, then so be it.

He crouched in front of me, resting his arms on my knees. "You wouldn't believe me if I just told you right now that's not true, but I'm saying it anyway—that's bullshit. It's not about who's better than who. That makes no sense to me. Did you choose your start in life? Did I? If I was given your life, are you saying that would make you a better person than me?" He didn't wait for me to answer. "I know that shit you're feeling doesn't go away overnight. I just want you to promise to do one thing for me. Just one thing, okay?"

Leaning forward, I kissed him and took it as a good sign when he didn't pull away. "What?"

"Promise me you'll try." He breathed against my mouth.

"I promise." The words were out of my mouth before I even realised, and he smiled against my lips.

"Good."

I nipped his lower lip gently with my teeth as I slid my hands down his back to the waistband of his pants. "I should probably talk to Mitch."

He kissed me. "Let me take care of it. We'll deal with this, Quinn. I don't want you involved anymore. It's too dangerous."

"You can't just—"

Travis kissed me again. "Yes. I can."

"You can't control me by kissing me," I lied.

He ran his tongue along my bottom lip and slid it inside my mouth.

I moaned.

"Should I stop kissing you?"

"No."

"Good, 'cause I'm remembering how you kissed me last night." He grabbed my hand and put it on the hard bulge in his pants. "And how I returned the favour, and ..." He trailed off, groaning when I rubbed the straining length of him.

A tap came at the door, and I snatched my hand away. We both turned, Travis rising to his feet.

Jared stood there, phone in hand. "Mitch wants to talk to you. He's been in touch with Melbourne's AFP and they're sending over a fed. They want to know what the fuck is happening with this assignment—"

"Jared!" Travis cut him off loudly, frowning.

Jared looked from Travis to me and shook his head.

"What's going on?" I asked.

Travis snatched the phone from Jared's hand, glowering. He turned to me, his eyes softening for a moment. "Nothing, Quinn. Get some rest. I'll be back."

He waited for my nod before he left the room.

Jared watched his retreating back for a moment before turning to me.

"So... I haven't been able to talk to you without big mouth or big ears around. How goes the party planning?"

Of course I'd agreed to help him plan Evie's party after my plans to leave fell by the wayside. Thankfully he'd put me on to Carol, the office administrator at Jamieson and Valentine Consulting. Between the two of us, we'd managed to put everything together in under a week.

"All done."

He raised his brows. "Already?"

I shrugged, a little bit smug at my efficiency. "Just waiting on numbers to get back to us."

"So the Florence Bar is booked?"

"Uh huh, as are the caterers, the cake, and music. We've organised a photo booth, a stylist—"

"Stylist?"

"Yeah, to pull the look together."

"The look?"

"Carol and I thought it might be nice to go with a vintage glamour look."

"What the hell is vintage glamour? Wait," he said and held up a hand, "I don't want to know. As long as we don't have to dress up, like in fancy dress."

I was about to tell him he'd need to at least wear a suit, when his eyes went wide with warning and he mouthed, "Big ears," at me just before I heard Evie say, "What's fancy dress?"

I smothered a laugh, watching Jared lean casually against the door frame as though we'd just been discussing the weather.

"Um…just the Christmas in July party that Jettison Records is having soon," I answered.

Jared gave me a discreet thumbs up in relief at my response. It soon turned to one of horror when she whooped with glee. "Yes! I love fancy dress," she said, not even considering it odd that after what happened earlier, Jared would be standing in my hotel room discussing fancy dress parties with me. "We could do a cutesy couple thing, Jared."

Jared folded his arms. "No way, baby."

I didn't have the heart at that moment to tell either of them that Jettison Records hadn't mentioned anything at all about their party being fancy dress. Evie was looking too excited, and it was just a little bit funny watching Jared squirm.

She arched a brow at him and said huskily, "I'll make it worth your while."

Not even I could miss the heat that had his eyes turning lazy. "Oh yeah?"

I cleared my throat and Evie shifted her attention to me. "Quinn, way to go. Mac said you were the one that threw the chair."

I shrugged modestly. "Well, I remembered Travis saying to be resourceful." I didn't mention that it hadn't hit anything besides the wall.

Three weeks of being permanently attached to mostly Travis and Casey came and went. On the minus side, I didn't really know what was going on. Travis said it was in the hands of the "proper authorities." On the plus side, Evie's party was keeping my mind occupied, and Travis and Casey were busy making sure I was safe at all times. It felt rude to complain about the lack of privacy. In fact, they were spending so much time shadowing me everywhere, I wasn't sure how to repay the gesture.

When I made that particular announcement to Travis and Casey last night in the loft, Casey choked on his drink. When I'd spun around from rummaging through the bottom shelving on the fridge, I caught two sets of eyes swivel quickly from my ass to my eyes. Mine narrowed as I watched Travis bite down on a smirk.

After several slurs towards men and their levels of maturity, I finished putting together my late night sandwich and stole the remote. Satisfied with my win, I flicked until I could find the girliest, most romantic love fest on television that ever existed and revelled in Casey's groans of "that guy's a total wimp" and Travis huffing whenever the hero did something "unrealistic." I admit to also revelling a little in sitting between the two of them. Both in worn faded jeans, Travis was bare chested and Casey wore a stretchy shirt that had seen better days.

Jared rang midway through the movie in a panic because Evie's birthday party was looming the next day. Sworn to secrecy, I had to abandon the couch reluctantly.

"I'll be back," I warned the pair of them with narrowed eyes and a waggle of the remote which I took with me while Jared spoke in my ear.

I giggled when I turned and saw I was getting chased. My heart thumped as I darted for the kitchen. Glancing behind, I saw Travis closing in on one side, Casey on the other. At the last minute I opted for the dining area and shrieked when Travis lunged for me and missed by a millimetre.

I gasped into the phone that I was still there when Jared called my name in irritation, but the last minute indecision cost me. I squealed when a pair of strong, tanned arms circled me from behind and grabbed for the remote. I tried to hold it aloft, but was no match for the strength that had me locked down.

"Shortie." Casey laughed in my ear as he snatched the remote easily from my hand. Breathless, I spun around and found myself only centimetres from his bright, blue eyes.

Casey jerked back. "Got it!" he whooped at Travis and took a running dive for the couch in victory.

"Dammit, Jared," I complained down the phone breathlessly. "You just cost me the remote."

No sooner had air filled my lungs when Travis slammed my body hard into the wall and planted his lips on mine.

"Travis, I'm on the phone," I breathed.

"I don't care." He groaned into my neck. "You're being cute. I like you this way. It gets me hot." Travis grabbed the phone from my ear. "She'll call you back," he announced and tossed my phone away.

"That was rude," I muttered.

His grin was devious as his hand slid swiftly underneath my shirt and trekked upwards. "I'll show you rude."

"Guys," Casey called out as Travis found my mouth again, gripping my thigh and tugging it around his hip as he ground his body against me. "That's not fair."

My face flamed as Travis grabbed hold of my hand and tugged me into his bedroom, slamming the door shut behind him. He advanced slowly, and shrieking with laughter I jumped on the bed. My hand swiped a pillow and held it in a threatening stance as I bounced from one foot to the other, waiting to see which way I needed to run.

Travis paused, tilting his head at me as though changing tactics. Lowering his lids, he moved his hands to the button on his jeans. He undid one slowly, then another, and I froze when I realised he wasn't wearing anything underneath.

My mouth went dry as his fingers slowly worked their way down until each one was undone and his jeans were tugged off. Heat slammed into me as my eyes ran over his chest, lean hips, long muscled legs, and everything in between.

"Like what you see?" he asked huskily.

"M-maybe," I stammered.

With laughter in his eyes, Travis leaped easily onto the bed. All I could manage was to hold the pillow aloft in defence.

Travis wrenched it easily from my hands. With a toss he threw it across the room. My hand flew to my mouth, covering the shout of laughter when it hit the lamp, sending it crashing to the floor.

Ignoring it, he advanced another step towards me, his eyes falling to my mouth when I bit my lip in anticipation.

In an effort to throw him off, I came at him and we went down in a tangle of naked limbs and laughter. It soon dried up when Travis slid his mouth along my skin, his tongue tracing lazy circles along my collarbone. Within moments, my own jeans were tugged off and his hand was tracing those same lazy, maddening circles up the bare skin of my thigh. I parted my lips when his tongue demanded entrance to my mouth while his fingers grazed my panties, teasing the edges of the lace material.

I moaned into his mouth, my body throbbing when they eventually slipped underneath the lace, teasing me playfully where I ached for him.

When those fingers inched inside of me, he groaned into my neck, letting out a shuddering breath as I moaned his name.

A loud rap at the door registered through the fog, and Travis cursed loudly.

"Umm, sorry, guys," Casey called through the door, "but Travis, it's the phone, mate. It's one of your work assignments."

Travis leaned his forehead against mine, his hands retreating reluctantly. "Quinn," he breathed against my lips. "Dammit. I can never get enough of you."

I watched my fingers trail down the side of his face while he watched me.

I love you.

Travis couldn't drag his eyes from mine. Could he see the love there?

I closed them. "Hurry back."

"Don't leave."

I opened them. "I won't leave."

He nodded once, relief softening his features and relaxing his shoulders. David had been released three days ago, but while Travis was worried about my safety, I was worried about his.

"Good. I don't want you going anywhere at all without me or Casey. No one else, okay?"

"Travis. I can't do that forever."

I had a job, bills to pay, a dog to walk. I couldn't have a permanent bodyguard.

"It's just for now. Trust me. He's caught up in the kind of shit that will see him going back in for a very long time."

"What shit?"

He pushed up off me but not before I caught the pained expression on his face. "We'll talk about it tomorrow, okay?" He picked up his jeans off the floor and pulled them on. A dark grey henley was dragged over his head, and he yanked it down, tucking his wallet and phone into the back pocket of his jeans. He paused. "Okay?"

I frowned and sat up. "Okay."

Travis leaned in and kissed me. "I want you naked so that when I get back so I can slide into bed and into you."

"Travis!" I called out when he reached the door and opened it. He looked over his shoulder. "Be safe."

He nodded and left.

With Casey promising not to bite, I slid on a pair of sleep shorts and joined him on the couch with a wine to watch the rest of the movie.

My head was tilted back, my eyes half closed when the credits started to roll. Casey turned a sleepy head towards me. "You 'kay?"

"Mmm," I mumbled. "That movie was shit."

A smile spread slowly across his face and he chuckled softly. "Wanna watch another one?"

Casey looked tired but reluctant to go to bed. Missing Travis, I felt that way myself, so I agreed. Stumbling towards the kitchen, I opened the fridge, feeling generous in letting him choose the next movie.

"Tea, coffee, beer?" I called out. With no answer I spun around and found him returning from his room in just a pair of sweatpants and nothing else. I averted my eyes back to the fridge.

"Beer me, Quinn." The words were close enough to my ear that I shrieked a little and jerked back. My elbow struck his bare chest and I leaped forward.

"Oh God, sorry."

Casey didn't even budge. "My fault."

He took a step back, and I rummaged in the shelf and grabbed a Corona.

"Here," I mumbled, holding it out behind me. He took it from my grasp and I grabbed the wine bottle.

He sat his beer on the kitchen bench and took the bottle from my hands too. "Let me pour it for you."

I yawned sleepily, scratching at my head as Casey poured me a glass and slipped the bottle back in the fridge.

We both wandered back to the couch and sagged into the soft leather. My mind on Travis, I glanced at Casey, his beer in one hand, remote in the other. "This job Travis got called out to. He's not in any danger, is he?"

Casey took a pull of his beer and exhaled loudly. "Nah. Just another sorry custody dispute. We get called in when it gets out of hand. You know you'd think it's good—both parents loving the kid so much they can't agree who gets to spend more time with them—but that's hardly ever what it's about."

"What is it about?" I asked softly.

"Winning. But for there to be a winner, there's got to be a loser, right? And we all know who that turns out to be." He pressed play on the movie as if to finish the conversation.

"Is that what happened with you? Travis says he does what he does because of you."

Casey chuckled but it wasn't a happy sound. "Travis and I have been friends since we started uni, so I know how you feel around the Valentines, Quinn. They'll all be quick to tell you they're not the perfect family, and they aren't. But they're not perfect in the way that it counts."

"What way is that?"

"Love of course." He shook his head. "They grew up with it. People like you and me, Quinn, we grew up with fear. Learning to love is work for us because we don't understand or trust it. We don't accept it so easily." He paused. "I'm sorry I wasn't there for you in Melbourne."

"Casey—"

"But if there's a next time, you get straight on your phone and ring Travis. If you can't get Travis, you ring me. You can't get me, you ring Jared, you can't get—"

"Casey." I held up a hand. "I've had this chat with Travis already. And Mitch. And Jared," I added. And even Evie's brother, Coby, who I didn't know all that well, not that he seemed bothered by that from the way he weighed in with his own chat.

"I know, but now it's my turn and this won't take long."

I nodded and my stomach flipped over when his blue eyes got a little fierce. I gulped down the last of my wine and set the empty glass on the coffee table.

"I know what Travis was like before you, and I know what he's like since you, and I like the latter." Casey's voice was firm as his eyes held mine. "He smiles like he means it, even after a long shitty day like he's dealing with today." Casey tapped a finger to his temple. "Up here, there's you at the back of all that, making his day not so shit because at the end of it, he gets you. You leave, he loses that and we lose him, and I don't like that. I already feel guilty enough getting him involved in what he does, but it doesn't come as easy for him to deal with because he hasn't lived it. So you understand me when I say don't ever think about leaving again."

I felt the wind go out of me, like his words were a verbal punch to the gut. The very idea it was me who had the ability to cancel out a shitty day for Travis made the argument for trying that much more compelling.

I nodded towards the television. "We're missing the movie."

His lips curled upwards and he saluted me with his beer.

We both turned towards the television and watched *The Fast and the Furious* play out on the screen.

"Paul Walker's hot," I blurted out. "He reminds me of Henry."

"So you think Henry's hot?"

"Well I'm not blind," I mumbled under my breath.

Casey smirked, his eyes telling me he heard my words.

"Oh shush," I muttered and slapped his shoulder.

His eyes sobered. "I like having you here, Quinn."

"You do?"

"Yeah." He cleared his throat. "I had a brother but I never had a sister."

Warmth flooded through me because when I was young, I would lay in my bed at night and pray to God to send me a brother—a big one, with lots of muscle that would strike fear in my stepfather's eyes just by looking at him. The older I got, the more I began to realise that prayers weren't going to get me anywhere. Drifting back to the present, my mind wrapped itself around Casey's words and my heart stuttered. "Wait. You *had* a brother?"

He nodded towards the television. "We're missing the movie."

Screw the movie and talk to me, I wanted to say, but sharing was never easy and Casey looked tired. Instead, I reached out and took his hand in mine. He glanced over at me and gave it a squeeze. I wasn't reassured because at the end of a shitty day, who did Casey have?

Chapter Nineteen

Sufficiently pruned from a long glorious shower, I hopped out with a blissful sigh and towelled myself off. The luxury of bathroom hogging didn't exist at the duplex, and after living on my own for so long, it had been a shocking adjustment. Henry lived in the shower. He was a no-holds-barred-I-don't-care-if-you're-a-girl-I'm-gonna-knock-you-down-to-get-to-the-shower-first. Mac spent hours taking long, hot baths to relieve the daily stress that was her life. Here at the loft the bathroom was my oyster, and I took full advantage.

I slipped on a robe and trailed steam on my exit. Casey was on the computer in the study nook by the dining table, and Travis was out dealing with the job that took his attention last night. He'd slipped in during the night, his weight depressing the bed and his warm hands sliding up my bare legs. When his mouth found its way between my thighs I woke slowly drowning in pleasure. His touch had been different to his usual relentless intensity. It had been slow and loving, and he held me close after, my face pressed against his neck until I fell asleep.

"I won't be long," I yelled at Casey in my rush back to the bedroom.

"Take your time," he called back.

That was good because I needed to get ready for Evie's birthday party, and when I said I wouldn't be long, I lied. In my defence I didn't really know any woman who said they would only be a minute and actually followed through.

An hour later I finally emerged from the bedroom in a long, backless dress in deep rose. My hair was pinned at the nape of my neck and glittery chandelier earrings adorned my ears.

When Casey emerged after showering and ready to walk out the door in five simple minutes *and* looking like a GQ model, I thought it was a little unfair.

"Don't blame me," Casey said, tucking in his wallet and picking up keys when I complained. "You women are the ones who insist on…" He turned around and trailed off.

"Insist on what?" I asked, picking up my clutch, colour-coded folder, iPad, and bag of last minute party supplies.

"Well I was gonna say insist on torturing yourselves with all those hair devices and whatever, but maybe it's more a case of torturing us."

His eyes trailed down the excessive amount of skin on display where the back of my dress cut low. I was nervous about how daring it was, but I knew Travis would like it.

My phone rang so I put down my folder, iPad, and bag and rummaged through my clutch for the phone. Clutches were really devil bags in disguise. Everything was so jam-packed inside it I couldn't get to my phone.

By the time I yanked it out, it stopped ringing. A second later, Casey's phone rang. He handed it to me wordlessly. I looked at him and then at the phone.

"You better answer it," he warned.

I grabbed it from his outstretched hand.

"Hello?"

"Quinn. Next time answer your damn phone," Travis said irritably.

"I beg your pardon?" I said, giving him time to think about what he just said and consider revising it.

"Your phone. Answer it," he repeated.

It was tempting to hang up on him in the interests of throwing that rudeness back in his face. "You know when you speak to me like that it makes me not want to answer it in the future."

"Quinn—"

"I've spent all day holed up in your godforsaken loft…" It wasn't really godforsaken. I actually loved being there, and I *had* made a minor escape to go shopping with Casey for my dress, but he didn't need to know that. "…trying to deal with the final preparations for Evie's party from afar, and I haven't heard from you once. The minute we make a move for the door and I have an armload full of crap is the moment you ring."

"Quinn—"

"No, Travis. The past three weeks I've been doing everything you asked. Is this how it's going to be? Because Casey's taking me to this party and when it's over, *he* can take me home."

Casey raised a brow.

"Drop me off," I added. "At home. My home."

Silence.

I cleared my throat, wondering if Travis was still on the line.

"I was worried about you," Travis said softly.

I flinched because the sweet words had more of an impact than his angry ones.

"Every second your phone rings and you don't answer, I imagine all sorts of scenarios. None of them good. I saw the evidence of what David is capable of, and with shit going on right now, I need to know I can get hold of you and that you're safe. I'm sorry I can't take you to the party. I'd rather be with you than stuck here."

"Where's *here*?"

"At the office. Just winding up a few small things and I'll be done. I'll duck home for a shower and meet you there, then you're coming home with me," he added firmly.

"Okay," I replied, surprised at the ease of my agreement.

It's because you're happy, Quinn.

I closed my eyes and took a deep breath. I wasn't happy, but I was almost happy. So much so I could taste it on the tip of my tongue.

"So…you're all dressed and ready to go, huh?"

"Uh huh."

"What are you wearing?" His voice turned husky.

"A long silk dress."

"Yeah?" he murmured. "What colour is it, sweetheart?"

"It's deep rose. And backless," I added.

"So I get to see every inch of your creamy skin all the way to your ass?" Travis exhaled loudly. "I'm imagining tracing every inch of it right now with my tongue."

I moaned. "Trav—"

The phone was snatched from my hand by an annoyed looking Casey.

"Travis," he spoke into the phone impatiently. "We're on our way out the door, unless you want me to take over with Quinn where you just left off?"

I laughed and fiddled with the strap of my clutch as I heard him end the conversation.

Soon after, we arrived at the Florence Bar, and Carol and I delved into final preparations with Casey glued to my side.

"Wow, look at you, Quinn, you belong at the Oscars!" I turned from talking to Vince at the bar to see Mac bearing down in her usual fashion.

Dressed in a shimmery floor length gold number, she said hello to Casey and Vince before sweeping her gaze around the private function area.

"Vintage glamour. How did you manage this without me knowing?"

I snorted. "I can be sneaky." She raised a brow, obviously remembering the suitcase incident. "Sometimes," I added. "But Evie almost caught Jared and I talking about it. Don't ask, but Evie now thinks the upcoming Jettison Records party is fancy dress."

Mac shouted with laughter. "Oh this is too good!"

She called Henry over and when he got close she told him, and then they were both standing there gasping for air.

"You're gonna help her pick her costume out, right, Mac?" Henry asked.

Casey shook his head at both of them as Henry gave a brief wave to Vince and asked for a beer. "You three are like an episode of *Gossip Girl*."

Vince placed a wine for me and a beer for Henry on the bar while Mac gaped. "You watch *Gossip Girl*?"

Casey narrowed his eyes on her.

"I was stuck in the loft all day," I offered. "Travis was out on a job. We…" Casey turned those eyes on me. "*I* had a *Gossip Girl* marathon." Henry and Mac were watching me. "Then we…" I glanced at Casey "…then *I* dragged Casey shopping so I could get a dress and shoes. And earrings," I added.

"Wow." Mac grinned. "Sounds like you had a busy day playing big sister, Casey." Henry laughed as Casey handed me my wine. "Tim'll be pissed he wasn't there for that. I'd avoid him tonight if I were you. In fact, I see him heading this way right now. Can you see your life flashing before your eyes?"

"Thanks for that heads up, Mac," Casey muttered while everyone laughed. He grabbed hold of my elbow and muscled me away from the group of people forming around us.

I leaned in closer to be heard. "Am I ruining your badass reputation, Casey?"

"I can handle it," he said, eyes carefully scanning the crowd.

I was quite certain Casey could handle just about anything. "How about I get you a drink?" I started back for the bar.

He grabbed my forearm and hauled me back to his side. "No. Not while I'm looking after you without Travis here. Later."

I didn't mind. I wasn't exactly the expert at working a crowd. Relieved, I stood by Casey as people came over to chat to us. Mac and Carol worked the room for me, and Casey pointed out who was who as I sipped at my wine.

"How the hell do you know all these people?"

"He doesn't. Jared gave us the guest list," came the voice behind me.

I jolted when a hand touched the small of my back. Lips brushed my ear. "You're not gonna tip your wine over me again are you?"

"You made it," I murmured with pleasure, and holding tight to my glass, spun around to face Travis. My body flushed as I took in his navy dress pants and matching jacket. His collared shirt wasn't buttoned at the neck, and my eyes rested where his blood pulsed visibly. "Not this time."

"Pity. I kinda liked how our night ended up the last time you did that." He trailed his fingers lightly down the naked skin of my back to where it dipped a little dangerously low.

"So..." I cleared my throat and aimed for safer conversation. "Jared gave you the guest list? I thought the party was a surprise."

"It is."

"So you know?"

"Know what?"

"About the...thing."

"What thing?"

I pressed my lips together. "Oh. Nothing."

Travis raised a brow at me.

"Really," I insisted, averting my eyes and fiddling with the backing of my earring. "There's no thing."

Casey nodded at Travis. "There's definitely a thing. Jared rang Quinn at least five times today."

I frowned at Casey. "How do you know how many times he rang me?" I faced Travis. "It's a surprise."

"What's a surprise?"

"Ouch." I winced when my earring backing jammed in with force.

"Here." Travis handed his drink to Casey and swatted my hand from my ear. "I'll fix it." He turned me so he had my back, and he started fiddling with the clasp of my earring. "What did you do to it?"

"If I knew, I could fix it, couldn't I? I can't tell you."

"Tell me what?"

"About the surprise. Then it's not a surprise anymore."

I felt the backing of my earring loosen and I sighed. "Thanks."

Casey handed Travis back his drink and left us alone to go and chat with Mitch and Coby.

"You mean about Jared proposing to Evie?" said Travis.

My eyes widened. "You know?"

He ignored my question and ran his eyes over me, making sure to take his time. "I need an excuse to drag you from this party, take you home, and fuck you until neither of us can move for a week. You sure about not tossing that drink at me?"

"I…" That sounded like a really good plan. I actually found myself eyeing my glass with consideration. "Your brother would kill me if I ditched this party and left it all in his hands."

Travis ducked his head and nibbled lightly on my bottom lip. "Let him try," he said against my lips before pulling away. "I can take him."

Carol approached me from the right. "Caterer crisis," she advised. I made a grab for my colour-coded folder and clutched it to my chest. "Excuse us," she said to Travis.

Travis slipped his hand in mine and laced our fingers together, not letting me budge.

"He knows," I told Carol.

She eyed me cautiously. "Knows… what?"

"About the proposal."

"Oh. Well, no caterer crisis then. It's a Jared crisis."

Following Carol, we detoured the kitchens until we reached the back room and a pacing Jared. He looked similar to Travis in a dark suit, but whereas Travis was relaxed and smiling, Jared's face was pinched in fear. Travis leaned up against the doorjamb and folded his arms while Jared ceased his pacing at our arrival.

He ignored Travis. "Thank God you're here. I need to get this over with. Right now."

My eyes widened as he resumed his back and forth motion. "You can't!"

He stopped his pacing again and looked at me, eyes rounded with panic. "I can't? Why not?"

I bit down on my cheeks to hold back the laughter. "Well, because Evie isn't here yet."

"Right. I knew that." Jared cleared his throat and resumed pacing. "That's good. I need a few minutes to-to..." He took a deep breath and exhaled slowly. "God. I thought I'd be so much cooler than this."

Jared's shoulders were broad, his biceps flexed under his jacket as he clenched his hands together in a fist, yet the vulnerability rolled off him in waves.

Not sure what else to do, I grabbed at his arm to stop his pacing. I wasn't really the mother hen type and found myself suddenly floundering in the new found role. "Well..." I licked my lips. "I guess you don't need to be cool, just...be yourself." I eyed Travis warningly. "Right, Travis?"

Travis nodded. "Absolutely." The firm assurance warred with the smile he was visibly fighting.

"You're not Superman after all," I added.

"I am." Jared pointed at me. "My nerves are hardcore fucking steel." He resumed his pacing. "Except when it comes to Evie," he muttered. "Then I turn into a giant douchebag. I can't help it. Being with Evie is like being on a roller coaster ride that I don't want to ever get off." He stopped and looked at me. I stared back, thinking that maybe he'd gone a little around the bend. "What the fuck am I talking about?"

"That's a good question. Maybe I should go get you a drink."

I made to leave when once again my arm was grabbed, and I was hauled to Travis's side.

"I don't want a drink. I don't want her thinking I needed it to get through asking her to marry me."

"Okay," I agreed.

Jared stared at me a moment. "Maybe just a beer. That won't hurt. Right?"

Travis slid his arm from around me. "I'll go get you a beer," he offered and with a soft kiss at my temple, he was gone.

"So you and Travis, huh?" Jared watched him go then turned back to me. "I know we haven't really had a chance to talk—"

"We had our chat the other week," I told him. "I'm all out of chats right now. If I had a dollar for all the chats I've had these past three weeks, I could retire. I could buy a boat and spend my days drinking champagne and cruising the harbour."

"Quinn, stop." My breath caught at the anger in his tone, and he grabbed both of my hands in his. Then he paused. "Wait. You wanna buy a boat?"

"Well, not really. I've never thought about it. Doesn't everyone buy a boat when they're rich?"

"Who's everyone? Jesus. Just…never mind." Jared frowned at me. "You think about running again, don't."

"I got your sister involved. She could've been hurt. You should be mad at me. All of you should be pissed as hell."

"She handled herself pretty well, and so did you."

Jared looked over my shoulder and saw Travis returning with his drink. He let go of my hand and took a step back, his green eyes changing instantly from fierce to teasing. "Anyway, welcome to the family, Quinn. Mac's always been the runt of the litter, but that crown passes to you now."

"Thanks for the talk." I folded my arms, a little irritated at having to listen to another lecture and then getting called a runt on top of all that. "Just remember, I did all this for you." I waved my hand around, my attempt at encompassing the whole venue. My eyes narrowed. "You owe me."

"Interesting," he murmured.

"What is?"

"Well when the crown passes, apparently so does the attitude."

I gasped. "You…"

He cocked a brow. "I…"

I let out a weak laugh. "Oh my God, you're right."

"Shut your mouth, Quinn. Rule number one of surviving the Valentine family, and you can consider this little piece of advice payback for the party, never and when I say never, I mean *never*, concede defeat. You do that, you'll get walked on. And no Valentine gets walked on. *Ever.*"

"But…I'm not a Valentine."

Travis reached my side and handed the beer to Jared.

Jared looked at Travis and then at me. "Yes you are." I watched in amazement as he gulped down half the glass in one go. Then the hand holding his glass pointed at me. "There's no escape for you now."

"No escape from what?" Travis asked, taking my now empty wine glass and replacing it with a full one.

Jared winked at me. "From planning all the Valentine birthday parties in the future of course, seeing how she's done such an amazing job tonight."

Rumour on the street according to Evie when she took me aside later that night was that Jenna had a dream. As the sharp and all-knowing mother of the Valentine clan, I really liked her, but her dreams didn't bode well for me. They included healthy, bouncing grandbabies and lots of them. That was off the table for me. If Travis and I remained together, it was off the table for the both of us.

I rubbed at my chest.

The thought of Travis never having his own babies gave me indigestion.

Travis looked down at my wince. "Okay?"

"Indigestion," I replied, moving my glance from Jared climbing the stage to look up at him.

"Can I get you something?" His gaze softened as he smiled down at me. He'd make a great dad. Of that I was sure.

Crap, were those tears lurking in the back of my eyes?

I blinked them away, hearing everyone clap after Jared said something. My hands clapped numbly.

Standing on the other side of Travis and Jenna was his dad, Steve. Steve had his arm around Jenna, forming a strong family unit.

"Thanks everyone for coming tonight and sharing Evie's birthday with us."

I blinked again and focused on Jared as the crowd around us clapped wildly, all eyes turning to Evie when the spotlight hit where she was standing. She gave a bright smile and waved her glass in a jaunty salute.

I looked around the entire room, suddenly breathless.

"No Valentine gets walked on. Ever."

"But I'm not a Valentine."

"Yes you are."

"Travis?"

He looked down at me, concern in his eyes. "Sweetheart?"

"I think I need some fresh air."

In a matter of moments I was out the back of the bar and sucking in lungfuls of it. I wish I could say it was fresh, but it was the back of the bar. The air was cool at least, soothing the embarrassment burning my cheeks from freaking out.

Travis looked down into my gasping face. "What's wrong?"

"Nothing," I puffed and waved airily, certain I was about to vomit. "I'm just...having a moment."

"Talk to me, Quinn."

"Family," I blurted out under the pressure of his burning eyes. "I've never had one. Not really. It's a bit overwhelming."

"Sweetheart, our family is a bit much for anyone. It's not just you."

Travis reached out and tucked my hand in his, and the nausea took a back seat to his touch.

I cleared my throat. "I need to ask you something, and I need you to be honest with me. A hundred, no...two hundred percent honest with me."

His eyes searched my face. I had no idea what he could see besides my red cheeks, the fear in my eyes maybe, because what if he wasn't okay with what I was about to ask?

Travis nodded, patient, a little cautious.

"If you're asking me to try, for us, then I figure that means you want us to have a future." I looked down at my hands and forced the words out. "But you know I can't give you a family. What I need to know is if you're okay with that."

"Quinn—"

"Travis," I cut him off as I looked up, focusing somewhere over his shoulder. "Maybe you should take some time to think about it. Not just answer based on how you feel right now. What about in five years, when your brothers and Mac are all having babies. All of a sudden, it's nappies and cute baby talk. Then all they're talking about is how little Dean is doing with potty training, or how little Juliet got an A on her spelling bee. Years later, their weekends are all caught up in taking their kids to soccer or netball and dealing with kids' parties and raging sleepovers. Then it's teaching them how to drive, glaring down potential boyfriends for your daughter, or seeing them graduate from university. You would be watching all of that happen to everyone close to you. What if one day you resent me for not giving that to you. For having to stand on the sidelines and watch it happen to everyone else...but you."

Saying that out loud sounded so much worse than how it sounded it my head. It wasn't indigestion. It was goddamn agony.

"How can I deal with being the one that couldn't give that to you?"

My chest burned as I tried not to look at Travis. Maybe I was having a heart attack.

He stepped forward, right in my space, until his face was all I could see. "Lucky for you I'm going to ignore the fact you think I'd only be with you for what I could get from you. Why does this have to be so hard?"

"I...what?"

"If one day we wanted kids together, why can't we just adopt? Or be foster parents? There are so many beautiful children out there just thrown away. Why can't we be the ones to love them? Give them parents, grandparents, cousins, aunts and uncles, friends."

Foster kids? The very thought had the next breath I sucked in lodge tight in my lungs until I thought I'd pass out.

"Quinn?"

"Huh?" His voice sounded far away because suddenly I'd been shown a way to give to someone else what had been taken from me, and that was huge. *Huge.*

Travis said something else but I didn't catch it. Instead I said, "You...you want that?"

Even I could hear the wonder in my voice.

Travis tilted my chin until his eyes held mine.

"I would love that. There's only one thing I love more than the idea of doing that with you."

Silence fell as a cool wind gusted through, ruffling my hair around my face. I could hear the tinny noise of music coming from inside and the tinkle of glassware and laughter going on around us.

"You," he said.

"Me?" I tried to say. I felt my mouth move, but I didn't hear anything come out.

"I love you."

Travis reached out and squeezed my hand, and for some reason he may well have just moved heaven and earth. I wasn't whole, I wasn't sure I ever would be, but Travis loving me made me realise that no one ever really was. If we were, how did it explain the need for someone to fill us with their love?

"Perfect is for people who don't know how to be real, and I don't want any of that. I want you."

I swallowed, feeling tears spill over. Travis was the peace I'd been struggling to find since as long as I could remember.

"Travis."

He slid his hand around my neck and pulled me in. His lips touched my forehead for a brief moment before he pulled back. "Sweetheart, I promise, soon David will be a memory and then we'll have time for us."

I wiped at the tears on my face. Travis swatted my hands away and tilted my head as he took over. "It's not a party without a few tears," he offered.

"Well." I chuckled. "Glad I could help out."

"Just don't start throwing chairs," he joked.

I straightened my shoulders because finally I was finding my place. Quinn. The survivor. Jesus. I sounded like a television show.

"I could totally Jackie Chan your ass."

His eyes crinkled. "Oh you could, could you?"

My eyes narrowed at his patronising tone. I bit down on my lip enticingly and lowered my lids. "Uh huh. When you least suspect it, I'll have you laid out flat and begging for mercy."

Chapter Twenty

The next morning I was in the kitchen making a cooked breakfast when the knock at the door of the duplex came. It was Sunday and even with the sun already high in the sky, everyone was still bunkered down in bed.

Not for much longer, I thought as I filled the frypan with bacon and the scent overtook the kitchen. All I'd done was remove the packet from the fridge, and already Peter and Rufus were banging at the back door, frantic to get inside. Rufus was letting out intermittent powerful barks amidst Peter's desperate yips, both of them busy informing me they were famished from the morning walk Travis and I took them on.

I peered out the blinds. Seeing Casey standing there, I swung the door wide. "Casey! How did you know I'd just put breakfast on?"

He shrugged. "I know everything."

I rolled my eyes and he grinned, stepping inside and following me back into the kitchen.

Travis came down the stairs dressed in a T-shirt and jeans, tying his wet hair back after his shower. My heart swelled as I turned back to the kitchen counter and started removing eggs from the carton.

"Did you get my message?" I heard Casey ask Travis.

"Yeah," he replied unhappily.

I tuned out as they spoke, busying myself with putting bread in the toaster and getting mugs down from the top cupboard.

"Oh, Quinn? Did you know your car's leaking oil on the drive?"

I spun around. "What?"

"Your car. Leaking oil," Casey told me.

My eyes narrowed and I balled up the tea towel and tossed it on the counter. "That horrible mean bitch," I muttered angrily and started for the front door.

Travis snatched my wrist.

I gave him a look. "Travis. I won't go further than the driveway."

"Don't care if it's the front door or the goddamn moon. I'll go move your car onto the street and then I'll have a look at it. Probably just needs a new oil filter or something."

He snagged the keys off the hook by the front door.

"Thanks, Travis!" I called out.

Travis rolled his eyes. "I'm buying you a new car."

"What?"

"You heard me."

"I know, but I was giving you a chance to take your words back. You can't buy me a car."

He waved his hand in an "I can't hear you" gesture and pulled the door shut behind him as the toast popped.

I looked at Casey. "He wouldn't really, would he? Buy me a new car?"

"We are talking about that piece of yellow scrap metal out there currently falling to pieces on the front drive?"

I sighed. "Yes."

He shrugged and then grinned. "If someone said they were buying me a new car when I owned that, I wouldn't complain. You know he lo—" He halted his words.

"Loves me?" I put down the butter knife and leaned up against the kitchen bench. "I know," I said softly, feeling an idiotic smile creep over my face.

"Well that's what you do for the people you love. You look out for them. Anyway, I'm glad he told you. I know he was worried about the whole assignment thing but I told him once he explained—"

"Wait…what? What assignment thing?"

Travis walked in the door and hung up the keys. He smiled at me. "You're right, Quinn. Your car does hate you. Looks like it's the rear seal. That's gonna cost a stupid amount of money to fix because the engine will have to be removed to be able to replace it."

That sounded bad. Really bad. He was smiling because it was just another reason for me to get rid of her and get something new and safe, but all that was beside the point.

"What assignment is Casey talking about, Travis?"

Travis froze, his eyes steady, the green in them dark as he stared at me. Something didn't feel right, and I opened my mouth but nothing seemed willing to come out. My chest was starting to rise and fall a little faster in the silence. The fact that Travis remained motionless only escalated the feeling of unease.

"Travis." My eyes pleaded with him to talk to me. "What assignment?"

Casey folded his arms and looked down at his feet. Travis shifted his eyes between the two of us.

"You."

"Me?" I whispered, not understanding the hard edge in his voice.

He gave a single nod.

"What about me?"

"You're our assignment."

"You...you mean what, bodyguard duty since the whole Melbourne incident?"

Travis rolled his shoulders. The gesture was a nervous one that set my stomach churning. He lifted his chin and met my eyes. "No. Since the beginning."

The world faded around me, blocking out everything but the guarded expression in his face. I opened my mouth but I couldn't seem to form the next question.

"The AFP hired us to watch you. They've had feds on the inside of a crime group they've been trying to bring down for well over a year.

These are the people that David is caught up with. When the AFP heard he was due out of prison, they assigned our firm to you."

Casey cursed softly but I ignored it because my entire focus was on what Travis was telling me.

"Who…who is the AFP?"

"The Australian Federal Police."

"The entire time you've been with me is because I've been an assignment?" I couldn't breathe. What I had with Travis wasn't real. His entire reason for being with me was a… a *paid obligation*. A job. A fucking *duty*. I licked my suddenly dry lips.

"To what, keep me safe?" My heart pounded as I tried to process what I'd been told. "All this time you knew I was in danger, and you didn't say a word?"

"No," Travis began and the hand that rubbed at his brow shook a little. "Not that…"

"Then wh…" Oh my God. My stomach turned over. "You weren't assigned to keep me safe at all. Your job was to get information. You thought I was involved," I said accusingly.

I should've known.

I really was stupid and just like Beth said, my life really was fucked. She'd known it all along, but something inside of me that I'd squashed for so long had rebelled against the painful words. I'd been battling so hard to let go of my past. Then Travis had asked me to try. He had touched me so tenderly that I ached from it, and asked me to *try*. Yet all this time, not just Travis, but all of them, had suspected me of being involved, had been sitting back and waiting for what, me to give them an in? Prove myself as one of the bad guys? The thought was utterly ridiculous, and I might not have had many friends, but I knew what friendship was and this wasn't it.

"Quinn, it's not like that."

Travis took a step forward, walking further into the house, and I took a step back. I barely noticed Mac and Henry both stumbling down the stairs.

"I might have kept things from you because I was scared of people I cared about getting hurt," I told him, "but you lied to me. You sat there and looked right in my eyes when I told you I was scared, and you asked me to try. And I was so stupid, because I did. I tried," I choked out. I blinked back burning tears because damned if I was going to let him see me cry. "But what was the point? Why would you ask that of me?"

"Quinn," he whispered.

I could feel everyone's eyes on me, and I fought against all the instincts that were telling me to run. Instead, I straightened my back and lifted my chin.

"I didn't want to hurt you. If we hadn't taken on the assignment, then it would have been someone else that—"

"Bullshit!" I yelled, balling my fists, because if he thought this wasn't hurting me then he was a right fucking idiot.

He reached out a hand towards me, and I swatted it away. "Don't touch me. I don't need your excuses."

"I didn't trust anyone else with the assignment, dammit."

I shook my head when he opened his mouth to say more. "So tell me what it is I'm caught up in. What is this AFP or whatever, trying to bring down?"

"Drugs and human trafficking."

My head tilted back as I choked on a laugh of disbelief. "And you thought I would be involved in that? Poor little girl from the wrong side of the tracks, beat up by her stepdad half her life until she's so damaged no one will ever want her. I'm just trash, right? The daughter that got thrown away and tried to take something back for herself. So what part was I involved in?" Some part of me was screaming at me to shut up, but the anger was spewing out and I couldn't stop. "Was I handling the paperwork and making the bank deposits for the big bad crime lord? Or was I on the other side of the desk prostituting myself for the—"

"Quinn!" Travis barked. The vein in his neck pulsed angrily.

"You and I were a lie. All this…" I swept out a hand to indicate the duplex and everyone currently standing in it watching me break apart "…was nothing but proof of how little I belong in a world like yours."

Travis shook his head, his eyes pleading. "We weren't a lie, Quinn."

"Don't." Travis had a way with words, somehow manipulating them to always sound like the truth and something I could believe in.

My heart squeezed painfully.

"Quinn. Look at me."

I wanted to but I didn't trust myself.

God. That night at the bar when I'd spilled my drink all down his shirt, it must have been all he could do not to laugh at how easy I'd made the assignment for him.

My eyes sought out Henry. His lips parted in shock, then Mac, her hand at her throat, and Casey, who just the other night had me believing my wish for a big brother might finally have come true.

"Quinn, please," Travis pleaded, his voice hoarse. "Look at me."

I didn't need to look at him to know what he was feeling because the anguish was clear in his voice. I hated that I took satisfaction in hearing his pain.

"I can't."

Because I don't see you. You're not my Travis. You're someone else. I don't want to look at you and see a stranger.

Mac reached out for me, and I took another step back, my eyes focusing on her and her alone. "Mac…" I swallowed. "I quit."

"You can't quit. Travis!" she yelled. "So help me God, you better fix this."

"No!" I blurted out. My eyes found Travis and I flinched. There was no colour in his face. "I don't want *this* fixed. I just want to leave."

I backed towards the door.

Travis took a step towards me. "It's not safe. You can't go out there."

The air left my lungs in a huff of laughter, and I turned and kicked the side table next to the couch, sending it clattering across the floor. "I've never been safe!" I shouted through tears.

I stalked for the door and threw it open. Looking over my shoulder I saw Casey holding Travis back from coming after me. "No, Travis. You don't get it. What it's like for people like us to have trust shattered like that."

I shook my head because in that moment that was how it felt. There were people like me and there were people like him and never should the two mix.

I made it out the front door and to the side of the house before I had to lean against the weatherboard for support. I'd never seen Travis so pale or his hands shake like that. I'd never heard an ache in his voice like it had been just before.

The front door opened and I closed my eyes, but the voice calling my name was Casey, not Travis. I dug my fingers into the pocket of my jeans and hurriedly yanked my car keys out. The only person I wanted to wrap their arms around me until it hurt to breathe was the one who'd just broken my goddamn heart.

"Quinn!"

I ignored Casey and unlocked the car door, sliding inside and jamming the key into Suzi-Q's ignition with trembling fingers.

The passenger door swung open, and Casey jolted hard into the seat. The agony must have been clear in my eyes because he glanced away and said softly, "It's okay, Quinn. Just drive."

We were halfway down the street before I could let a breath out of my lungs. I felt Casey glance my way, but I kept my eyes on the road. He must have understood my need for quiet because he didn't speak, allowing me to focus on calming the wild rage of emotion.

I pulled into a park by the beach and without acknowledging Casey, I dodged cars, making my way across the road to the rail that looked down a rock shelf and onto the beach. Spying a public seat, I sat down.

When Casey sat down next to me, I sighed.

"I just want to be alone."

He rested his elbows on his knees. "I know. I'm sorry."

"It's so much better being alone."

"Better or easier?"

The breeze fluttered over me, and I hugged my arms around myself. My eyes remained trained on the horizon. The waves were choppy, the beach quiet. "Easier."

"You know you mean more to him, to all of us, than just an assignment, right?"

"I don't know what to think. I keep getting the urge to run. Always, there's the urge to run, but I don't know what I'm running from. David? The bad guys? Travis? Myself? Who are the bad guys anyway?"

"I'll let Travis explain it to you."

"I don't want—" The rest of my words choked in my throat because suddenly Travis was standing in front of me. "How did you know I was here?" My eyes turned to the traitor sitting next to me.

Casey shrugged under the full force of the glare I aimed his way.

"Sorry, Quinn." He stood up and slammed a hand on Travis's chest and shaking his head, growled, "You and Jared. Christ. Tired of it. I'll be across the road getting a coffee."

Travis sat down in his place.

I didn't say anything.

He didn't say anything.

It felt like a bloody standoff, and I started to fidget because I was fighting the urge to curl into him and cry, and that just set off another wave of anger.

"Do I really know you, Travis?"

"If you're asking me that, then maybe you don't." His voice was low and wounded.

"Maybe you should start from the beginning," I said coldly.

"Okay," he agreed and rubbed his palms along his thighs. "The AFP approached us the day Mac hired you, and we met with them the next day."

227

I remembered back to the day when I'd barricaded myself in the toilet, so utterly embarrassed to find out that Travis was Mac's brother. When he walked out, talking on the phone, the relief had made me weak, but it was his phone conversation that pinged my memory.

"Can't today, Tim. Tell the AFP to set the meeting up for tomorrow morning, okay? Did they say what it was about?"

"So that night at the bar—"

"Had nothing to do with anything but you and me."

My chest loosened a little as I waited for him to continue.

"They've been building up a case against this group of traffickers for so long. They have agents so deep undercover with the Zampetti crime group that *no one* has a clue who they are. Jesus, Quinn, men, women, kids. *Kids.* They've got all their best investigators on this operation, so they had to outsource for every possible lead. The minute they pegged your connection to us was when they approached us. We didn't know anything about you, about the abuse. They told us David was in for assault, but they didn't say why. They just told us you were his stepdaughter and they wanted to know your level of involvement. But Quinn, we don't like to fly blind. We pulled up his records and found out it was you he assaulted, but the release date on the paperwork was wrong. It told us he was due out on early parole three weeks after he was actually released. I don't know who fucked up there, but if we had've known he was out, he wouldn't have gotten anywhere near you. It wasn't until after we told the AFP what happened that they released the photos of the assault and we found out how bad it really was. No one knew he'd been abusing you, but after seeing those photos, I don't know how anyone could not. Why didn't you tell anyone?"

I shrugged. "Who was I supposed to tell?"

"Fuck," Travis muttered and rested his elbows on his knees. "We managed to put some pieces together and found out that David was friends with someone called Angelo. Angelo got him involved in their international trafficking ring. He was helping transport victims, setting them up in housing. Turns out though that David has a bit of a gambling addiction and after borrowing huge amounts of money from some of the bigger players, he couldn't pay up because he ended up in prison."

"Oh God." I pressed my palms against my eyes. "Them coming after me for the money is my fault."

"Jesus fucking Christ, Quinn. It's David's fault. All of this fucking mess," he growled. "The reason we took the contract was because we *knew* without any doubt that you knew nothing about it. I've told you to trust your gut, and mine was telling me you had no idea about any of it. I didn't tell you about the assignment because I didn't want you thinking any of us doubted you for a single second. But also..." He swallowed and looked out at the ocean. "The AFP wanted to find a way to use you. Their information says David was the one that sent the Zampetti crime group your way to either get the money in cash, or get their use from you some other way. They went for the cash option first. Trafficking a local female isn't as easy for them as getting immigrants who don't know anyone and can barely speak English. When a local girl goes missing, there's more press and local police involvement. That's something they don't want to attract if they can help it, but the AFP were thinking that maybe if they used you, it might help them rack up more charges. The Zampetti drug and trafficking operation is so slick they're trying to get them on anything they can, and you were just another option."

"But no one from the police ever approached me."

"That's because I wouldn't let them. They're not using you, but that stunt in Melbourne only increased their aim to get you involved."

Jared stood there, phone in hand. "Mitch wants to talk to you. He's been in touch with Melbourne's AFP, and they're sending over a fed. They want to know what the fuck is happening with this assignment—"

Oh God. How could I not see?

"If I told you what they were asking of you, what would you have said?"

I looked down at my hands and thought hard. Getting David permanently out of my hair? Having a hand in helping save thousands of lives from the hands of traffickers—people suffering worse than what even I could comprehend. "I appreciate you keeping me safe, Travis, but there's a bigger picture, isn't there? I think it's my decision to make, and I would have agreed to do whatever I could to help," I said softly.

"No." He spun to face me and grabbed my hands from my lap. "No."

"Travis you can't—"

"No!" he shouted hoarsely. "Quinn, this isn't just about drugs. It's exploitation of the worst kind. Women forced into prostitution against their will. How could I let them get you caught up in that? I'm not seeing you suffer anymore. No more," he shouted.

"At the least I need to hear what they might have in mind, don't you think?"

"No, I don't think. No. Dammit." Travis tightened his grip as though scared of letting me go.

I focused my gaze on the waves, the dark blue of the ocean. The sun was bright, but not warm against the chill. The last time I'd been here with Travis was probably one of the best days I could ever remember living.

"When I was young I used to think I deserved it. The suffering. The pain David inflicted. These women, kids, taken by the traffickers...they're suffering too. Are they sold into this? Stolen? Putting up with the suffering because it's the only roof over their head they think they're going to get? I can relate to that. Remember when you told me that night that *if you weren't there to help those kids, who would?* How can I turn my back if I'm able to help in any way?"

Travis ran his eyes over my face and reached out to tuck a strand of hair behind my ear. The gesture was soft and loving. "Do you remember what you said back to me?"

"Dammit, Travis."

"Tell me what you said back."

I looked down at our linked hands. "You can't save everyone."

Travis nodded.

"But does that mean you stop trying?"

I took in the rigid line of his shoulders and the tension in his jaw and cleared my throat. "Can I...I need to think, Travis. I need to be alone."

He went to speak and I held up my hand. "Please."

Travis let go and stood, looking down at me, his eyes dark and wounded. I shielded my eyes from the glare of the sun behind him. "I know you're still angry, Quinn, and you can be for as long as you want, but it won't change what I feel for you. That was never a lie and because of that, I won't let you do this." He paused. "Two minutes, okay? Then I'm taking you home."

With that he was gone.

God.

What a fucking mess.

I pulled the car keys from my pocket.

Running again, Quinn?

I pushed up off the seat and started for the car.

Yeah, that figures. No backbone in you at all. It's pathetic that you can't face your fears.

My body froze in the act of opening the car door.

What do you fear the most?

Losing everything all over again, I answered the voice in my head.

And what are you losing by running away?

I closed my eyes.

Everything.

My chest ached with how much I loved Travis and the knowledge of how much he loved me. It was clear in his eyes yet I had doubted it. That must have hurt. How could I blame him for wanting to keep me safe? I had done the exact same thing.

I shut the car door and put the keys back in my pocket just as my arm was grabbed in a vice.

"You fucking bitch."

I turned, breathless. David was right in my face. He grabbed both my biceps with his hands and shook me hard. I winced, knowing it would leave bruises.

"We put a roof over your goddamn head and now you've got yourself a job and friends in high places, you can't repay what we gave you." David shoved me backwards, and I went down hard on the pavement.

"David. These people aren't good," I said, scrambling backwards and trying to regain my feet. "You can go to the police. Talk—"

He gripped my biceps again and yanked me to my feet, backhanding me with a loud crack. My vision dotted and I swallowed down the familiar nausea and bitter tang of blood. "Don't be stupid. If you can't give them the money, I'll just hand you over."

I turned, searching frantically for Travis and saw him across the road. Before I could call out, David kicked my feet out from underneath me and unable to brace myself in time, I went down hard on my stomach. My head slammed into the pavement with force. Dizzy, I lifted a hand to my head, feeling blood streaming down my face. I blinked and it pooled in my eye as my hand came away, red dripping from my fingers.

"*You're* stupid," I whispered without turning around. I licked the blood from my lips. "The police are only moments from taking down the entire Zampetti crime group. You're not immune. You'll go down too."

I forced a chuckle and grunted when David jammed his knee in my back, pinning me to the ground. I turned my head from the blurred vision of waves and faced the street.

"Travis," I whispered.

The click of a gun loading was loud in my ears and the cold press of metal in my neck sent chills twisting down my body.

Casey stepped out of the coffee shop door at the same time Travis turned to search for me.

I met his gaze, swallowing blood as fear swept across his face. He yelled my name as they both started to run.

I tried to push up off my hands, but my arms were pulled behind my body, and I cried out when something tore in my shoulder.

"Stay back," David screamed as they got closer. "I'll fucking shoot her, I swear it."

The cold metal pushed harder into my neck but Travis didn't stop running. He was fast. So fast he was on David before I could even blink. The crack of his fist in David's face was louder than the waves crashing in the ocean.

Casey reached my side and ran his hands over me frantically. "Jesus, Quinn."

I winced and whispered, "I'm fine. Go help Travis. Please."

He shook his head, yanking his phone from his back pocket.

Travis slammed David against my car, his eyes wild as rage engulfed his body. David grunted, his head cracking back before falling to the ground. Then Travis was on him, knuckles slamming into his face again, and again.

My head pounded and I moaned, trying to struggle up from the ground, crying out when white hot agony ripped through my shoulder.

"Stay down." Casey put a gentle hand to my chest as he spoke into his phone for an ambulance.

I struggled, moaning as the world tilted. I called out for Travis and in the split second he tilted his head to make sure I was okay, David grabbed at him and they were rolling and as daylight flickered out, a gunshot went off with a loud crack and my heart exploded with fear.

Chapter Twenty-One

I roused from unconsciousness to a hospital room and the blotchy tear-stained face of Lucy. My stomach pitched.

"Lucy," I croaked and swallowed. "You look like you've been crying."

"Rubbish," she replied angrily. "And ruin my beautiful face? You look like you've gone ten rounds with Mike Tyson and lost. I warned you that you were no Rocky."

I struggled to sit up when my stomach pitched again. She started to lean back when my arm snapped out and grabbed her with panic. "Travis?"

Her eyes filled with tears.

"Oh," I murmured and swallowed hard, but tears climbed my throat and spilled down my face before I could take another breath. I snatched my hand back. "No. Oh no."

My mind swam with the image of him laughing at me when we joined the other idiots swimming in the ice cold ocean. Travis had looked so beautiful in that moment, and I'd thought nothing could ever hurt him. Clinging to him in the water with his arms holding me tight against him, I'd thought he was infallible.

"Quinn," Lucy whispered.

"No," I shouted, holding stubbornly to the image of Travis brimming with life. "Shut up."

I swung my legs over the bed and screamed with pain, not knowing what hurt more, my body or my heart.

"Quinn, he's okay," Lucy shouted as I panted past the pain, feeling sweat pop along my brow.

A nurse dashed in as I sat on the edge of the bed. Her cardigan was flapping in her rush, her brow pinched with harried irritation. She picked up my chart from the end of the bed and without looking up, asked, "What's your pain level between one and ten, love?"

My eyes were stuck on Lucy. "You mean he's not...not..."

"No!"

"Then why—"

"Because he's—"

The nurse cut Lucy off. "I'm afraid you're going to have to leave the young lady to rest." She directed her stern gaze on me. "Now, Miss Salisbury, what is your pain level?"

I turned a glare on her. "A hundred." My eyes found Lucy again. "Luce?"

"He's been arrested," she told me.

"What?"

"Excuse me, miss," the nurse said determinedly to Lucy, "but you're going to have to come back."

"Arrested for what?" I asked breathlessly.

Lucy ignored the nurse and reached out to take my hand. She gave it a squeeze. "Honey. Travis shot David. He's been arrested for manslaughter. Casey rang to tell me you were here. He'd told me everything, about the assignment, the police handcuffing Travis and taking him away. Oh, Quinn." Her eyes were sad. "How could you believe he didn't love you?"

I stared at her waiting for the words to sink in. I licked my lips. "David's dead?"

She winced and I realised my nails were digging in to her hand.

"Lucy, that's...crazy. David was...Travis didn't mean... It was an accident!" I burst out, remembering their tussle with the gun. "Travis wouldn't have done it deliberately."

"Are you sure about that? If it were me I would have shot him myself." Her nostrils flared dangerously, and Rick walked in looking tired, his eyes red, as she said, "Have I told you how much I motherfucking love Travis? I'm glad David's dead. He's hurt you for the last time."

"But at what cost?" I whispered. For Travis to languish in prison for the rest of his life? "If I hadn't taken off this morning in an emotionally induced panic, this whole mess wouldn't have happened."

"Here." Lucy shoved a cup of water under my nose. "Have a sip."

"Fuck water." I smacked it out of her hand. "I need to get out of here."

The nurse bustled around my IV, and within moments I felt myself drifting, her capable hands tucking me back into bed. "What did you do?" I slurred in accusation.

"Eased your pain, love. I'll be back later."

"Rick," I whispered. He stood stoically against the wall, and I tilted my head to watch him step closer to my bed. His eyes were sad as they raked me over. I indicated for him to lean close and he bent right down.

"Listen to me carefully," I slurred. "Go...car...bring...dammit."

"I can hear you clear as day, Quinn," Lucy called out. "And we're not helping you bust out of here."

"Travis," I muttered.

Tears rolled down my cheeks that I wasn't able to wipe away. Rick reached out and wiped them with his thumbs. The touch was soft and a giggle bubbled out of me before I could swallow it.

"Oh shit," I sobbed.

"It's okay, sweetie," Rick said. "It's just the drugs. Get some rest."

"Mistake, Rick. Travis and David. Accident. I don't have time to be high, dammit," I growled.

"Yes. You do," Lucy snapped from over Rick's shoulder. "God. You fight at everything. Just this once will you bloody well be quiet and close your eyes."

"You can tell us what happened later, okay?" Rick said and patted my good shoulder.

"Okay," I lied. There wouldn't be time for telling later. I needed to get hold of the federal police and get Travis out.

I must have mumbled something because when Rick pulled back from my bed, Lucy snorted. "This isn't *Prison Break*, Quinn. Besides, it took them a whole season to bust out. What are you going to do?"

I ignored her and instead asked, "Where's Casey?"

I lost consciousness before anyone could reply.

Later that afternoon I woke groggy to a commotion at the door. It flew open loudly, swinging back and clicking into the doorstop behind it with a loud thunk.

"Mac, for God's sake," came Evie's exasperated voice. "Can you just try for a little less force next time?"

"Shut up, Sandwich," she snapped. "If you didn't decide you had to make a food stop on the way here, then I wouldn't have had to rush."

They both halted simultaneously when they saw my face. Tears filled Evie's eyes; anger narrowed Mac's to slits.

Evie came around one side of my bed, Mac around the other, and she put her bag down to take my hand in hers.

"What happened?" Mac barked.

"Mac! She's tired. Save the inquisition for when she's up for it." Evie turned back to face me and nudged a small packet onto my bed. "Here," she muttered. "I brought you a burger and chips. I've seen my fair share of shitty hospital food, so I figured you'd be hungry."

My stomach pitched terribly at the idea of food, but I didn't have the heart to tell her considering she'd made such an effort.

"Thanks," I said and nudged the packet a bit further down the bed. "You two don't know what happened?"

"No. So tell us. All I got was some vague message from Jared saying shit had gone down and you were okay but in the hospital."

"Travis has been arrested for manslaughter."

Mac's mouth fell open. "What?"

237

"David's dead."

I waited for the relief those words would give, but no matter how much I wanted to see him pay for his actions, it wasn't this way. "We need to get down to where Travis is being held." I swung my legs over the bed and bit down on my tongue to stop the whimper. "They said I could be released..." I lied "...so we really should get a move on to make sure this mess gets sorted out."

Evie gave me a doubtful look. "You don't look like they should be releasing you."

I wiped casually at the sweat on my brow. "Are you saying I look like shit?"

"Pretty much," Mac confirmed.

"Thanks a bunch," I snapped. The pain and fear for Travis was making me irritable, but Mac and Evie appeared to be taking it all in their stride. "Help me find my clothes. I hate feeling naked in these hospital gowns."

"You're a shitty liar, Quinn. What's the plan—bust you out of the hospital and then bust Travis out of prison? Seems too easy. What's the catch?" Evie asked.

"There's no catch," I replied. I just couldn't bear the thought of Travis being behind bars any longer than necessary. How could the police have arrested him? I didn't like to think shitty thoughts towards the police, but their actions were stupid. I couldn't understand how Casey, Jared, or Mitch hadn't sorted any of this mess out.

"The catch," Mac said, rummaging through the little cupboard on the left of my bed, "is that you have to retract your resignation. In fact, it wasn't really official and I didn't accept it. So once you're fully recuperated I want you back in the office." She pulled out a plastic bag of clothes.

Unfortunately they were the same clothes I was wearing earlier and covered with dirt and blood. Evie helped me dress while Mac went and collected a wheelchair. Soon after I was standing outside the busy hospital entrance with Mac while Evie went to get her car and bring it around. When a man came and stood beside me I thought nothing of it. The entrance was busy and it looked like quite a few people were loitering or waiting for their respective rides. That was until I felt something hard press into my side. The man leaned in a little and said softly, "Lose your friend. Now."

Without moving my head, my eyes shifted down and saw the gun. My heart hammered hard in my chest, and I closed my eyes.

Shit.

"Mac," I croaked and cleared my throat. "I've just realised I left my phone on the counter where we signed the release papers. Would you mind ducking in to get it for me?"

Mac rolled her eyes. "It's not like you to forget shit, Quinn. Stay put. I'll be right back," she called over her shoulder as she disappeared through the automatic doors.

They whooshed closed behind her as a black BMW slid to a halt in front of me. The driver got out, came around, and opened the back passenger door.

"Get in," the man beside me ordered quietly and nudged me forward.

I stepped towards the door and ducked my head. What greeted me was a shock. In my limited experience, which was based mainly on action movies, the bad guy was never attractive. His face usually featured an identifying scar or a tattoo across his knuckles that said MOM while hatred blazed from his evil eyes. Whatever it was, it was a screaming beacon that told you he was the bad guy—avoid this man at all costs! The man sitting in the back of this car was none of those. His hair was short and light brown, his suit sharp and fresh—right down to the gold monogrammed cuff links on his shirtsleeves.

He grinned, showcasing a dimple that would melt any woman's heart and winked at me with his light blue eyes. "Hop in, Quinn. I don't bite."

"Sure you don't," I muttered under my breath and slid inside the car.

No matter how friendly or how good looking he was, my stomach still rolled when the door slammed shut behind me.

The car accelerated smoothly out of the hospital zone and into traffic, stopping soon after at a red light. Being high on painkillers, the decision to take a leaping dive out of a moving vehicle might possibly be the best option in this scenario. My hand reached for the door handle as we began to accelerate, but no matter how many times I yanked on it, the damn thing was determined to see me fail.

The man chuckled before saying, "Put your seatbelt on."

"Fuck you." I folded my arms, not without a measure of pain. "Who are you anyway?"

"Nice of you to offer..." he looked me up and down "... but you look a little too sweet for my tastes. Now put your seatbelt on," he enunciated clearly. "If I have to tell you again, I promise you won't like the way I do it. I hate having to repeat myself."

My eyes narrowed but I slid the seatbelt carefully over my aching shoulder and fumbled awkwardly as I clicked it in place.

"Happy now?"

"I am, thank you. I have a vested interest in keeping you alive. It wouldn't do to see you harmed before we arrive at our destination."

"Who are you?" I ground out.

"No need to be rude, Miss Salisbury, it doesn't suit you, but I'll answer your question. My name is Luka Zampetti."

My eyes went wide. "You...you're..."

"Oh." Luka's eyes crinkled in pleasure. "You know of me then?"

"David was the one that sent the Zampetti crime group your way to either get the money in cash or get their use from you some other way. They went for the cash option first."

"I-I don't have any money."

"Quinn." He tutted. "You could have gotten the money if you tried hard enough, but as it turns out, I have another use for you."

"Quinn, this isn't just about drugs. It's exploitation of the worst kind. Women forced into prostitution."

I shivered in horror. "I won't... I won't do—"

"No, no, I wouldn't be so horrid as to subject you to that distastefulness, even though you would fetch a good bit of money. I leave all that with my father to deal with. No, Quinn, you're like a little diamond in the rough that has fallen into my lap. I have a much greater use for you than that." He waved his hand as though dismissing the subject. "You'll find it all out later. First I want to talk about this morning." He grinned and it was almost childlike in delight. "Did you like what I did for you?"

My brow furrowed. "What you did?"

"Wow, you're a bit slow, aren't you? Never mind. You *have* been in the hospital and a bit out of the loop I suppose. I got rid of David for you. The stupid bastard. Kept attacking you at every turn. So predictable. Once we realised who you were, we couldn't have him go off on one of his rages and accidentally kill you. You're far too important. So I had him shot. How bloody marvellous it was that your cowboy happened to be in the way. The police who arrived on scene were so daft they arrested him for it. Soon enough they'll work it out, but it got them out of my hair long enough to get to you, didn't it? Bloody Jamieson and Valentine getting their fingers into every pie in Sydney. It's not good for business."

I was completely lost. "You realised who I am? I don't understand?"

My phone vibrated from my back pocket and I froze, having forgotten it was there.

"Quinn, I really don't like repeating myself. As I said, you'll find it all out soon enough. Now hand over your phone."

"I have no idea what you're talking about."

The slap was hard and fast, and I cried out as my already pounding head copped another round of agony.

"Hand over your phone, Quinn."

I used my right arm to reach behind me, struggling to get to the back left pocket of my pants as tears smarted my eyes. The phone stopped ringing, starting again only moments later. I could only hope that if it was Travis and he was still locked up, he wasn't wasting his one phone call on me.

Luka snatched it from my hands, looking at the display before answering with a smile.

"Mr. Valentine."

I swallowed, wondering which Mr. Valentine it was.

The voice on the other end was loud and forceful, but I couldn't make out the words over the rumble of the car engine.

"You're speaking with Luka Zampetti."

"Fuck!" came the reply. *That* I heard.

"Such language you people have." He said *you people* as though we were lower class thugs. "Yes we have Quinn if that's what you were trying to ask me. We're absolutely delighted with her. She's so very pretty."

There was a pause while the voice on the other end spoke.

"What was that? You want to talk to her?" Luka shrugged. "Why not."

He held the phone out towards me, and I took it gingerly, my shoulder twinging at the casual movement. "Hello?"

"Quinn! Are you okay?" came the hoarse voice of Travis.

"Oh, Travis," I murmured, my heart pounding hard as I tried to sound calm. "You wasted your phone call."

"What?"

"Your one phone call," I repeated patiently.

"Quinn, Jesus. It was a misunderstanding. They let me go when they realised it wasn't me who shot David. Have they—"

I cut him off. "Are you okay?"

"I'm fine." He didn't sound fine. I could hear Casey in the background yelling. He didn't sound fine either. "Have they hurt you?"

"No," I lied. "I'm fine too."

"Hold tight, sweetheart. I'm coming for you. I promise." Hot tears filled my eyes because I knew Travis would be moving Heaven and

Earth to fill that promise. "Just…I need to know we're okay—you and me," he pleaded hoarsely. "I need to hear you say it."

The BMW purred along the streets, but the scenery was a blur. I didn't know where I was being taken or why I was so valuable to the Zampetti's. My future suddenly wasn't so certain.

"I'm sorry I didn't trust in us. That I didn't give you a chance to explain before I ran. Nothing we have is a lie," I whispered, knowing the love I'd seen in his eyes was clear long before he'd said the words. I was scared I'd never see that again, or tell him he was beautiful and strong and so damn relentless, and that he was my whole world. A tear spilled over and rolled down my cheek. "I love you."

"Oh, God, sweetheart," he choked out softly. My knuckles went white on the phone. "I love you so much."

"I…Travis—" I cried out when Luka took the phone and covered my mouth with my hand to smother the sob.

"Mr. Valentine," Luka said into the phone. "Quinn is going to prove very valuable to us, but we're going to be busy from here on in. I'd appreciate it if you didn't bother us again."

Luka depressed the button on the door and the window slid down. He casually tossed my phone out onto the road and slid the window back up. Travis had told me they could track me anywhere as long as I had my phone. I had just watched my last chance of seeing him again tossed out the window and my heart sank.

Feeling numb, we eventually pulled into the driveway of a suburban middle class house. Nice lawns, rendered brickwork painted beige, black wrought iron fence—completely nondescript—nothing that screamed evil-doers lived within.

Luka led me through the front door, down an entryway, towards an open style living, dining and kitchen area at the back. Our soft footfalls echoed through the open, empty space. With dusk coming on, it was eerie and cold.

There were no furnishings apart from two single high back chairs that sat facing each other and a solitary man. He was standing, facing out into the yard, lost in thought. He was tall, broad shouldered, with pale blond hair cut short and styled carefully. Hearing our steps, the man spun around. My knees buckled, and I reached out to grab hold of the chair as I sank down into it, my eyes unable to look away.

His eyes went wide as he looked at me, and the colour leached from his face.

"Luka," he rasped. "Who…"

Luka stepped further into the room, and standing to our right, he folded his arms. "Eric. I'd like you to meet Quinn Salisbury. Quinn, this is my right hand man, Eric Donovan."

Eric stumbled towards the chair opposite me and sank into it. We sat there facing each other like two mirror images. His hair was the same shade as mine, his brown eyes large in his face, his lips full and soft, his skin fair and smooth. Despite the obvious muscle and wide shoulders, he was pretty, his features feminine.

"I-I don't understand," I stuttered.

Eric sat reeling. "Beth," he whispered. "Beth Salisbury."

"That's my mother," I told him. I wanted to add that *mother* was a loose term, but under the circumstances, it didn't really seem the best time to start explaining her fetish for vodka and money.

"Oh my God," he moaned. The hands he rested on his thighs dug in until his knuckles turned white. "She told me she had an abortion. I didn't want her to do it, but we were so young and then she moved away. God, that was a lifetime ago."

"Y-you…you're my…" This was the second time today that my world had been flipped upside down, and I didn't think I was coping overly well. A hysterical giggle bubbled out of me that turned into a sob. I swallowed it with effort and forced my eyes from Eric to Luka. Luka was smirking at the both of us. "He's my father?"

I faced Eric. "You're my father?"

Eric reached out, his eyes on the butterfly tape on my forehead. I flinched backwards.

"Sorry," he mumbled. "Beth and I... She was my girlfriend back in high school. We were only together for three months but I... I dumped her." He swallowed and closed his eyes briefly before opening them again. "I didn't realise until after that the feelings she had for me were so much more. I-I think I broke her heart. We were only sixteen." His eyes pleaded for me to understand. "Young and stupid, that was me, but when she came to me and told me she was pregnant, I said I'd support her. She...she told me not to bother and she was getting rid of it. 'It' she called the baby. She sounded so cold and so determined that I believed her. She was only sixteen too, so I didn't feel like I had any right to force her to keep the baby. I went round to her place almost every night, but she wouldn't talk to me, and then one day she was gone. Just like that. I had no idea..." he trailed off, his eyes unfocused and lost. "How...how old are you?"

"Twenty-two," I whispered.

"I'm thirty-eight," he replied. It was hard to believe because he didn't look a day over thirty. In fact, he looked just like Luka with his carefully styled hair and clothes.

"Oh no," I moaned. I had a father but he was worse than David—obviously much higher up in the chain than David ever was.

I lifted from the chair. This time I truly felt my instincts to run were spot on.

"Not so fast."

Luka stepped up behind me, his hands coming down hard on my shoulders. "You see, Eric here has worked hard for me for so long. He's practically married to the job. So much so, he doesn't have a wife or kids of his own. When I stumbled across your photo, Quinn, it was obvious you were both related somehow. After a few well-placed questions to David, I had my answers. I can't tell you how delighted I was personally because that made you very valuable to us." Luka fixed his blue eyes on Eric. "Don't you think so... *Seth*?"

Eric closed his eyes and his lips muttered a soft curse.

"I-I don't understand?" I looked around when four men, all obviously armed, walked into the room and surrounded us in a distant circle. One of them stepped forward and placed both hands on Eric's shoulders.

"Quinn. Run," Eric yelled, struggling against the hold. *"Run!"*

Without hesitation, I bounded to my feet.

"Sit down," Luka growled.

I was halfway out of the room before he got in my way, backhanding me across the face. I fell to the floor, the room spinning as my stomach rolled.

"You bastard," Eric yelled.

"I'm not," Luka replied, dragging me to my feet. "I've been nothing but nice. I told Quinn I didn't like to repeat myself. How could it be my fault that she didn't listen when I told her to sit down?"

I was forced back into the chair, seeing with surprise that one of the men was now holding a gun to Eric's shoulder.

"Well now that everything's out in the open, Seth, I think you know what to expect next."

"But...I don't understand," I wheezed breathlessly.

"Your daughter's a bit slow," he said to Eric as though it was some sort of joke. Luka faced me. "You see Eric here, isn't really Eric. It's Seth. Agent Seth McKinnon of the Federal Police. Isn't that right, Seth?"

Eric... Seth remained silent, his jaw ticking.

"They have agents so deep undercover with the Zampetti's that no one has a clue who they are."

My mouth fell open. "You...you're the..."

Oh my God.

Seth was the undercover agent. And he was my *father.*

"Well anyway," Luka continued. "Seth is going to talk because we need to know what he knows. That's why you're so valuable, Quinn. You're going to get him to talk for us."

"H-how am I going to do that?"

Luka stepped behind me, replacing the armed man who shifted further to my right. He rested his hand on my shoulder and trailed his fingers softly across my collarbone until his hand reached my neck. Suddenly his fingers dug in. The strength of his hold was immense as he squeezed, and I struggled, fighting for breath as my fingers clawed desperately at his hand.

"Let her go," Seth yelled, struggling against the men who held him down.

"Look at that." Luka laughed throatily as he squeezed. "How quickly the protective daddy instincts kick in."

He let go and I wheezed, sucking in huge gulps of air as my eyes watered from the lack of oxygen.

Luka clicked his fingers and one of the men handed over a sheaf of papers wordlessly. Luka stepped from behind me, another armed man quickly taking his place, and dropped the papers in Seth's lap. Seth slid his eyes downwards, and he moaned as his eyes took the contents in.

"You remember David, Agent McKinnon? The man we had killed this morning? He was Quinn's stepfather. Do you like what he used to do to her? That's evidence of the wonderful childhood Quinn grew up in." I swallowed, pissed off the photos of my assault were doing the entire rounds of Sydney.

Seth hung his head. "I'm so sorry," he whispered, and even though his eyes were focused on the papers on his lap, his voice held a world of hurt.

"You should be," Luka told him. "If you want a chance to get to know your daughter, Agent McKinnon, then you're going to be busy telling us what we want to hear."

For the first time, Luka's voice was cold and harsh. As though his nice persona was shattering around him, revealing his true identity beneath the handsome face and slick clothes. He took the gun one of the men handed over and with his arm out straight, fired without hesitation. It was cold, calculated, and scary as hell.

I flinched and cried out, watching a bright red spot bloom on Seth's right shoulder. He was visibly fighting not to cry out in pain. His face was red, his eyes screwed shut as he panted hard. Seth tilted his head back, eyes focusing on the ceiling, biting down on his lip as he fought the scream that came from deep in his chest.

"This, Quinn..." Luka lifted the gun again and my heart hammered so hard in my chest I thought it would split wide open. He aimed it at my leg. "...is how we're going to get Agent McKinnon to talk."

Chapter Twenty-Two

TRAVIS

Earlier the same day...

There were only two things in my life I'd ever fought hard for.

The first was my job as a consultant. The word was broad but the work was extremely specialised. It paid well because there was no one else who did what we did, and we were the best at it. To put it simply, I was a trained negotiator that also dealt in kidnapping and security. Mostly I rescued kids from custody situations turned dangerous. When two parents divide, so does the child. Right down the middle. Their life sliced in two with the blink of an eye. When that division escalated into potential or actual violence, my firm got called in to sort it out. We tracked, located, negotiated, talked, or used excessive force, depending on what the situation called for. I'd been spat on, bitten, scratched, knifed, beaten, and shot. I wouldn't take any of it back either, because all of it led to the safety of someone unable to save themselves. There was no greater satisfaction in that, yet it took its toll. I started smoking more, sleeping less, and constantly questioned my ability to remain emotionally detached from the job.

The second was Quinn—the most precious gem to ever enter my life. That she'd been hurt and so severely damaged she'd lost the strength to live and hope, just about broke my fucking heart. She was sweet and endearing, made me laugh and left me in tears. She had me hard just watching her, and there was nothing I loved more than crushing her slight, naked body to my chest, holding on tight, and feeling the beat of her heart against my skin.

When I first saw her sitting in the bar, I wanted her. When I first kissed her, I knew her taste would never be enough, and the moment I realised I was sleeping more, smoking less, and laughing hard, I fell in love and fought to keep her.

Turns out that was a full time job in itself, especially now, as I struggled against the officer slapping me in handcuffs.

"Christ," I growled, knowing they'd get me for resisting if I didn't calm the fuck down. My eyes remained locked on Quinn until she disappeared inside the ambulance. "Casey," I shouted.

About to get in the back of the ambulance to follow with Quinn, his eyes found mine.

I nodded my head. That was my unspoken word not to leave her side for a second. He lifted his chin, catching my message, and disappeared.

My chest burned at not being there with her and the moment this shit storm was cleared, we needed to work out who the hell shot David. It was a shame the bastard died before I got my fifteen minutes of pounding him into the ground. Adrenaline had burned through me until I'd pushed his dead weight off and got to Quinn. The shooter would've been long gone by then, but it would ultimately lead back to the Zampettis. Federal narks infiltrated their operation from the ground up, and according to Mitch, those slimy, dirty fucks were about to implode. Couldn't happen fast enough for my liking.

Three hours later, locked up in City Central, I felt tired, edgy, and raw, but right now Quinn was all that mattered. She was everything, *my* everything, and it broke my heart this morning when she'd acted like I was her nothing. I knew it wasn't true. I'd hurt her—bruising the fragile trust I'd worked so hard to gain. I just wanted her safe. I loved her—and I don't care how sappy it sounded—I just needed to hear her say it back.

I needed it to untie the knots in my chest, have her look at me so she could see nothing I felt for her was a goddamn lie.

"Trav."

I tensed and turned to the voice. "Casey. Mate, what the fuck are you doing here?"

Jared stepped up beside him.

"They wouldn't release you until I came down, gave my version."

"Quinn?"

"Fine. Wrenched shoulder, few scrapes, concussion, but fine. Sleeping."

"Who's watching her?"

"Uniform on the door. Lucy and Rick were there when I left."

I nodded at Jared while another uniform stepped up next to him and unlocked the cell door and slid it across with a clang.

"You know the drill, Valentine," he told me as I signed my name on the release forms at the front counter. "Don't leave town yadda yadda."

I glared. "I didn't shoot the sonofabitch."

He held up his hands. "Ain't accusin' you. Just doin' my job."

I nodded, Jared and Casey following behind as I walked outside. Jared went off to get the car while I put my phone to my ear. As it rang I locked eyes with Casey. "I've got a really shitty feeling in my gut right now."

The call connected. "Yeah?"

"Mitch. This has Zampetti stink all over it. What do you know?"

"Fuck," he growled. "Those agents are all tighter than a cat's asshole. From what I hear, only two people in the whole fucking federal division know who the nark on the inside is, and they're so high up I can't get close to find out. I have no fucking idea."

"They've been after Quinn, but now they've targeted and taken out David and left her alone. Not that I'm really fucking unhappy about that, but it doesn't make sense and my gut is twisting in the wind."

"I'll do some more digging," Mitch returned.

"Do that. I'm headed to the hospital. Meet me there."

"Right."

I disconnected and after checking the GPS of Quinn's location, tracked the signal to St Vincent's Hospital as Jared pulled up out front.

I opened the passenger door and ducked my head in. "You brought the Porsche?" It was more a complaint then a question. I folded back the seat and nodded at Casey to get in the back.

"How am I supposed to fold my ass in there?" he bitched.

"How the fuck should I know? You're the twats who thought bringing the matchbox car would be the idea of the century. Just suck in your fat gut and get in the car."

Casey wedged himself in, and after adjusting the seat, I slid in and slammed the door.

"Easy on the car," Jared growled irritably.

"You'll have to get rid of it soon," I pointed out.

"No way." Jared's mouth tightened as he accelerated in to city traffic. "Mum's been harping on at me to get rid of it ever since Evie and I got engaged," he told Casey.

Casey's brows flew up. "You only got engaged last night."

"I know," he snapped and rolled his eyes. "It's not a good car for babies she says."

I chuckled. "She'll take you shopping for an SUV soon."

Jared took his hand off the steering wheel to punch me in the arm. "Take that back, asshole."

My phone rang and ignoring Jared, I put it to my ear. "Yeah?"

"Trav, thank God," came Mac's tense voice. Considering Mac always sounded tense, it didn't ring alarm bells. "Quinn said you'd been arrested."

I chuckled. "Christ, she isn't worried is she? It's all been sorted out. I'm on my way to the hospital now. Are you there?"

"I am, but there's a problem. A really big, horrible problem."

My stomach sank. "What?" I barked.

"Quinn's gone."

I gripped the phone tight to my ear. "What the fuck, Mac!"

"Don't shout at me," she shouted. "I already know I fucked up. Oh God," she moaned.

I twisted in my seat and eyed Casey and Jared. "Quinn's gone."

Waves of tension rolled through the car, and Jared planted his foot, just catching an orange light.

I put the phone down and hit a button. "You're on speaker. Talk."

"We were out the front of the hospital. Evie went to get the car and bring it around and—"

"Why the hell was Quinn leaving the hospital?"

"I…she…you were locked up, and it was all a mistake. She said they were releasing her anyway and that we were going to bust you out. Well, not bust you out but clear everything up and get you released."

"Christ, Mac," Casey snapped from the back. "The doctor said she'd be in at least overnight if not two nights."

"Well obviously she's a big, fat liar."

"Never mind," I growled. "Just tell us what happened."

"Evie went to get the car and then Quinn told me she left her phone on the counter inside where we signed the release paperwork, so I said I'd duck in and grab it and to wait right there. The uniform at the door was dismissed because we were leaving. When I came back out, she wasn't there."

I banged the back of my head hard on the headrest, twice. "Okay. How long were you gone?"

"Five minutes maybe."

Casey shoved his phone towards me. "I've got a trace on her phone. It's tracked her to the M4 heading west."

Without hesitating, Jared checked his mirrors and swung the steering wheel hard left. The back end fishtailed wildly as we started for the most direct route to the M4.

I gripped the dash as I spoke to Mac. "So obviously you didn't find her phone. Did you see her speak to anyone or see anyone that was suspicious?"

Jared accelerated, screaming down the road nowhere near fast enough for my liking, as he fought through thick afternoon traffic.

"No! I wasn't paying attention to anyone else because Quinn's body was pumped full of painkillers. She wasn't steady on her feet."

"Where are you and Evie now?" Jared asked, changing gears and checking his mirror as he shifted lanes.

"We're still at the hospital."

"Both of you back to the duplex now," he ordered. "Whatever you've got on tonight, cancel it."

"But we can—"

"No." I cut her off. "You can't. Just do it and ring us when you're there."

She replied with a muffled okay, and I disconnected the call.

"Jared, give your phone to Casey. Casey, get Coby on the line. Tell him what's going on and to get over to the duplex and stick with the girls."

I dialled Quinn's number. It rang out. I dialled again.

"Mr. Valentine," answered the male voice.

"Who is this?"

"You're speaking with Luka Zampetti."

"Fuck!" I yelled as my stomach rolled in fear. Sonofafuckingbitch. "The Zampetti's have her," I muttered to Jared as Casey spoke to Coby from the back seat.

"Such language you people have. Yes we have Quinn if that's what you were trying to ask me. We're absolutely delighted with her. She's so very pretty."

"You better not harm a hair on her head, Zampetti. You're about to have every police officer in the damn state on your ass. Put her on the phone."

"You want to talk to her? Why not."

There was a muffled fumble and then the sweet sound of her voice answered the phone. I closed my eyes for a brief second.

"Quinn! Are you okay?" My voice cracked. I leaned over and held my head in my hand.

"Oh, Travis," she murmured. "You wasted your phone call."

"What?"

"Your one phone call," she repeated.

"Quinn, Jesus. It was a misunderstanding. They let me go when they realised it wasn't me who shot David. Have they—"

"Are you okay?"

"I'm fine."

"Motherfucking Zampetti's," Casey yelled from behind me and kicked the back of the centre console in frustration. I held up a hand, indicating for him to shut the hell up. "Have they hurt you?"

"No. I'm fine too."

I didn't believe her. Her voice was shaky and she sounded so damn scared.

"Hold tight. I'm coming for you. I promise." I swallowed hard. God. If anything happened to her I don't... I pushed the thought away. "Just...I need to know we're okay—you and me," I pleaded. "I need to hear you say it."

There was a pause.

"I'm sorry I didn't trust in us. That I didn't give you a chance to explain before I ran. Nothing we have is a lie," she told me with a voice thick with tears. "I love you."

"Oh, God, sweetheart," I whispered hoarsely, my heart swelling as I stared blindly out the window. "I love you so much."

"I... Travis—" she cried out and then she was gone.

"Mr. Valentine," Luka said into the phone. "Quinn is going to prove very valuable to us, but we're going to be busy from here on in. I'd appreciate it if you didn't bother us again."

The line went dead and hot tears filled my eyes. After a deep breath I handed Casey back his phone and picked up Quinn's signal on my own.

"Casey." I cleared my throat. "Ring Mitch. Fill him in and tell him where we're headed."

The scenery flew by as we hit the M4 Freeway, and Casey spoke in the background on his phone. I blanked his words and tried to clear my mind and stay calm, but when Quinn's location stopped moving passed the M7 Westlink, my heart stuttered.

"Hell," I muttered.

Jared glanced across at me as he drove. "What?"

There was nowhere to turn off and stop along that freeway. It could only mean one thing. "He's dumped her phone." And I lost the only link to tracking her. "I promised her we were coming for her," I whispered.

Rage built up like a force inside of me.

"Trav," Casey said from behind me.

"Fuck!" I roared and slammed my fist on the dash. The brief burst of pain was a welcome relief. I threw my phone on the floor, my body shaking from the effort to contain the desperate fury. "Sonofabitch!"

"We're going to find her," Jared said. "We need to work out where Zampetti would be heading."

"Mitch said the AFP isn't talking."

"Maybe once they know they've got Quinn they might start," Casey muttered.

I bent over and grabbed for my phone. We'd reached the signal for Quinn but as my eyes took in everything ahead, all I could see was empty road. Rubbing my forehead wearily, I started to dial Mitch when he rang me at the same time.

I answered. "Yeah?"

"Here's the deal," he began. "The AFP have a nark high up. He's sent a signal to get the police ready to close in. His last location was at a safe house in Penrith. If your heading west on the M4 it sounds likely that Zampetti could possibly be heading to that safe house right now."

I twisted in my seat and indicated for Casey to give me his phone. He handed it over, and Mitch spelled out the address as I typed it in the phone and called up the map.

"Thanks, Mitch. We're heading there right now."

"Travis, wait," he said quickly before I could hang up. "I'm right behind you, but...be safe. This shit is a big deal. They're calling in choppers left and right. No matter what, we'll find her, okay?"

Even though he couldn't see me, I nodded anyway. "Okay."

After hanging up I ran the coordinates of the safe house with Jared and sat back in my seat, fighting the urge to tell Jared how to drive. My legs were cramped from the tiny matchbox car, and I needed a cigarette. Quinn first, but a cigarette straight after to calm the itchy nerves would be really fucking good right now.

After what seemed an eternity, we arrived at the address in time to see two unmarked sedans and agents busting down the door.

I glanced across at Jared as he squealed to a halt, parking sideways across the driveway. "Guns?" I yelled.

"Boot," he replied.

We both bailed out and I slid the front seat forward for Casey to get out before running for the boot. I grabbed one of the two handguns Jared held out and engaged the slide with a quick, efficient movement.

The three of us approached the house at a jog, and stepping through the open door, heard the agents yell 'clear' even as my eyes took in the empty room.

"Back here!" one yelled and I followed the sound, leaving Jared to pass on our identification.

"Oh God," I moaned when we stepped through to the dining area. I swallowed the nausea from the sight that greeted me, the effort causing a sweat to break out on my brow. A window had been shot out, shards of glass scattered across the floor. The room was empty apart from two chairs, one was kicked over, but both were covered in blood. I spun around. Blood spatter trailed up the wall. It smeared across the floor and pooled on the timber flooring. The metallic tang of it filtered the air. My body dropped to a crouch, and I hung my head in my hands, the gun still clasped tight in my fingers as I fought to breathe past the waves of fear that rolled through me faster than I could repress them.

A hand landed on my shoulder. I shook my head, my body starting to shake with the sobs I couldn't contain.

"Travis," Casey croaked, the heartbreak in his voice staggering, dragging me further into despair. "This doesn't mean anything."

After a moment I stood, and disengaging the gun and tucking it into the waistband of my jeans, strode blankly from the room and straight out the front door. Dusk had arrived. The sky was tinged with pale blues, yellows, and pinks, the air cold, the street lit up with flashing police cars as uniforms stormed the house, setup up police tape, and took over the street.

One hand on my hip, the other wrapped around the back of my neck, I stared blankly at the paved driveway, my mind working frantically to decide on our next move.

"Travis!" A car door slammed and I looked up.

Mitch jogged towards me, his partner Tate on his heels as Casey and Jared reached my side. He spread a directory over the bonnet of the nearest car, and we huddled around while he hurriedly flicked pages.

He pointed and said breathlessly, "Here. Old man Zampetti has a wife. Her sister has a company that owns a rural property along this road. You need to get back on the M4 and head farther out towards the Blue Mountains. The place has a private airstrip. The crew I was talking to think that's where they could be headed next. Luka drives a black BMW 760 sedan." He rattled off the registration number. "Those cars can move bloody fast."

I committed the location and registration to memory and looked up, relieved to have a focus. Mitch met my eyes and gave a nod. "Let's go."

We sprinted to our cars and moved out, taking the most direct route to the property, having no idea how far we were behind them, or even sure it was the direction they were heading in.

Jittery, I tapped my hand on my thigh, my eyes peeled to every car in front of us that we eventually reached and overtook. My phone buzzed a message from Mac.

M: Any news? Lucy and Rick are here at the duplex.

I replied as quickly as possible.

T: Working a lead.

We hit a quiet winding road, thick with tall trees and scrub, making the dark nightfall approach that much faster. Mitch and Tate were behind us, two cars of agents not far behind them.

I checked the map on my phone.

"Close," I muttered.

"Fuck!" Casey shouted and pointed at a right angle through the two seats. I followed his line. Down an embankment, crushed against a tree, was a black BMW and in the fading light I could just make out a partial on the registration Mitch had given us. The entire front and left side was crumpled inwards, the bonnet steaming, headlights blazing deep into the forest.

Jared tore off the side of the road, and I was out of the car and sprinting at a dead run before the car had even peeled to a full stop.

"Quinn!" I shouted breathlessly, my heart in my throat. I grabbed the handgun from my waistband and engaged the slide, skidding my way down the embankment. "Quinn!"

Chapter Twenty-Three
QUINN

"This, Quinn…" Luka lifted the gun again and my heart hammered so hard in my chest I thought it would split wide open. He aimed it at my leg. "…is how we're going to get Agent McKinnon to talk."

Seth swept his leg out, connecting with the man standing to the right of his chair. The sudden movement had Luka swivelling the aim of his gun from my leg to Seth, but Seth was a blur. He ripped the gun from the man he took down and fired twice.

I sat dumbstruck, my heart thumping as the man's body jerked from the force of bullets tearing into him.

"Quinn!" Seth yelled before another man was on him. They fought and another shot was fired, splattering blood up the wall and over my face and chest. I glanced downwards, disconnected from the horror playing out before me. No amount of bleach would save my shirt. A tear trickled down my cheek.

Huh.

Why was I crying over a ten dollar tank top?

"What are you doing? Get out of here!"

I blinked.

"Quinn, goddammit!"

Standing on shaky legs, I wiped at the blood, feeling it smear across my face. Seeing my hands covered in red, cold adrenaline rushed through me. Wiping them on the back of my jeans, I reached out and

260

grabbed the back of the chair I'd been sitting on, and for the second time in my life, I yelled and swung hard with everything I had. It connected and Luka staggered backwards before he could take a clear shot at Seth. The chair splintered from the force, and I stood frozen, holding the empty remains as I met Seth's eyes for a single moment that stretched for an eternity.

"Run, damn you," he panted as he struggled against the last two armed men standing. The other two were down, bodies still, blood pooling on the floor.

I dropped the chair as Luka made a recovery too swift for my liking and lunged for me. I turned to run, but his arms locked around my waist and in my ear, he breathed, "Little bitch."

"Fuck you," I grunted and kicking my legs, tried to push off against the wall with my feet to unsteady him, but he jerked me backwards towards one of the dead men on the ground. I closed my eyes as I panted and struggled. Reaching into the man's pocket, Luka dug out a length of rope and started binding my wrists together before dragging me outside and into the back of the BMW. I drew in a breath to let out a scream, but he backhanded me until I saw nothing but stars before it all faded to black.

When I came to, the car was moving along a windy road. It was getting dark so I could see my reflection in the window. It wasn't pretty. In fact, I looked like utter rubbish, but my whole day had been utter rubbish from the moment I woke up so that was only to be expected. In the passenger seat in front of me sat Luka, the driver was one of his armed thugs, and to my right sat Seth. He was unmoving and watching me.

"I'm sorry," he mouthed.

My eyes searched his face.

This man was my father. Was I supposed to feel an immediate connection to him?

All I could feel was defeat, the taste of it bitter and harsh.

"Hold tight. I'm coming for you. I promise."

I'm holding tight, Travis, and I know you're coming for me, I stared bleakly out the window at my bloodied reflection, *but I think my time is finally running out.*

Tears spilled over my cheeks and our bodies jerked, the driver cursing as the car bounced over a pothole. The action pulled at my bound arms and I felt the knot loosen.

My breath quickening, I jerked them again and realised my slender hands were slowly working free of the knot. I caught Seth's eyes and nodded behind me.

He frowned so I nodded again.

He shook his head.

Did he not understand? I pursed my lips. Wasn't the head nod the universal language of all men?

The car was speeding along and despite seeing it in the movies, actually considering the leap from a moving vehicle seemed impossibly daunting. My hands free, I wriggled them. Seth saw and widened his eyes. He looked at me and then nodded at the car door.

I rolled my eyes at him, frantically trying to think of an alternative. There was no way I could untie Seth without being seen but damned if I was going to sit back and await my doom *or* watch the man who was my father die.

My eyes fell on the driver and breathless, I realised there was only one other option, and it was a really stupid one. I was sure Travis wouldn't condone it, nor Casey, or Seth for that matter. But I knew Lucy would, and so would Mac and Evie.

"I can only fight for you for so long before you have to start fighting for yourself."

Well, Travis, you said to fight, and I'm pretty sure you didn't mean it like this, but here goes nothing.

Leaping forward between the two front seats, I grabbed at the steering wheel and swung it hard. Surprised, the driver grappled as the car spun. Luka grabbed my arms and pulled but I hung on like a goddamn barnacle, screaming as he yelled and tore at my fingers. Even when the tyres caught loose gravel and started spinning out of control, I held tight.

Seth shouted something at me as the car hurtled down the embankment, but I couldn't hear through the blood roaring in my ears. I was thrown back in my seat. Breathless, I grabbed for my seatbelt, fighting with trembling fingers to click it into place as trees hurtled towards us at amazing speed. The scream of metal crunching in my ears deafened me, and I lost consciousness.

"Quinn!"

Hands were running over me.

I blinked.

"Quinn!"

With effort, I turned my head towards the sound and blinked again.

"We've got to get you out of here."

"Travis," I mumbled.

"No. It's Seth," he panted as strong hands gripped me and pulled me from the crumpled car.

"Where's Travis?" I moaned.

My body was flung up and over a shoulder, and my stomach rolled as the jostling flared up all kinds of pain.

"Who's Travis?"

Did he just ask me who Travis was?

My eyes closed and a chuckle came from deep within me.

Travis was light and safety, beauty and passion, laughter and love...and hope.

Travis was *everything*.

"Why are you carrying me?" I mumbled. "You got shot. I should be carrying you."

"I'm fine," Seth panted as we staggered through the dark forest.

"Where are we going?"

"The driver was killed in the crash, Quinn, but Luka is behind us. We've got to keep moving."

"Oh God," I moaned. "Why can't this day end?"

It was his turn to chuckle, but it came out more like a hiss. "Quinn?"

"Hmm?"

"If I knew—"

"Don't." Tears threatened again. "I have a family now, and I'm trying to stop living in the past and move on…but…dammit Seth, I can't have this conversation while I'm hanging over your shoulder."

"You can't walk," he breathed out, pain etched in his voice as his feet crunched over dried leaves, twigs and rocky ground.

"I can't?"

"You've got a deep gash in your leg, Quinn. You can't feel it?"

My brow furrowed. "No. It feels kinda numb." I licked my dry lips and swallowed. "Is it… bad?"

"Not at all. You'll be fine."

He didn't sound like it was fine. His voice shook, but he *had* been shot. And in a car accident.

"Don't move!" I heard Luka yell.

"Fuck," Seth cursed softly and halted.

"Turn around."

Seth turned, softly lowering me to the ground and that leg that felt so numb, didn't feel so numb anymore. I screamed as pain ricocheted upwards through my body and I crumpled to the ground.

Seth shifted in front of me.

"All this time, Agent McKinnon, you stood with me, worked by my side. Now you have blood on your hands." He looked up as a chopper came over, circling slowly above us, blinding lights spearing the ground over and over. "But you know I can't allow you to live. That would send the wrong message. It's just a shame you'll die with all those black marks on your soul, and knowing the daughter that was never yours will die along with you."

A shot rang out.

My breath stuttered in fear, but Seth didn't jerk back, or fall down. That honour belonged to Luka, and he looked surprised before he didn't look like anything at all.

"Quinn!" Seth crouched and picked me up, cradling me in his arms and a fresh round of sweat broke his brow from the effort. "What a fuck of a day."

"Put her down or I shoot."

My mouth fell open. Behind where Luka lay stood Travis, gun in hand, pointed directly at Seth. Slightly dazed, I took a moment to admire him. His green eyes were hard and locked on Seth, his fitted white shirt dirty and torn, his legs braced as though he was prepared to take down King Kong and win, and in that moment I would've believed he could.

"Travis," I whispered.

"This is the man who's your everything?" Seth whispered softly to me.

My heart swelled because not only was he my everything, I was his too and never had I felt more whole. "Did I say that out loud?"

Ignoring my question, Seth looked down at me. "Travis Valentine? Really?"

I raised a brow. "You know him?"

"Every single Government agency and police force in Sydney, hell, in Australia, has heard of the Valentines. Fucking cowboys," he mumbled.

"Put her down," Travis yelled, inching forward, gun steady, every movement and word corroborating Seth's opinion without him even realising it.

"I can't," Seth returned. "She's hurt. She can't walk."

Travis flicked his eyes from Seth to me. "Quinn?" he called softly.

"I'm okay. Just a scratch on my leg." I reassured him. I waved a hand towards Seth. "You can put the gun away. This is Seth. Agent McKinnon," I added.

"You're the nark?" Travis said to Seth.

"That would be me," he replied.

Travis wasn't convinced. "Put her down gently and back way."

Without hesitation, Seth knelt, gently sat me down and backed away, hissing as each movement caused him pain.

Travis moved forward, lowering himself to his knees before me, his eyes running the length of me. They fell on the makeshift bandage around my thigh, and he checked it carefully. Satisfied the pressure was tight enough on the wound, his eyes found mine and they were wet with tears of relief. "Oh, Quinn, baby."

He wrapped the upper half of my body in his arms and tucking his head in my neck, breathed deeply.

"Travis," I murmured, waves of emotion rolling through me.

His body started shaking and I wound my arms around his neck and held on.

"I'm sorry I didn't get to you sooner."

My fingers gently caressed the back of his neck. "That's okay. I took matters into my own hands."

He jerked back and looked at me. "More chair throwing?"

I bit down on my lip. "As a matter of fact…"

Travis groaned.

"She saved us. Quinn got herself loose in the car and jerked it off the road. If she hadn't done that, we would've been dead by now. Luka was heading to his private airstrip. We were just bargaining chips until he got there and got rid of us." Seth knelt on the other side of me. "Her leg's pretty bad—"

"You said it wasn't," I accused just as Travis cocked back a fist and slammed it in Seth's face. Seth crashed backwards into the ground from the force, and it didn't look like he'd be getting up again anytime soon. "I told you to stay back. Until I can verify who you are, I don't trust you," he raged.

"Oh my God," I moaned, staring in disbelief at the prone Seth. "Travis, I…uh…know who he is."

He frowned at me as he tucked his gun into the waistband of his jeans and pulled out his phone.

"Don't believe anything he says, Quinn."

"Oh I think I believe what he's told me."

Travis put the phone to his ear. "And what did he tell you?"

"He didn't even need to tell me. Look at him. He's my father." I stared at Travis. His eyes held mine as I heard his phone dialling. "You just punched my father. In the face."

Travis looked from the prone Seth to me and back again. His mouth fell open.

The call connected. "Hello? Travis?" came the tinny voice of Casey.

"And then I said, 'No one messes with the Valentines. *Ever*' before I reached forward and grabbed the steering wheel," I told Lucy, Mac, and Evie from my hospital bed where I lay propped against mounds of pillows, munching on a pile of hot chips, and slurping noisily on my large strawberry shake.

Well I didn't really say that, but I would have if I'd thought of it. I was just a little bit preoccupied at the time trying to save lives. I recounted the entire story for them, starting from the moment I woke, not missing out a single thing, from my decision at the beach not to run to David getting shot to Seth pulling me from the wrecked car to me telling him Travis was my everything—which evoked sighs—to the way Travis looked as he stood there, gun pointed at Seth. Lucy's gleam of happiness was bright enough to take out an eye.

"… and then I stared at Travis in utter shock," I continued, "and said 'That's my father. You just punched my father. In the face.'"

Shrieks of laughter broke out, and Mac started gasping for breath. "Oh my God," she wheezed. "What an asshead! That's brilliant. I can live on that for *years*."

The door to my hospital room burst open, and Travis strode through, Casey hot on his heels. His frown was fierce and he made sure it took in all of us.

The chuckles died off.

A false cough rang out.

"What the hell is going on in here?" he thundered. "Quinn..." he pointed at me, and I bit the insides of my cheeks to hold back the laughter "...is supposed to be resting, and you're all having a bloody party."

Mac made a noise that sounded like the high-pitched whine of a dog, forcing everyone to turn and look at her. Her face was a tad red, her eyes watering a little.

"You punched Quinn's father," she choked out, unable to help herself. "In the face."

Casey cleared his throat.

Evie choked on a chip.

I giggled.

Instead of the expected irritable retort, Travis swung his eyes to me and the anger in them softened. He chuckled. "Yeah. I did."

Mac's mouth fell open.

"Close your mouth, Mac."

She closed her mouth.

"Everyone out," he ordered, his eyes never leaving mine, just like they never left mine in the ambulance ride to the hospital last night, and when they put fifteen stitches in my upper thigh and he squeezed my hand hard as he sat with me. Even as I lay in my hospital bed in the dead of night, freshly showered, exhausted and drifting off, his eyes held mine until lost in them, I fell asleep.

There were grumbles and rustles of paper as Evie gathered up the last of the chips. Kisses were pressed on my cheek, "be back later's" were called out, and then it was just Travis and me.

He leaned in, touching his lips to mine.

It wasn't enough. I pressed harder, tasting his lips with my tongue. He groaned, opening his mouth, and took over the kiss.

Pulling back, he said, "You taste like strawberries," and sat on the edge of my bed.

Patting at my hair with one hand, I held up my shake in reply with the other. He stole it from my hand and wrapping his lips around the straw, took a sip. I watched breathlessly as he swallowed and eyes crinkling, said, "You know how much I love strawberry ice cream."

I shivered, remembering him tasting it from my mouth after our date. "Me too."

"So …" He grinned. "I looked like I could take on King Kong and win?"

"You were eavesdropping," I accused and whacked his chest with the back of my hand. "How much did you hear?"

"Casey and I heard it all." He chuckled but it died off. "I'm your everything."

I flushed wildly and picked at the hem of my blanket.

Travis tucked his thumb and forefinger under my chin until I couldn't avoid looking at him any longer.

"You are," I agreed softly. "You gave me everything that helped me find myself. Your support gave me confidence, your determination made me fight, and your strength helped me find my own." He wiped softly at a tear that spilled over and streaked down my cheek. "I love you so much, Travis."

His eyes filled and he blinked. "I love you too, sweetheart."

Spreading out on the bed next to me, his feet hanging off the edge at an angle, he pulled me into a tight embrace, and I drifted off in his arms.

Travis shifting and the clearing of a throat woke me from my nap. Travis sat up and swung his legs over the edge of the bed, wiping at tired eyes as my own found Seth standing by the door. His brow and jaw were swollen and bruised, his blond hair mussed, his shoulder wrapped up in a sling. He was pale and sweaty and looked in no condition to be out of his own hospital bed and trekking around the hallways.

"Seth," I murmured.

He hesitated, not knowing what the appropriate greeting was for a long lost daughter. Unfortunately, I was in the same boat.

Travis solved the problem. "Agent McKinnon." He nodded at the visitor chair. "Why don't you take a seat before you fall down."

Seth glared, no doubt remembering Travis throwing that now infamous punch. Travis returned the glare, no doubt remembering my recount to him of yesterday and blaming Seth for getting me caught up in everything.

I sighed because we weren't off to a good start.

"Travis, why don't you go grab a coffee?"

He folded his arms. "I'm good."

I smiled at him meaningfully.

"I think she was politely asking you to leave," Seth offered as he dragged the chair closer by the bed and seated himself carefully.

"I know that, but having dealt with Quinn's *family* in the past, I'm not inclined to ever leave her alone with any of them again."

By the way he emphasised family, I knew he considered it a loose term just as I did. The single word didn't encompass much except a mother who wasn't worth knowing and a father I didn't know at all. At twenty-two, I wasn't sure I was in need of a father anymore. Frankly I didn't know what on earth to do with one now that he was here, but maybe it was something we could work out together.

"Travis." I reached out and squeezed his hand. "I'd really love a coffee."

He returned the squeeze and looked into my eyes. I needed to talk to Seth, and I needed the space to process whatever came of it. I hoped he could see that in my eyes and understand.

Travis nodded and with a quick kiss, he was gone.

Over the next hour, I learned I had more family than I knew what to do with. Seth was the youngest of three. I had two uncles, grandparents, and cousins scattered over the countryside. It made me ache, my chest burning at knowing everything I'd ever prayed for had been right at my fingertips all along, and my mother had known. She'd *known* and never bothered to tell me.

Was it because Seth broke her heart like he believed? A silent "fuck you" to Seth that he was never supposed to hear?

"I hate her," I whispered to him after I explained my upbringing, saving most of the details for another day. "And I hate that I hate her. I thought I didn't feel anything for her but this...this *burns*," I whispered, my voice thick with hurt.

Seth stood up and folded me awkwardly in his free arm. The kindness had me slumping into his shoulder.

A loud curse came from the doorway, and I pulled away as Travis strode forward and got in Seth's face.

"What did you say to her?"

I pulled away, suddenly exhausted. "I have a family."

Travis frowned at me, sitting a coffee on my tray table and taking hold of my hand. "Of course you do. Us."

"I'll see you tomorrow, Quinn," Seth cut in, and with a nod to Travis, he left my room.

I scooted over in my bed a little to allow room for Travis. He sat down, handed me the coffee, and I told him everything Seth told me.

Chapter Twenty-Four

"You know," I said, and paused, looking up at Travis from beneath my lashes where we lay in my bed. Morning sunlight streamed through the window, making me squint a little as I rolled to my side and propped my head in my hand. "I think you should hire me at Jamieson and Valentine Consulting. I'd make a really good employee."

"Yeah?" Travis scratched lazily at his neck and yawned as I trailed my fingers up the ridges along his naked chest. He appeared to give it serious thought. "Well you could fetch me coffee I suppose, pick up my dry cleaning, do all my paperwork. I could even bend you over my desk whenever I wanted." His lips twitched. "When can you start?"

My eyes flashed in annoyance, but I quietly smothered it. Instead, I changed direction, trailing my fingers downwards, and this time when I looked up at him from beneath my lashes, I bit down on my lip. He sucked in a breath and I hid my smirk. "Well I was kinda thinking that—"

"That what? You helped dismantle an entire drug and human trafficking cartel and now that you're on a roll and have a taste for adrenaline, you want more?"

"Well life with you and the badass brigade is never going to be dull, is it? Maybe Mac was right and I need to learn how to shoot."

"Newsflash, sweetheart. You're the ones that are causing the mayhem and leaving a trail of destruction behind you."

A loud bang on the door interrupted our chat.

"Quinn!" Mac yelled through the door. "Are you ready to go yet?"

The door flew open before I could reply, and I whipped the sheet up to cover my naked chest.

"Seen it before," she sing-songed as she sailed into my wardrobe.

"Jesus Christ, Mac, haven't you heard of fucking privacy," Travis growled.

"Sorry!" she yelled, her voice muffled as rummaging and banging noises came from deep within. "Ah ha!" She stalked out, waving a bag around. "I knew you had my lemon tote." Pausing at the end of the bed, she said, "What the hell are you doing anyway? Hang on...let me rephrase that. Mum is downstairs. Did you forget we were going shopping today?"

"No," I lied.

I did forget. When I was with Travis, he made me forget my name, forget to breathe, and forget I had seen people die. He made me forget everything. But Travis couldn't be there all the time. When he wasn't, my friends rallied, but it was high time the cotton wool that had cocooned me for two weeks was unwrapped so I could move on with the rest of my life.

That was supposed to start today, with shopping, because my stitches were out, my crutches were gone, and Mac had told me the feel good endorphins from spending lots of money was the first step on my road to recovery. I was told it would be epic. Evie and Tim were coming, Lucy was meeting us there, and Evie had Jared book us a late champagne and seafood lunch at Mr. Chow's. Unfortunately, it couldn't drag late into the night because tonight was my first night back at work—Jamieson would be playing at the White Demon.

"You're lying," Mac announced.

"No I'm not," I lied, shifting when Travis sat up a little and reached for his phone from my bedside table.

"Yes you are," she returned. "You have a tell."

Travis chuckled as he unlocked his phone and began scrolling through his emails.

"What?"

He shook his head in reply.

"I don't have a tell," I told Mac, folding my arms over the sheet.

She raised a brow.

"You do," Travis said as he flicked through his phone. "Everyone does."

I looked at Mac as Travis tapped out an email reply. "What's Mac's tell?"

"She widens her eyes a little," he replied, putting his phone back and joining me in looking at Mac, only he was frowning. "You can leave now."

Mac flared her nostrils. "Whatever. Downstairs, Quinn. We're leaving soon."

She closed the door behind her, and I turned back to Travis. "Now as I was saying—"

Travis interrupted me by pulling down the sheet, rolling over, and grabbing my hips.

"Travis, I'm trying to talk."

"So talk." He leaned down and began licking and biting my neck, running his hands up my torso until he held my breasts in his hands, his thumbs rubbing across my nipples.

"Travis," I moaned and arched my back into the touch.

"You like me touching you?" he whispered into my ear.

I grabbed his naked hips and yanked him down, feeling the length of him harden against the soft skin of my belly.

"Yes," I breathed.

He slid a hand down between my thighs and chuckled in my ear as I squirmed against the feel of his roughened fingers.

"You're not talking."

A tear leaked out my eye and Travis froze.

"Did I hurt you, sweetheart?"

Another tear leaked out and he drew back.

"I'm sorry," I whispered thickly.

He rolled over, dragging me with him, until I was sitting above him and the tear rolled down and dripped onto his chest. I reached out to wipe it away, and he grabbed my wrist. "Don't. Do you need to talk? I know your first counselling session with Jude isn't for another few days, but I'm here now."

"Travis!" Another bang came at the door, this time from Henry. "Casey and Evie just got in from a surf. He says you two had something to do today?"

"Be right there!"

Travis slammed his head back into the pillows. "Christ. We need to get our own place." He gave me a speculative look. "Move into the loft with me?"

"Oh God," I whispered, and as another tear threatened, I blinked it back with considerable effort. "I can't."

Disappointment shadowed across Travis's face before he schooled his features. "It's too soon. I'm sorry."

"No," I protested. "It's not about time. I want to be with you. I miss you when you're not there." My face flushed wildly at the admission. I was not used to putting myself out there as much as I had been lately. Travis reached out and took my hands, giving them a squeeze.

"I…it's Rufus. He can't live in a loft."

"He's a big dog," Travis agreed. "Needs space."

Reaching up he pulled me down against his chest, one hand holding me close, the other skimming down my back. He pressed a kiss against my head where it was tucked under his chin. "Maybe we can get somewhere together."

I thought quietly for a moment, feeling my lashes brush softly against his skin as I blinked. "What about Casey?"

"We'll work something out." Travis exhaled softly. "Now tell me why the tears?"

"Because."

"Because why?"

I knew Travis wouldn't let it go. "I love that about you," I whispered.

"Love what?" he asked gruffly.

The vibration of his voice against my chest had me sighing in pleasure. "That you don't let me close myself off from you. Most of the time I don't even realise I'm doing it, but you never let me."

Travis rubbed his hand in circles on the small of my back, warming me. "You know what I love about you?"

"What?" I whispered.

"Your biscuits."

I sat up a little so he could see my glare. A chuckle rose from deep in his chest as he grabbed my ass in both hands. "I love this too."

"Travis!"

He rolled us both over until we were side by side and brushed a thumb gently across my cheek, silent for a moment as his eyes drank me in. "Quinn," he said softly. "I also love knowing I have you to look forward to at the end of the day, and I love knowing that when I open my eyes in the morning the first thing I'll see is you."

"I remember the first morning I woke up and all I saw was you."

"Yeah?"

"I was horrified. Not at first, because you were lying on your stomach, one arm curled under the pillow and the ahh…sheet wasn't quite covering you. You were the most beautiful man I ever saw, and I panicked because I was quite the opposite—"

Travis frowned. "Quinn—"

"Let me finish. So I ran, but obviously not far enough because there you were again, and I cursed my luck. How was it fair that someone I wanted so much was never meant to be mine? Everything that was ever beautiful in my life was always taken from me, and it was scary to think you'd be the same. But you never stopped fighting for me, and you forced me to see that maybe I really was worth fighting for. You took away all the ugly on the inside, Travis, and you made me beautiful."

There was a slight quaver in my voice because saying that wasn't easy, but the way he was looking at me made my heart want to burst.

"Christ, sweetheart." Travis crushed his mouth down on mine, kissing me wildly, his hands fisting in the back of my hair as his lips moved over mine until he broke away, breathing heavily. "Have I told you how much I fucking love you?"

Later that night in the dressing room of the White Demon, Jamieson on a set break, Mac was fiddling with my hair. Turns out today was not only an epic shopping day, but a semi-makeover day too. My hair was freshly cut. Not only that, it was done by Evie's hairdresser who, according to her, was shit hot. Looking at Evie's glossy mane I could only agree. The past few months my hair had grown, but I really liked the shorter style. Now it was choppy and styled in messy waves and sat just above my shoulders.

Lucy, here with Rick for the show, met my eyes in the mirror. "Does it look okay?"

Her eyes softened as she reached out and ruffled my hair. "You look perfect."

"It's shorter than Trav's hair now." Mac turned from playing with my hair to smirk at Travis where he stood leaning against the wall talking with Jared and Henry. "When are you cutting your hair? People might start mistaking you for a girl."

I turned from my seat to look at Travis, and just like every time, my mouth went dry. His wide chest and muscled arms were on display in his fitted Jamieson shirt, golden stubble covered his jaw, and his hair barely fit into the tie that was holding it off his face. He was utterly beautiful.

"Travis isn't cutting his hair," I announced.

He raised his brows at me. "I'm not?"

"Neither is Jared," Evie told the room as she uncapped a bottle of water.

Everyone looked at Jared. Another inch and he'd be tying it back too.

Cooper nudged Frog, knocking him off his perch on the arm of the couch. "I told you. Chicks dig guys with long hair."

"Why the fuck do you think I haven't had my hair cut for three months?"

Ignoring the chatter around all of us, Travis pushed off against the wall, and watching him stride towards me took my breath away.

"Ordering me about already?" he asked.

I stood up. Tilting my head to meet his eyes and sliding my arms around his neck, I grinned. I couldn't help it.

"You have a problem with that?"

"No. I like it." He leaned in and rubbed his nose against mine. "I spoke with Casey today and Coby. Coby has a big house in Coogee he lives in on his own. Said he could rent it to us and he could move into the loft with Casey. At least until we worked out what we wanted to do. We could build a house or buy one and renovate."

From her nearby vantage point, Evie obviously overhead Travis speaking and shouted, "No! Don't do it, Quinn. Just buy one all ready to move into. Renovations are more painful than being shot."

Jared rolled his eyes. "Baby, I've been the one doing all the work while you're the one standing by causing drama because you keep changing your mind."

Evie raised her eyebrows at me as if to say "see my point?"

Travis smiled down at me. "Well we have plenty of time to make a decision. Still not too soon?"

"No!" I bit my lip, thinking of how it would be to live with Travis. The past two weeks we hadn't slept apart, but to have our own space? No interruptions, no fights for the bathroom, quiet lazy mornings in bed.

"Oh," I breathed, "I can have my hands and lips on you in any room in the house, whenever I feel like it. When can we move in?"

Travis slid his hands down my back, gripping my ass firmly, his eyes dropping to my lips. "Tomorrow."

The door flew open and chatter died off. Seth stood there in dark jeans and a navy collared shirt with the sleeves rolled up. There was a hard edge in his eyes that took away from the pretty appeal of his features.

He eyed Travis and growled, "Get your hands off my daughter."

My mouth fell open and if anything, Travis pulled me tighter against him.

Then Seth curled his lips a little. "Just kidding. Sort of."

"Alright!" Mac clapped loudly. "Set break over. You lazy assheads get your butts back on that stage."

"We've still got ten minutes," Cooper protested.

Jake slapped him up the back of his head. "Ouch."

The room cleared out and with Travis pressing a soft kiss against my lips with sad eyes, he told me to find him by the stage after. Brow furrowed, my eyes followed his retreating back until he was gone too.

The moment of silence was deafening until Seth shrugged. "Sorry. I didn't mean to clear the room."

"Umm...that's okay. Have a seat." I indicated to the couch and then waved at the bucket of ice filled with beer, soft drinks, and water. "Drink?"

"Sure. Beer's good."

I plucked out a beer and a soft drink for myself and handed it over.

"So..." I murmured, feeling awkward. Seth was my father, but I didn't really know him yet. Despite seeing him a few times since the drama, this was the first time I found myself alone with him without people shooting at us.

Seth uncapped his beer and took a sip. "So...this is your job, huh?"

The muffled thump of a beat started pounding through the walls, indicating Jamieson had taken to the stage for their last set.

"It is. I worked for Jettison Records before Mac hired me, but I love this. It's exciting. Hearing them perform, watching the crowds go nuts.

No day is ever the same, and I get to travel for the first time in my life. Well…actually I've only been to Melbourne so far and uh, I discovered I'm not a good flyer."

"I'm not either."

"Oh." Remembering the glance Travis shot me before he left the room, I cleared my throat and asked, "So what are you doing here?"

Peeling away at the label on his beer bottle, he offered me a reassuring smile, but it didn't appear genuine enough to reassure me. "I'm leaving for work. I…can't tell you where. Can't tell anyone really."

"Oh," I muttered again and forced my own smile. "Well, for how long?"

"I don't know. Six months… a year maybe."

"Huh."

Funny. I'd just found my father and now I was losing him. I thought maybe we were heading towards a new road together. Seth was already looking for the exit. I guess that made me wrong.

Then I looked at his knuckles—they were white, and his face, I could see it on his face. There was no choice.

"I'm sorry. I spoke to your…to Beth. I went and saw her."

I exhaled shakily and rubbed sweaty palms along my jeans. "I'm not sure I want to hear..." I indicated for him to tell me anyway.

"She's… it was difficult seeing her like that, knowing that was what you lived with. Not that I knew her all that well, Quinn, but she's hard and coarse and well, frankly, she's a bitch."

I nodded my agreement. "A douchebag."

"A poor excuse for a mother," he added.

"A selfish cow."

"She's someone who never deserved you."

I searched his eyes and found nothing but honesty. "You're absolutely right."

Seth cleared his throat. "My career always came first with me. I'm two years shy of forty, and I've never been in love or married or had kids of my own. I've watched on as my brothers did all that, and I never felt I was missing out because I was the one making a difference. Meeting you made me realise how much I was sacrificing. I know you're a full grown woman in your own right, but you...you're my daughter, and I want a chance to learn how to be father. I want you in my life, so I...this job is my last one. I've handed in my resignation." He stood as he spoke, starting to pace the room. "Is that okay? I mean, I realise now that I've gone and done it without even thinking about you and what you want. God." He paused and looked at me. "That's really selfish, right? I'm sorry. We're not off to a good start. Not at all."

He started pacing again and I watched him silently, my heart tripping over itself.

I stood up.

I had a father. One who wanted me. I had friends, a great job, a lazy dog, and a man who loved me, all because one night my best friend dragged me to a bar and I locked eyes with a man who took me home and showed me something beautiful.

I made a mental note to put up with listening to Lucy say "I told you so" a thousand times and to buy her round trip tickets to Paris. Then I caught Seth in a hug. He hesitated before his arms came around me and held on.

"When are you leaving?" My voice was muffled against his shirt.

"Two weeks."

I pulled away so I could look at him. "What are you going to do when you get back?"

He shrugged casually. "I don't know."

"Will I be able to ring you?"

"Probably not."

"You'll be safe then, right? I mean, I can't go rescuing you from all your operations, you know."

He chuckled. "I'll be safe."

The door opened. "Everything okay?" Travis asked, his eyes on me first.

"I should get going," Seth said.

"You can't stay?"

He looked from Travis to me. "Maybe next time. I just wanted to see where you worked, but I'll see you both tomorrow anyway, right? The family's looking forward to meeting you both."

I was nervous and excited, but mostly nervous, and maybe a little bit sick. I'd planned a day of baking tomorrow, trying out a new recipe: orange and almond cake. I'd planned to bake extra because I thought it might be something Jared would like. Also, part of my shopping expedition today had been a "finding the right outfit to wear to meet the family you never knew you had and really wanted them to like you."

"They're gonna love you," Seth told me, no doubt seeing fear in my eyes. "Promise."

With a kiss to my forehead and nod towards Travis, Seth left.

"You knew he was leaving."

Travis leaned down and picked me up. I wrapped my legs around him and he sank back into the couch.

"I did," he agreed. "He told me today. He was worried it would upset you."

"Did he tell you he also quit his job?"

Travis looked at me with some surprise, his brows raising a little, so I told him what Seth told me.

When I finished, Travis said, "Maybe he could come work with us."

"I don't think so."

"Why not?"

"Seth said you were a bunch of cowboys which probably means he doesn't think you're as all that as I think you are."

"As long as you think I'm *all that*, then that's all that matters."

I brushed a kiss against his smiling lips.

"Now, back to this morning. Why the tears?" I sighed and he laughed. "You said you loved that I didn't let shit go. Having a change of heart?"

I pursed my lips. "No."

"Then…?"

"Because I realised that this was my life now."

"And that made you cry?"

"Yes." I knew it would sound stupid, but how do you explain that you were crying because you were happy without it sounding lame when the tears felt anything but. "Somehow, even after everything I've been through, I feel like a very lucky person."

Travis nodded and his eyes crinkled. "Because you have me."

I held his face in my palms. "Because I have you."

Epilogue
TRAVIS

The alarm blared like a fucking freight train, and I rolled over and slammed it with my fist. The noise died a fast and satisfying death. Happy, I rolled back over, dragging Quinn towards me and wrapping my arm around her middle.

I slept naked and the best part about that was Quinn did too. Frowning, my hand patted her belly and I realised she was wearing her cotton robe. Not only that, the knot she'd tied was tight enough to make it impenetrable to my searching hands. The closest bit of naked skin I could find was the back of her neck. Her pale blonde hair tickled my nose as I leaned in and tasted it with my lips and tongue. I nipped the skin lightly with my teeth, just the way I knew she liked it.

She moaned and rolled towards me, the cotton robe gaping open slightly at her thighs from the movement. Happy, my hands found the smooth, naked skin and trekked their way upwards. Still sleeping, she wriggled towards me, and it was all I could do not to growl in pleasure. Even when my arms were wrapped around her as tight as I dared on her slight frame, it never felt close enough.

Feather light, her hands trailed down my chest, her fingernails scraping my nipples just the way she knew I liked it. I closed my eyes, groaning softly and growing hard at her touch.

A pounding fist came at the front door, and Quinn's hands stilled. "Tell me it's not Saturday morning."

"It's not Saturday morning."

She burrowed further into my chest, unable to open her eyes to greet the early hour. "You're lying," she mumbled.

"I don't lie."

The lips she currently had pressed into my neck curved in a smile. "You have a tell."

"No, I don't."

"Everybody does. That's what you told me."

Rolling Quinn over, I pinned her arms to the bed and ground my hips into hers, making sure she knew I was hard and I wanted her.

"Except me. Did I forget to mention that?"

I touched my lips to hers and smiled against them as she strained upwards into my touch, making me harder if that was possible.

The pounding at the door came again.

"Dammit, Quinn! I know you're awake," came the muffled yell.

"Will you forgive me if I strangle Lucy, weigh her body down and let her sink to the bottom of the ocean?"

"Are you kidding?" she groaned into my neck. "I'll supply the cement bricks. I know exactly where I can get some."

She was, of course, referring to the leftover blocks from our newly constructed rendered fence. We'd moved into Coby's house a year ago. During that time, to much protest by Evie, Mac, and even Quinn, who rarely protested about anything, I bought us a dilapidated four bedroom house in Manly Vale. I liked to think I was smarter than Jared though, and our renovations were undertaken over the six months we lived at Coby's house before we moved in.

"Maybe we can just pretend we're not home," I said with a small degree of hope.

Quinn rolled from beneath me, swinging her legs over the edge of the bed she sat up, looking back at me over her shoulder. I loved Quinn's back. Seemed an odd body part to fall in love with, but her hair was short enough I could see the delicate line of her neck and it led down a creamy satin expanse of skin to an ass I never got tired of watching or holding in my hands. I frowned because in this instance she was wrapped up like Fort bloody Knox, and I couldn't see anything, making this a really shitty start to my day.

"That didn't work the last time we tried, remember? *You're* the one that bought a house just two blocks away from where Rick and Lucy bought their house."

"Maybe we can play the blame game. She's *your* friend."

Quinn raised a brow as she dragged her sweet, delicious body out of bed. "*Our* friend."

I reached out to drag her back, but she danced from my reach and waggled the ring finger of her left hand, diamonds glinting every which way in the morning light. My lips curved in a smile of pure male satisfaction at the sight, even while she was smirking at me. "We joined forces in case you forgot. Everything became *ours*. Including Lucy."

That was true. Quinn was now my wife, and I never got tired of introducing her to everyone that way. Mrs. Valentine. This is my wife, Quinn Valentine. It suited her, being mine. The wedding, according to Quinn, was going to be nothing like Jared and Evie's. Theirs had blown out to major proportions. It hadn't helped that Evie was now being recognised wherever she went. Magazines wanted scoops and access to her private life. Quinn didn't want the show. She tried to rope me into it by asking what I wanted, but I wasn't stupid. Whatever she wanted was what I wanted—as long as she was happy. That wasn't the right answer apparently. According to Mac, I needed to have an *opinion*. So I asked Mac what Quinn wanted. Mac told me she wanted a quiet wedding, close family only. So I told Quinn I wanted a quiet wedding. "You don't want a big wedding?" she'd asked me with wide eyes. I looked helplessly at Mac. I thought the problem was fixed. Had Quinn changed her mind and wanted a big wedding? It was all too hard. It seemed to be universal that when we told women we wanted whatever they wanted, they didn't believe us, but it was true. Our lives were happy when they were happy. Happy equals happy. Simple math. Women liked to complicate it by dragging algebra and long division into the equation.

In the end we had our quiet wedding. Jared stood on my right and Lucy on Quinn's left. Quinn had daisies wound through her pinned hair and a white lace dress that flared out to her knees. She was simply perfect.

Propped up on one elbow, my focus immersed in her, she peeled off the pink robe and replaced it—entirely too quickly—with her jogging gear. She propped a leg up on the corner chair, the one that was great for flinging all my clothes on, and started lacing up her shoes before furrowing her brow at me in worry.

"Are you sure you're gonna be—"

I cut her off. "Yes! We'll be fine." A kitchen cupboard opened and then slammed closed and my brows flew up in disbelief. "You gave her a key?"

She shrugged. "Just for emergencies."

Sighing heavily, I swung my legs over the edge of the bed. Scratching idly at my chest, I said dryly, "I can see how this morning's jog could constitute an emergency where Lucy would need to breach the premises."

Her eyes tracked the movement of my hand as it rubbed lazily over my chest and my lids lowered a little. "See something you like?"

"Quinn! Hurry up," Lucy yelled from somewhere in the vicinity of the kitchen.

I stood up and waved her away when she hesitated. "Go. The sooner you leave, the sooner I get you back. Take your phone," I added. Never could be too careful.

"I can take care of myself, you know," she called out over her shoulder as she left the room.

"Not unless you find a few stray chairs along the sidewalk to whack people over the head with as you jog on by," I called back teasingly.

Lucy must have heard me because she let out a shout of laughter then it followed with a muffled "ouch."

"Are you sure you got this on your own?" Quinn called out from the front door as I shuffled towards the ensuite.

"Yes! Just relax!" I yelled back.

An hour later, Quinn returned to chaos.

I was sure I had it. How hard was it supposed to be?

It was just unfortunate the yard had yet to be renovated along with the house. With the light rain this morning over the mud pit that constituted our backyard, Rufus had broken through the back door and trekked it all through the gleaming timber floors. Shaking his fur, mud spatters covered various cream painted walls throughout the house.

Breakfast had seen me go through four different cereals until the favourite of the day had been chosen, leaving milk and flakes scattered on the bench, floor, and breakfast table, along with the dishes from my eggs on toast. Cartoons blared at dangerous levels from the television, and a trail of toys littered the living room floor. Stuck indoors, the decision to move on to forts had been made. That involved shifting the couch and dining chairs to create tunnels and covering them with all the plush blankets Quinn kept for guests.

Quinn chose that moment to return—shutting the front door just as I got too vigorous demonstrating how to kick a soccer goal, broke the blinds, and watched them crash to the floor. What was I supposed to do with it raining outside?

Sam let out a giggle.

Quinn's mouth fell open as she stared.

So did mine.

Sam hadn't uttered a word the entire week we'd been taking care of him. At three years old, he'd watched his father overdose and die and his mother almost follow. She was in the hospital, but it wasn't looking good for her. Sam was the first kid in our care since we'd signed up as foster parents six months ago—the first thing we did when we moved into our Manly Vale home. The process had taken that long. Six months of paperwork, screening checks, home interviews, training, and home inspections.

It was looking likely that Sam may be with us for a while. Quinn and I had talked about adoption, but we knew we had to be able to establish a stable, long term relationship so the process might take some time. Though with the possibility of Sam's mother being mentally unstable, the Supreme Court could move proceedings along that much faster. We wanted to be free to love Sam without the fear of having to let him go. Sam was endearing and hesitant and little, just like Quinn, with his choppy short blond hair and dark hazel eyes. It would take time and love and stability for him to be able to use the voice that was shocked right out of him. I'd been encouraging him to draw his feelings with pictures, but just now, his giggle was the first sound we'd heard.

Quinn cleared her throat and looked at me. Immediately I knew the mess and the damage to the blinds was already forgiven. I grinned. We talked about the fact that when Sam started to verbalise again we were not to make a big deal of it so that he'd feel comfortable.

Even with the emotion running riot across Quinn's face, I could see her force a smile through imminent tears, put her hands on her hips and say, "Well. What a mess, huh?" and it made me so fucking proud of her.

Sam giggled again.

Later that morning, closer to lunch, we arrived at Jared and Evie's house for the Sunday barbecue. They'd finished renovating five months ago and I was honestly surprised with how well Jared did. I'd taken one look at the house and thought it would have been better to drive a bulldozer straight through the middle of it. The two story structure was painted weatherboard in stone with white trim and lush green lawns and hedges. I saw Quinn eyeing the landscaping with frustration.

"Must be nice to have a lawn," she murmured longingly. "The soft scratchy feel of grass between your toes. The smell of freshly mowed lawn on a warm afternoon." She opened the passenger door of the Subaru and sucked in a lungful of air for effect. "Pretty flowers making everything…pretty. Space to kick a soccer ball without tearing apart a clean house."

"You know we can't do anything until the excavators come in and start digging for the retaining wall." Out of the car, I unbuckled Sam's car seat and settled him on my hip. With a wink at Quinn, I beeped the locks and we walked up the driveway. "You can always come over here when you feel the need to be at one with nature."

She snorted, juggling a cooler of beer and container of biscuits baked this morning while I cleaned the chaos, and rang the bell. Someone yelled to "come in."

"If I did that, Jared would tell me I had to mow the lawn or weed the gardens for the privilege."

Through the door, Mum ran towards us as though we'd been schlepping lost through war torn Afghanistan for a year and returning home alive had been doubtful.

"Mum," I warned when she kissed both Quinn and I on the cheek and reached immediately for Sam. Sam burrowed into my chest, latching his little arms around my neck.

Undeterred, Mum smiled wide at him and asked him if he wanted to go for a swim in the pool. Not looking at her, he shook his head.

"I'll take him swimming later if he wants to, Mum."

"Okay." She sighed, taking the bags from Quinn as we walked further into the house. "Did you bring him something to swim in? I was at the shops yesterday with Mackenzie and saw the cutest little boardshorts. They were on special. I had to buy them."

I raised my brows at her in reply.

"Just a couple of pairs. I've left them in the guest room, okay?"

Holding Quinn's hand, Sam in my arms, we wandered outside where everyone was gathered around the outdoor seating, pool, and barbecue.

Mac swooped in. "Where have you been? You're late, you lazy assh—"

I cleared my throat.

"Lazy people," she amended.

She grabbed Quinn by the elbow after pressing a kiss to Sam's forehead and patting his back softly. He squirmed but otherwise seemed to enjoy the affection.

"Evie's been busy. Busy throwing up all morning. Tonight is the biggest night of Jamieson's life. They have to play at the awards in eight hours. *Eight hours*," she hissed, her voice slowly fading out as she dragged Quinn away.

Grabbing a beer, I stood chatting with Dad, Jared, and Mitch by the barbecue for a few minutes before Jared dragged me away.

"Listen," he said. "Evie and I…" He folded his arms. "We uh…"

I chuckled because he looked nervous. "Spit it out, mate."

"We haven't told anyone yet because we only found out this morning. I didn't want to spring it on you, but…Evie and I are having a baby."

Shock punched through me until I smiled slowly, feeling it overtake my face. I pulled him towards me and slapped his back. It was a little awkward because I was still holding Sam, but I offered my congratulations.

Jared looked worried but it eased a little into relief as I asked him how Evie was, and he told me she'd been green for an entire week and it didn't look like letting up anytime soon.

"I appreciate you telling us first," I told him, "and…well, we haven't told anyone this yet either. Quinn and I saw a specialist a few months back. Turns out they *might* be able to reverse some of the damage with surgery but…" I glanced down at Sam. He appeared to be dozing off a little. "…with all the weddings, renovations, the foster parenting process, Quinn busy at work with Jamieson's two singles going platinum, there's been no time to organise it." I paused when I heard Mac swearing loudly from somewhere upstairs. Jared rolled his eyes. "Anyway, we've got Sam. He's our focus for now."

"You're going to adopt him?"

I nodded. "We'd like to if we can."

Quinn could now be heard swearing loudly from upstairs. "What the hell is going on up there?"

We wandered inside as Henry tore down the stairs, phone to his ear. Taking our questioning glances in, he muffled the speaker and said, "It's

Frog and Cooper. They've been in a car accident on their way here," before returning to his phone call.

Mac followed behind him, Quinn behind her. "It's a goddamn disaster. The awards tonight and Evie is up there looking like death city, throwing up a lung and a kidney, and now Frog and Cooper."

I grabbed Quinn's hand as she reached the bottom step.

"They're okay. Some idiot went through a stop sign, but they weren't going fast. Cooper has a couple of scratches but Frog's broken his arm."

"Oh shit," I muttered.

"Shit is right," she agreed.

"Fuck shit," Mac growled. "It's a goddamn disaster. This is the biggest night of Jamieson's life and Frog's gone and cocked up his arm and Evie, well..." She threw up her hands.

Mum came in from outside just as Casey came through the front door. "We'll be out of beer soon, can one of you go?"

"Mum," Mac shouted. "We've got bigger problems."

"What could be bigger than being out of beer?" Casey chuckled as he did the rounds of kissing Mum, Mac, and Quinn on the cheek in greeting. He reached for the stirring Sam in my arms, and Sam went willingly, having taken to Casey the couple of times he'd visited the past week. He swung Sam onto his hip and tucked his tired head under his chin, and I wasn't about to admit that my arms were a bit tired from holding the little champ.

"Actually, we have a replacement bassist for Frog all lined up thanks to Henry," Quinn told us. "Maybe you can pick her up from the airport and grab the beer at the same time for us?"

"Airport?" I asked.

"She's dropped everything to fly in from Melbourne for us. Would you mind?"

Casey sat the now fully alert Sam at his feet and jangled his keys. "Blocking the Subaru in."

I nodded my head towards the door. "You can drive then. You'll be right with Sam, Quinn?"

Quinn took hold of Sam's hand, passing over the printed flight details in the other. "Of course. Mac and Henry are going to collect Cooper and Frog, and Sam and I are going for a swim in the pool."

Sam looked up at me with wide eyes. I ruffled his hair. "Be back soon, bud, okay?"

He nodded.

Ducking my head, I took hold of Quinn's chin gently and touched my lips to hers and whispered in her ear what I wanted to do to her later tonight that I'd missed out on doing this morning. "Later, sweetheart."

"Later," she breathed, her cheeks flushing pink.

With a grin and short wave, Casey and I left for the airport. The flight from Melbourne to Sydney only took an hour but we arrived with ten minutes to spare and stood waiting as passengers started flowing in from the arrivals gate.

Towards us came a girl with a guitar case slung over her back. Deep red tangles of hair flowed down her back and a colourful tattoo wound along the length of her bare arm and towards her neck. Encased in tiny black leather shorts and a sleeveless shirt, she strode directly towards us.

"Holy fuck," Casey breathed beside me. "Do you think that's her?"

I checked the photo of her that Quinn had messaged through and checked the girl coming towards us again. The tattoos weren't in the photo, neither was the smoky eyes, painted lips, and wild red hair—just a fresh faced girl with dark brown hair and a smattering of freckles across her nose.

"I think so."

"Who is she?"

"Henry's sister apparently."

I chuckled at Casey's open mouthed expression. "Close your mouth," I muttered. "You'll catch flies."

"What did Quinn say her name was?"

I checked my phone and looked back up.

"Grace."

The End

Acknowledgements

A HUGE thank you to my readers for reading my books. I hope you find them as entertaining to read as they are to write!

To my husband for your encouragement.

Terrena and Julie—two of the most beautiful women in my life. Your enthusiasm, love and ability to cut through the bullshit makes you both two very rare gems that I am so lucky to have.

Max, Max, Max. Holy shit woman. No words except no one will ever take you away from me. You're mine.

BJ Harvey. PTFD and SMYD. I am so blessed to share this journey with you.

To Trisha Rai and Tammy Zautner. The two of you got me through this book. I wouldn't have survived it otherwise. Thank you both so much for being you. I love you both so very dearly.

To Claire Haiek—the superwoman of the proofreading world. Remember—you were mine first.

To my beta reading team—thank you for being on board the crazy train! Your feedback kept me going and made this book so much more than it could be.

To the bloggers who are willing to take on board and read an ARC from indie authors like myself, thank you. To Devoured Words, Reviews by Tammy & Kim, Must Read Books or Die and Give Me Books, the most supportive bloggers an author could hope for.

To my group of super fantastic sexy ladies—my counsellors, friends and cheerleaders.

Thank you to Sarah at Okay Creations for putting together a cover that I couldn't love any more than I already do.

About the Author

Kate McCarthy lives in Queensland, Australia.

Facebook:
https:/www.facebook.com/KateMcCarthyAuthor

Check out Kate's blog:
http://katemccarthy.net/

Follow Kate on Twitter:
https://twitter.com/KMacinOz

Friend Kate on Goodreads:
http://www.goodreads.com/author/show/6876994.Kate_McCarthy

CPSIA information can be obtained
at www.ICGtesting.com
Printed in the USA
FFOW04n0859190116
20599FF